The Bird of Time

***

A Story of Friendship

John Isaac Jones

"Come, fill the cup! The bird of time has but a short way to fly, and lo! The bird is on the wing."
- Rubaiyat of Omar Khayyam

Dedicated to

Llewellyn Hiawatha Downs

1 – Calvin and Lamar

October, 2021

In the predawn stillness, the Golden Years retirement home loomed dark and silent against the silhouetted background of tall Georgia pines. Its inhabitants—those whose lives had progressed beyond the point of self-care—were sound asleep. They were dreaming of their grandchildren, social security checks, dead husbands and wives, and lives that were growing ever nearer to their inevitable end. Slowly but surely, the cloak of darkness edged away and faint glimmers of soft pink light began to seep over the eastern horizon, and by twilight—the crack between the two worlds—lights began to pop on in individual rooms here and there across the facility. Moments later, there were more lights, more voices, then even more voices that finally gave way to the clattering sounds of wheelchairs, walkers and other such devices designed for the non-mobile. By then, the sprawling wood structure was bathed in morning sunlight and one could see the fullness of the lily-white frame building, its lofty spires, and its gabled roof.

A car pulled into the parking lot at the front of the building. Calvin, a tall black man in his early thirties, emerged from the driver's side. Seconds later, Lamar, another black man, stocky and barely in his twenties, got out on the passenger side, then together they started walking along the sidewalk to the building entrance. Both were dressed in white. They were orderlies at the facility. Lamar, who knew Calvin was not very talkative while driving, had been saving his questions for now.

"Why didn't I see you at church yesterday?" he asked.

"I'm not much for church. If it wasn't for my wife, I

wouldn't go at all."

"Why not?"

"I just don't believe in it. Jonah and the whale and the Garden of Eden… all that sounds like fairy tales to me."

"But you sit in amen corner…"

"That's all for show."

They walked quietly for several moments.

"How's my try-out going?" Lamar asked.

"God damn it! You asked me that five minutes ago."

"I'm asking again," Lamar said.

Calvin was quiet for a moment, then he spoke.

"You just need to pay more attention to little things."

"Little things like what?"

"Let Mr. Chance get out and walk more. He's in better shape physically than most of the others."

"You have to watch these old people," Lamar said. "They can fall and break a leg… or an arm."

"I know, but sometimes you have to make an exception. Mrs. Cleveland likes a slice of lemon with her water. She complained to the supervisor about it yesterday."

"I can't go running to the kitchen to get lemon every time she wants a glass of water."

"The supervisor says we're there for them, not the other way around."

Lamar shook his head indecisively.

"I sure hope I get this job."

They walked quietly.

"We're going to have to fill out the report on Mr. Abernathy today," Calvin said finally. "You remember the old man that broke his hip last week in the shower?"

"What are we going to tell the supervisor?"

"Not sure yet," Calvin said.

"It's not my fault if that old white man was too old to stand on his own two feet."

"We're going to have to keep the insurance company happy."

"There's always the insurance company."

The two orderlies had reached the entrance. Lamar opened the front door and held it open for Calvin.

"What are we going to tell the supervisor?" he said as he closed the door behind him.

Seconds later, the two were inside.

***

Two hours later, the Georgia sun was high in the eastern heavens and, on the facility's veranda, the door swept open, and eighty-one-year-old John David Chance emerged. Tall with a drawn face and a shock of silver hair, he walked unsteadily across the veranda with the help of a cane. Directly behind him was Calvin, carefully watching his every move.

"You all right, Mr. Chance?" Calvin asked.

"I'm fine," John said. "Can we go down to the lake today?"

"Let me ask Mr. Sanders if he wants to go."

Seconds later, the door behind them opened again, and Lamar, pushing a wheelchair, appeared. In the wheelchair was seventy-seven-year-old George Sanders, a frail, sickly-looking man with bony hands and a bald head. Once the wheelchair was clear of the door, Calvin turned to George.

"Mr. Sanders, John wants to go down to the lake today. Do you want to go?"

"Oh, yes. I would like that."

Calvin turned to John.

"Should I get a wheelchair for you?"

"I can walk with my cane," he said.

"The doctor said you shouldn't be exerting yourself because too much stress and strain could cause you to have a heart attack."

"The doctor be damned!" John said.

***

Ten minutes later, the two orderlies and their charges were trundling down the concrete walkway from the retirement home to the lake some 50 yards away. Lamar was pushing George in the wheelchair. John, leaning on a cane, was walking slowly but steadily in front with Calvin at his side.

"I saw some Canadian geese fly into the lake yesterday

afternoon," John said.

"I hope they're still here," George replied.

Ahead of them, they could see the lake. It was a sprawling body of blue water that stretched backward some 200 yards on either side to thick woods beyond. Along the lake's front edge, the entrance was guarded by a white picket fence and a tall white door with a rounded top.

They walked quietly for several minutes.

"Did you hear about Mr. Abercrombie?" George said finally.

"The man in room 214?" John said.

"Yeah."

"What about him?"

"He died yesterday afternoon."

"That's too bad," John said. "For over two weeks now, he's been at death's door."

Now the group had arrived at the lake entrance.

Calvin stopped.

"Let me get the door."

Instantly, he stepped forward to the door. Then, as he grasped the handle, the knob refused to turn.

"It's locked!" he said.

He turned to the others, a puzzled look on his face.

"Who locked the door?"

"I don't know," George said. "Never been locked before."

For a long moment, Calvin studied the situation.

"Strange!" he said. "Oh well, so much for the lake. Let's go back."

Instantly, the two orderlies and their charges turned around and started back up the walkway.

Calvin still seemed puzzled.

"Now who would have locked that door?" he said again.

"I don't know," George said. "It's a mystery to me."

***

Ten minutes later, the two orderlies and their charges had arrived back at the retirement facility. John, still using the cane and moving under his own power, walked unsteadily across the

4

veranda and took a seat in a rocking chair along the railing. Lamar pushed George's wheelchair up the ramp to the veranda, then carefully maneuvered it to a point directly beside the rocking chair where John was seated.

"Now don't get me too close to the railing," George said. "I like to stretch out my legs."

The orderly repositioned the wheelchair as instructed.

"How's that?" Lamar asked.

"That's fine," George said.

The two orderlies, having done their job, stood in front of the two men to address their needs.

"Will y'all be okay now?" Calvin said.

"We'll be fine," George said.

"Okay," Calvin replied. "If you need us, just give us a holler."

"We will," George replied.

The two orderlies went back inside.

John and George were quiet for a long moment.

"Going to be another beautiful day in South Georgia," John said finally.

"Looks that way. What were we talking about yesterday?"

"You were finishing the story about your friend Charley," John said. "You were talking about the last time you saw him.

A pause as George marshalled his thoughts.

"Oh, yes," he said, his eyes lighting up with recognition. "I remember now. I went to visit him in a hospital in Houston. He looked bad. Really bad. I remember him saying the radium treatments were worse than the cancer. When I left the hospital that day, I knew he didn't have long. Two weeks later, I got a call from his daughter saying he died in his sleep. I cried when I heard the news."

George paused for a moment, then wiped away a tear.

"Of all the people I ever knew in my life," he continued, "he had more influence on my life than anybody else. When I was with Charley, I would do things I could never possibly do on my own. It was almost like I was a different person when I was around him. You ever have a friend like that?"

A long pause.

"Well, now that you mention it, I did."

George turned to John.

"What was his name?"

"Jesse!"

"Oh yes, Jesse. I've heard you mention that name many times in our talks. You want to tell me about him?"

"It goes way back yonder," John said.

"I like way back yonder," George said.

John seemed hesitant.

"Go ahead!" George urged. "You listened to my story, now I want to listen to yours. Tell me about you and your friend Jesse."

"It's a long story."

"I got all day."

John laughed, then began to slowly rock back and forth in the rocking chair.

"All right," he said finally. "This is the story of me and Jesse."

2 – Blood Brothers

1945

I was born to be alone. Ever since I can remember, it seemed like every time I loved somebody, they suddenly disappeared from my life. My mother was the first. Oh, with such glorious delight do I remember those early, happy days. Nothing on this earth meant more to me than to look into my mother's eyes. Her visage was the rising sun; therein rested heaven and earth, the moon, and the stars and all of the vast, infinite galaxies beyond; therein lay peace, serenity and pure, unadulterated joy.

When my mother was cooking, there was always a smile in my heart. The kitchen was filled with the mouth-watering smell of apple pies, fried chicken, green beans, hot biscuits, and banana pudding. On Sundays, she would dress me up and take me to church. We would sing church songs and listen to the sermon and, as the plate was passed, she would press a nickel into my palm and instruct me to place it among the other coins and bills.

During the endless summer afternoons, we would play ball in the backyard of our Columbus, Georgia home. My mother would sit on a thin strip of plywood with the long end protruding between her legs, then bend the plywood downward with her thumb to create tension. In the other hand, she would hold an old tennis ball and, when the tension was released, wood would strike ball and send it soaring high into the air. If I failed to catch it, she would say, "Oops! Try again!" When I caught it, she would squeal with delight like a spectator at a baseball game. "Great catch, Johnny! Great catch!!" Nothing on this earth warmed my heart more than my mother's approval. Then one day, when I was five, she was gone.

It had been an unbearably hot day in late August and, around midmorning, my mother and I had gone to the family garden to pick okra. My mother said she had to pick eight rows and I should play with my circus toys at the end of the rows until she was finished. She stayed within sight while picking the first few rows, but after she started the fourth row, she became lost in the sea of head-high okra plants. I was preoccupied with my toys, so when she didn't return after some thirty minutes, I wondered what had happened. Finally, fearfully, I went searching down the rows. The minute I saw her lying on the ground, the half-filled bucket of freshly-cut okra spilled around her, I knew something was wrong. I ran to her.

"Mama!! Mama!" I cried in horror.

I knelt beside her. She was breathing hard and not moving.

At first, I was gripped with paralyzing fear and didn't know what to do. Finally, I gathered my thoughts and ran across the broom sage patch to our neighbor's house.

"Oh, Mrs. Dunn!! Mrs. Dunn," I cried, pulling her arm when she finally came to the door. "There's something wrong with Mama. Come quick! Come quick! Please come quick!"

Together we ran back through the broom sage patch and Mama was lying still at the end of the okra rows.

"Let's go back and get Thomas," she said, referring to her husband. "We'll go to the crossroads and call the doctor."

An hour later, an ambulance arrived, took my mother away, and I never saw her again. The doctor said the cause of death was heat stroke. I didn't know what heat stroke was. All I knew was that I didn't have my mother any longer.

And my father.... Well, there really wasn't a lot to say about Homer.

After my mother died, he just kind of froze up inside. Even before that, I didn't really have a father. He was there in body, but never in spirit and certainly not emotionally. When he was sober, he would go through the motions of being a parent, but when he was drinking, he became a different person, and being a father was the last thing on his mind. My mother had

provided a direction, a sense of purpose to his life, but after she was gone, the spark that drove him onward disappeared.

***

After Mama died, Daddy's mother Rhoda came down from Macon and stayed with us for a while, but having her there was worse than having nobody. All she wanted to do was cook and clean and give orders and make me ashamed of being alive. Even something simple like making a banana and peanut butter sandwich would bring down the wrath of Hell upon me.

"Look at you!" she would scream. "Look at the mess you made! Twenty minutes ago, the kitchen was clean as a pin and now it looks like a pigsty. Get up from there and go outside to eat."

Every time she washed my clothes, there was a new set of rules. If there was mud on my pants legs, she would say I shouldn't play in the dirt. If there were beggar lice, she would say I shouldn't run in the fields. If there was black tar from creosote on the telephone pole I climbed to get crabapples, she would say it was poisonous and would make me crazy. It was as if she didn't want me to be alive. Then there was her Bible quotes and the dire warnings about Hell and the hereafter.

"And the smoke of their torment goes on forever and ever," she would read aloud. "They shall have no rest, neither day nor night; those who worship the beast and his image, and whomever receives the mark of his name."

That was me: "no rest, neither day nor night." I had heard about the eternal fires of Hell for so long, I suddenly realized I was living in it. Finally, when she told Homer that she was going back to Macon to "work for the Lord," I was so happy. Maybe I could have some peace for a change. At least I could be alive.

***

When I turned six and started school, I always dreaded the days when I missed the school bus and Daddy would have to take me to school. He always put Nathan, his redbone hound dog, in the truck first.

"Come on! Hurry up!" he would say to me impatiently as he led the dog around the side of the house to the truck. "I ain't got all day."

Once inside, he would always sit the dog between us in the front seat.

"You okay, Nathan?" he would say as he playfully stroked the animal under its throat. The dog would lick his arm, then Homer would turn to me.

"Are you ever going to learn to get into bed at a decent hour?" he said, pulling his whiskey flask out of his pocket.

"I was in bed at 8 p.m.," I said. "I was sick. I took medicine and I was asleep by 8:30."

"Yeah! Yeah!" he said impatiently. "All I know is I've got to take you to school when I should be over in Albany working."

"But, Daddy," I protested.

"Shut up!" he said angrily, turning to swat me on the side of the head with his open hand. "I don't want to hear your damn excuses."

He turned to his dog. Then using one hand to steer the truck, he used the other to play with the dog.

"Ain't that right, Nathan," he said, scratching the dog under the throat again.

Then he turned to me.

"You know you got a smart mouth on you."

"Daddy, I didn't do anything."

"When I tell you to shut up, you're supposed to keep quiet. You're six years old now. It's time you learned to respect your elders."

I didn't reply for fear of being hit again.

"If I'd talked back to my daddy like that, he'd a busted my head wide open."

"Daddy, it hurts when you hit me..."

"Aw, them little old licks ain't nothing. You should have felt some of the licks I took off my father."

I looked at him and said nothing.

"Anyway, them little licks will make a man out of you," he said, taking another swig from the flask. "You DO want to be a man someday, don't you?"

I didn't reply.

"And if you don't get up in time tomorrow to catch the school bus, you'll get a few more. Understand?"

I was afraid to reply.

"Did you hear me?"

"Yes, Daddy."

Moments later, the old pickup slowed down and turned off the main highway into the schoolyard. Once the pickup stopped, I got out.

"Bye, Daddy. I'm sorry I made you mad."

He looked at me took then took another swig from the flask in the seat.

"You got a lot of learning to do."

"Bye, Daddy," I said again.

"Go on, boy. Git to school!" he said, not looking at me.

Then he turned to the dog.

"Ain't that right, Nathan?"

Then, without a good-bye, he playfully jostled the dog again, revved the engine, and the truck pulled back out on the highway. He loved Nathan more than he did me.

***

When I turned nine, Homer brought a new woman into the house. Her name was May Nell Whitfield, a thin, tough, not unattractive woman in her early thirties with hard eyes and a sad, drawn face whom Homer had met at the J&S truck stop over at the crossroads. When she first moved into our house, she said she would be there "just a little while," just long enough to save money to have her own place and get custody of her daughter, the offspring of her broken marriage to a truck driver in Tennessee. She was rough around the edges, not particularly intelligent, and she smoked a lot, but she had a good heart.

"Now don't you go making no mama out of me," she said when she first arrived. "I'll cook for you and wash your clothes and try to help you, but don't get to loving me because I might be gone tomorrow."

In my heart, I wanted to tell her that I wouldn't dare make a mama out of her because every time I loved somebody, that was when I lost them. Love just didn't pay off for me; that was what I wanted to tell her, but I didn't. So I kept my mouth shut because, in my heart, I would take just about anybody I could get.

"I had to fight all my life," May Nell would say while she was washing dishes. "When I was little, even my own daddy would come into my room and touch me in forbidden places and I would tell him to stop, but he wouldn't. Then one day, when I was in the seventh grade, Odessa Franklin told me her father had been doing the same thing to her and she told the school principal, and the principal went to the law and it stopped. That's the story I told my daddy and that's when he finally stopped."

Even though she told me not to expect her to be a mother, her maternal instinct was stronger than she was and she became quite good as a surrogate mother. Most of all, Homer was happy to have a warm body to do the "woman's work" of keeping house and raising his child.

Every morning, she made me pass inspection before I went to school.

"Washed behind your ears, combed your hair, and brushed your teeth," she would say, eyeing me closely. "You did good."

She would straighten my collar and pat down my shoulders. My hair was never combed to her satisfaction.

"My! My! You're such a fine-looking boy," she would say admiringly as she raked a comb through my blonde hair. "Lord only knows how many hearts you'll break with them blue eyes."

Finally, when she had finished combing, she would replace the cowboy hat.

"Now you're ready for school," she said, smiling proudly.

"Can I have a nickel for a popsicle?" I asked.

"Tips haven't been good lately," she would say, "but I can always come up with a nickel for you."

Then she would press a nickel into my hand and say, "Git on to school now."

But the loneliness was always there. Like an old suit of

clothes, I could remove it for a while with school friends and May Nell, but once I left their presence, it always returned.

***

Like most nine-year-old boys in the late forties, I was caught up in the cowboy craze that was sweeping the nation. Everywhere you looked, cowboys—the Lone Ranger, Roy Rogers, Gene Autrey, Tom Mix, Rex Allen, Bob Steele, Cisco Kid and all the others—loomed vividly in the forefront of youth consciousness. Post-war American youth needed some romantic semblance of the past to remind them of a simpler, gentler time before the days of mass genocide and the atomic bomb. As a result, all healthy-minded boys under the age of ten were rabid fans of cowboy radio shows and movies; they cut out the photos of their favorite cowboy heroes and plastered them on walls, lunch pails, and school books; Saturdays became a religious ritual to go to the movies and watch their favorite cowboy blow away the bad guys. Major food companies, seeking lucrative marketing opportunities, plastered the faces of popular cowboys on bread, ice cream, cereal boxes, donuts and such. Devoted fans had to have the latest toy gun and holster set signed by their favorite cowboy hero; they had to have blue jeans with extra-long legs so the wearer could roll them up in thick cuffs like Bob Steele and Hopalong Cassidy.

Of course, this craze spilled over into schools. Every morning before class began at my elementary school, the younger boys, armed with their favorite cowboy paraphernalia, would gather on the playground to play cowboys. The moment I got off the school bus, I would take my books inside, then race off to play cowboys and reenact the daring deeds I had seen our heroes pull off in comic books, the radio and movies.

***

When I arrived at the playground one morning in late May of 1949, the games were already in full swing. On that particular day, the leader of the "good guys" was a taller older, dark-haired kid named Jesse Trubble. I had seen him in class; he had been at Columbus County elementary for only a few weeks, but he had quickly gained the respect of his fellow students. Everybody wanted to be his friend. Since his cowboy paraphernalia was more lavish and more expensive than that of the other boys—he had two six-shooter cap pistols and holsters with a silver bullet-laden gun belt—he was elected leader of the "good" guys.

On the top of a hill, I joined the "good guys." Then, with Jesse in the forefront, we gathered at the top of a hill to launch an attack upon the "bad guys" at the bottom.

"All right, men," Jesse said. "That's black Bart and his men down there among those rocks. They've robbed the stage over at Abilene and it's our job to bring them to justice. Are you men ready?"

A murmur of yeses rolled through the group of eight- and nine-year-olds.

"Draw your guns!" Jesse shouted. We pulled our cap pistols from their holsters, then the leader, pistol at ready, raised his right hand and shouted, "Charge!!" His pistoled right hand shot forward like a cavalry sword and, in unison, me and the other boys went racing down the hill in a tumult of "Bang! Bang! Bang!"

At the bottom of the hill, the "bad guys," defending themselves as best they could, responded with "Bang! Bang! Bang!!", then seeing they were outnumbered, retreated from the rocks and escaped into the nearby woods. Moments later, the others and I were right behind them.

In the thick undergrowth, Jesse, myself and the other "good guys" moved quietly in search of our adversaries. I spotted Billy Jenkins behind an oak tree. When he peeked around the side of the tree, I gave him a "Bang! Bang!" And he fell over in mock death.

"They're hiding in the bushes over there," Jesse said, indicating the thick brush and trees beyond the playground. "I'm going up this tree to spot them and then you men can pick them off one by one."

As I watched, he shinnied up the tree, then perched himself on one of the lower limbs. Standing on the limb and holding

the trunk to support himself, he peered into the undergrowth.

"There's two behind that pile of brush there," he whispered to me, indicating a clump of pine brush some twenty feet beyond our hiding place.

Quietly, I slipped through the woods and came up behind them. It was Tommy McCartney and Alton Overby.

"Bang! Bang!" I shouted.

Tommy fell over instantly in mock death.

"You missed me!" William said. "Bang! Bang! Now you're dead."

Suddenly, at the school, we heard the first bell ring and our fantasy of violence was at an end. Instinctively, I went back to the tree where Jesse had perched himself.

"Stand back," he said. "I'm going to jump."

As instructed, I stood back and, with a single leap, he jumped out of the tree to the ground.

"Ow!!!" he said upon hitting the ground. His feet had landed on huge roots protruding from above the ground. His face was screwed up in pain as he sat on the ground and held his ankle.

I knelt down to inspect it.

"I think it's sprained," he said. "Let me see if I can stand up."

Tentatively, holding one hand on my shoulder, he stood up and put his weight on the foot.

"Ow!" He grimaced in pain, then fell back to the ground helplessly. "Will you help me to the school?"

Facing him, I put my hands under his armpits and hoisted him to his feet.

"Come on," I said. "Just hold on to me."

At the first step, he grimaced in pain.

"Oh!" he said loudly, his face twisting up again in pain.

"Come on," I replied. "Put your arm around my shoulder so we can walk."

With that, he put his arm around my shoulder. Then, taking a few halting steps at a time, we started out of the thicket.

"Go slow," he said. "It hurts. It hurts so bad."

Slowly, we made our way out of the thicket and down the hillside.

Once we were down the hill, the playground was empty and we heard the tardy bell. As we started across the playground, we saw the fearsome form of Lois Strickland, the school's no-nonsense, stone-faced principal, awaiting us.

"I think we're in trouble," I said.

"We'll just tell her what happened," he replied.

Finally, after they arrived at the school entrance, I carefully helped Jesse seat himself on the schoolhouse steps.

"Why aren't you two in class?" Miss Strickland asked gruffly.

"He was hurt," I said. "I couldn't leave him. He couldn't walk."

"That's no excuse!" she replied sharply. "You should have come to my office and I would have gotten the school nurse."

"I didn't know what else to do," I said, shrugging innocently.

"All students are supposed to be in class before the tardy bell," she said coldly. "That's the rule."

"Yes, ma'am," I said obediently.

The principal turned to Jesse.

"Let me see that," she said, bending over to examine Jesse's ankle.

"Don't touch it," Jesse said, grimacing in pain. "It hurts."

"Wait here and I'll get the nurse."

Then she turned to me.

"YOU come into my office, young man," she said. "You're going to get a paddling!"

With that, she grabbed me by the arm and led him up the schoolhouse steps.

Inside the principal's office, she closed the door and ordered me to have a seat. Then she picked up the phone and ordered the school nurse to go to the front steps and attend to Jesse. Once she hung up the phone, she wasted no time reaching into her desk and withdrawing a small oak paddle. Instantly, I recoiled at the sight of the paddle. Although it was only three inches across, it looked like ten inches.

"Bend over!" she said coldly.

I bent over, then anticipating the first lick, I stepped forward and the blow glanced off the edge of my hip. Instantly, she jerked my arm and spun me around.

"Do I have to put you over my knee?" she asked, raising her voice.

"No, ma'am! No, ma'am!" I said. I could feel myself trembling.

"Then bend over!" she ordered again.

She forcefully twisted my arm behind me and pushed me into a bending position. I gritted my teeth and awaited the blows.

Whack! Whack! Whack! Whack!

The sound of each blow reverberated across the room. The first blow sent stinging pain from the top of my head to my toes. Once the pain of the first blow had set in, I hardly felt the others because my buttocks had been so numbed with the first one. Then, she spun me around.

"Now go to your class!"

***

When I saw Jesse at school the next day, he was on crutches. His right ankle was swollen to twice the size of the left one and it had been tightly wrapped with an elastic bandage.

"Thanks for helping me," he said. "Sorry you got in trouble."

"It's okay," I replied. "When will your ankle be well?"

"Doctor said a week, maybe sooner," he said. "I was talking to Daddy last night. He wanted to know if you want to come to our house one night?"

"Sure, I'd love that," I said. "What night?"

"This Friday night," he said. "We can stay up late because there is no school the next day."

That night, I reported the invitation to May Nell. She approved.

"You've got to be home by nine," she said. "Your father is coming in from the job in Albany and he'll expect you to be here. Now mind your manners and make a good impression."

***

I couldn't wait for Friday. On Thursday, Jesse left school early to go to the doctor. He was no longer using the crutches and he said the doctor was going to remove the bandage. When he returned to school on Friday, the bandage was gone and Jesse could run and play cowboys with me and the others again. I was so happy. That afternoon, Jesse and I were waiting when the big Ford sedan pulled into the schoolyard. All of the other kids watched enviously as Jesse and I got inside. Once inside, Jesse introduced his father Charles, a medium-built man in his forties with dark hair, glasses and a quick smile. He thanked me for helping Jesse and said I was welcome to visit anytime.

"A friend of Jesse's is a friend of mine," he said.

Some thirty minutes later, the shiny black Ford sedan pulled off the main highway into the Green Acres subdivision on the outskirts of Columbus and into the driveway of a new, modern brick home. Once we were inside, Jesse's father turned to his son.

"Now you and Johnny go ahead and play in your room," the father instructed. "I'm going to put a pizza in the oven and listen to Eric Sevareid. What do you boys want on your pizza?"

"I'll have pepperoni and black olives," Jesse said.

"What about you, Johnny?"

I didn't know what pizza was.

"I'll have the same as Jesse," I said, trying to appear knowledgeable.

Mr. Trubble disappeared and I followed Jesse into his room.

"Wow!" I said as I walked in. Here was the room I had always dreamed of having for myself. On the wall over the bed, there was a big poster of Superman and an array of other comic book/movie heroes including the Lone Ranger and Roy Rogers. All around the room, there were stacks of comic books. Little Lulu, Lash Larue, Roy Rogers, Frankenstein, Dracula, the Count of Monte Cristo, and many more. There was a bookshelf lined with children's books along with board games, travel souvenirs and boys' toys of every imaginable description.

"And you even have your very OWN radio," I said with glee, my eyes stopping on an old upright, forties-style radio in the corner.

But there was more. Nearby, a huge bookcase was filled with all sorts of books for boys.

"Look at these," I said happily, falling to my knees on the floor in front of the bookcase.

"*James Whitcomb Riley, Boy Poet; Lou Gehrig, Boy of the Sandlots; Thomas Edison, Boy Inventor*," I said, reading the titles. "Have you read all of these?"

"Yep!"

I took down the copy of *Thomas Edison, Boy Inventor*.

"I've never seen one of these except in a library," I said, thumbing through the pages. "Can I read it?" I asked. "I'll take good care of it."

"Sure," Jesse said. "Come look at my comic book collection."

"Swell!" I said, glancing over at the stacks of comic books. "Boy, your daddy must be rich to buy you all these."

"I've got a great daddy," he said.

Suddenly, he jumped up.

"It's time for the *Lone Ranger*."

Moments later, we fell down in front of the stand-up radio in Jesse's room. We peered at one another with pure delight as the "William Tell Overture" came up and the words: "Return with us now to those thrilling days of yesteryear, when out of the past comes a fiery horse with the speed of light and a hearty Hi-yo, Silver..."

Suddenly, Jesse's father put his head inside the door.

"Pizza's ready," he said.

"We want to eat in here," Jesse said.

Moments later, Jesse's father brought in a tray filled with piping hot pizza and bottled soft drinks. As we listened, he sat the tray on the floor and left us to serve ourselves. Over the next thirty minutes, I was in heaven. As we ate the hot pizza and drank the ice-cold soft drinks and listened to the *Lone Ranger*, all at the same time, I could never have imagined a greater happiness. I had never dreamed that any kid in the world could have so much—their own radio, every comic book imaginable and a father who served pizza and cold Coca-Colas while he listened to the *Lone Ranger*—all at the same time.

Finally, after listening to the *Lone Ranger* and finishing the pizza, we talked about our personal lives. His full name was Jesse Solomon Trubble; at age ten, he was seven months older than me; he and his father had moved to Georgia six weeks earlier; he said his father fell in love with the South while he was in basic training in Columbus and when his father's company asked where he wanted to be transferred, he asked to be relocated near Columbus. He said, when his grandfather immigrated to the United States at the turn of the century, they were Polish Jews and his grandfather had changed their name from Trublinsky to Trubble so people would not recognize that he was Jewish.

"What's Jewish?" I asked.

"People of Israel," he said. "The descendants of Christ. Lots of people don't like Jewish people because they think that Jews own all the banks. I've seen poor Jewish people just like I've seen poor white people, Mexicans and black people."

I asked about his mother.

"I don't have a mother," he answered. "When I was three, she just up and left me and Daddy."

"Why?"

"Mother said the life Daddy provided for her wasn't good enough," he replied. "She was raised in a very wealthy family and she said she refused to live like a second-class citizen."

I smiled at that, then explained about the death of my own mother.

"Do you miss her?" he asked.

"Sometimes," I said thoughtfully. "It's been so long now that I don't remember much."

"I guess we're motherless children," he said. "But that's all right, we'll make it through."

I looked at him. Somehow, I found solace in his words.

Then he wanted to show me his scary faces in the mirror.

"Look at this one," he said. "This is Miss Strickland."

He drew his chin and nose up tight to give his face a lemon-tight, unsmiling look like the school principal.

I laughed.

"Now look at this one," he said. "This is my Frankenstein face."

Then, using two fingers of one hand to pull up his nostrils and two fingers of his other hand to distort the lower half of his face, he created a particularly grotesque effect that recalled the famous horror villain.

I rolled on the floor with uproarious laughter.

"You've got to come to my house this weekend," I said excitedly. "We can go fishing."

"I've never been fishing," he said.

I could see the excitement in his eyes.

"Let's go ask Daddy," he said.

Moments later, we were in the living room. His father was reading a newspaper.

"Daddy, can I go visit with Johnny at his house this weekend?" Jesse said.

Mr. Trubble looked up from the newspaper to me.

"Will it be all right with your parents?"

"It will be fine."

"You'll keep him safe?"

"Yes, sir!"

"He can go. Are you ready to go home now?"

"Yes, sir!"

***

Just before 9 p.m. that night, Jesse's father pulled the Ford sedan into the front yard of our home. The old farmhouse was silhouetted against a bright Georgia moon and, behind the house, I saw Homer's pickup. Quickly, I got out of the car, said my good-byes and, armed with Jesse's copy of *Tom Edison, Boy Inventor*, went inside.

Inside, the house was dark. Knowing May Nell was still at work, I opened the door and glanced into the living room. There I saw Homer, unshaven and dressed in his underwear, sitting in a chair sound asleep. An empty whiskey bottle sat on a table beside him.

"Daddy!" I said tentatively, touching his arm.

He didn't respond.

"Daddy!" I said again.

He awakened slightly. For a moment, he stared at me with dull, drunken eyes. Then he let out a groan and his head flopped back down on his chest. I turned and went down the hallway to my bedroom.

As I crawled into bed, I realized I had never had so much fun in one night. I had always dreamed of having a life like Jesse's. What more could any red-blooded American boy ask for… endless toys, comic books, my own radio, and eating pizza while listening to the *Lone Ranger*? As I drifted off to sleep, I dreamed that we were rich. I went into the kitchen and there was a big pile of money on the table. Homer and May Nell raked their hands through it gleefully, then threw it into the air with careless abandon. "I can buy a new truck," Homer said.

"I can buy a new dress," May Nell said. "We can buy Johnny all of the toys he wants."

But it was all just a dream.

***

The following Saturday, Jesse came to visit me at my house for the first time. When he arrived, we rigged up two fishing poles then went down behind the barn to dig bait. As I spaded back the black earth, Jesse eagerly gathered up the wiggling earthworms and placed them in an old tin can. Once the can was filled with worms, we went fishing at the little creek behind our house. Over the next three hours, we caught six crappie, four bream and several panfish.

"What are we going to do with them?" Jesse asked.

"We'll give them to May Nell and she will cook them for us."

"You mean we'll eat the fish we caught?" he said. "Just like we were living off the land?"

"That's right!" I said.

***

That afternoon, May Nell cooked the fish and we ate it with

ketchup and saltines. Once we had finished, we returned to the creek and went swimming. For almost an hour, we lay in the green grass along the creekbank to let our white undershorts dry out in the warm sunshine. As we waited, we peered up at the white clouds scudding silently overhead.

"Look at that one!" Jesse said. "It looks like an old woman smoking a pipe."

"I see her husband to the left," I replied. "He's bald-headed."

"Where?" he asked, gazing intently.

"Look just behind the old woman's right shoulder," I said, pointing. "See the outline of his shoulder?"

"Oh, yeah," Jesse said with instant recognition. "He IS bald-headed."

I laughed.

We lazed quietly in the green grass for several moments.

"What do you want to be when you grow up?" Jesse said finally.

"I want to be a cowboy," I said. "A real cowboy! I want to own a big ranch, tend my cattle all day, then ride off into the sunset when the day is done."

Jesse laughed.

"Just like the Lone Ranger, Roy Rogers and Gene Autrey?"

"Just like all of them."

We laughed at our tomfoolery, then we were quiet again.

"What about you?" I asked.

"I want to be an adventurer," he said. "I want to climb Mount Everest. I want to join the French Foreign Legion. I want to go down the Amazon River."

"The Amazon River? Where's that?"

"It's in South America. It's the longest river in the world and the rainforests have some of the strangest-looking creatures in all the world. Sloths, capybara, piranha, anaconda and giant leeches. Could you imagine a leech that's two feet long?"

"Where did you hear about the Amazon?"

"My Uncle Marvin bought me a book for my birthday. I'll show it to you next time you're at my house."

***

When Jesse's father arrived late that Saturday afternoon to take him back home, I realized I had never had so much fun. When Mr. Trubble got out of the car, he walked to the front porch where Jesse, May Nell, and I were waiting.

He turned to May Nell.

"Has he been behaving himself?" he asked.

"Oh, yes," May Nell replied. "A really good boy."

"Then we'll be going now," he said.

After good-byes, the father and son headed back to the car.

As they were getting into the car, Homer's pickup pulled into the yard.

Upon seeing Homer getting out of the pickup, Jesse and his father waved to him. Homer stared at them for a moment, then made a half-hearted wave of the hand. Moments later, the black sedan pulled out of the yard and onto the main highway.

"What was that Jew boy doing at my house?" Homer said.

"That's Jesse," I said. "He's a friend of mine from school."

"Don't ever bring him back to this house again," Homer said. "I don't like Jews and I refuse to allow them to come into my house."

"But that's Johnny's best friend," May Nell said.

"Shut up, woman!" he said.

Then he turned back to me.

"If I ever catch him in this house again, you'll get a whipping like never before."

I peered at him without answering.

"Do you understand me?" he said.

I looked to May Nell.

She didn't reply.

"Yes, Father," I replied.

***

During the summer of 1949, I spent almost every weekend with Jesse at his house. May Nell was happy to get me out of her hair; Homer didn't care if I was there or not and Jesse's daddy loved to have me. During those times, we would read comics, listen to the radio, eat homemade ice cream Jesse's father made and play cowboys in the woods behind his house. Our favorite cowboy heroes were the Lone Ranger and Tonto, and we spent endless hours playing out the roles we had heard on the radio. Jesse, who had a white cowboy hat, a mask and a cap pistol, and gun belt with silver-colored bullets, would play the hero. Me, I had an old buzzard feather we found in the woods and I tied it to my head and played Tonto, the Lone Ranger's faithful Indian companion.

"All right, Tonto," Jesse would say in mock seriousness, "that's the Cavendish gang down there in that valley. Our job is to capture them and bring them to justice."

"Me ready, Kemo Sabe."

Then, Jesse would loudly slap his thigh as if riding a horse.

"Hi-yo! Silver!"

Then he would dash down the hill.

I would slap my thigh.

"Get em up, Scout!"

Then I would go running down the hill behind him.

***

One night that summer, Jesse and I listened to the episode of the *Lone Ranger* when the Lone Ranger and Tonto became blood brothers.

"Since we're good friends," he said, "we should take the blood brothers oath like the Long Ranger and Tonto."

So, when darkness fell that night, we built a fire in the woods behind Jesse's house, then we stood over it facing one another. Jesse, using a hunting knife, made a small cut to his wrist. Once there was a trickle of blood, he handed the knife to me. Then I made a cut to my wrist until it was bleeding. Then, looking into one another's eyes, we clasped one another's forearms and held our two wrists together so that the blood of each intermixed with the blood of the other.

"We are now blood brothers," Jesse said.

"Yes, Kemo sabe."

"Blood brothers for all time," Jesse said. "Now that we are blood brothers, we must have a secret distress call known only to us. If one ever needs the other, all he has to do is make the distress call."

"What will be our distress call, Kemo sabe?"

Jesse cleared this throat then made a special sound by rolling his tongue against the back of his teeth.

"Yooodle, doodle, doodle, doodle, doodle, doodle, doodle."

"How do you do that?" I asked.

"By rolling your tongue against the back of your teeth," he said, demonstrating. "You try it."

I put the tip of tongue against the back of my teeth and tried to duplicate the sound.

"Yooodle, doodle, doodle, doodle, doodle, doodle, doodle."

"Very good," Jesse said. "Remember! Say 'doodle' six times."

"It is a good distress call, Kemo sabe. We must remember it for later years."

Then, ceremony over, we stared silently into the fire for several moments.

Finally, I spoke.

"Jesse, how can we be blood brothers for all time? We can't be blood brothers after we die."

"Why not?"

"We'll be dead."

"Nobody ever really dies," he said. "They just return to the great beyond."

"The great beyond?"

"Yeah. That's where everything comes from and that's where everything returns when you die. Living is only a short visit."

I peered curiously at him.

"How do you know things like that?"

"I just know it."

"Did you read it in a book or did somebody tell you that?"

"No. I just know it."

"Sometimes, I don't understand you," I said.

***

Four years passed. During that time, Jesse and I became the best of friends. We were constantly together at school and went through grades three, four, five and six together. When I turned ten, thanks to May Nell, Jesse started visiting my house again. One morning while May Nell was cooking breakfast, she told Homer Jesse was coming to visit. Naturally, he threw a fit.

"That's the only friend Johnny has," May Nell said. "I'm not going to see you deprive him of that boy's friendship because he's a Jew."

"I will not allow a Jew to come into my house," he said. "Now, or ever!"

For a moment, like an angry tigress, May Nell peered at him in livid anger.

"Then you can have it!" she said angrily, flinging off her apron. "You're the most selfish, unreasonable human being I have ever met! I'm finished with you!"

May Nell turned and strode out of the kitchen.

"Where are you going?" Homer asked.

"I'm leaving you."

Moments later, she was in the bedroom packing a suitcase.

"Wait! Wait!" Homer said. "You don't have to leave over some little thing like this."

"Then go in there and tell your son that his friend can come visit him. It's the only fair thing to do."

Homer looked away. He inhaled.

"All right! All right! That Jew kid can come here to visit," he said. "But you just keep him away from me. I don't like those people and I never will."

May Nell looked at me.

I smiled from ear-to-ear.

***

So, from that day forward, our summers were spent visiting one another, fishing and swimming in the creek behind my house, eating pizza, listening to the radio, reading comic books, going to movies and just being together. Over those years, our fascination for cowboys and Indians slowly faded away and we took up new interests. There was baseball, basketball, marbles, collecting baseball cards, flying kites and, finally, horror comics. When I would spend the night at Jesse's house, we would turn off the lights, then using a flashlight, read comic books in a pitch-black room to see how much we could frighten ourselves. There were comics about Dracula, Frankenstein, Tales from the Crypt and other such tales of terror. Those were such happy days.

Then, when school was out in May of 1953, and Jesse and I were thirteen years old, we created a private refuge for ourselves. In April of the previous year, the US Government bought the 500 acres of virgin woodlands behind our house. The thick forest of oaks, elms, pines and cedars began at the property line at the back of our house and stretched westward almost a quarter mile to the banks of the Chattahoochee River. Ever since I could remember, the Copeland Family, a wealthy family in Columbus, had owned the land, and they forbade anyone to set foot on it. When they owned it, there were signs warning "No Trespassing," but once the government bought it, the signs came down. At the time the government purchased the property, the intent was to use the land to train soldiers for fighting in thick forests, but it was never used for anything. So, the "government woods," as everybody came to call it, sat there unused. For years, Jesse and I had wanted to go exploring among the trees and the river banks. Now that the signs were gone, we had an opportunity.

Over the first few weeks of that summer, we beat a path from our house to a huge stand of water oaks located some 100 yards inside the forest. There, using scrap lumber and tarpaper and planks we gathered from Homer's endless scrap pile, we built a tree house some twenty feet high complete with a floor, a roof and a window on one side. We made a rope ladder like we had seen in jungle movies to enter and exit our refuge. We got some old quilts and pillows from the house, and, on hot summer nights, we would go to the treehouse, eat, cook fish we had caught in a nearby creek, sleep, read comic books and remain free of the outside world and its madness. The only reason we needed to go to the house was to get food or listen to the *Shadow* and *Sky King* on the radio. In our treehouse,

Jesse and I thought we were the kings of the world.

One Saturday morning, I proposed that we go exploring in the deep woods all the way back to the Chattahoochee.

"That's a long way back," he said.

"Maybe half a mile," I said. "We can set out some trot lines."

"Let's go!"

So, armed with fried apple pies and egg salad sandwiches May Nell had prepared, we set off through the woods to the river. Once we got into the thickest part of the forest, we discovered a well-worn road with intermittent signs proclaiming "No hunting! By order of the state game warden." Promptly, we dubbed it "the game warden road." It had been used quite frequently and Jesse and I followed it to see where it would lead us. We followed the trail for more than an hour through thick stands of black oaks, elms, and white oaks hanging heavy with Spanish moss and air plants. Intermittently, a rabbit would jump up and race across the trail or we would interrupt squirrels nibbling on acorns and, upon seeing us, they would dash off up the trees to the safety of their nests.

Over the next thirty minutes, we followed the road to the river. Even before we saw it, we could hear the Chattahoochee's mighty roar. At that point, the river was more than a hundred feet wide and a raging torrent of water that roared over giant white and gray rocks before plunging over a waterfall, then dropping some thirty feet down to rejoin the main channel below.

Jesse peered across the river.

"What's that?" he said, pointing toward a white building on the top of the mountain on the Alabama side.

"That's the Skyline Club," I said. "A honky-tonk. At night, men and women drink whiskey and beer and dance."

"How do you know?"

"May Nell told me."

"How would she know?"

"Everybody knows it. Tonight, after dark, we'll come back and I'll show you. It will be all lit up."

Moments later, we were downstream in the quiet part of the

river and I was busy setting out trot lines among the low-hanging tree limbs using small pieces of bream we had caught in the creek for bait.

***

That night, armed with a flashlight, we retraced the "game warden road" back to the river. Finally, we stopped at the point along the bank where I had set out the trot lines. On the Alabama side, high atop the mountain, we could see the Skyline Club, a massive, rectangular white structure bathed in red and white lights at the very top. Along the river's edge, we watched as cars, their bright lights tracing through the darkness, turned up the mountain road, their engines groaning and straining to make it up the steep mountain grade. From the jukebox at the club high above, we could hear faint mournful strains of Hank Williams singing "Your Cheating Heart."

We were quiet for several moments.

"I thought alcohol was illegal," Jesse said.

"It is," I replied, "in Georgia, but that's Alabama over there. They're crazy in Alabama!"

I could see I had piqued his interest.

"Let's go over there."

"To the Skyline Club?"

"Yeah."

"Are you crazy? They'd run us out in a minute."

"Who wants to go in?" he said. "All we want to do is see what they're doing."

For several more minutes, we watched the line of cars groan up and down the mountainside. Then suddenly, we heard the engine and saw the lights of a car coming down the "game warden road" behind us.

"Quick! Quick!" I said, dousing the flashlight. "Let's hide."

Moments later, we were crouched inside the thick undergrowth along the river's edge. The car stopped at the end of the road near the water, not more than twenty feet from our hiding place. We heard car doors slam and men's voices.

"Let's get this booze unloaded and get out of here," we

heard one man say.

"Hold your horses!" another man said. "Help me get this raft off the car!"

"Bootleggers!!" I whispered to Jesse. "Shhhh!"

His eyes were wide with interest as he raised his head to peek through the thick undergrowth toward the two men. As he did, he broke a twig.

"Did you hear that?" the first man said.

"Hear what?"

"That sound," said the first man said. "I heard a sound over there."

"It's your imagination," the second man said. "There's nobody within a mile of here. Come on."

We listened quietly, then we heard the splash of the raft as it went into the river. In the moonlight, we could see the silhouettes of the men carrying the boxes of whiskey to the raft, the bottles inside clinking with a glass sound as they rattled about. Finally, they were finished.

"You got paddles for the main channel?" one man asked.

"I got paddles," the other man said impatiently. "Help me push the raft away from shore."

Then we heard the sounds of the men wading in the water and grunting as they pushed the raft into the water. We waited.

"She's all yours." one man said. "I'll meet you on the other side."

Then we heard the car start, turn around and head back up the "game warden road" to the highway. Finally, certain that the raft was far out into the river, we left our hiding place and went back to our fishing spot. There, in the bright moonlight, we could see the silhouette of the raft and its whiskey-laden load crossing the river. Once it disappeared in the darkness on the Alabama side, we returned to our treehouse.

"Wow!!" Jesse said excitedly as we bedded down for the night. "Bootleggers!! Real bootleggers!!"

***

At the river the next morning, I started checking the trot lines. On a long water oak branch that extended far out over the water, I had set four lines at two-foot intervals. I checked the first three; two of the hooks were clean. The fish had taken the bait and escaped. On the third line, I had three hand-sized crappie. On the fourth line, however, I could see I had a big fish. The line from the tree limb was taut and swirling vigorously in the water. I climbed out on the limb and lifted the line. Then I caught sight of my catch; it was a whoppingly huge catfish, at least ten to twelve pounds. I took it off the line.

"Look at this!" I said proudly.

"Swell!"

Then, with me carrying the big catfish and Jesse carrying the crappie, we started back up the "game warden road" to the treehouse. After we had walked some 100 yards, we came to a bend in the trail. Then, as we made the turn, we saw a youngish black man walking toward us. When he looked up and saw us, he froze in his tracks with fear.

"Howdy!" I said.

"Howdy!" he replied. "What you going to do with that catfish?"

"Take it to our treehouse and cook it," I said.

"I love catfish," he said, eyeing my catch. "I hadn't eat in three days."

"Why haven't you eaten?" Jesse asked. "You have family?"

"Yeah, but they're not around here."

"Why don't you come with us to our tree house?" I said. "We'll cook it and you can have some."

"I can't do that," he said. "Somebody might see me…"

He studied me for a moment.

"Why don't y'all go with me to my place?" the black man said. "We can cook it there."

"Your place? Where do you live?" Jesse asked.

He looked around ominously as if someone might be listening.

"Can you boys keep a secret?"

"Sure!" I said.

He looked at Jesse.

"What about you?"

"Wouldn't tell a soul," Jesse said.

He studied us again.

"Come on," he said finally. "I'll show you."

For over thirty minutes, we followed the black man through the woods. As we walked, I could see that he was leading us into the deep woods far down the river to places we had never been. We scrambled through dense bushes, gnarly vines and thick undergrowth, ducked under huge, hanging tassels of Spanish moss, and finally stopped in a small clearing under a canopy of white oaks. Then we stepped into a thick grove of bamboo, maybe twenty feet high, and then into another clearing. There, nestled inside the bamboo grove, was a cave.

"Wow!" I said with wide-eyed wonder. "That is sooooo neat."

"Yeah!!!" Jesse said.

"This is my house 'til I can find something better," the black man said. "What's your name?"

"My name is Johnny," I said.

"And I'm Jesse."

"My name is Roy," the black man replied. "Can I have that catfish now?"

I handed him the catfish, then the three of us seated ourselves on a log in front of a fireplace at the front of the cave. Quickly, Roy started gathering small sticks and leaves to start a fire. Once he had a bed for a fire, he lit it and the flames arose quickly. Then, as we watched, he sat down on the log and, with a pocket knife, expertly removed the outer skin from the catfish then, with sure, even strokes, cut open its belly, removed the entrails and sliced off several filets for cooking. Finally, he strung several pieces on a small spit and placed them over the fire.

"I wish I had some ketchup," he said, watching as the fire seared the fresh meat.

"I got some at the treehouse," I offered.

"No, I'll make do."

A pause.

"You boys won't tell nobody you saw me," he said.

"Oh, no," Jesse said. "Let's be friends. I've never had a black person for a friend before."

"I would like that," Roy said.

"Why are you so afraid?" Jesse asked.

He studied us for a moment before he answered.

"Guess I can tell you white boys."

He paused again.

"I got in trouble with the law over in Alabama," he began. "I been hiding over here for over a month."

"You can't stay here forever," Jesse said.

"No, I won't be here forever. Someday, I'm going to go back across that river, get my little Sugar Cane and we going up to Detroit. Ever been to Detroit?"

"No," I said.

"They say that white people are better to black folks up north," Roy said.

"I never had nothing against black folks," I said. "They seem just like white folks to me."

"I've heard that black people are not treated fairly in courts in the South," Jesse said. "Have you got a lawyer?"

"Lawyer?" he asked as if it were a dirty word. "Never had no lawyer," he said. "Couldn't afford one."

Jesse studied him for a moment.

"I wish there was some way we could help you," he said.

"If you boys had a boat," he said, "you could take me back across that river."

"You can't swim?" Jesse said.

He laughed.

"Swim ain't no name for that river," he said. "Why, that current would take you down so fast, you'd be drowned before you knew it."

Jesse looked at me.

I nodded that he was correct.

By now, the pieces of catfish on the spit were cooked. We watched as Roy gingerly picked the hot morsels of fish from the spit, then gobbled them down as fast as he could. Tall and unshaven, I guessed his age at thirty to thirty-five. He had a small scar under his right eye, which he attributed to his "wild, younger days." He said he had a job over in Alabama putting roofs on houses. It was hard work, he said, but it paid well. Then one day, he came home and his girlfriend said the law had come to her house looking for him. She said the sheriff claimed he stole a car and killed a white man.

"I never killed nobody in my life," Roy said. "I got scared when Sugar Cane told me that. Real scared. I had twenty-two dollars to my name, so I grabbed some clothes and an empty five-gallon gas can and jumped in that river and came to the Georgia side. Once I hit that main current, that gas can was all that saved me. Without it, I'd have been a goner."

He stopped, cut off another slab of catfish and held it over the fire. We could see he had been living in the cave for a while. There were old empty plastic jugs for water, some empty bottles of Gentleman's Pleasure hair tonic, old wrappers from loaf bread, empty cans that once held sardines and Vienna sausage, old lunch meat wrappers and a pile of empty soda bottles. Inside the cave, there was a piece of old carpet he used for a floor and a metal soft drink advertising sign that read: "Wrenn's Grocery." Apparently, he had been scavenging at Wrenn's, a country store I knew about a half mile through the woods on the main highway.

We talked for over an hour. Jesse told him about living in New Jersey. Roy asked questions about the north and the living conditions of blacks in the north. Jesse politely answered all of his questions. Finally, I stood up to leave.

"Well, we got to go now," I said. "Jesse is visiting me this weekend and we got lots to do. Can we come back and visit you again?"

"Sure," he said. "If you come back, can you bring me some eggs? And some ketchup?"

"Sure," I said. "And maybe another catfish."

"Oh, I'd love that," he said with a big smile.

We turned and started back along the trail to the tree house.

"Good-bye!" he said. "Thanks for the catfish."

"You're welcome," I said.

We turned and started back up the trail.

"Hey, boys!" he called.

We turned.

"Y'all won't tell nobody?"

Both Jesse and I drew our hands across our mouths to indicate our lips were sealed.

He smiled and waved good-bye.

"Wow!!" Jesse said as we walked back along the trail. "A black man in the south running from the law. Just how exciting is that?"

"I've heard about the way black folks are treated by the courts in the south," he said. "It's very unfair and many times black people will be accused and convicted of things they didn't do."

"Do you think he's telling the truth?"

"Yes," Jesse said. "He said he never stole anything from anyone until he came to live in those woods. Now he's got to steal to eat."

He looked at me.

"I believe him," Jesse said. "I wish there was some way we could help him."

***

Thirty minutes later, we were sprawled on the ground outside the tree house with our comic books. I was reading *Little Lulu* and suddenly burst out laughing.

"What is it?" Jesse asked.

"Tubby and his friends are camping in the backyard when it starts to rain and his mother makes them come inside," I explained. "Inside the house, Tubby doesn't want his friends to be disappointed, so he tells them to just imagine the water from the bathroom sink is a cool mountain stream…"

Suddenly, Jesse burst into laughter.

"Oh, yeah, I remember that one," he said. "Later, Tubby tells them to imagine that the sound of the police siren they hear is the call of a lonesome wolf high in the mountains..."

"Yeah," I said, bursting into laughter.

We were quiet for several moments.

"I'm never going back home," he said. "We're going to stay right here and live in this tree house for the rest of our lives. We can live off the land and be perfectly happy."

"We've got to go back sooner or later," I said.

"No. We'll stay right here."

***

The next morning, I was awake at the crack of dawn. As I started down the ladder to the ground, Jesse suddenly awoke.

"A raft!! A raft!" he said excitedly. "We can build a raft like the bootleggers had to help Roy get across the river."

"Yeah," I said. "Then, after we help Roy, we will have it for ourselves."

After gobbling down some more of May Nell's fried apple pies for breakfast, we took an axe from Homer's woodshed and started through the woods to the river. There, along the banks, we started collecting old logs. After we had ten to twelve, we cleaned them up so they could be tied together.

"Now we need some rope and some inner tubes," Jesse said.

Back at the house, I found two lengths of grass rope. Taking them in hand, we returned to the river and, after lashing the logs together with the rope, we had the platform for a raft.

"Where are we going to get some inner tubes?" he asked.

"I don't know," I replied. "We'll have to think of something."

Jesse peered up at the afternoon sun.

"Don't you think we should be getting back?" Jesse said. "Daddy will be at your house to get me at 3."

"What about our raft?"

"Let's hide it in the brush," he said. "We'll finish it next weekend."

***

That night, I didn't see May Nell. Usually, she was home by just after 9 when the truck stop closed, but tonight, she didn't come home. Around 10 p.m., I was awakened by the sound of Homer's pickup in the yard. I looked at the clock. It was 10:30 and still no May Nell. I wondered where she was, then went back to sleep.

The next morning, she was in the kitchen washing dishes when Homer came in. He was on the warpath.

"What time did you git in last night?" he said.

"Must have been about 10:30," she said. "Me and Doris closed late, we had some late customers, so when I got off at 10, I come straight home."

"I was wide awake at 10:30," Homer said. "I got up and went to the kitchen. You were nowhere to be seen."

"I might have been a little later than that," May Nell said absently, "but it was somewhere around 10:30."

Homer stared suspiciously at her. I could see he was fuming inside.

"Now don't you start on me," May Nell said, a warning sound in her voice. "If you got problems, go take them out on somebody else."

Homer didn't answer.

"Did you hear me?" she pressed, raising her voice.

"I heard you," Homer said. "There was a pack of Chesterfields in your purse this morning..."

"So...?" May Nell replied.

"You smoke Pall Malls..."

"Homer, will you quit it?" May Nell said. "I run out of cigarettes last night and Doris give me part of a pack she had. She smokes Chesterfields."

Homer eyed her suspiciously.

"You seeing another man, May Nell?"

"No! I wasn't with nobody last night but Doris Thompson. Now will you just let me be?"

"If I ever catch you with another man, I'll kill both of you," he said. "Do you understand?"

"Nobody else is crazy enough to have me. Homer Chance, you're the most jealous man God ever made."

"You just remember what I said."

Then Homer stalked out of the house to his truck. Moments later, we heard the engine start and the truck pull out of the yard. Over the next few days, Homer disappeared again.

***

The following weekend, Jesse was back at my house. That afternoon, we went to Wrenn's grocery, the little store on the main highway near the government woods. Upon arrival, we

went to the garage next door and asked about some old tire inner tubes we had seen in the back. The man said he wanted a quarter each and Jesse gave him a dollar for four of them. Once we had pumped them up, we returned to the river. There we tied the inner tubes to the bottom of the platform. We made push poles from two ash saplings, then a crude rudder out of a long pole and a wide piece of lumber. I told Jesse I thought we were ready. Then, with Jesse on one side and me on the other, we carried the raft to the river and put it in the water. With a deep sense of pride, we peered at our creation.

"Look at that!" he said. "There's nothing me and you can't do."

"Yeah," I said.

We spent that afternoon on the raft in the river learning to use the push poles and the paddles to maneuver it in and out of the different parts of the river. At sundown, we returned to the Georgia side and checked the trot lines. I had three bream, a big carp and two crappie, maybe five pounds of fish.

Back at the treehouse, we cooked the fish, ate, then lay quietly in the grass under the treehouse, looking up at the stars and listening to the sounds of the night. Somewhere in the distance, we could hear the plaintive cry of a screech owl.

"What's that?" Jesse asked.

"That's a screech owl. Somebody is dying somewhere," I said, recalling a story I had heard as a child.

"Death?" he said. "There's no such thing as death."

I turned to him.

"What?" I said in profound disbelief.

"Nothing ever really dies," he said. "It just goes back to the great beyond. Being alive is just a little visit."

"How do you know that?"

"I just know," he said.

***

The following morning, we were back at Roy's cave. We took a bottle of ketchup, three fish we had left over and a dozen eggs we had bought at Wrenn's. When we arrived, he was snapping green beans he had stolen from someone's garden.

"My goodness!" he said when he saw the fish. "You white boys sure know how to fish."

"We built a raft," Jesse said. "We're going to help you get across that river."

He looked at us.

"Will it float?" he asked.

"Oh, we tested it out yesterday afternoon," Jesse said. "When do you want to go back across the river?"

"I'll have to talk to my Sugar Cane and see when she's ready. Can you boys take a message to her?"

"Sure!" Jesse said. "What's the message?"

He went back to the cave and returned with an old, broken pencil. Then he tore a label off an empty tin can and started scribbling. Finally, he finished.

"She lives in the holler with her mother behind the Skyline Club," Roy said. "Think you boys can find her house?"

"What does it look like?" I asked.

"It's just a shanty. There's an old Ford truck rusting in the yard and she's got a garden and a red chicken house in the back. You can't miss the red chicken house."

"What's her mother's name?" Jesse asked.

"Dilsey!"

***

Thirty minutes later, we were back at the raft. Message in hand, we loaded water and sandwiches and headed across the river. The water was quiet and we quickly navigated the raft out of the eddies into the main channel. Once we arrived on the Alabama side, we hid the raft among the thick bushes along the river's edge and started up the mountainside. As we neared the top, we heard the sound of music from the Skyline Club. We skirted the parking lot, then made our way some 200 yards behind it where we could see a settlement of shanties.

"This must be 'the holler,'" Jesse said.

As we walked along the dirt road eyeing the houses, black children and their parents peered at us suspiciously. Finally, we saw the home with the red chicken house and the old Ford pickup in front. On the front porch, an old black woman was eyeing us suspiciously.

We stopped.

"You know Nancy Williams?" Jesse asked.

"Who wants to know?" the old woman asked.

"We got a message from Roy."

She studied us for a moment, then got up and went into the house.

Moments later, a young black woman appeared on the porch.

"You know Roy?" she asked.

"Yes, ma'am," I answered.

"How you know Roy?"

"He's our friend."

"He's friends with two white boys?"

"Yes, ma'am," I said.

She still wasn't satisfied.

"What does Roy look like?"

"He's tall and got a scar under his eye."

"Lots of black men got scars, which side?"

"The right side!" Jesse said.

She still wasn't satisfied.

"What else?"

"He's got a gold tooth he sure is proud of," Jesse said

"Which side?"

"Well, neither side," Jesse said. "It's almost in the middle."

"What's he call me?"

"Sugar Cane!!"

She smiled.

"You DO know Roy."

"He said to bring you this."

I handed Roy's note to her.

She opened it and read it.

"You boys wait right here."

She went back inside. A few minutes later, she returned with pen and paper and started scribbling. Finally, she finished.

"Will you take this back to him?" she said, handing the folded paper to Jesse.

"Yes, ma'am!"

"And take this."

She handed Jesse a ten-dollar bill.
"He'll like that!" Jesse said.
"You white boys come back any time. Hurry on now!"
We turned to go.
"What's your names?" she asked.
"I'm Johnny," I said.
"My name is Jesse."
"Thanks, Johnny and Jesse!"

***

Back at the cave, we gave Roy the money and the message.
"Hot diggitty dog!!" he said after reading the note. "She is preparing for our trip."
"What does the note say?"
"She's going to save one hundred dollars and buy two bus tickets to Detroit."
"When will that be?"
"About two weeks."
He stopped.
"Would you boys go to Wrenn's and buy me some things? I got a list."

***

Twenty minutes later, we were back at Wrenn's. We bought three bottles of Gentleman's Pleasure hair tonic, two loaves of bread, a big jar of mayonnaise, ten cans of Vienna sausage, two pounds of baloney and twelve cans of potted meat. We paid the clerk and he loaded everything into two bags.
Outside the store, I turned to Jesse.
"Why do you think Roy wanted so many bottles of hair tonic?"
"He's drinking it."
I laughed. Then, with Jesse carrying one sack and me the other, we started across the grocery store parking lot to the woods. As we neared the trail head, we heard a sharp call.
"Jesse!"

We turned. A well-dressed, middle-aged woman was staring at us. Nearby, a middle-aged, stern-faced man was leaning on a new black sedan.

"Mother!" Jesse said. "What are you doing here?"

"I want you to go with me," she said. "I want to take you out of all of this."

"I'm not going," Jesse said.

"You can't spend your life around people like this," she said, indicating me.

"You shut up," Jesse shouted. "Johnny is my friend."

"Jesse! I'm your mother! I love you and I want you to come and be with me."

"Not after what you did to Daddy," he said. "You're not my mother! Do you understand? You're not my mother!"

"I can show you a life better than this," she said. "These country people have no future and, if you stay here, you will have no future."

"No!" he shouted. "Go away! I want nothing to do with you."

With that, Jesse turned, and together we headed down the trail.

Instantly, the woman motioned to the man standing beside the fancy car. Quickly, he rushed forward, knocked the sack of groceries from Jesse's arms and threw him on the ground.

"Turn me loose!" Jesse shouted. "Let go of me!"

For a moment, the man and Jesse wrestled on the ground. Finally, the man, who was much stronger, had Jesse pinned to the ground and was sitting on top of him.

Instinctively, I laid aside the groceries, picked up a large rock from the trail and rushed at the man. As I drew near, I could see a small bald spot directly on the top of his head. With all my might, I slammed the rock against the bald spot. The man's head wobbled side to side for a moment, then he looked back at me with bleary eyes and fell on the ground.

"Come on!" I said, helping Jesse to his feet.

Quickly, we gathered the groceries and bounded off down the trail into the woods.

"Jesse! Jesse!" the woman called. "Come back here! I'm your mother…"

***

Back at the cave, we gave Roy the two sacks of groceries and his change. He put the money in his pocket and wasted no time making a huge baloney sandwich. As he ate, we talked.

"How we going to know when Sugar Cane is ready for me?"

"What are you saying?" Jesse asked.

"In the note, she said she'd have the money in two weeks. What if she's got the money gathered up and we don't know it?"

"Well, we can go over and ask her."

"Would you boys do that for me?"

***

That afternoon, we took the raft back across the river, climbed the mountain and ventured into "the holler" once again. When we arrived at the shanty, Nancy's mother said she wasn't home.

"She's cooking over at the Skyline. How's Roy doing?"

"Roy's fine," Jesse said. "He can't wait to get Nancy and be gone."

"Nancy can't wait either," the old woman said.

Then she peered down the road.

"Look yonder! Here she comes now."

The two boys turned.

The minute Nancy saw them, she came running.

"I'm so glad you white boys are here," she said. "I want y'all to take a message to Roy."

She went into the house and came back with pencil and paper. Then she furiously scribbled a note and handed it to them.

"Take this to Roy."

We started to go.

"Wait!" she said. "Tell him I'll have clean clothes for him once he gets across the river."

"We will," Jesse said.

Back at the cave, Roy anxiously opened the note.

"Hot dog!" he said. "She says she'll be ready this Saturday. She wants us to meet her at Miles Landing. Do you know where that is?"

"That's about a mile down the river," I said.

"She says she and her brother will be waiting in a black car at the boat launch. Can you boys get me there?"

"We sure can," Jesse said.

"It's best if we do it in the afternoon," Jesse said. "Remember the bootleg patrol comes up the river about noon every day."

"Yeah, I know," Roy said. "I've seen them on the river."

***

A week passed. The following Friday night, Jesse was back with me in the treehouse. Most of that night was spent making plans for the following day. When I awoke the next morning to a bright, sunny Saturday, I didn't realize it, but it would be a day that would live forever in my memory. At the river, we had prepared the raft; we had fishing poles and bait to make it look like we were going fishing; we threw an old piece of canvas over our water jug and sandwiches to protect them from the sun.

"We're ready," Jesse said. "Let's go get Roy."

At the cave, Roy was ready. He had bathed and shaved.

"How do I look?" he asked.

"Look like you're ready to go to Detroit," Jesse said.

He smiled.

"I been ready to leave for a long time," he said. "Thanks to you boys, it's finally going to happen."

"Let's go!" Jesse said.

Roy picked up a sack containing several cans of Vienna sausages and crackers and turned to face the cave.

"Good-bye, old cave," he said. "Your darkness has kept the rain off my head for almost two months. Now I'm going to get my Sugar Cane and we're going to Detroit. Bye-bye, old cave."

Then Roy turned and started back through the woods with us to the river. Once we arrived at the raft, we started to load up.

"You can't sit on the raft," Jesse said. "You'd be spotted in a second by anybody that looked out on the river. You're going to have to stay in the water and hang on to the raft. If we see the bootleg patrol, duck under the water and breathe through this."

Jesse produced a long plastic pipe.

"Think we'll see the patrol?" Roy said.

"I don't know," Jesse said. "If we do, we'll be prepared."

"How will I know which side of the raft to be on?"

"Johnny will rap on the side of logs that's the safe side," Jesse said. "Just keep your head under the edge of that canvas. That way, you'll be hidden."

"I got it," Roy said.

Roy slipped into the water and grasped the edge of the raft. With Jesse at the rudder and me using the push pole, we maneuvered the raft through the slowly spinning eddies of water outside the main channel.

"Keep an eye peeled for the river patrol," Jesse said, manning the rudder with both hands.

Moments later, the raft was in the main channel.

***

Over the next fifteen minutes, Jesse expertly maneuvered the raft down the middle of the river in and out of the gentle swells, staying clear of rocks and washes of tree limbs.

Suddenly, we heard the engine of a motorboat downriver. It was the bootleg patrol. They were coming straight toward us. I tried to contain my fright.

"Stay calm," Jesse said. "Just stay calm."

The patrol boat pulled up alongside the raft. My heart dropped into my mouth as the first officer grabbed the side of the raft and pulled us toward their boat. Both men had gold badges on their breasts and big pistols strapped on their hips.

"What you boys doing on this river?" the first man asked.

"We're going fishing over at Miles Landing," Jesse said, indicating the cane poles and can of worms. "You wouldn't happen to have any extra hooks with you, would you?"

"No," he said. "We're not out here to go fishing."

"You boys been playing in those government woods?"

"Yes, sir!" Jesse said.

"You know there's a fugitive from Alabama over there," he said, reaching for a paper on the boat's dashboard. He unfolded the paper. It was a wanted poster for Roy.

"Have you seen this man?"

Jesse peered at the wanted poster.

"No, sir!" Jesse said. "Never seen him."

The officer turned to me

"What about you?" he said. "Ever see this colored man?"

He showed me the poster of Roy.

"No, sir."

The officer's eyes scanned the raft.

"What you boys got under that piece of canvas?"

Jesse leaned over and pulled back the canvas.

"A jug of water and some chicken sandwiches," Jesse said. "You want some?"

"No," the officer said disinterestedly. "We're not hungry… Are you boys sure you haven't seen this man, a tall Negro, early thirties, got a scar under his right eye…"

"No! We haven't seen him," Jesse said.

He looked at us one final time.

"Okay! You boys have fun. Hope you catch some fish."

Jesse started to push the raft away from the patrol boat.

"One more thing," the officer said.

"Yes, sir?"

"If you see that fugitive," he said. "Don't go around him. He's armed and dangerous and he'd kill a white boy faster than you can say Dixie. If you see him, you contact us."

"Oh, we will," Jesse said. "We don't want any trouble."

The main patrol officer pushed the raft away from the patrol boat and Jesse held the rudder firmly as the raft descended back into the main channel. We waited and watched nervously, saying nothing until the patrol boat was far upriver, then I jiggled the plastic pipe. Roy's head popped up.

"Everything okay?" he asked.

"Yep!" Jesse said.

Now we were at the edge of the main channel on the

Alabama side. Some fifty feet downstream, we could see the boat launch at Miles Landing.

Then I used the paddles against the river current at the front of the raft to maneuver it through the eddies. Moments later, the raft bumped into the shoreline at Miles Landing. Once the raft was tied up in the thick brush along the river's edge, Roy came out of the water. He was soaking wet. Then the three of us started up the steep bank to an old boat house some fifty yards from shore. About halfway up, we saw Nancy and a black man and a car. She was all dressed up.

"Oh, my sweet little Sugar Cane," Roy said as he sloshed up to the car in his wet clothes. "Do you have everything?"

"Yes!" Nancy said. "I've got dry clothes in the car. Hurry and let's get on the road."

She turned to me and Jesse.

"Thank you boys so much!!" she said. "Can you do one more thing for me?"

Sure!" Jesse said.

"Will you go back up to the holler and tell Mama we got Roy and we're headed to Chattanooga. Tell her we're safe and I'll write when we get to Detroit."

"We'll tell her," Jesse said.

Then we watched as Roy, Nancy and the other black man hurriedly got into the car and it headed back up the mountainside.

"Come on," Jesse said. "Let's go talk to Nancy's mother."

***

Over the next thirty minutes, we headed the raft back up the river to the point where the Skyline Club was located. Once it was tied up, we started up the side of the mountain. When we reached the top, we would hear music and laughter coming from the Skyline and, moments later, we were in "the holler."

When we arrived at the shanty with the red chicken house, we saw Nancy's mother sitting on the front porch peeling apples. As we approached, she saw us coming.

"You got word about Nancy?"

"She's safe," Jesse said. "She's in the car with Roy and her brother and they're going to Chattanooga. She said she would write you when they get to Detroit."

"Oh, thank God!" the old woman said, folding her hands and looking heavenward. "And thank you two boys for helping us. This never would have happened without you. You two are little white angels."

"We were glad to help!" Jesse said. "We better be going now."

"God bless you boys."

We acknowledged the thanks and started back down the dirt road out of "the holler."

"Come on," I said. "Let's go back across the river."

"No!" Jesse said, "I want to see inside the Skyline."

"We can't go inside," I said. "They'll throw us out in a heartbeat."

"Let's just look in the window."

"Okay," I said. "But we'll have to be careful."

Ten minutes later, staying hidden in the thick underbrush, we maneuvered ourselves to the parking lot in full view of the building entrance.

"Let's sneak up to the side window," I said. "Then you can sit on my shoulders and I'll lift you high enough to see inside…"

As we watched, a couple holding hands emerged from the entrance. I peered at them for a long moment.

"Isn't that May Nell?" I said as I watched the couple cross the parking lot to a car.

"Where?" Jesse asked.

I pointed to the couple about to get into the car.

"Yes!" Jesse said. "It IS May Nell!"

"Oh, my God!" I said as we watched May Nell and the strange man stop beside a shiny, late model Buick not more than thirty feet from our hiding place. Then, as we watched, the strange man took May Nell in his arms and kissed her, all the while pressing his body against hers. I was dumb-struck at what I was seeing. Then we watched as the man unlocked the back door of the Buick and he and May Nell crawled into the back seat.

"What are they doing?" Jesse asked.

I shook his head. I was afraid to answer.

For several minutes, we watched May Nell and the strange man moving around in the back seat of the Buick. Finally, we saw May Nell lie down in the seat and one of her legs, with a white high-heeled shoe, was sticking out the window.

We listened for several moments.

"Frank! Frank!" May Nell moaned. "Oh God! Oh...Oh...Frank!"

"He's hurting May Nell," I said. "He's beating her!"

Suddenly, I leapt out of the undergrowth and raced to the Buick. For a moment, I looked around for a weapon. Unable to find anything, I grabbed the high heel shoe, then reaching inside the open car window, I started hitting the strange man in the back with the shoe.

"You leave May Nell alone," I shouted, thrashing the man's back and head with the shoe. "You quit hurting May Nell!"

Suddenly, the man stuck his head out the window.

"What the hell are you doing?" he said.

"You quit hurting May Nell!" I shouted angrily. "You leave her alone!"

Seconds later, May Nell, holding her arms over her bare breasts, appeared in the open car window.

"Johnny!" she said. "Get away from here!"

"This man was hurting you," I said.

"He's not hurting me," May Nell said, obvious irritation in her voice.

Suddenly, the man burst into raucous laughter.

"Get out of here!" May Nell said. "Get out of here! Now!"

Suddenly, we heard a voice nearby.

"Hey!"

We turned to the sound of the voice. It was the club bouncer, a fat burly man with a shaved head, and he was headed straight toward us.

"You kids get out of here!"

"Come on!" Jesse said. "Let's go!"

Without another word, we raced off down the side of the mountain. When we reached the river bank, Jesse stopped, turned to me and burst out in laughter.

"What's so funny?" I asked.

"That man wasn't hurting May Nell," he said. "They were screwing."

I peered at him.

"May Nell wouldn't do something like that to Homer."

"Looks like she has already done it," Jesse said. "Come on! We've got to be back at your house by 3. Daddy will be waiting to take me home."

***

As we navigated the raft back across the river, my head was spinning with confusion and uncertainty. Was May Nell leaving Homer? And me? I wondered how long she had known this Frank. What was she going to do now?"

When we arrived back on the Georgia side of the river, we tied up the raft and raced through the woods to my house. Just at the moment we arrived, Jesse's father was pulling into the yard. He was happy to see his son. Moments later, Jesse was in the car. I waved good-bye and went into the house.

An hour later, May Nell appeared. The moment she was through the door, she hurried straight into her and Homer's room, threw a suitcase on the bed and started packing.

"What are you doing?" I asked.

"I'm leaving," she said, throwing clothes into the suitcase. "I don't expect you to lie to your daddy about what you saw today."

"May Nell! May Nell!" I pleaded. "I would never mention what I saw today. Honest!"

She inhaled, shook her head resignedly, then continued throwing clothes into the suitcase.

"It's best if I go on," she said. "I've put up with the drinking and the fighting for too long already. I thought that was the way things were supposed to be. I know different now."

"Please don't leave!" I said. "You're all I got."

"Honey, I told you a long time ago to not be making a mama out of me…"

Suddenly, it dawned on me that she was saying good-bye.

The suitcase was now full and she slammed it shut.

She turned to me.

"I just wanted to tell you..."

Her voice broke. She looked at me, then burst into tears. She rushed to me and took me in her arms.

"Now whatever happens," she said, holding me tightly. "You've got to be strong and take care of yourself. You hear me?"

"Please don't leave!" I pleaded.

"You're a smart boy... and a good boy... and a handsome boy. Remember all those things. Most of all, you've got to stay strong."

I could feel her tears dripping on the top of my head.

"I don't want you to leave!" I pleaded. "I want you to stay here! Please stay!! Please stay!!"

"Honey, I'm sorry," she said. "Please try to understand."

"I love you, May Nell," I said.

"I love you too," she said.

For several seconds, she held me in her arms, rocking and consoling me. Suddenly, outside, we heard Homer's truck pull into the yard. Then we heard the door slam.

"Damn!! He's here!" she said, quickly breaking the embrace.

I turned from her and went into the living room as Homer came in the front door.

"Where's May Nell?" he asked.

I shrugged.

Instinctively, he went into the bedroom. There he found her packing the suitcase.

"What's going on?" he asked.

"I'm leaving," she said.

"No, you're not," he said. "You ain't going nowhere."

Then he went to her and grabbed both of her arms and held them firmly in his hands.

"Turn loose of me," she shouted. "You son-of-a-bitch, turn loose of me!"

With all her strength, she wrested her arms from Homer's grasp, then grabbed the suitcase and shot out of the bedroom. Homer was right behind her. Moments later, she was out the front door and started across the yard. Instantly, Homer burst through the front door, ran across the yard and tackled her. For a moment, they fell together and the contents of the suitcase spilled on the ground. May Nell, like an enraged tiger, jumped up to her feet.

"You son-of-a-bitch," she said, gritting her teeth, livid fury in her face. "Get away from me."

Then she started gathering up the contents of the suitcase.

"May Nell, I'm sorry!" he said. "Please don't leave. I need you. I need you!" He was pleading like a little child. "Please don't leave me! I'll do anything."

May Nell quickly stuffed the clothes and other personal items back into the suitcase.

"If it hadn't been for Johnny," she screamed, "I'd have left years ago."

Suddenly, the shiny new Buick Jesse and I had seen at the Skyline Club eased into view out on the highway. Homer looked up and saw it.

"So THAT's the way it is," he said. "You've got another man. Let me git my pistol."

Instantly, Homer turned and rushed into the house.

By now, May Nell had all the spilled items stuffed back into the suitcase. Hurriedly, she closed it, then started across the yard to the Buick.

Moments later, Homer burst through the front door, waving a pistol.

"You sorry, two-timing bitch!" he screamed.

At the road, May Nell had reached the Buick. Quickly, she threw the suitcase in the rear seat.

"You bitch! You bitch!" Homer screamed, rushing across the yard.

May Nell slammed the car's back door then got into the front seat. As the Buick's engine roared, Homer fired several shots.

"Blam! Blam! Blam!" the pistol sounded.

It was too late. The Buick was gone.

For a moment, Homer stopped, then dropped to his knees, sobbing like a little child. I started toward him.

"Daddy! Daddy!" I called.

As if he hadn't heard, he stumbled to his feet, pistol still in hand, then strode across the yard and into the house. Instinctively, I sensed something terrible was about to happen. I raced off after him.

"Daddy! Daddy!" I yelled.

As I burst into the living room, I saw him turn, go into the bedroom and close the door. I rushed to the door and tried to open it. It was locked. For several seconds, I pounded on the locked door.

"Daddy! Daddy! Daddy!" I called.

Then I heard a single shot: *Blam!*

***

Eight days later, suitcase in hand and dressed in my best Sunday suit, I was seated on a bench in the boarding area of the Columbus train station. Seated beside me was a middle-aged, stern-faced woman in a 1950s-style women's business suit. She was reading a newspaper.

Suddenly, I heard someone call.

"Johnny!"

Instantly, I turned and saw Jesse and his father coming into the train station.

The stern-faced woman looked up from the newspaper.

"Who's that?" she asked.

"That's my friend Jesse. Can I talk to him a minute?"

The stern-faced woman peered at Jesse, then turned back to me.

"Go ahead!"

Once I started toward him, he ran to me.

"I came to say good-bye," he said. "Where are you going?"

"To Valdosta. To live in the state orphanage."

"An orphanage? What's it's like in an orphanage?"

"I don't know," I said. "The state people said I'd be going to school and working. They said as long as I work hard and follow the rules, I'll be fine."

"Will you be able to watch *Superman* and *The Cisco Kid* on TV?"

"Yeah, but no TV after 8 p.m."

Jesse peered over at the state employee.

"Who is that?" he asked, almost in a whisper.

"That's Miss Hester."

"She looks kind of weird," Jesse said, still whispering. "I wouldn't be giving her any sass."

"She's been nice," I said.

"I'll bet she can paddle hard," he said. "Look at the muscles in her arm."

Johnny looked out of the corner of his eye at the woman's arms.

"You're right," I said. "I'll bet she CAN paddle hard. I'll be watching my step."

"I brought something for you," Jesse said, offering a brown paper bag.

I took the bag, then pulled out a hardback book.

"Wow!" I said. "*Thomas Edison, Boy Inventor*! I can't take this," I said, handing it back. "This is your only copy."

"No," he said. "I want you to have it. You're my best friend."

I looked at the book again.

"Thanks!" I said. "And you're MY best friend."

We looked at one another.

"John David Chance!" the woman called.

"Yes, ma'am."

"We must go!"

I turned back to Jesse.

"Goodbye," I said.

"You have my address?" Jesse said.

"Yes, do you have mine?"

"No!"

I fished in my pocket and withdrew a letter from the orphanage. Then I tore off the letterhead, which contained the address and handed it to him.

He glanced at it, then put it in his pocket.

For a long moment, we peered at one another, not knowing what to say

I was about to cry and I could see that he was too. Quickly, I turned and started walking back to the boarding platform. There, I was joined by Miss Hester, then together we boarded the train. Peering through the train windows, Jesse watched as me and the woman made our way through the passenger car and took a seat at a window facing the platform. As the mighty steam locomotive started to strain, I turned to the window and waved good-bye one final time. From the platform, Jesse sadly waved back. Then, as the engine gathered steam and the train started to move slowly forward, he stopped waving and, using both hands, made his crooked Frankenstein face. Instantly, upon seeing the face, I broke into spasms of uproarious laughter. He could always make me laugh over the stupidest things. So I was alone again. As the train moved southward past the cotton fields and pecan orchards of South Georgia, I knew that I would never forget Jesse. Of all the people I had ever known, he was the only one who had the same sense of adventurous madness inside him I did. I never dreamed I would see him again.

3 – High School

1957

In late September of 1954, I was enrolled into the Baldwin Home for Boys in Valdosta. Located just north of the Georgia-Florida line, the 200-acre facility was a working farm with tractors and cattle and goats and sheep and a population of more than 200 boys. Upon arrival, I was housed in a "group" barrack with four other boys. Each of us had our own bunk, a private locker for personal items and we shared a bathroom. Rules were plentiful and strictly enforced. All of the boys attended Valdosta County Schools and the daily schedule was rigid. Up at 6 a.m., chores until classes began at 8; classes until 3 p.m., then more chores and study until 9 p.m.; lights out at 9:30; no exceptions.

When I enrolled, my group counselor, Mr. Wainwright, said I would be expected to form "positive relationships" with the other boys and integrate myself into the school's "functional family environment."

"We don't offer a normal family environment at Baldwin," he said, "but it's fairly close. Most of all, we offer a sense of structure and belonging. If you follow the rules, get along with the other boys and work hard, you'll be fine."

And, I must say, I did develop a certain "sense" of family at Baldwin. Early on, I became friends with Billy Joe Royal, a member of my group who was from Milledgeville. Billy Joe's parents had been killed in an auto accident when he was 10 and he had been at Baldwin for three years when I arrived. He knew the ropes and he helped me acclimate. He quickly became my best friend and I loaned him money to go into town on

Saturdays. Billy Joe taught me to wiggle my ears, make a hickory sap whistle and play rock, scissors, paper. He knew more dirty jokes than anyone I ever knew and he was goodhearted, but he had a secret daredevil living inside him.

My first chores were feeding the animals and loading hay onto a tractor-pulled trailer for delivery to the barn. After I became adept at loading hay, Billy Joe, who had been driving a tractor for two years, told the field supervisor I would be good on a tractor. With Billy Joe's help, I mastered the tractors in about two days. After that, I got another fifty cents a week in my responsibility allowance. Some days, if there was no need to use the tractor, I would milk cows with the other boys, mend fences or kill chickens for the night's evening meal. There was always something to be done.

Life at Baldwin was not bad. I had a roof over my head, clean clothes to wear, three squares a day and lots of male companionship, but it was not the same as a nuclear family. You never really formed a "loving" relationship with anyone in an orphanage. During my stay, several of the other boys were adopted and placed in "outside" homes. Some boys returned, some didn't. Alton Griffin, a member of my group, had been adopted by a family in Louisiana. He was gone for three months, then suddenly reappeared. When he returned, he was filled with hate. I wasn't sure what happened and never asked him, but he was a different person when he came back. Then, when Bill Winston, a boy from Augusta whom I worked with in the school laundry was adopted, I never saw him again.

Over the twelve months of 1955, my second year at Baldwin, I saved my "responsibility allowance" and bought a Hereford calf, which was my farm project for the year. He had his own stall in the barn and I spent the year feeding, grooming and caring for the animal. That fall, at the annual Georgia state fair at Tifton, I won second prize in the competition and received a blue ribbon and twenty-five dollars. Mr. Wainwright said I was destined to be a farmer.

Christmases were always a grand time at Baldwin. The facility had 200 acres of cotton in cultivation and when the crop was harvested, a percentage of the proceeds went to the boys for Christmas gifts. During one Christmas, each boy in my group received fifty dollars to spend. At Christmas, 1956, I got a total of one hundred dollars in "responsibility money." Each year, the school erected a massive tree in the auditorium and all of the boys pitched in to get it decorated. Dangerous gifts like BB or pellet guns were prohibited, but virtually everything else was allowed. One Christmas, Billy Joe and I spent all day and most of the night playing an electric football game the school gave me. Of course, there was always plenty to eat and, on Christmas Day, we all devoured the turkey and dressing and giblet gravy liked starved peasants.

***

During my days at Baldwin, I kept trying to reconnect with Jesse. Early on, I wrote a letter to his Columbus address, but it was returned. Several months later, I tried to call him in Columbus at his old number, but the operator said the number was no longer in service. When I tried to find a new number, there was no listing. I wondered what had happened to him. Two weeks later, I was in Valdosta and went to the office of the local Liberty Life Insurance Agency and asked if he knew of an agent named Karl Trubble in Georgia. He looked at his records and said he could only find one agent with that name in the entire company and it was in Tullahoma, Tennessee. I didn't think it was Jesse's father, but I got the address and sent a letter anyway. I never heard back. Two years later, I was back at the Liberty Life office in Valdosta asking about an agent named Karl Trubble. The man said there was one in Dallas, Texas and gave me the office address. I wrote another letter to that address, but again, I never heard back.

***

One day in early spring of 1957, my fifth year at Baldwin, Mr. Wainwright called me into his office.

"I have some news," he said. "The school administrator has been communicating with a man in Texas, a Mr. Charles Trammel, who is interested in adopting you."

I was shocked at his words. Somehow, it hadn't crossed my

mind that someone would want to adopt me.

"He's wealthy, has a thriving business in Dallas and wants to come to Baldwin and meet you. He'll be here next week."

***

Charles Trammel was a stocky man, maybe five eight, in his early fifties with thinning hair, sad eyes and a quiet, unassuming demeanor. When he arrived at Baldwin, he was modestly dressed in faded jeans, an open collar plaid shirt and fancy cowboy boots. He looked older than his years and he had a slight nervous twitch. During our private lunch in the school cafeteria, he asked about my life at Baldwin. I told him it met my needs, but I longed to be part of a real family. He asked about my ambitions in life and whether I knew anything about running a business. I answered his questions as honestly and politely as I could.

After lunch, I took him on a tour of the school and he seemed quite impressed. When he left, he shook my hand and said he would be in touch with my counselor. Two weeks later, Mr. Wainwright received a letter from Mr. Trammel requesting that I be allowed to come and spend the summer with him on a "trial basis." A week later, I was on a train to Dallas, Texas.

***

When the train pulled into the station, Mr. Trammel was waiting. Although he tried to put on a happy face when he greeted me, I could see he was not well. His personal aide, a middle-aged Mexican man, loaded me and my bags into a station wagon. The Trammel home was comfortable but not extravagant. Located on a quiet, tree-lined avenue near downtown Dallas, it was an older, nondescript ranch-style home with a picture window, well-manicured lawn and four bedrooms.

Upon my arrival, his wife Margaret, a bulky, unsmiling middle-aged woman, showed me to my room. She explained that dirty clothes should go into a red hamper in the corner by the bureau and maids would wash my clothes and clean the room on Saturdays and Wednesdays. She cautioned me that, when taking a shower, I should be sure the curtain was inside the stall because, otherwise, the bathroom floor would flood. As a school teacher, I could see she was a woman who lived with lots of rules.

***

That first night at dinner I met Benji, their frail, thirteen-year-old son who was in a wheelchair. Benji was born was spina bifida; he had shortened legs and forearms and nerve damage from the birth defect, which left him unable to walk. When his mother wheeled him to the dining table that night, I could see he didn't like me.

"Benji, this is Johnny," she said. "He has come to live with us."

The teenager pushed his glasses up on his nose, peered at me, then a sneer slowly formed across his face.

"You mean he'll be staying here and sleeping in a bed in our house?"

"That's right," she said.

"You and Father don't like me anymore?"

"Oh no," she said. "It's not that. We wanted a bigger family. Your father needs help with the business."

"I don't like him," Benji said. "One child is enough for this family."

***

After dinner, Mr. Trammel and I retired to his study. He tried to explain Benji's attitude.

"He'll be okay," Mr. Trammel said. "I think it's just the shock of having someone new in the house. More than anything, he's lonely and refuses to come out of his shell. He spends all of his time alone in his room reading books and watching TV. The only person he has any contact with outside the family is his tutor. He's a very intelligent child."

"I can see that," I said.

"I hate it that he's like that," Mr. Trammel continued. "The

61

doctor warned my wife about having a child after 40, but she wanted to get her education first."

He shook his head sadly.

I didn't pursue the subject.

***

The following morning, Mr. Trammel laid out my schedule for working in the family's paint supply business. During the summer, I would be working from 9 until 7 Monday through Saturday. Sundays would be free. He said he wanted me to work closely with the store managers so I could learn every nook and cranny of the business. Once school began, he would buy me a car and I would enroll at the nearby Crockett High School.

"Someday I want you to be able to run the business on your own," he said. "We'll get started in the morning."

***

Mr. Trammel owned four paint supply stores. The main store was in Dallas and served as the staging point for the others. Located in a busy shopping center, the Dallas store was stacked floor to ceiling with paint—both enamel and water-based—of every imaginable color. There were brushes, thinners, drop cloths, mixers, ladders… everything a painter or a do-it-yourselfer would need for a painting job. Mr. Trammel said he wanted me to work first in the main store and learn its operations, then he would familiarize me with the other stores. So, I set about learning the paint supply business.

Working at the counter, I quickly learned to present a polite, accommodating attitude toward customers. Once I had proven myself at the counter, Mr. Trammel showed me the books and explained that here was where most business decisions were made. Keeping the business operating was a constant juggling act, he said. Inventory had to be weighed against sales. New supplies had to be ordered to replace old ones; distributors had to be pressured to deliver popular, fast-moving items. So I pitched in to learn the business. I wanted to

make Mr. Trammel happy. It was new, it was different and I was having fun.

In mid-August, near the end of the summer, Mr. Trammel announced he wanted to legally adopt me. He said I didn't have to do anything; his attorney would handle all of the papers with Baldwin School for Boys.

That was the end of my orphanage days. As I look back now, I always remember those five years with both sadness and nostalgia. Baldwin had been good for me in several ways. Never had I had that level of daily discipline in my life. At home in Columbus, I had no authority figure to dictate my daily activities. All I was expected to do was go to school. Baldwin added a sense of responsibility and discipline that I would never have had had I not attended there. Baldwin taught me a work ethic, which paid off handsomely when I began working for Mr. Trammel. Sometimes, fate has a strange way of rewarding one.

***

So, I settled in with the Trammels. Margaret was always preoccupied with the upkeep of the house, fussing with maids, gardeners and deliverymen. She had an opinion about everything; the "loose woman" across the street, the mailman that had body odor, and her brother who couldn't "keep his nose out of a bottle." Benji kept his distance. At the dinner table, he never spoke to me. If he and I were in the same room, he wouldn't address me. At the stairs, a special apparatus had been installed to allow him to go up and down the stairs on his own in the wheelchair. Sometimes, he would get stuck halfway down. When that happened, he would never call on me to help. He always called one of the maids, his mother or his father. As a result, I was at Mr. Trammel's side most of the time.

***

Once summer ended, Mr. Trammel bought me a car, a 1954 Chevrolet Bel-air, and I enrolled at Crockett High School. That was when, on the first day of high school, a miracle happened.

That's all you could call it, a plain, out-and-out miracle.

Crockett High was located at the corner of Tenth and Oakmont Streets in downtown Dallas. On the opposite corner, directly across from the high school, sat a small grocery store, and next door was Steven's Drug Store. "Stevens," as the students called it, served as a convenient hang-out each morning before class for all the students who wanted to chat with friends, buy a pack of notebook paper, leer at members of the opposite sex or simply have a shake and an order of fries before class. As a result, the corner was a bustling beehive of loitering high schoolers each morning from around 7:30 until 8 a.m. when classes began.

On that particular September morning, decked out in my penny loafers, jeans and white tee-shirt, I waded into this beehive of high school students for the first time. The moment I rounded the corner, the first thing I saw was two other students—a big, burly, blonde teenager with a crew cut and a smaller one with a shaved head—leaning on a yellow hotrod parked directly at the corner.

The moment the smaller one saw me, he jeered.

"Hoo! Hoo! Hoo!" he called, imitating a monkey.

For a moment, I stopped and glared at him.

"Well, look who we have here!" he said. "The new kid on the block."

The burly crew-cut one snickered at his friend's words.

"Look at those shoes!" the smaller one said. "Only faggots wear shoes like that."

The larger one snickered again.

"What's your name?" he said.

"Kiss my ass!" I replied.

"Faggot! Faggot!" the smaller one yelled.

Instantly, I made a move toward the smaller youth. As I did, the bigger one stepped forward and blocked my path.

"Watch it, punk!" he said gruffly.

For a moment, I looked from the large one to the small one. Then, thinking the better of it, I turned abruptly and started into the drug store.

"Chicken, say chicken!" the smaller one called after me, waving his arms. "Cluck! Cluck! Cluck!"

I didn't look back.

Inside the drug store, the booths and aisles were packed with groups of teenage girls, many dressed in high school sweaters and bobby sox, giggling and chattering among themselves. In the corner, a jukebox was blaring:

"Who walks in the classroom cool and slow, who calls the English teacher daddy-o, Charley Brown, he's a clown, that Charley Brown, hc's a clown…"

Stepping through the crowd, I made my way to the soda fountain.

"What'll it be, buddy?" the soda jerk asked, wiping the slick, polished marble countertop with a wet cloth.

"Cherry coke, no ice."

"Coming right up."

A group of girls at the front table were eyeing me. I smiled. They giggled.

"That'll be twenty cents," said the soda jerk, sitting the cherry coke on the counter.

I fished through a handful of change and placed two dimes on the counter. Then, taking the cherry Coke, I started back outside. As I passed the group of girls seated at the front booth, one of them, a dark-haired beauty, looked up and smiled.

"Hi, handsome," she said.

I smiled. This brought a ripple of nervous giggles from the other girls.

Outside again, I settled against the brick wall at the corner of the building. As I sipped the cherry Coke, my eyes wandered through the crowd of students. Nearby, two male students were busy reading a copy of *MAD* magazine, pointing to the pictures and laughing. There were scattered groups of students here and there, chatting, laughing, talking about the new school year and eyeing members of the opposite sex.

At the street, in front of a parking meter, I saw two male students—one, a tall, dark-haired student with long hair and ducktails and another, a chubby, blonde-headed student wearing glasses, matching quarters. For some reason, my wandering eyes instinctively homed in on the dark-haired student matching quarters. For a moment, I studied him. The build, the black, wavy hair, the way he held his chin, the way he stood all seemed familiar to me. Very familiar. Quickly, I gulped down the remainder of the cherry Coke and tossed the paper cup in a nearby waste basket. As I approached for a closer look, the dark-haired student was oblivious to my presence. I watched as he flipped a quarter into the air.

"Even!" he said, catching the quarter, then holding it flat on his arm.

The chubby student went through the same motion, then each exposed their coin.

"Damn!" the chubby youth said, then handed over his quarter.

As the two started to flip new coins, I saw an opening.

"Excuse me!" I said.

"Huh?" the dark-haired teenager said distractedly. Then he turned to face me.

For a moment, the dark-haired student and I stared at one another in disbelief.

"Jesse?" I said tentatively. "Jesse Trubble?"

He was as shocked as I was.

"Johnny? Johnny Chance!" he replied.

"Yeah!" I said with a hearty laugh.

"Jesus Christ!" he said. "Are you going to Crockett High?"

"I sure am!"

"Aw, man," he said. "This is wild. I mean, this is just too wild."

The chubby student who had been matching quarters turned toward Jesse.

"You going to match quarters or have a family reunion?"

"Robert, I got to break it off," Jesse said.

"You're into me for six dollars," the chubby kid said.

"You'll get it back tomorrow," Jesse said.

"You always say that," the other youth said disgustedly, then, shaking his head, he turned and walked away.

"Great to see you again," Jesse said.

"Same here," I replied.

Across the street at the high school, we heard the sound of the first bell.

"Let's go to class," Jesse said.

Then we turned and started walking toward the high

school.

At the corner, I pointed out the two students sitting on the yellow hotrod.

"Who are those two?"

"The big one is Wooten Watson," Jesse said "He's a football star and a big man on campus. He thinks he's a bad man."

"And the smaller one?"

"That's Shooter Copeland, Wooten's shadow," Jesse said. "He's quick with the insults. Best to just stay away from him."

"Somebody is going to kill him one of these days."

"You're probably right. I just hope it's not me."

***

As we walked across the high school lawn, we chatted.

"I never dreamed I'd ever see you again," he said. "What are you doing in Dallas?"

I explained about being adopted by the Trammels.

"What about you?" I asked.

"After my father died, I came to live with my Uncle Marvin here in Dallas. I've been here three years."

I peered at him.

"Sorry to hear about your dad," I said.

He shrugged and changed the subject.

"What classes are you taking?"

"Algebra, biology, English, PE and Latin."

"Latin?"

"Yeah," I said. "Mrs. Trammel says it will help me in my medical studies."

"Who you got for biology?" Jesse asked.

"Abston."

"I got Todd," Jesse said.

"What about algebra?"

"Davis," Johnny said.

"Damn! I've got Faulkner."

"English?"

"Abercrombie!"

"You got 'Sack' Abercrombie for English?" Jesse asked

excitedly. "Great! We'll have a ball in that class."

"Why do you call her 'Sack'?"

"Because she's got big knockers."

I laughed.

For several moments, we walked quietly.

"I still can't believe I met you again," he said with a laugh.

"Neither can I," I said, shaking my head incredulously.

"What period you got lunch?" Jesse asked.

"Fourth."

"So do I," he said. "We got lots of catching up to do."

As we walked along the sidewalk to the school entrance, I studied him. Instantly, I could see the same crazy magic I had sensed the first time I met him. At nineteen, he was tall for his age, maybe six one; he had long dark hair, ducktails and sideburns like Elvis and, when he walked, he had that same confident carriage, a swagger that told the world he was fearless. As I watched him mount the first step to enter the school building, I could see he was the epitome of late fifties "cool."

***

Three hours later, we were in the high school cafeteria chowing down on meatloaf, macaroni and cheese, potato salad and chocolate milk.

"What happened to your dad?" I asked.

"My mother broke his heart one final time," Jesse said. "In the fall of 1953, my mother's mother called him to ask about me and, while they were talking, my father asked about my mother and she gave him a phone number. A few days later, Daddy called the number and talked to her. She asked about me. She wanted to know what I looked like and how I was doing. Finally, she said she wanted to come visit. After the phone call, Daddy got his hopes up. He told me, when she came to visit, they might be getting back together. A week later, when he called again about her travel arrangements, the number had been disconnected. She had disappeared again."

Jesse stopped to take a swig of chocolate milk.

"Then he started drinking," Jesse continued. "Real hard. It

wasn't beer this time, it was the hard stuff and he started missing time at work. This went on for about a month, and finally, they laid him off work. One morning, I got up to go to school and noticed that Daddy hadn't got out of bed. When I went into his room, he wasn't breathing. The doctor said later he had had a heart attack in his sleep. He was holding a picture of my mother when I found him."

"It must have been tough," Johnny said.

"Oh, it was," Jesse said. "I loved my father."

"Your father was good to me," I said. "I'll always remember all the times he transported us around Muscogee County in that Ford sedan."

We ate quietly for several moments.

"Has your mother ever tried to contact you again?" I asked

"Oh, no!" he said, a note of bitterness in his voice. "If she did, I would tell her to go to hell in a minute."

"You would say that to your mother?"

"Oh, yeah," Jesse said. "I could never forgive her for what she did to my father. I'll never let a woman do that to me. Never!"

Jesse glanced up at the lunch room clock.

"Come on," he said. "We better hurry or we'll be late for our first English class."

***

Ten minutes later, we were climbing the stairs to the second floor for our English class. As we started up the stairs, three girls were going up the steps ahead us.

Jesse motioned with his head at one of the girls ahead of them.

"The one in the middle is Barbara Troncalli. She's Italian. A perfect cup and saucer ass."

I glanced at the girl he was indicating. She did have a beautifully-shaped rear end.

"What's a cup and saucer ass?"

"If she lies on her stomach, you could put a cup and saucer between her back and her hips and the bottom of the saucer wouldn't touch anything."

I laughed.

We walked quietly for a moment.

"Look!" Jesse said. "She's going into our English class."

Inside the classroom, Jesse glanced around for desk. In the back corner, he spotted a chubby, dark-haired teenager wearing glasses,

"Come on!" he said. "Let's sit back here with my friend Edward."

Edward Latimer was a rotund, cherubic-faced teenager with glasses who never stopped smiling. Almost as wide as he was tall, Edward was one of those people who did everything slowly. Each morning during PE class, when students were required to run a mile around the football field, Edward was always last. If one of Edward's classes went on a field trip, you could always be sure that Edward would bring up the rear. At school assemblies, Edward always arrived after everyone else was seated.

Once we were seated, Jesse couldn't take his eyes off the girl we had seen in the hallway.

"Edward!" he whispered. "Check out the butt on Barbara Troncalli."

Edward pushed his glasses up on his nose and peered uneasily at the girl. His face formed a cherubic smile.

"Cup and saucer ass!" Jesse said. "Now, Edward, would you like to just tear her clothes off and let her have it? Ooooooo-weeee! Wouldn't that be too much?"

Edward smiled from ear to ear.

"How'd you become friends with him?" I asked.

"Last year, when we were in PE together, another student kept picking on Edward and making fun of him. After he pushed Edward down, I jumped him and put the other kid in his place. He never messed with Edward again. Edward has been my friend ever since."

***

The following Friday night, Jesse came to the Trammel home to meet my new family. I knew Margaret, the eternal school teacher, would disapprove of his appearance. Mr.

Trammel greeted him cordially and made polite table conversation. When Jesse offered his hand to Benji, he looked at the hand, then turned away coldly.

Jesse was unfazed. He knelt beside the wheelchair.

"What's that behind your ear?" Jesse said.

Annoyed, Benji put his hand to his ear.

"There's nothing behind my ear."

"Yes, there is," Jesse said, reaching behind his ear and pulling back a quarter. "A quarter was hiding behind your ear."

Benji was mystified. He smiled.

"How'd you do that?"

"I didn't do anything. There was a quarter behind your ear."

"No, there wasn't."

"Now there's an ace in your shirt pocket."

"No, there isn't," Benji said, looking into his pocket and seeing nothing.

Jesse pulled an ace of hearts from out of his pocket.

"Wow!" Benji said. "That's cool. How did you do that?"

"It's magic."

"Will you teach me?"

"Someday. Maybe."

Benji was impressed. He smiled.

"I like your hair," he said. "Just like Elvis. If I were like you, I'd let my hair grow like that."

Over the course of the dinner, Benji kept asking Jesse questions: where he was from; how long he had known me; what books he had read. Never had I seen Benji open up to someone like that. Before he left that night, Benji pressed Jesse to show him the trick with the quarter and, once he learned it, he had to try it on everyone in the family. When he got ready to leave, Jesse said his good-byes, then offered his hand to Benji again.

"It was swell to meet you," Benji said, shaking Jesse's hand.

"Good to meet you!" Jesse replied.

Once Jesse was out the door, Mr. Trammel turned to his wife.

"How did you like Johnny's friend?"

"He shows a lot of anti-social behavior with his hair and his flippant careless ways."

"Mother, why do you say that?" Benji asked

"Everything about him speaks of disrespect for his elders. Especially the long hair and ducktails."

"That's the style," Benji said. "If I was like him, I'd have hair like that."

"No, you wouldn't."

"Oh, Mother, you're so old-fashioned."

"The sort of behavior he is exhibiting is going to land him in reform school."

Mr. Trammel laughed.

"Every generation has its quirks the previous generation doesn't approve of."

"That's right, Father," Benji said.

***

The following Monday morning, I met Jesse in the high school parking lot. Then together we started across the street to "Stevens." As we rounded the corner, the first thing we saw was Wooten and Shooter leaning on the yellow hotrod at the corner. Instantly upon seeing Jesse and me, Shooter started.

"Hey, look!" he called. "It's the new kid with the faggy shoes."

"And the Jew boy!" said Wooten.

Jesse peered at Shooter.

"Watch your mouth, punk!" Jesse said. "Or I'll close it for you."

"Yeah, sure, Jew boy!" Shooter sneered. "You and whose army?"

Jesse glared angrily, then stepped toward him.

"I wouldn't do that if I were you," Wooten said, holding out his arm to block Jesse's path.

Jesse didn't budge.

"Are you his protector?" he asked, glaring into Wooten's face.

"That's right," Wooten said.

Jesse stepped back, then, with a sudden swing, he slammed

his right leg into the back of Wooten's crossed legs, which were supporting his weight on the hotrod. Instantly, Wooten's butt was flat on the street curb.

"Now what you going to do, Mr. Protector?" Jesse asked.

Jesse's reaction had taken the larger youth by such total surprise that it took several seconds to register.

"Why you...!" Wooten said, still sitting on the ground and glaring up at Jesse.

Suddenly, Wooten was on his feet and he and Jesse faced off to fight.

"Come on, fat boy," Jesse shouted, ready to mix it up. "Show me your stuff!"

Instantly, Jesse and Wooten became the focus of attention at the corner and the other students started backing away to give them room to fight.

Suddenly, Shooter called out to Wooten.

"Woot! Woot!" he said, pointing to the corner. "Here comes Lamon!"

Both Jesse and Wooten looked to where Shooter was pointing and saw Robert Lamon, the school's head football coach. For a moment, the coach, seeing the two were paired off to fight, stopped.

"Are you students having a problem here?" he asked.

"Oh no, Coach!" Wooten answered, forcing a smile. "Just a friendly discussion."

The coach turned to Jesse.

"Is that right?" he asked.

"That's right, Coach," Jesse said sheepishly. "Just a friendly discussion."

The coach looked from one to the other.

"Make sure it stays *friendly*," Lamon said, emphasizing the word. "Now break it up!"

Then he turned and started into the drug store.

Across the street, the first bell for classes was sounding.

***

The following Sunday, I asked Mr. Trammel if I could spend the day with Jesse. He approved. An hour later, when I pulled up in the yard of his Uncle Marvin's brick home, Jesse was waiting.

"Come on!" he said, heading to his hotrod parked nearby. "I want you to meet Bobby and Vavaloo."

"Vavaloo?" I asked.

"Yes! Vavaloo!" Jesse repeated. "That's his 1954 Studebaker Golden Hawk."

Twenty minutes later, we pulled up in the driveway of a plush, multi-story home on Dallas' upscale North side. Ahead of us, in the garage, I could see a young man working under the hood of a 1954 Studebaker.

"That's Bobby Cottle," Jesse said. "Come on."

We got out of Jesse's hotrod and started walking up the driveway to the garage. When Bobby raised his head from under the hood, I was taken aback. He was a dead-ringer for movie star James Dean. Not only did he have the lean face, the small mouth and the high, well-chiseled cheek bones, but he had the searching, hurt-animal eyes of the famous actor.

"Jesse!" Bobby called.

"Bobby!" Jesse said. "This is my friend Johnny."

Bobby, a cigarette clenched in his teeth, looked at his hand.

"Hope you don't mind a little grease," he said.

"No problem," I said, shaking his hand.

"What are you doing?" Jesse asked.

"I got a new four-barrel carburetor I'm trying to install," Bobby said, "but I can't figure out the linkage."

With that, he ducked back under the hood and started tinkering again. Moments later, frustration in his eyes, Bobby withdrew his head from under the hood.

"Let me see what I can do," I said, ducking my head under the hood.

"You've got to connect each linkage in the same order in which the barrel kicks in," I said. "The linkage for the first barrel is connected first. Then, the second, then the third..."

Bobby turned to Jesse.

"I didn't know your friend was a hotrodder," he said.

"Neither did I," Jesse said.

I still had my head under the hood.

"Look at this," I said.

Bobby stuck his head under the hood again.

"This one is connected first," I said.

With that, I held the linkage and Bobby connected it to the lever on the first barrel.

"Now I got it!" Bobby said.

Over the next thirty minutes, I held the linkages for each carburetor barrel while Bobby connected them. Once the last one was connected, he wiped his hands on an oil rag and turned to me.

"You're pretty good," he said.

"I made all A's in auto mechanics at the orphanage I attended in Georgia," I said.

"You learned your lessons well," Bobby said.

I stood back and admired the hotrod.

"What'll she do in the quarter?"

"Thirteen seconds," Bobby said.

"That's pretty fast," I said.

"She should do better now that she's got the four-barrel," Bobby said. "Come on, let's take her down to the Sand Pits."

***

In the late forties, a sandy, tabletop area along the banks of the Trinity River on Dallas's west side was the site for Consolidated Industries, an internationally-known company that specialized in services related to the oil industry. The company, which specialized in building refineries and providing reservoir, drilling and production services, took up almost twenty acres along the river's edge where it had administrative offices as well as storage areas for drilling, pipelines and metal fabrication equipment. The principal road in and out of the property was directly along the river's edge and, through the years, the trucks and other heavy equipment that passed over it had compacted the fine sand into a hard, smooth surface. In 1954, the company moved to Oklahoma and, in doing so, the spot where the old buildings had stood became little more than a deserted expanse of weeds, bushes and rusting metal. By 1956, the only visible sign of the company that remained was the hard-packed strip of sand along the river's edge. Before long, local teenagers discovered the area and dubbed it "The Sand Pits." It was the place where they could park with dates, drink beer and shoot the breeze. Also, they discovered that the strip of hard-packed sand along the river's edge was perfect for drag racing.

When we arrived at the Sand Pits, Jesse and I got out and Jesse prepared to line up Vavaloo's front bumper with the track's starting line.

"Time me!" Bobby said.

As Bobby edged the car forward, Jesse held up his hand.

"Right there!" he said. "You're on it."

Then Jesse turned to his watch.

"I'll drop my hand at 12."

With that, Bobby revved the Studebaker's engine and watched Jesse, waiting for the signal. At the drop of Jesse's hand, the car's mighty engine roared, then in a flurry of squealing tires and white smoke, the hotrod with "Vavaloo" stenciled on the front fender roared off the line and shot off down the strip.

"Holy moly!" I said. "That thing will fly."

Moments later, the Studebaker returned to the starting line.

"What was my time?"

"Fourteen seconds."

"I can do better than that. I'm going to have to tinker with the carburetor some more."

"What was she on when you crossed the finish line?" Jesse asked.

"Ninety-five miles an hour," Bobby said, smiling from ear to ear.

Jesse shook his head.

"You got the fastest car in town," Jesse said, patting the hood. "I mean, this baby here is the fastest rod around."

"Wait 'til I race Wooten again," Bobby said with a big smile. "I'm going to kick his ass."

***

At Crockett High, Bobby Cottle and Wooten Watson were

known to be the two premiere hotrodders. When Bobby was a senior at Crockett, he owned a 1948 Mercury with a V-8 that would outrun anything at the Sand Pits. Then, after Bobby graduated, Wooten souped up a 1952 Ford cut-down with a V-8 engine, solid lifters, special heads and a high-speed rear end, and he became the man to beat. Now, for over six months, Wooten had held the title.

***

The following Saturday night, when Bobby, Jesse and I arrived at the Sand Pits, the drag races were already underway and, as usual, Wooten's Ford was cleaning everybody.

"You going to run that piece of crap against me again?" Wooten called out when he saw Bobby, with me and Jesse inside, pull up in the Studebaker.

Bobby smiled.

"You're mine tonight!" he said.

"Yeah, sure," Wooten said sarcastically. "Who are those two punks you got in the car with you?"

"To hell with you!" Jesse said, shooting Wooten the bird.

At the starting line, Janice Dickerson, Crockett High's known wild child, was flagging cars off the starting line. With a beer in one hand and her brassiere in the other, she stood bare-breasted, and waited for the Studebaker and the Ford to pull up to the line. Finally, once the bumpers of both cars were aligned, she held up the brassiere.

"Okay, boys," she said with a big smile. "Keep your eyes on the track and not on these."

With that, she swung her bare breasts from side to side.

"Ready?" she asked, raising the white undergarment.

Both cars, engines revving, were straining.

Suddenly, she jerked the brassiere downward.

With that, the Studebaker and the Ford shot off the line in a roar of screaming tires and churning engines. Off the line, Wooten's Ford got the jump, but once they shifted into second gear, the Studebaker shot into the lead. Then, after shifting into third, the four-barrel kicked in and, on the straightaway, Bobby easily won by three car lengths. Moments later, the two hotrods returned up the track.

"Luck!" Wooten shouted, a note of annoyance in his voice. "Pure luck! Let's run again!"

Once again, Janice, between swigs of beer, aligned the two cars' bumpers on the starting line, then raised the brassiere.

"Hey, baby!" Janice said to Bobby. "That Studebaker is a fast boogie-woogie."

"Vavaloo is the fastest car in town!" Bobby said confidently.

"Come on!" Wooten said impatiently. "Cut the bullshit and start the race!"

Seconds later, Janice brought down the brassiere again.

Once more, in a flurry of screaming tires and roaring engines, the two cars shot off the line. Then, exactly as before, Wooten got the jump, but when he shifted into second, Bobby took the lead. Once they shifted to third, the Studebaker was ahead of the Ford again by three car lengths at the finish line.

Back at the starting line, Wooten pulled up beside the Studebaker.

"What you got under that hood?" he asked.

"I'll bet you'd like to know," Bobby said with a big, victorious smile.

***

On Monday night of the following week, Bobby, Jesse and I went into the Smokehouse Pool Hall, the hangout for local high school boys on weeknights. Located next door to a cab company at 14th and Woolsey, students could shoot pool and get updates on the local high school scene. When we walked in, we saw Wooten and another teenager playing pool. "Shooter" Copeland, his shadow, was seated nearby.

"Who's the guy shooting pool with Wooten?" Jesse asked.

"That's Tommy Martin," Bobby said. "He's a pretty good pool player."

Moments later, the three of us had each selected a cue stick and Jesse broke the rack to play rotation pool. Over the next forty minutes, the three of us played rotation pool and Bobby won every game.

"Where did you learn to shoot pool like that?" I asked.

"When I was growing up, we had two pool tables in the basement of our house. By the time I was 14, I could beat my father, who was a champion in his own right."

I glanced across the pool room.

"Look who's coming," I said.

Jesse turned and saw Wooten and Tommy coming toward us.

"Hey, rich boy!" Wooten said. "Want to play my friend here some short rack nine-ball?"

Bobby looked at his would-be competition, then turned back to Wooten.

"How much?" he said.

"Five dollars a game."

Bobby looked to Jesse.

"Got any cash?"

"Yeah!" Jesse said. "Go ahead and play him. I think you can beat him."

Bobby hesitated.

"Well?" Wooten said. "Chicken...say chicken."

Bobby glared at Wooten, then turned to the house man.

"Rack 'em up!"

With that, the house man racked the balls for short rack nine ball. Wooten flipped a coin and Bobby won the toss. On the first break, Bobby made the three ball, then ran the one and two balls. After Tommy made the four and five balls, he had a very difficult bank shot on the nine and missed, leaving Bobby an easy shot for the winner. With that, Wooten handed Bobby five dollars.

On the second break, Bobby made the five, then ran the one and two balls. After Tommy made the three and four, but missed the five ball, Bobby was set up perfectly for a run. With that, Bobby ran the last two balls and won the second game. Wooten handed Bobby another five-dollar bill.

In the third game, Bobby made the five ball on the break. Then, after making the two, he had an easy three-on-nine combination for another winner. Wooten handed Bobby a third five-dollar bill.

Over the next two hours, Bobby and Tommy played

twenty-two games of short rack nine ball. Of those, Bobby won eighteen. After the twenty-second game, Wooten called Tommy aside. Then he turned back to Bobby.

"That's enough," Wooten said, throwing another five-dollar bill on the table.

"No more money?" Bobby asked, obvious sarcasm in his voice.

"That's right," Wooten said sullenly.

"No have money, no can play," Bobby said.

With that, Bobby started pulling five-dollar bills out of his pockets. For several minutes, he sorted and counted the money on the table.

"Seventy dollars!" Bobby said. "Not bad for a couple of hours' work."

With that, Bobby folded the wad of money, put it in his pocket and the three of us started out of the pool hall. As we reached the door, Bobby looked back at Wooten and his boys. All three were glaring at us. For a brief moment, Bobby smiled, then gleefully applauded before going out the door. Wooten, Shooter and Tommy were fuming.

***

Later that night, Jesse and I were with Bobby at his house until almost midnight. The son of a former school teacher and a well-to-do oilman, Bobby Cottle truly had a life of leisure. At age twenty, his wealthy parents had set up a trust that gave him a handsome stipend each month, so there was no need to work. Although he had enrolled at Texas A&M, his mother's alma mater, he dropped out after the first semester, bored and unsure of what he wanted to do. Although there were six bedrooms in the spacious Cottle home, Bobby lived in the garage. Already equipped with a bathroom, he had built a small closet and installed a small cot in one corner for sleeping. The garage walls were covered with stills from James Dean movies. There were scenes from *Giant*, *Rebel Without a Cause* and *East of Eden*. The one still that particularly caught my eye was a scene from *East of Eden* in which the James Dean character is talking to his mother, the local brothel keeper. The woman, dressed in a severe Victorian hat and a black veil, was staring knives at the James Dean character.

Later that night, as Jesse and I rode back to his Uncle Marvin's house to get my car, I commented about Bobby.

"Being around Bobby is like being in a James Dean movie," I said. "Everything around him seems larger than life."

"I know," Jesse said. "He's a trip. He really likes you."

***

Every morning on school days, at the end of third period, Jesse and I would meet briefly in the first-floor restroom of the science building. After two months of the same routine, we learned to predict the traffic in and out of the restroom at the beginning of the third period. At 11:01, one minute after the bell, the place was flooded with smokers who, having spent three hours in class without a cigarette, would duck in to light up, take a few quick puffs then duck back out. At 11:05, Jesse's pal Edward Latimer, who had a free period, would come in and take a seat in one of the stalls. Ten minutes later, a flood of guys would come in to take a leak, comb their hair and freshen up a bit. Finally, around 11:30, Coach Lamon would arrive to do his business. By then, all the smokers and hair-combers would be gone.

The following Monday morning, when Jesse and I rushed into the restroom, we saw Wooten and Shooter, who was a smoker, standing at the urinals. After finishing his business, Wooten glared at Jesse.

"I'm going to have your ass for the other morning, Jew boy," Wooten said, looking menacingly at Jesse. "I'm just biding my time."

"Sure you are, fat boy!"

Moments later, Jesse ducked into the stall beside Edward's. When he came out, Wooten and Shooter immediately went into the stall.

By then, Jesse and I were at the sinks washing our hands and combing our hair. Behind us, Wooten and Shooter quickly emerged from the stall and headed for the door. Then, just as

Jesse and I stepped away from the sinks, there was a sudden enormous explosion, the sound reverberating against the restroom walls. There was the sound of breaking ceramics and spewing water and the students could see that the restroom floor was rapidly flooding with water.

Instantly, panic broke out and some twelve students, including Jesse and me, made a mad rush to the door. Then, when we reached the door, the rush of escaping students came to a sudden stop. Coach Lamon, who was coming in, blocked their entrance.

"Back inside!" he shouted. "All of you! Back inside! Now!"

With that, the coach herded all of the students back into the restroom. Inside, while keeping an eye on his suspects, the coach surveyed the damage. The commode in one of the stalls had had its belly blown away and water, toilet paper, human waste, and urine were pouring out on the restroom floor.

"Jeez!" he said. "What a smell!"

Then, anger and resolution in his face, he turned back to the students.

"All of you!" he ordered. "Go to the conference room in the principal's office. Now!"

Ten minutes later, the twelve suspects, including me, Jesse, and Edward Latimer, were gathered in the school conference room.

"Somebody is going to pay for the damage to that restroom," Coach Lamon began. "I know one of you flushed a lit cherry bomb down the commode. Now who was it?"

For a moment, he scanned the group.

Each of the students looked around at the others. Nobody raised their hand.

"Does anybody want to confess and save all of us a lot of time and trouble?" Coach Lamon asked.

Again, nobody raised their hand.

With that, the coach went down the list of names and personally asked each student, including me, Jesse and Edward, if they had done the deed. All of us, one by one, denied it.

"Okay," Coach Lamon said finally. "I intend to get to the

bottom of this. I want all of you back here at 3 p.m. when classes end. All of you are going to stay after school until somebody confesses."

***

That afternoon, when we went to English class, Edward pulled Jesse aside.

"I know who flushed the cherry bomb down the commode," he said.

"Who?" Jesse asked.

"Wooten and Shooter," Edward said. "They wanted it to look like you did it."

"Why didn't you tell Coach Lamon?" Jesse said.

"I'm afraid," Edward said. "If Wooten and Shooter found out I told, they would beat me up."

"No," Jesse said. "Me and Johnny wouldn't never let that happen. How do you know it was Wooten and Shooter?"

"I heard Wooten tell Shooter to give him the lighter."

"You've got to tell Lamon!" Jesse said urgently. "Don't worry about Wooten and Shooter; me and Johnny can handle those two."

"Are you sure?" Edward asked. "I don't want to get beat up."

"Just trust us!" Jesse said reassuringly.

***

That afternoon, in the conference room at the principal's office, Lamon was unrelenting in his pursuit of the culprit.

"I mean it!" he said. "Somebody is going to pay for this. It's going to cost several thousand dollars to repair the restroom."

"Can we talk to you, Coach?" Jesse said.

"What do you want to say?"

"Can we talk privately?" Jesse said.

Coach Lamon looked at us. Then he motioned us outside into the hallway.

"Did you two flush the cherry bomb down the commode?"

he asked.

"No, but we know who did," Jesse said.

"Who?"

"Wooten Watson and Shooter Copeland."

"That's what I expected you to say," the coach said. "You two have been having some problems with Wooten and Copeland. Right?"

"Not really," Jesse said.

"Oh yes, you have!" the coach continued. "You and Wooten were about to fight down at Stevens the other morning before I broke it up."

"That was no big deal," Jesse said.

The coach studied Jesse for a moment.

"Ask Edward Latimer," Jesse said finally. "He'll tell you the truth! He was sitting on the throne in the next stall when the whole thing happened."

"Are you sure?" the coach asked.

"I'm sure," Jesse said.

Moments later, Coach Lamon, Jesse and I returned to the conference room.

"Latimer!" the coach said.

Edward perked up. The coach motioned him out into the hallway.

For fifteen minutes, as the other suspects waited, Coach Lamon and Edward Latimer were out in the hallway. Finally, they returned.

"Okay," the coach said. "Everybody here is off the hook."

***

The following morning, when Jesse and I arrived at Stevens Drug Store, Wooten and Shooter were absent. We asked several other students about their whereabouts, but no one knew.

That afternoon, before English class, Jesse pulled Edward aside.

"What happened to Wooten and Shooter?"

"They got expelled. They're going to Clara Barton High now."

Jesse looked at me.
We giggled with sheer delight.

*****

Two months passed. During that time, my and Jesse's lives changed. In late September, Bobby went to visit with an uncle in California and the drag racing came to an end and girls entered the picture. In English class, Jesse had met Brenda Cherry, a petite brunette, and they started dating. After Jesse arranged a date for me with her younger sister Emily, we started double dating, and throughout the months of October and November, our lives became an endless string of sock hops, drive-ins, movies, parking at "Lover's Leap" and high school football games.

*****

In early December, Jesse announced that Bobby was back in town and he wanted to go see him. The moment Bobby saw us, he broke into a big smile and hugged us. The first thing Jesse told him was that Wooten and Shooter had been expelled.
"They're going to Clara Barton now?"
"That's right," Jesse said.
"Well, let's go over and see if we can foment some turmoil," Bobby said. "Next Friday night is the big game between Crockett and Barton High."

*****

In mid-December of each year, the biggest high school event in east Dallas was the annual football contest between Crockett High and their cross-town archrival, Clara Barton. In the town, Crockett was considered the upscale high school since most of the students were the children of wealthy professionals, prominent businessmen and community leaders. The students at Clara Barton, however, were mostly the offspring of factory workers, tradesmen and other blue-collar types who toiled in the machine shops, the plastics factories and pipe foundries on the other side of town. As a result, the haves vs. have nots mentality had generated a genuine hatred between the students of both schools and resulted in an intense football rivalry. Clara Barton's football team could lose every game in a season, but if they beat Crockett, the students and the alumni considered the season a winning one.

On the night of the big game, Bobby, Jesse and I arrived at Barton High a full hour before the game began. Already a huge crowd from both schools had gathered in front of the school building, shouting insults at one another. At the statue of Clara Barton in front of the school building, Barton students had erected huge banners proclaiming support for their team.

"Look!" Bobby said as we cruised past the crowd in his Studebaker. "There's Wooten and Shooter. Come on!"

"What are you going to do?" I asked.

"We're going help Clara Barton hold her breasts up," he said.

Thirty minutes later, Bobby, Jesse and I walked out of a department store with a large-sized woman's brassiere and two cans of spray paint. One can was blue and the other was gold, the Crockett High's school colors. Before returning to Barton High, Bobby stopped and spray-painted one cup of the brassiere blue and the other gold.

"Check this out!" Bobby said, holding up the painted brassiere. "Wooten and Shooter are going to just love this."

Back at Barton High, the crowd of Barton students, including Wooten and Shooter, were still shouting insults at Crockett students. Finally, Bobby parked the Studebaker on a side street. Then, with the painted brassiere in hand, Bobby, Jesse and I walked back to the statue of Clara Barton in front of the high school.

"I'll climb up and fit it on," Bobby said. "Jesse, you go around behind and connect the strap."

At first, Wooten, Shooter and the other Barton students didn't know what was happening when they first saw Bobby, holding the white undergarment, climb up on the pedestal of their beloved statue. The moment he fitted the blue and gold brassiere over the statue's breasts, however, and Jesse snapped the strap, they got the message.

"Hey!" Wooten yelled. "What the hell do you think you're doing?"

With that, Wooten, Shooter and some nine or ten other Barton students stormed across the high school's front lawn toward Bobby, Jesse and me.

Wooten, who was leading the charge, went straight for Bobby. As he approached, Bobby pulled a motorcycle chain out of his hip pocket. When Wooten came within striking distance, Bobby lashed out with the chain in a whip-like motion.

"Aaaaaaeeeiiii!" Wooten screamed in pain as the motorcycle chain slapped him across the right side of his face, cutting a huge gash and drawing blood.

Wooten stopped and grabbed his face.

Instantly, Bobby turned to confront Shooter and, with another sudden whip-like motion, he swung the chain, clipping Shooter across the right cheek with its very tip. Instantly, Shooter stopped and put his hand to his bleeding face.

Now the other Barton students, seeing what had happened to Wooten and Shooter, suddenly stopped in their tracks and looked at Bobby.

"Any more takers?" Bobby asked, whirling the bloody motorcycle chain over his head. "Just come on!"

With that, the other Barton students, thinking the better of it, backed away.

Wooten, holding his bloody face, got up slowly.

"Your ass is mine, rich boy!" he shouted angrily at Bobby. "Just wait! Just you wait."

***

For Benji's fourteenth birthday, Mrs. Trammel threw a lavish party. Among those present were his tutor Mr. Maddox, Jesse and I, and the Trammels. There was a huge chocolate cake, a festively garlanded house, and gifts. When Benji opened his gift from Jesse, it was a baseball and a glove.

"Now what's he going to do with that?" Mrs. Trammel said.

"We're going to play catch," Jesse said.

"Catch?" she replied. "He can't get out of that wheelchair."

"We can give it a try," Jesse said.

Once the birthday festivities were finished, Jesse turned to Benji.

"Come on! Let's go play some baseball."

"I can't move around much," Benji said, "but I'll try."

"That's all I ask," Jesse said.

Ten minutes later, me, Jesse and Benji were outside on the front lawn.

"Here," Jesse said. "Try on this glove."

Jesse fitted the glove on Benji's left hand.

"How does it feel?"

"Fine!"

Jesse handed him the baseball.

"Throw the ball into the glove a few times to get the feel of it."

Benji did as instructed.

"Now throw the ball to me," Jesse said.

Benji, with his shortened arms, threw the ball to Jesse.

"Good job!" Jesse said.

He turned to me.

"I'm going to back up some and, when I throw up the ball, I want you to push his wheelchair under it so he can catch it."

I took a position behind the wheelchair.

Then Jesse threw the baseball high in the air and I maneuvered the wheelchair under the ball so Benji could catch it. When it plopped into his glove, Benji was delighted.

"I caught it! I caught it!" he said excitedly.

Over the next thirty minutes, the three of us played catch. Finally, Benji grew tired and asked to go back inside.

As we started up the ramp into the house, Benji turned to Jesse.

"The only time I feel like a regular person is when I'm around you," he said. "Everybody else, all they see about me is this wheelchair. There's a lot more to me than this wheelchair."

"I know," Jesse said.

Back inside, Benji, Jesse and I sat down at the table for

another piece of birthday cake and a glass of milk. As we ate, Benji turned to Jesse.

"Will you do something for me?"

"Sure. What's that?"

"Will you take me around some girls? I want to be near some girls and talk to them. Just because I'm in this wheelchair, doesn't mean I don't like girls."

"I don't approve of that," Mrs. Trammel said.

"What can it hurt?" Mr. Trammel said. "He needs to get out. Just because he's in a wheelchair doesn't mean he has to be in prison."

"That's right, Father," Benji said. "That what it's like being in a wheelchair. Being in prison."

A long pause, then Jesse spoke

"Next time me and Johnny go on a double date to Hamburger King, you can go with us."

"Where will I ride?"

"We'll put the wheelchair in the back and you can sit in the rumble seat."

"Swell!" Benji said, smiling from ear to ear.

When Jesse left that night, Mr. Trammel and I walked with him back to his hotrod.

"I can't express my appreciation enough for the way you and Jesse have brought Benji out of his shell," he said. "It's like a miracle."

"It must be really tough to live like that," Jesse said. "I'm glad I can bring some happiness into his life."

"Thank you so much!" Mr. Trammel said.

***

Once Jesse was gone, Mr. Trammel and I started walking back up the walkway to the house. Suddenly, he stopped and grabbed his chest.

"Oh," he said.

"Mr. Trammel?"

His face screwed up in excruciating pain.

When we reached the porch, he stopped and took a seat on the steps.

"It's my heart," he said. "Go up to our bedroom and get the bottle of white pills on the bedside table. Hurry!"

Seconds later, I was in the house, up the stairs and back down to the front porch. Mr. Trammel was still clutching his chest.

"Give me two of the pills."

Quickly, I opened the bottle and handed him two of the little white pills. He put them under his tongue.

For several moments, we waited.

"Are you okay?"

He didn't answer at first. He continued holding his chest, severe pain still in his face. Finally, he spoke.

"I'm okay now. One of these days, this angina is going to kill me. I don't know when, but it will happen someday."

He arose unsteadily from the steps.

"Can I help you?"

"No, I'll be okay now. Let's go inside."

***

The following Sunday night, Bobby, Jesse and I were back at the Sand Pits. As usual, everybody wanted to race Bobby's Studebaker. Tommy Harmon, a hotrodder from Fort Worth who had had been beaten by the Studebaker five times, kept after Bobby to race him again and again.

"Tommy," Bobby said. "I've raced you five times and the closest you've come was one car length. You can't beat me."

"One more time!" Tommy pressed. "Just one more try!"

"Okay," Bobby said finally. "One more and that's it!"

With that, each racer went to his hotrod and brought his machine to the line as Jesse and I watched.

Janice Dickerson, fully-clothed this time, prepared to line up the bumpers.

"Whoa!" Janice said. "Right there!"

She raised her hand.

"Are you ready?" she asked, looking at both drivers.

Bobby nodded.

Tommy nodded.

Then, suddenly, Janice lowered her hand.

Both cars, wheels spinning and engines grinding, shot off the line. In the darkness, Jesse and I could see the two cars side-by-side streaking down the track. Then they saw the Studebaker, in the lane next to the river, slowly pulling ahead of Tommy's Mercury.

"Bobby's going to beat him again," Jesse said as he and I peered at the tail lights vanishing into the darkness.

Suddenly, we heard a loud crash, then the heart-sickening sound of a car rolling over and over. In the darkness, less than a quarter mile away, Jesse and I could see the Studebaker's headlights, twisting and turning in the darkness as the car rolled over again and again. For a moment, the crashing sounds stopped, then, seconds later, there was a loud splash in the river.

"Oh, God!" Janice said. "That was Bobby. He went off into the river. Come on!"

Quickly, Jesse and I jumped into Janice's car and we sped off down the drag track. As we neared the finish line, we saw a huge log in the lane next to the river.

"Look out!" I shouted. "There's a log!"

At the last moment, Janice swerved and narrowly missed the log. Then she parked her car and together, she, Jesse and I ran to the river's edge.

Some forty feet below us, we could see the headlights of the Studebaker, bright as ever, slowly sinking in the murky river water. Janice ran to the edge of the river.

"Oh, my God!" she said. "Can't we save him?"

"It's forty feet down to the water and the car is already totally submerged," Jesse said. "A rescue attempt without scuba equipment would be futile."

Janice suddenly broke down in tears, then she turned to Jesse, who embraced her.

"Oh, Bobby!" she said as Jesse held her. "We'll miss you!"

Moments later, Janice dried her tears and we walked back to her car.

"We better call the cops," I said.

"Who would have put that log there?" Jesse asked.

I shook my head.

"It couldn't have been Wooten; he was racing."

"Have you seen Shooter and Tommy Martin tonight?"

"No," I said. "They're the logical suspects."

Moments later, when Jesse and I returned with Janice to the starting line, we saw Shooter and Tommy Martin in Wooten's hotrod, high-tailing it out of the Sand Pits.

"There go the two culprits," Jesse said. "They're the ones that put the log in Bobby's lane."

"What are we going to do?" I asked.

"There nothing we can do. We have no evidence. We didn't see anything."

Later that night, members of the Dallas Police Department came to investigate. Detectives took a report and explained that it would be futile to call out divers at that time of night. The next morning, a police dive team pulled the 1954 Studebaker Golden Hawk from the bottom of the Trinity River, but there was not a body inside. Three days later, a fisherman some five miles down the river saw a strange red object caught in some trees. He called police. When they investigated, they recovered the body of Robert William Cottle III.

***

Three days later, Jesse and I attended Bobby's funeral at the Episcopal Church in east Dallas. The undertakers had Bobby all laid out in a gray suit, impeccably combed hair and a faint smile on his face. He looked every inch like James Dean lying in the coffin. After a brief service, Jesse and five other pallbearers delivered Bobby to his final resting place. As the coffin was lowered into the cool black earth, Jesse wept like a little child.

On the way back from the funeral, I asked Jesse if we should tell the police about what we witnessed the night of Bobby's death.

"Nothing can be done," he said. "The coroner's report listed his death as accidental drowning. We know who did it, but we could never prove it. All we can do is let it slide."

***

Christmas was always a grand time at the Trammels. For Christmas of 1957, they bought a giant Douglas fir tree and placed it in front of the picture window in the living room. Benji and his mother decorated it with a colorful array of balls, fake icicles, bright lights and memory tokens of the previous year. Mrs. Trammel had the gardeners string Christmas lights around the front of the house and Mr. Trammel placed a replica of Rudolph the Red-nosed Reindeer in the front yard.

On the morning of Christmas Eve, the four of us went into town to shop for family gifts. Mr. Trammel asked me if there was anything in particular I wanted and I told him I wanted a kayak, a green one, and some new jeans. Over the next three hours, we bought the kayak and the jeans, board games, books and a transistor radio for Benji as well as an assortment of women's gifts, dresses, perfume and kitchen utensils, for Mrs. Trammel.

When we arrived back at home, I helped Benji out of the car and into the house, then I went back to help Mr. Trammel unload the gifts. When I got back to the family car, I found Mr. Trammel slumped on the ground. He had his bottle of white pills in his hand, but they were spilled on the ground.

"Mrs. Trammel!" I yelled.

She didn't hear.

I rushed into the house.

"Mrs. Trammel!"

She was in the kitchen.

"What is it?"

"Call an ambulance! Mr. Trammel has had a heart attack!"

"Oh, God!" she said.

Instantly, she ran to the porch and saw her husband lying on the ground, then she rushed back to the phone to call an ambulance.

***

That night, at the hospital, Mr. Trammel was in a coma. When Mrs. Trammel, Benji and I entered the hospital room, he looked him a dead man. His face was white, there were huge black spots under his eyes, plastic tubes were running in and out of this nose and arms, and heart-monitoring machines were connected to his wrists and chest.

Benji started to cry when he saw his father.

"Father is going to die, isn't he, Mother?"

"We don't know yet," Mrs. Trammel said.

Later, when we talked to the doctor, a smallish, Italian-looking man in his late thirties, he said Mr. Trammel's heart was "near its end" and explained, if Mr. Trammel came out of the coma, he could never lead a normal life again.

"His heart can't handle the stress of daily living," the doctor said. "It's too weak."

Mrs. Trammel burst into tears at his words.

***

Back at home, Mrs. Trammel and I tried to placate Benji.

"Is Daddy going to die?" he kept asking over and over.

"We don't know yet," she replied. "We're going to have to wait and see if he comes out of the coma."

Finally, when Benji was asleep that night, Mrs. Trammel took me into the living room for a talk.

"Now I'll have to depend on you more than ever," she said. "You're the man of the house now. I don't expect you to manage the stores, but I do expect you to keep tabs on managers and bring the monthly sales report to me so I can enter them in the ledger. You're the only one I trust."

"You can depend on me," I said.

"And I want you to try to comfort Benji all you can," she said. "This is going to be very hard on him. He was always close to his father."

"I'll do that," I said. "Did the doctor say how long Mr. Trammel will be in a coma?"

"Nobody knows the answer to that."

***

Three months passed. During that time, Mrs. Trammel, Benji and I returned to our daily routines and Mr. Trammel remained in a comatose state in the hospital. During the first week of March, Jesse and I were back at the Hamburger King with Brenda and Emily. This time, we had Benji in the hotrod with us. Jesse had put the wheelchair in the back seat and Benji in the rumble seat. We were chatting and having burgers, shakes and fries when Wooten and Shooter showed up in the drive-in stall next to us.

"Who's that cripple you got with you, Jew boy?" Wooten said.

"None of your business, lard-ass," Jesse said. "Now you leave him alone."

"A cripple is a cripple," Wooten said. "He can't walk, he can't talk, he can't see, he can't screw…. what's he good for?"

"I can see and I can talk," Benji said.

"Well, I'm shocked," Wooten said. "I guess he can talk. What else can he do?"

"Didn't your mother ever teach you that when you make fun of disabled people," Jesse said, "you will end up in the same condition."

Wooten burst out laughing.

"That will never happen to me, Jew boy," Wooten said. "I'll always have my strength and my muscles."

"I wouldn't be so sure if I were you!" Jesse said.

"You leave Benji alone," Brenda said. "He can't help if he's like that. He was born that way."

"Poor little thing!" Wooten said. "He might as well have been born dead. He's useless to the world."

Jesse looked back into the back seat.

Benji was crying at Wooten's taunting.

"Come on!" Jesse said. "We didn't come here for this."

Jesse started the hotrod's engine.

"Leaving so soon?" Wooten said. "Don't like my words about your crippled friend?"

Jesse's hotrod started to back out of the stall.

"I'm not through with you, Jew boy," Wooten shouted. "You hear me? I'm not through."

***

When Jesse learned I had received a kayak for Christmas, he said he was going to buy one for himself and we were going kayaking at the Sand Pits.

"That's something I've always wanted to do," he said.

So, when the warm days of April rolled around, Jesse and I went into town and bought another kayak. Once we had it in tow, we returned to the Trammel home to retrieve mine. When Benji saw us loading up the kayaks, he asked Jesse if he could go with us. Jesse approved.

Once we had everything loaded, Jesse said he wanted to stop by the Hamburger King and grab a sandwich, shake and fries. Fifteen minutes later, when we pulled in, we saw Wooten and Shooter sitting in Wooten's hotrod in the nearby stall. We ordered our sandwiches to go.

"You going to put that cripple in one of those kayaks," Wooten asked. "He'll get drowned."

"That's none of your business, lard-ass," Jesse said.

"Like I told you, Jew boy, I'm not finished with you."

By then, our order had arrived, and immediately, we left the premises. As we pulled out on the highway, Wooten's car pulled out behind us.

"Now why would he be following us?" Jesse said.

"He's up to something," I said.

"I'm going to lose him."

Once on Highway 17, outside of town, Jesse put his hotrod up to 90 miles per hour until Wooten's hotrod was out of sight. Then he quickly pulled off on a side road and waited for Wooten's car to pass. Once he saw the yellow hotrod shoot past, he turned back onto the highway in the opposite direction and took a roundabout way to the Sand Pits.

***

Twenty minutes later, we were parked along the banks of the Trinity River just north of the drag strip. Jesse explained our plans to Benji.

"Me and Johnny are going to take our kayaks out to Bear Island," he said. "We won't be gone more than thirty minutes. Can you entertain yourself until we get back?"

"I'll be fine! I'll listen to my transistor radio. Can you park me on the bank in the wheelchair?"

Moments later, Jesse had Benji out of the car, in the wheelchair and parked near the river's edge. At that point, along the river's edge, there was sharp drop-off, maybe twenty feet, from the top of the bank to the water's surface.

"Will you be okay here?"

"I'll be fine," Benji said. "Y'all go ahead. Don't worry about me."

Then Jesse and I launched the two kayaks into the water and started paddling out to Bear Island, a small sand bar in the middle of the river. It was a beautiful April day. The morning sun had warmed the water, fish were jumping and the early blooms of water lilies were beginning to show along the water's edge. After we had paddled out maybe thirty yards, we suddenly heard a scream. When we turned, we saw Benji and his wheelchair plunging over the river's bank to the water below.

"Oh my God," Jesse said. "Something happened to Benji!"

Now all we could see was Benji floundering helplessly in the water.

"Jesse! Help me!! Help! Help!"

Quickly, Jesse began paddling furiously toward Benji.

After several seconds, seeing the kayak was too slow, Jesse jumped out and started swimming. With strong, sure strokes, he needed only a few seconds to reach Benji.

"Hold on to my arm," Jesse said. "I'll take you to shore."

Instantly, Benji grabbed Jesse's arm and held on tightly. Moments later, the water was shallow enough that Jesse would wade. Once he and Benji were safely on shore, Jesse turned to me.

"Get the wheelchair!" he shouted, pointing to the edge of the water where the wheelchair had been caught on a protruding limb.

Moments later, I retrieved the wheelchair and started up the embankment.

When I reached them, Benji was coughing, spitting up water and gasping. Finally, he had regained his breath.

Benji looked at Jesse. There was horror in his face.

"Hold me!" he said.

Jesse picked up Benji and he wrapped his arms around Jesse's neck and his short legs around Jesse's waist.

"I was afraid I would drown," Benji said. "I can't swim."

Then, clasping Jesse's neck with all his might, he began sobbing.

Jesse looked at me as he held the fourteen-year-old in his arms like a little baby.

"It's okay now," Jesse said. "What happened?"

"I don't know," he said, still trembling with fright. "I was listening to my transistor radio and suddenly someone was behind me pushing my wheelchair toward the water."

"Who was it?"

"I don't know. It happened so fast, I didn't see anyone."

Jesse looked at me.

"Where are your glasses?" Jesse asked.

"I lost them in the water. Who would want to treat me like that?" Benji asked.

Jesse looked at me knowingly, then he turned back to Benji.

"You must never mention this," Jesse said.

"Why not?"

"Because your mother will never again let you go out with us."

Benji studied Jesse for a moment.

"You're probably right," he said. "I won't tell. I'll never tell anyone else."

"Promise?"

"Promise."

"What will we tell your mother about what happened?"

"I'll tell her I dozed off and fell into the water."

"What about your glasses?" Jesse asked.

"I'll tell her I lost them in the water."

"That's a good idea," Jesse said. "Okay, let's get the kayaks loaded. I'm going to take you home."

***

Thirty minutes later, Benji was delivered safe and sound

back to the Trammel home.

Mrs. Trammel met us at the door. Concern crossed her face the moment she saw Benji.

"Why are your clothes wet?" she said.

"I fell into the water," Benji said.

Instantly, she turned to me.

"I thought you two were going to take care of him."

"It wasn't their fault," Benji said. "I dozed off and fell into the water. The fault was all mine."

"And your glasses?"

"I lost them when I fell in the water," Benji said.

Obvious disapproval in her eyes, she looked from me to Jesse, then turned back to Benji.

"Come on!" she said. "Let's get some dry clothes on you."

***

Moments later, we left the Trammel home and went straight back to the Hamburger King. Upon arrival, we saw Wooten's hotrod in one of the stalls. We pulled in beside him.

"Hey, Jew boy? Back so soon?"

Jesse glared at him.

"Have you heard the news?" Wooten asked.

"No. You tell me."

"I heard that the cripple you been hauling around went for a swim down at the Sand Pits today."

Both Jesse and I froze at the words.

"Is it true?" Wooten continued.

"Did you shove Benji off that cliff?"

"Oh, no!" Wooten said with a big laugh. "I would never do anything like that."

He turned to Shooter.

"Would I?"

"Oh, no!" Shooter replied. "The Woot would never do such a thing."

Then together they had a big laugh.

Jesse looked at them, then calmly started the engine, backed out of the stall and pulled out on the highway. Moments later, we were cruising down Highway 17. We were quiet for several minutes.

"We're not going to let this one slide," Jesse said.

"What do you want to do?"

"Let's kill him."

"How do you want to do it?" I replied.

"Let me think about it."

***

The following afternoon, a Monday, Jesse and I were in the Dallas City library going through medical books. Jesse, who had been poring over a copy of *Gray's Anatomy*, was looking down at a graphic displaying the parts of the human skull.

"The human skull is mostly solid bone," he said, "but it has different parts separated by little cracks, which allow for the pieces to expand and contract."

For a moment, he pointed to the graphic, then continued.

"See how the little cracks run sideways at the front and back, then down through the center?"

I peered at the graphic.

"So what's your point?"

"Those little cracks are weak points in the skull, which means they can be easily pierced to get to the brain."

"So, what do you propose?"

As if he hadn't heard, he turned from the book.

"Let's take a look at this skeleton," he said, getting up and going to the replica of a human skeleton standing in the corner of the library.

I followed him and watched as he ran his fingers over the top of the skeleton's skull.

"Do you see there are three fissures that intersect in the front?" he said. "If you had something that could pierce one of those cracks, you could do some major brain and nerve damage."

"What kind of instrument?"

"The tip of a Phillips screwdriver or maybe a nail. It would need to be about four inches long and fixed on a handle so it could be thrust forward and downward in an overhand motion."

"But you would have to hit the fissure directly. It would take a strong blow to pierce solid bone."

"That's why I've got to practice," he said. "Let's see how far above the top of the eyes it is to the intersection of the three fissures."

I peered closely at the skeleton's head.

"Looks like about four inches," he said. "That means the best place to strike would be where the three intersect."

"Yeah," I replied. "There would be a much better chance of hitting a crack and entering the brain."

"Also, you would be directly on the cranial midline, the bundle of nerves which carries signals from the body to the brain."

"That's my point," I said. "How are you going to pinpoint that exact spot?"

"I'm going to practice."

***

Two days later, we were in the garage at Jesse's house. He had cut four inches off the pointed end of a Phillips screwdriver and fitted the piece to a thin, round piece of wood that would fit into the palm of a hand.

"That's four full inches of metal tip," he said. "More than enough to do some major nerve damage. Let's try it."

On a table, Jesse had a watermelon with a face drawn on. With the melon set upright on its end, he marked an X at a point above the eyes where the intersection of the front and side fissures were located. He was ready to make a thrust.

"Now remember," I said. "Wooten is a little taller than you, so the melon should be a little higher."

"You're right," he said.

We adjusted the height of the watermelon by about three inches.

"Yeah, that's better," he said.

Then Jesse tried a mock overhand blow with the instrument. I examined the watermelon.

"You missed by about an inch," I said.

I studied the situation.

"You've got to have a reference point. If you're facing him in a fight, the best way is to pick a spot four inches directly above the center point between the eyes."

"That's it," Jesse said. "Four inches directly back from the center of the eyes. Let me try it again."

This time, Jesse's blow was spot on. He hit the designated mark on the watermelon exactly.

"Bingo!" I said.

Jesse smiled. Then he practiced the overhand blow several more times. Each time, he was perfectly on target.

"I'm ready. Come on, let's go take care of that son of a bitch."

***

Twenty minutes later, in Jesse's 1955 Chevrolet, we were cruising past Tommy's Grill, the cheap greasy spoon of a restaurant that served as a hang-out for Clara Barton students. In the parking lot, we saw a group of teenagers sitting on cars and talking, but no sign of Wooten and Shooter.

"Where do you think they are?" Jesse said.

"Let's go to Shooter's house," I said.

Twenty minutes later, the 1955 Chevrolet was cruising through the quiet suburban neighborhood near Crockett High where Shooter Copeland lived. I peered out the window. No sign of Wooten and Shooter.

"Let's check out the Sand Pits!" Jesse said.

Twenty minutes later, we were cruising down the dusty road that led to the Sand Pits. Once we arrived, however, the place was deserted.

"Where could they be?" I said.

Jesse shook his head slowly.

"The pool hall!" I said suddenly. "I'll bet they're at the Smokehouse."

***

Twenty minutes later, Jesse and I were cruising slowly down 14th Street behind the pool hall.

"Slow down," I said. "Usually, Wooten parks behind the cab company."

Jesse eased the car slowly along the street.

"There it is!" Jesse said, pointing out Wooten's yellow hotrod down the alley. "They're in the pool hall."

Instantly, Jesse pulled the 1955 Chevrolet to the curb and parked. Jesse opened the trunk and I took out a tire iron.

"I'm going into the pool hall and pick a fight with Wooten," Jesse said. "When he comes out back, Shooter will be right behind him. I'll depend on you to take care of Shooter."

"I'll be happy to. You got your punch?"

"I got my punch!"

***

I watched as Jesse went into the back door of the pool hall. The only light behind the pool hall was a dim street light at the end of the alley. For some ten minutes, I waited in the shadows between the cab company and the billiard parlor. At the cab company, some new construction was going on; a foundation had been poured and some framing, studs and plates had been installed, but wall covering had not yet been started. I watched as taxi cabs intermittently pulled in and out of the cab company parking lot. Suddenly, I heard the back door of the pool hall open. Jesse and Wooten were coming out.

"I've been waiting a long time for this, Jew boy," Wooten was saying as they came out the door. "Your ass is mine this time."

In the darkness, I could see them squaring off to fight. Wooten came at Jesse swinging wildly with both fists. Jesse stepped aside, then Wooten came back at him again. This time, Jesse ducked and went inside and took a hard punch to the side of the head, but as he did, he threw the overhand blow with the punch, but Wooten was unfazed.

Now Wooten rushed into Jesse again, swinging wildly. Jesse side-stepped, but the momentum of Wooten's heavy frame sent him crashing into the new construction at the cab company. Jesse waited for Wooten to get up.

Suddenly, Shooter came out the back door of the pool hall into the darkness.

"Shooter! Come up behind him!" Wooten said.

With that, Shooter maneuvered himself behind Jesse so they would have Jesse from both sides. Once they had positioned themselves, I came out of the darkness and slammed the tire iron into the side of Shooter's head. He went down instantly.

Now, Wooten and Jesse were wrestling in the dirt of the back alley, rolling one way, then the other.

"Cranial midline!" I shouted. "Cranial midline!"

Then, in the dim light at the end of the alley, I saw Jesse bring his right hand around into the top of Wooten's head once more. Suddenly, Wooten groaned in pain and fell to the ground. For a moment, he lay dazed, then, when he tried to get up, he fell helplessly back to the ground. For a moment, he looked up at Jesse in the dim light and mouthed the words "Jew boy," then slumped down unconscious into the dirt and gravel. Jesse got up. There was blood over his right eye.

Suddenly, we heard a voice from the shadows in the cab company parking lot. A light went on and we could see a short, middle-aged man appear.

"Hey, what's going on back here?" the man called, peering into the shadows down the alleyway. "I'm going to call the cops."

With that, we watched as the man disappeared back into the cab company office, then we ran back down the alleyway to Jesse's car. Moments later, we crawled inside and the 1955 Chevrolet hotrod shot off down the darkened street.

Inside the car, I turned to Jesse.

"What are you going to do with the murder weapon?"

"Throw it in the Trinity River," he said.

***

Two days later, on Monday, I was in my second period algebra class in the science building when an administrative assistant came to the door.

"John Chance!" he called. "You're wanted in the

principal's office."

Ten minutes later, when I reported to the principal's office, a member of the Dallas Police Department was waiting.

"You're under arrest!" he said.

"For what?" I asked.

"Assault and battery," he said, snapping on the handcuffs.

***

That afternoon, I was lying on the bunk in a county jail cell when I heard the cellblock door open.

"John David Chance?" the turnkey asked.

"That's me," I said.

"You got a visitor," the turnkey said.

Ten minutes later, as a deputy led me out of the jail to the visitor's area, I could see Mrs. Trammel, frantic with fear, arguing with two police officers. She was ballistic. One of the officers had to restrain her and she was protesting with all her might. Then she looked up through the glass and saw me. Suddenly, she broke away from the two policemen.

"Johnny!" she screamed as I was led into the waiting area. "What's going on?!! Tell me what's going on!!"

I raised my hand. "Stay calm," I said, turning to the deputy. "Can we go in here and talk?" I asked, indicating a nearby visitor's room.

"That's fine," the deputy said.

Moments later, Mrs. Trammel and I were seated in the visitor's room. She was frantic.

"I want to know what's going on!" she shouted. "Is this the pay I get for taking you into my home and trying to make something out of you?"

"Stay calm!" I said. "Please stay calm."

For a moment, she looked at me. Then she took a deep breath.

"Okay," she said, calmer now. "Tell me why you have been arrested for assault and battery."

"Me and Jesse got into a fight with these two guys at the pool hall."

"Stop!" she said, holding up her hand. "Hold it right there!

I should have known it! This Jesse is the one behind all this, isn't he?"

"No!" I said. "It was both of us."

"Oh, God!" she said, wringing her hands. "How could you get involved in something like this?"

"I had to stand up for myself," I said.

Mrs. Trammel turned from me and held her face in her hands. For several moments, she didn't speak. Finally, having regained her composure, she turned back to me.

"Tomorrow, I'm going to get a good lawyer," she said. "I'm going to get you out of this mess. I've put too much time into you to see you turn out to be a criminal."

***

Two days later, I was arraigned in Dallas County Criminal Court. When I was led into the courtroom, I could see Thomas Hayes, the Trammel family attorney, standing at one of the counsel tables. In the gallery, I saw Mrs. Trammel.

"John David Chance," the judge began. "You have been charged with assault and battery against the person of Charles Matthew Copeland on the night of April 16, 1958. How do you plead?"

"Guilty!" I said.

"Your honor," the attorney said, "I would like to point out that John David Chance has no prior arrest record. Also, it should be noted that the injuries received by the victim were only minor. An hour after the incident occurred, the victim was treated at a local hospital and released."

"Is this true?" the judge asked, turning to the prosecutor.

"That's correct, your honor," the prosecutor said. "However, it should be noted that the accused used a tire iron, a deadly weapon, to inflict the injuries."

"Whatever instrument was used is beside the point," Hayes said. "The important fact is that no permanent injuries were sustained by the victim."

The judge looked at me, then at the attorney.

"Do you have anything to say before sentencing?"

"The accused's legal guardian would like to address the

court," the Trammel attorney said.

"Proceed!" the judge said.

With that, Mrs. Trammel went to a small podium in front of the court. She was sworn in.

"Your honor," she began, "I would like for the court to know that Johnny is a brilliant student. As a professional educator, I have seen few students with the intelligence he has. I can tell you now that this young man has a bright future ahead of him. The terrible crime for which he stands accused is the result of being led astray, not of his own making. He was only a follower. As a result, I ask that you show leniency and not blemish a young man who heretofore has a perfectly clean record."

With that, Mrs. Trammel returned to her seat.

"Anything else?" the judge asked.

"No," the prosecutor said.

"Anything else from the defense?" the judge asked.

"No," the Trammel attorney said.

For a moment, the judge looked at the police report, then turned to me.

"The crime of which you are accused is a very serious one," the judge said. "Eighteen-year-old boys should not be attacking other eighteen-year-olds with tire irons. That kind of behavior is reserved for animals, not human beings."

I looked up at the judge, expecting the worst.

"However, in light of the fact that you have no prior arrest record and the injuries sustained were only minor, I'm going to sentence you to one year's probation. Also, I am remanding you to the custody of your legal guardian."

With that, I turned and peered at Mrs. Trammel. She smiled.

***

On May 21, 1958, when Jesse's trial began in Dallas County criminal court, the public gallery included me and Marvin Trublinsky, Jesse's uncle and legal guardian. He was a balding, overweight man in his early fifties with a hooked nose and a double chin. At the defense counsel table, Jesse was sitting with his attorney, James Stockwell, a tall, late thirties man with blonde hair and glasses. Across the aisle, the prosecutor, a stocky, early fifties man with the face of a bulldog, was shuffling some papers.

Moments later, the judge took the bench.

"The criminal court of Dallas County, Texas is now in session," the bailiff said. "With the Honorable Howard L. Turner presiding. All please rise."

Everyone in the courtroom stood up when Judge Turner, in his flowing black robe, entered and took a seat on the bench. Then, after thumbing through some papers, he examined the docket sheet.

"In the case of the State of Texas vs. Jesse Jacob Trubble, let's begin," Judge Turner said. "Mr. Prosecutor, call your first witness."

"The state calls Walter Kilpatrick."

Moments later, a middle-aged man with gray hair, glasses and a paunch took the stand and was sworn in.

"State your name and occupation," the prosecutor said.

"Walter Kilpatrick, owner of the Smokehouse Billiard Parlor."

"Please tell the court what happened in the billiard parlor on the night of April 16, 1958 between the defendant and the victim."

"Wooten was playing pool with his friend Shooter when Jesse Trubble came in and started arguing with him. After a few minutes, the argument escalated and they went out back to fight."

"Was it the first time you have seen an argument between these two?"

"Oh, no! These two were always quarreling and insulting one another for several months. They are sworn enemies."

The prosecutor studied the witness for a moment.

"When they went outside, did you go with them?"

"No. I had to tend to my business."

"Did anyone else go out with them?"

"No. It was a slow night and there were only a few patrons."

"So you didn't witness the fight?"

"No."

The prosecutor paused, then took a deep breath.

"Dismissed!" he said.

He turned back to the courtroom.

"The state calls Hobart Winton."

A slight, middle-aged man with a drawn face and the unlit stub of a cigar in his teeth took the stand and was sworn in.

"State your name and occupation."

"Hobart Winton, owner of Metro Cab Company."

"Can you tell the court what you witnessed behind your place of business on the night of April 16, 1958."

"When I heard loud voices and cursing in the parking lot, I went out back to investigate and I saw these two teenagers on the ground fighting. When they got up, I saw Watson strike the defendant and knock him to the ground. Then, when the defendant was back on his feet, he went right back at Watson and knocked him into the scaffolding."

"Scaffolding?"

"Yes. I'm having an additional room built at the back of the cab company."

"What happened then?"

"When Watson fell back into the scaffolding, he didn't get up."

"Did the defendant have a weapon?"

"I didn't see one."

"The medical examiner's report stated the victim's injuries were caused by a sharp instrument which pierced the top of his head."

"That's what I heard," Winton said. "But I didn't see anything in the defendant's hand. It was dark."

"Where do you think the injury to the victim's head came from?"

"The only thing I can think of is the victim fell back hard against the scaffolding."

"I ask you again," the prosecutor said. "How do you think the victim received the hole in the top of his head?"

"Probably from a nail in the scaffolding that went into his head."

Jesse's attorney interrupted.

"So my client may not be guilty at all," Stockwell said. "The paralysis the victim is suffering may have been caused by a stray nail."

"No matter!" the prosecutor shot back. "Your client provided the force which sent the victim's head into the nail, so that is not a mitigating circumstance."

"This was an accident which occurred in the course of a fist fight," Stockwell said. "My client had no intention of causing the victim's death."

"That is clear cause for a charge of involuntary manslaughter," the prosecutor said, raising his voice.

"Gentlemen! Please remain calm," the judge said, rapping his gavel.

Then he turned to the prosecutor.

"Do you have any further need of this witness?"

"No."

He turned to Jesse's attorney.

"What about you?"

"The witness can be dismissed," Stockwell said

The judge turned to the witness.

"You can step down," he said, then he turned to Stockwell.

"Call your first witness," he said.

"I have no witnesses."

"Not even the defendant?" the judge said.

"Our case stands as is."

The judge turned back to the prosecutor.

"Anything further?"

"Yes, your honor. I want to call the victim to the stand."

"I object, your honor," Stockwell said. "What purpose could it possibly serve for the victim to appear in this courtroom?"

"The state of Texas, as well as the jury, has a right to witness the true extent of the injuries inflicted," the prosecutor said.

"Objection overruled," the judge said. "You may bring in Wooten Watson."

Two hours later, Wooten was brought into the courtroom in a wheelchair. When the jurors first saw him, they gasped in horror and pity. All the hatred and spite and malice that had been encased inside the bad boy was now encapsulated in a helpless, wheelchair-bound vegetable. Paralyzed on the left side, his left arm was permanently straight and, due to the nervous twitching, had to be strapped to the wheel chair's armrest. His eyes rolled uncontrollably in their sockets. One side of his chin rested permanently on his chest and his tongue lolled out of his mouth spastically.

"Members of the jury," the prosecutor said. "As you can see, this poor man has been rendered a vegetable. He can no longer speak, read or write, make love, enjoy the singing of birds or even eat a simple meal without assistance."

The prosecutor waited for his words to seep in with the jurors, then he turned back to Wooten and called his name.

"Wooten!"

"Awggg! Awggg!" Wooten replied. "Wakk! Wakk!"

Suddenly, Jesse burst out laughing. Then, unable to control myself, I joined in the raucous laughter. Everyone else in the courtroom turned to peer at me and Jesse. The murmur of loud voices spread across the courtroom.

"Order! Order!" the judge said, rapping his gavel.

At the counsel table, Jesse turned and winked at me. In that single instant, we realized we had accomplished our mission. The mighty Wooten was now a helpless vegetable and would remain so for the rest of his life. Whatever price must now be paid, we had accomplished what we set out to do.

"Your honor," the prosecutor said, "the defendant is making fun of the victim's condition."

The judge peered at Jesse for a long moment.

"Mr. Trubble! Were you mocking the victim?"

"Oh, no!" Jesse said. "I was laughing about something else. Sorry, your honor."

The judge studied Jesse for a moment, then returned to the prosecutor.

"Mr. Prosecutor, I fear the victim cannot further your case beyond this point. He is unable to respond to the questions of either you or the defense attorney."

The prosecutor studied the judge for a moment, then turned to the bailiff.

"Will the bailiff kindly remove the victim?"

Moments later, after Wooten was wheeled out of the courtroom, the judge turned to the attorneys.

"Anything else?" the judge asked.

"The state rests, your honor," the prosecutor said.

"Nothing else, your honor," Jesse's attorney said.

The courtroom was quiet for a moment as the judge shuffled some papers. Then, he turned to address the jury.

"Ladies and gentlemen of the jury," the judge said, "you have heard all the evidence in this case. Jesse Jacob Trubble has been accused of causing great bodily harm in a common street fight. If you feel that the evidence presented here is sufficient to draw the conclusion of guilt, then that is the verdict you must return. If, however, you feel that the evidence does not prove beyond a reasonable doubt that Jesse Jacob Trubble did in fact commit this crime, then you must return a verdict of not guilty. Is that understood?"

"We understand," said the jury foreman.

"Bailiff!" the judge said. "Take the jury to begin deliberations."

***

Two hours later, the judge was informed that the jury had reached a verdict and the five women and seven men returned to the courtroom. The bailiff took a slip of paper from the foreman and delivered it to the judge.

The judge unfolded the paper, cleared his throat and read the verdict.

"We, the jury, find the defendant, Jesse Jacob Trubble, guilty of involuntary manslaughter in the death of Charles Matthew Watson on the night of April 16, 1958."

Jesse, sitting with his attorney, didn't bat an eyelid. In the public gallery sitting beside me, his Uncle Marvin buried his face in his hands and wept.

"Ladies and gentlemen," the judge continued, turning to the jury. "Thank you for your decision. Mr. Bailiff, please return the jury to the assembly room so I can pass sentence."

With that, the jury, led by the bailiff, filed out of the

courtroom.

"From what I've heard in this case," the judge said finally, "I can only conclude that you, Jesse Jacob Trubble, are a violent and undisciplined teenager. As a result, I feel that you need the guidance and counselling of an institution like the state prison at San Antonio. There you will be taught to respect your fellow humans and obey the laws of our society. Therefore, I hereby sentence you to the Texas State Prison at San Antonio for six years."

With that, he rapped the gavel.

"Case closed!" he said.

***

The following morning, at the little brick home with the green shutters and the white picket fence on Whitehurst Street, Mrs. Trammell was reading the morning newspapers.

"Thank God!" she said, putting down the newspaper. "I see that your friend Jesse is going to the state prison in San Antonio for six years. I told you that's where he would end up."

She looked at me for a response. There was none.

"For you, it's the best thing that could have happened," she continued.

"Jesse is not a bad person," I said.

She studied me for a moment.

"He has some kind of control over you," she said. "It's as if you become a different person when you're around him."

I shook my head.

"Why is it so hard for you to admit that this Jesse was destroying you?"

I looked away.

Miss Trammel could see she wasn't getting through.

"Why won't you let me help you?" she asked. "You're going to graduate high school in two weeks. You have the intelligence to be a good student. Nothing would make me happier than to see you enroll in college."

"There is more to life that getting an education and making a living. There is a huge world out there. It is too varied and too vast to spend your life preoccupied with money."

"Johnny, do you realize what you're saying? Nothing, absolutely nothing on this earth can give you the freedom that money can."

I didn't look at her.

"So what do you want to do with your life?"

"I'm not sure," I said. "I'm just not sure."

***

Seven months later, I drove the 275 miles from Dallas to the Texas State Prison at San Antonio. After I had parked my car, a guard ushered me inside and, after some paperwork, I was escorted into a reception room. Moments later, the door opened and Jesse, fit, trim and smiling, entered.

"Hey!" I said.

"Hey, yourself!" he replied.

We hugged one another.

"How you doing in here?" I asked.

"It's not too bad," he said. "It's very structured. Up at a certain time, work at a certain time, eat at a certain time, bed at a certain time."

"How do you spend your days?"

"They keep me busy," he said. "I spend a lot of time reading; I work in the mess hall five nights a week. There is a rigid structure to everything."

A pause.

"What are YOU doing?" Jesse asked.

"I'm going to college."

"Uh, oh!" Jesse said, a warning sound in his voice. "I think I smell Mrs. Trammel."

I nodded.

"She wants to put me through medical school," I said. "She has my life all planned for me."

"You mean she's got your life planned for HER!" Jesse said.

I took a deep breath.

"It could be worse," I said. "She wants me to enroll at the University of Texas this next spring."

Jesse looked at me.

"Are you going through with it?" Jesse asked.

"I haven't decided," I said.

Jesse didn't reply.

"By the way," I asked, "what happened to your uncle? I drove by the house last week and there was a For Sale sign out front."

"He moved back to New York."

"New York?"

"Yeah," Jesse said. "His old business partner opened a brokerage house on Madison Avenue. Uncle Marvin joined the firm as a vice-president."

"What did he say when you were sentenced?"

"He wasn't happy," Jesse said. "In fact, he felt like it was his fault. I told him that I did the crime and now I would do the time. Then he started raving about 'I don't know where all the violence in you comes from. Nobody else in the family has that kind of violence in them...' and on and on. I let him have his say and kept quiet."

"Your uncle did his best," I said.

"I know," Jesse added with a note of finality. "But it's all in the past now. I have no regrets."

I nodded.

"I can tell you one thing..." Jesse added.

"What's that?" I asked.

"Wooten Watson will never call me 'Jew boy' again."

I laughed.

"That bastard got what he deserved."

With that, I stood up to say good-bye.

"Take care!"

With that, he offered his hand and I shook it, then I hugged him.

"You'll be hearing from me," I said.

***

That night, I drove the 275 miles back to Dallas. The next morning, I apologized to Mrs. Trammel for what had happened. I told her I knew I had brought shame and embarrassment on her and her family. I told her I appreciated her concern for my future and I wanted to take a new approach to life. I told her, as she had planned, I would enter the pre-med curriculum at the University of Texas in the fall.

"Thank God!" she said, hugging me. "You have finally come to your senses. Thank God!"

I was biding my time until Jesse got out of the state prison.

4 – Vietnam

1964

On the morning of November 12, 1964, I was waiting quietly in the reception area of the State prison in San Antonio for Jesse to be released. In a phone call several weeks earlier, he said he would be released at noon on that date, but, if he didn't appeared promptly, I should wait for him. I couldn't wait to see him.

Over the past six years, I had been a professional student. After graduating from Crockett High in late May of 1958, Mrs. Trammel had enrolled me in the pre-med school at the University of Texas's Dallas campus. There, while working part time and on weekends in the family paint stores, I completed the basic courses in biology, chemistry and math required for the university's medical curriculum. After my last class, I was four credits short of having a bachelor's degree. Mrs. Trammel was very happy with my accomplishments. Mr. Trammel had died in the fall of 1962. He had been in coma for almost three years. Actually, he didn't die in the standard sense of the word. His life expired when Mrs. Trammell instructed the hospital to remove the life support. In truth, I believe she kept him alive all those years for Benji's sake.

Over the years that followed, I became very close to Benji. Mrs. Trammel said he needed a male figure in his life. During that time, I discovered how intelligent he was. He had a mind like a steel trap. He could read a book and quote exact lines months later. We played a lot of chess and I discovered quickly I was no match for the reach of his mind regarding strategies, moves and counter-moves. He entered college in the fall of

1962 and was a straight-A student. As always, he was fascinated with Jesse. Every time I got a letter, Benji asked about him and his life in prison.

My ears suddenly perked up when I detected the sound of a clanging, closing metal gate inside the main reformatory facility. Instantly, I rose from my chair and peered through the glass window into the hallway leading to the reception area. As I shaded my eyes to see inside, I saw two figures, a prison guard and Jesse, carrying a suitcase and a shoulder bag, passing through the final door. My heart leapt with joy.

When he appeared outside the door, I stared at him for a moment. He smiled.

"Hey!" I said.

"Hey, yourself."

We shook hands and hugged one another.

"Are you ready?" I said.

"Let's go!"

With that, the guard, using a huge four-inch key on a heavy ring, opened the door to the facility's front entrance and escorted Jesse and me outside the reformatory walls.

"You're on your own now," the guard said. "I hope we don't see you again."

"Oh, don't worry," Jesse said. "You won't be seeing me again."

Then Jesse and I turned and started walking across the facility parking lot to my 1958 Chevy.

"This is her!" I said, patting the car on the hood. "I call her 'Buddha's Buggy.' She's got a 342 with a two-barrel and a high-speed rear end."

"Think she'll get us to California?" he asked.

"I don't see why not."

I opened the trunk and Jesse threw his bags inside. Moments later, the car's engine roared to life and we pulled out of the correctional facility parking lot.

***

Five hours later, back in Dallas, we arrived at the Trammel

home. The moment we pulled up into the driveway, we saw Benji and Mrs. Trammel sitting on the veranda. As we got out, Benji had a look of joyful surprise.

"Jesse!" he shouted.

Instantly, Jesse rushed forward.

"Pick me up!" Benji said.

Instantly, Jesse reached down and lifted Benji out of the wheelchair. They hugged one another. Benji was nineteen now. There was a new maturity to his face. He had started to shave and he had grown a small mustache.

"It's so great to see you," he said.

"Good to see you!" Jesse replied.

Jesse replaced Benji in the wheelchair.

"Where are you and Johnny going?" Benji asked.

"To California."

"Why California?"

"There's a whole new way of living out there."

"I've read about the flower children and the Beatniks," Benji said. "They want to do their own thing."

"That's right," Jesse said. "Me and Johnny want to see it for ourselves."

Jesse turned to Mrs. Trammel.

"Good afternoon!" he said.

"Hello!" she said coldly.

Then she turned to me.

"Johnny, can I speak with you privately in your room."

Moments later, I was in my room. When I pulled down a suitcase and started packing clothes, Mrs. Trammel was furious.

"What in God's name are you doing?"

"Jesse and I are going to California."

"Have you lost your mind? For the past four years, I have tried to guide you to a future which will make a positive contribution to society. Now you're throwing it all away."

"I appreciate what you've done, but I've got to do what makes me happy."

"What's going to make you happy in California?"

"I'm not sure. I've got to discover that for myself. I don't want my life packaged like I was a piece of meat to be cut, wrapped and delivered. The world is too big; there is too much to learn to spend my life in one place."

"It is through planning and discipline that you make something of yourself in this world."

I continued packing.

"It's that Jesse!" she said. "He brings out the worst in you. He's going to be your ruination."

"I have to do what makes me happy," I said. "You've been as good to me as I could have asked. I'm sorry things didn't work out the way you planned."

"Sorry?" she said. "Is that all you can say?"

Suddenly, furiously, she stormed out of the room and slammed the door behind her.

Thirty minutes later, I was packed and had my bags on the front veranda.

"Good-bye, Benji!" I said.

"Good-bye, Johnny! I'll miss you!"

"I'll miss you too."

"Bye, Jesse!" Benji said. "Will you pick me up again?"

Jesse lifted Benji out of the wheelchair again and the two hugged one another. Benji, tears rolling down his face, kissed Jesse on the cheek. Jesse replaced him in the wheelchair.

"If I wasn't stuck in this wheelchair, I'd go with you," Benji said, wiping away the tears.

"I'll send you a postcard!" Jesse said.

Benji smiled.

"Good luck!" he said.

Then we turned and started walking down the walkway to my car. At the car, I threw my duffel bag into the rear seat and slammed the door. We waved to Benji one last time, then I started the engine.

Suddenly, Mrs. Trammel rushed out on the front porch.

"John David Chance!" she shouted. "Don't ever come back to this house! Do you hear me! You're not welcome here ever again!"

Benji drew back at her words.

"Mother! What are you saying?"

As I backed the car out of the driveway, Mrs. Trammel,

livid anger in her face, rushed off the veranda into the yard, shaking her fist.

"You ungrateful little whelp! Don't you or that piece of trash ever come back to this house!"

"Mother! Mother!" Benji shouted.

When I pulled out on the street, I could see Mrs. Trammel still standing at the end of the driveway, shaking her fist. For a moment, I was touched with a bitter sadness, remembering all the hope and promise she had placed in me. Once I was on the road, however, the sadness was short-lived.

Thirty minutes later, as Jesse and I were cruising westward across the plains of West Texas toward the badlands of New Mexico, my heart was singing with excitement at the prospect of being with Jesse again. I was going to touch the madness once more.

***

We drove until midnight, stopping twice to eat and gas up. Around 2 a.m., we pulled into a service station in Truth or Consequences, New Mexico and slept in the car for several hours. At daybreak, we were on the road again and, by early afternoon, the 1958 Chevy was sailing across the eastern edge of the Mojave Desert, over the Colorado river and into the Golden State. By noon, we were passing through the little desert towns—Indio, Palm Springs, Banning and Fontana— that greet a traveler before they arrive in metropolitan LA. Two hours later, we were cruising past the cluster of skyscrapers that made up downtown Los Angeles.

"There she is," I said. "The City of Angels."

"First thing I want to do is go to Malibu," Jesse said. "I want to see the surfers, feel that California sun beating down on my brow and wiggle my toes in the sand."

Twenty minutes later, the Chevrolet was cruising along the Pacific Coast Highway past Santa Monica Pier, the palisades, the Getty Museum and Malibu City Hall.

"How much money you got?" Jesse asked.

"About seventy dollars. What about you?"

"About fifty dollars."

"Can we afford a hotel room?"

"No," I said. "Let's save our money for food. We'll sleep in the car."

"That's a good idea," Jesse said.

"First, let's get some fruit and water and hang out at the beach."

"That's music to my ears."

Thirty minutes later, armed with a bag of fruit and water, we were lounging on towels at Malibu beach. Jesse was reading Jack Kerouac's *On the Road* and I was catching some rays and watching the surfers skim along the surface of the Pacific Ocean. After we had been there some thirty minutes, we saw two young women, a tall, thin, long-legged blonde and a shorter, big-breasted brunette, walking down the beach toward us. As they neared, the blonde glanced over at Jesse.

"Excuse me!" she said, "Isn't that Jack Kerouac's *On the Road* you are reading?"

"Yes," Jesse said.

"Could you settle an argument?"

"Sure!" he said.

"Was Kerouac born in 1921 or 1923? My friend says Jack Kerouac was born in 1921 and I say he was born in 1923. Could you check the biography in the back of the book?"

Jesse flipped through the pages.

"He was born March 12, 1922. Are you two Kerouac fans?"

"Oh yeah," the blonde said. "I've read *Dharma Bums* four times."

"So what do you think about Kerouac's philosophy and lifestyle?"

"Oh, there is nothing like being free and wild and excessive," she said. "Especially excessive. That's why I loved *Dharma Bums* so much."

"Would you girls like to sit down and chat?" Jesse said.

"Sure!" said the blonde.

Moments later, after the two girls were seated on the beach towels, Jesse led off introductions.

"My name is Jesse," he said.

"I'm Daphne," said the blonde, "and this is Pamela."

The brunette smiled politely.

"My name is Johnny," I replied.

"I'm a singer and poet," Daphne said. "Sometimes I strip for extra money. My dream is to be an internationally-known folk singer like Joan Baez. I have a master's degree in English literature from Berkeley."

"What did you write your master's thesis on?" Jesse said.

"The schizophrenic overtones in Samuel Taylor Coleridge's 'Xanadu,' she replied.

"Must have been interesting," Jesse said. "Most of his poems were written while he was high on opium."

"If you'll look closely at most of his work," Daphne continued, "you'll see there is a certain schizoid quality to all of it."

"You will also find that quality in Poe," Jesse said. "Much of his work was written while he was drunk."

A pause.

Jesse turned to Pamela.

"Do you like poetry?" he asked.

"Pamela is a tree hugger," Daphne said. "She wants to save the world from pollution, carbon emissions, global warming and offshore oil wells."

Pamela turned to Daphne.

"I wish you wouldn't call me a tree hugger," she said. "It sounds so trite. If you don't appreciate my political perspectives, then don't ridicule them."

Over the next two hours, we chatted. Jesse and I told them about our lives in Texas and Georgia, our friendship and our dream of coming to California. Jesse and Daphne chatted about William Burroughs novel *Naked Lunch* and the Kennedy assassination. Pamela dragged on and on about how the government was responsible for all of the world's environmental problems.

"It's the God-damn government," she said. "They pollute the air, the water, the food and people's minds. They tax working people to death and start wars they can't win. If I had a chance to go to Washington and kill all of the politicians, I'd do it."

Finally, Daphne got up to leave.

"We need to get back," she said. "Do you guys have wheels?"

"Yes!" I said, nodding toward the beach parking lot.

"If you will take us over to our apartment in Pasadena," she said, "we'll treat you to some bean sprout sandwiches and red wine."

"Great!" I said.

"Wait 'til we get our beach stuff," Pamela said.

As the two girls started back down the beach, I turned to Jesse.

"Which one do you want?"

"The blonde."

"Perfect!"

Twenty minutes later, Daphne, lugging a guitar and a beach bag, and Pamela, carrying a rolled-up straw beach mat and a bottle of suntan oil, came tromping back up the beach.

"We're ready," Daphne said.

***

Some thirty minutes later, we pulled up in front of a small apartment building in Pasadena near the Glendale Freeway. Once we got out, Jesse and I helped the girls carry their beach gear to the door.

"This is our place for the moment," Daphne said, unlocking the door. "We're going back up north next week."

"Where's up north?" Jesse said.

"San Francisco," she said, opening the door. "The bitchinest place on earth."

Pamela and Daphne's apartment was a small, one-bedroom affair with a tiny kitchen and a small living area with pillows scattered about the floor. In one corner sat a bookcase made of bricks and wood planks and crammed full of books. The walls were covered with posters of Bob Dylan, Joan Baez and Jack Kerouac. Once inside, the girls served the promised bean sprout sandwiches and red wine. As we ate, we listened to Bob Dylan, in his patented nasal twang, wailing out a song from *The Free Wheelin' Bob Dylan* album.

"Oh, you masters of war, you that build the big guns, you that build all the planes, you that build all the bombs..."

Once the food and the Dylan album was finished, Pamela reached behind the bookcase and withdrew a carved wooden box. Then she opened it and withdrew a plastic bag filled with a dark green substance.

"What's that?" I asked.

"Weed! The herb superb!" she said as she doled out a small amount on the table and began rolling a joint.

"I've never smoked weed," I said.

"Then you have never touched your inner self," she replied, taking a long toke then passing the joint to me.

After a tentative puff, I passed the burning ember to Jesse. After he took a couple of deep drags, the joint went back to Pamela, then Daphne. Once it had been passed to me the third time, I could feel a sublime light-headedness taking over my senses.

***

For the next two hours, the four of us lounged on pillows, drank wine, talked about literature, politics, the state of the world and our lives. Toward the end of the evening, Jesse and I argued about Aristotle and Plato while Pamela and Daphne listened. Finally, around midnight, Pamela poured the last drop of wine and took a seat beside me. She was tipsy and, when I looked into her eyes, I knew what she wanted.

"Let's slip into the bedroom," she said. "I want to show you my coin collection."

"Just like that?"

"This is not Texas," she said. "You're in California now."

Then Pamela and I took our glasses of wine and got up.

"We'll see you two later," she said, turning to Jesse and Daphne, who were lying on the floor kissing. Pamela took my hand and led me into the small bedroom. Quickly, she threw off her shorts, her panties and her beach top, and stood naked before me.

"Love me!" she said, reaching out her arms. "Do with me as you wish..."

***

Thirty minutes later, Pamela lay naked in my arms, sweaty and still breathing hard. I could feel her heart beating rapidly against my own. Suddenly, there was a knock on the door. She sat up.

"Who could that be?"

She got out of bed, put on a robe and started to the other room. When she opened the door, I could see Jesse and Daphne lying naked on the floor in the corner.

"You guys cover up!" Pamela said. "Somebody's at the door."

Jesse and Daphne grabbed their clothes and began dressing.

Pamela was at the door, listening.

"Who is it?"

"The landlord!" said a voice outside the door.

"He's back to collect the rent," Daphne whispered.

"Christ!" Pamela said. "The agreement is in my name. I'll talk to him."

With that, she opened the door. The landlord, a balding, stern-faced man in his late sixties, started laying down the law.

"This is to notify you that you have until Tuesday to pay the one hundred forty dollars for the previous month's rent. If you haven't paid by then, I'm going to have you evicted."

"We haven't been working," Pamela said. "If you will just give us a little more time."

"That's what I've been giving you for the past three weeks," the man said. "Like I told you, pay by Tuesday, or you're out! Understand?!"

"We understand!" Pamela said.

Pamela closed the door.

"Screw him!" she said. "We're going back up north on Tuesday anyway. Let's get our stuff and leave tomorrow."

"That's a good idea," Daphne said.

She turned to Jesse and me.

"You two want to go to San Francisco?"

"What's in San Francisco?" I asked.

"The bay, good drugs, good conversation, good food and some of the most bitching people on the planet," Pamela said.

"Fine with me," I said.

"Why not?" Jesse replied.

"We'll leave tomorrow after breakfast," Pamela said.

***

Early the next morning, the girls prepared a breakfast of bagels and cream cheese, fresh fruit and instant coffee.

"Before we head up north," Daphne said. "You two are going to have to get cooled out."

"What do you mean?" I asked.

"You guys have got to change your look," Pamela said. "Leather jackets and boots don't cut it in San Francisco. The style up there is softer, more colorful and more.... humanistic."

"We'll do anything once," Jesse said.

Daphne went to the closet, took out a small suitcase then sat it on the bed. Moments later, she pulled out two black tee-shirts, cut-off jeans, and two long strings of multi-colored beads.

"These belonged to my last boyfriend," she said, holding up the beads. Then she turned to Pamela.

"Do you still have Robert's old sandals?"

"I think so," Pamela said. "I'll have to dig them out."

Moments later, Jesse and I, decked out in black tee-shirts, cut-off jeans and sandals without socks, looked at one another. We looked like we were ready for a flower-child demonstration.

"Now you're cool," Pamela said proudly.

"Oh, yes!" added Daphne. "And so handsome!"

I looked at Jesse. He looked at me, then both of us broke up in raucous laughter.

"No!" Jesse said. "We'll stick with our boots, jeans and leather jackets."

Daphne shrugged.

"Suit yourself!" she said. "We're going to the anti-war demonstration in SF tomorrow night and we wanted you to look the part."

"We're already cool enough," Jesse said.

***

The following morning, my 1958 Chevrolet was cruising northward along California Highway 101 toward the City by the Bay. Shortly after sundown, when we arrived in Santa Barbara, we decided to sleep on the beach. After building a fire and having a dinner of cheeseburgers and fries, we smoked weed and listened to Daphne play her guitar and sing folk songs. Around midnight, after more pot and some cheap wine, we spread out quilts on the beach and went skinny-dipping in the bitterly cold Pacific Ocean. Finally, dripping wet, the four of us, in all our nakedness, rushed back to the quilts and started drying off. Once we were dry, Pamela turned to Daphne.

"Is it okay if Jesse goes with me tonight?"

"You better ask him," Daphne said.

Pamela turned to Jesse.

"What do you say?"

"It's time Pamela and I got to know each other better," he said.

Pamela smiled.

"Come on," she said. "Let's take a quilt and go up the beach where we can have some privacy."

Daphne turned to me.

"Looks like it's me and you tonight."

***

Around noon the following day, we arrived in San Francisco. For years, I had dreamed of visiting the magical City by the Bay. I had read about Fisherman's Wharf, Alcatraz, the Golden Gate Bridge, Knob Hill, the Presidio and the city's colorful history. Now I was about to experience its mystique firsthand.

"I have a friend who has a small place we can crash for a few nights," Daphne said.

Over the next few minutes, she guided me to a luxury apartment building on Taylor Street. Daphne and Pamela got

out and went inside. After some thirty minutes, they reappeared. Before they got into the car, Daphne held up an apartment key.

"My friend said we can have it for three days. After that, we have to get out."

Twenty minutes later, I parked my Chevrolet in front of a small apartment building on Van Ness Street. Then, our personal belongings in hand, all four of us went inside.

"We work at night and do drugs by day," Pamela said as she started to unpack. "We want you two to stay with us. At least for a while."

***

Over the next two days, Jesse and I roamed the streets of San Francisco while Pamela and Daphne worked nights at a little strip club down the street. The first day, we explored Fisherman's Wharf, taking in the sights, sounds and the food along the harbor. The following day, we toured Chinatown and, that afternoon, we visited the Golden Gate Bridge and Sausalito. As we started back across the bridge to San Francisco, Jesse turned to me.

"I like that weed," he said. "It smooths me out."

"Same here," I said. "We'll have to get some."

We walked quietly for several moments.

"How much money you got?" he asked.

"About thirty dollars. What about you?"

"About twelve dollars."

"We're getting low," I said.

"We're going to have to do something. And soon."

***

That night, Daphne and Pamela arrived back at the apartment just after 2 a.m.

"Are you boys ready for some real drugs?" Daphne said, opening a small yellow box and taking out a tiny purple pill.

"What do you have this time?" I asked.

"Purple Haze! My friend that makes this stuff over at

Berkeley says the colors are outrageous."

"How many hits?" asked Pamela.

"Four!" Daphne replied. "Are you two going to join in?"

"We can't let it go to waste," Jesse said.

Daphne doled out one of the little purple pills to each of us.

"Let's ease into this acid with some wine and then some weed," she said.

Fifteen minutes later, after dropping the pill and taking the last puff of pot, I suddenly had an overpowering urge to lie down. Once I was on my back, I looked up at the tiny apartment's papered ceiling, but all I could see were bright, multi-colored stars shining in a clear, moonless night. Then, as I watched, the stars started changing colors into millions of hues of purple. Never in all my life had I seen so many shades of purple. I knew mauve and magenta, but now I was seeing hues of purple I had never dreamed existed. As I watched the ceiling in amazement, giant springs, like tiny slinky toys, formed around each of the purple-hued stars and began to slowly uncoil downward toward me. Then, at the precise moment I thought the uncoiling purple springs would touch me, they began their slow ascent upward again. For an indeterminate amount of time, I watched the springs moving up and down between the ceiling and myself. For some reason, I had an overpowering thirst for grape Kool-Aid.

***

All that night, the LSD surged through my body and nervous system, creating a dream-like world of unconnected purple images. Around ten the following morning, I was awakened from a deep sleep by someone's voice.

"Wake up! Wake up!"

It was Daphne. I sat up. Although the effects of the LSD had worn off, I could still feel the physical tiredness, the inner emptiness that comes after a hit of acid.

"What is it?"

"Pamela and I are going to the anti-war demonstration at Washington Square," Daphne said. "You boys want to join us?"

"You two go ahead," Jesse said.

"That's cool!" she said. "We'll be back in the early afternoon. Remember, we have to be out of here by tomorrow morning."

"We remember," I said.

After the girls left, Jesse and I showered and shaved, then we walked down the steep incline of Van Ness Avenue to a little deli shop. There, after having scrambled eggs, fried potatoes, sourdough bread and coffee, we strolled for almost an hour along Fisherman's Wharf. Finally, just after 1 p.m., we started walking back up Van Ness to the apartment. Once we had climbed back up the hill and turned the corner, we could see Pamela and Daphne standing at the apartment building's front entrance with their personal belongings. Beside them, we also saw our army duffel bags.

"What happened?" Jesse said.

"My friend said we have to vacate today," Daphne said. "She has renters that want to move in."

"Where are you two off to?" Jesse asked.

"Vegas!" Pamela said. "They need strippers. You two want to go?"

"No!" Jesse said. "Me and Johnny are going to stay in San Francisco for a while."

A long, awkward pause.

"Well… it's been fun," Daphne said. "You two take care."

"Same to you and Pamela," I said.

"Maybe we'll meet again," Pamela said.

"Maybe," I said. "Bye."

Then Jesse and I watched as, suitcases in hand, the two girls started walking down Van Ness Street. We watched until they had disappeared around the corner, then he turned to me.

"How much money you got?"

"About eight dollars. What about you?"

"Four dollars."

"What are we going to do?" Jesse said.

"Let's sell Buddha's Buggy."

"We won't have a car. We won't have a place to sleep."

"We need the money," I said. "And we need it fast."

***

An hour later, I pulled my 1958 Chevrolet into a used car dealership on Fremont Street. The firm's buyer, a bald-headed, middle-aged man in a green-plaid jacket, was driving a hard bargain.

"I'll give you one hundred twenty-five dollars," he said. "Not a penny more."

"The headers alone on that car costs sixty-five dollars," I said.

"I told you. One hundred and twenty-five is the most I will pay."

I inhaled, then looked at Jesse. Both of us knew we desperately needed the money.

"We'll take it." I said.

Twenty minutes later, money safely in hand, Jesse and I were lugging our duffel bags along Fremont Street. Suddenly, huge, intermittent drops of rain began to fall.

"Come on," Jesse said. "Let's get under the awning."

Seconds later, we were standing under a large green canvas awning in front of a doughnut shop and a US Army recruiting center watching the rain come down.

"What do you want to do?" I said.

"I don't want any more of this flower child crap. I like the idea of intellectual freedom, but this flower child business seems to be more show than substance. These people are exhibitionists whose only real desire is self-indulgence."

"So, what do you want to do?"

"I don't know," Jesse said.

Suddenly, a wind kicked up and cold rain began blowing up under the awning. Instantly, Jesse and I moved deeper under its shelter. As we did, we bumped into the wall of the building behind us, then we turned and saw a sign in the window: "Uncle Sam Wants You!"

I looked at Jesse.

"Are you thinking what I'm thinking?"

"Yep! Come on!"

***

Inside, Jesse and I introduced ourselves to the recruiter, a clean-shaven young man with an insignia on his breast that identified him as Sgt. Wayne O'Brien.

"Can I help you?"

"We want to enlist," Jesse said.

"Great!" the sergeant said. "Have a seat."

Over the next two hours, we filled out a mountain of forms listing all the personal information relevant to our lives. Every iota of personal information, education, parentage, medical history, food allergies, likes and dislikes, arrests, insurance coverages, mental illness; all of this had to be detailed. Once the forms were complete, Jesse went in for the interview.

Thirty minutes later, he reappeared.

"How did it go?'

"He asked about the time I spent in prison."

"Is it a problem?"

"He said it would make me a better soldier."

Moments later, I went into the interview room.

"As you know, the war in Vietnam is getting underway," the recruiter said. "Since it's a war like we have never fought before, we need men to train in our technical specialty programs."

"What kind of technical specialty programs?"

"Let's look at the list," Sgt. O'Brien said, rifling through a file folder, then withdrawing a sheet of paper.

"Let's see," he said, looking down the list. "Right now, they need specialists in infra-red equipment."

"Infra-red equipment?"

"It's the latest technology for night fighting," Sgt. O'Brien said. "Soldiers in this program are trained in the use of night vision equipment."

"I would like that."

"There are added incentives for new enlistees that want to join up under the buddy program," he continued "If you sign up to train as technical specialists under the buddy program, the army guarantees that you and your buddy will be together during your entire enlistment. Your friend says he wants to be part of the program."

"That's fine," I said.

***

Two days later, Jesse and I boarded a C-130 military transport that took us from San Francisco to Fort Riley, Kansas to begin basic training. Once we arrived at the induction center, our heads were shaved, we were provided uniforms and assigned quarters. That afternoon, we were standing in formation on the parade ground with other new enlistees.

"We're going to make men out of you pansies!" the master sergeant barked. "We have no time for wimps or candy-asses. In here, you either get strong and tough or your butts go back home to Mama. Got that?"

"Yes, sir!" shouted Jesse and I and the other new recruits.

***

Over the next eight weeks, we learned the fundamental skills of being an efficient soldier. On the firing range, we learned to shoot an M-16 and hit a moving target 100 yards away. We learned how to pack a backpack so tight that not a single inch of space went unused. We crawled through mud and barbed wire with machine-gun fire just inches above their heads. We learned to disarm booby traps, locate land mines and identify and interrogate enemy soldiers. In the technical portion, we learned the intricacies of the very latest night vision equipment. In practice, using an M-16 with an infrared scope in total darkness, I could hit a target six inches across from 400 yards.

"The enemy is never safe with these," the instructor said. "In fact, the moment he thinks he is the safest, he is in the most danger. Stealth is the key to winning a war like this."

***

On the morning of January 23, 1965, after eight weeks of boot camp, which included two weeks of infra-red classes, our preparation for soldiering was at an end. On the final day, the master sergeant, who had treated us like dirt the previous eight weeks, showed some respect.

"All right, men, your basic training is over," he said. "You are now soldiers. Tomorrow at 0900, you will board a C-130 transport for San Francisco. After an overnight stay, you will board another C-130 and be arriving in Saigon Tuesday night at 1830 hours. I want to offer my congratulations for a job well done. Good luck!"

With that, he saluted the new soldiers.

"Dismissed!"

Later that afternoon, at command headquarters, we learned that, in our battalion, we had been assigned to Company B, Platoon C. Our platoon was one of two squads in Company B, both created for special missions.

"Christ!" Jesse said as we left headquarters and headed back to the barracks. "We're going to Vietnam."

"Let's hope we don't get our asses shot off."

We walked quietly for a moment.

"I think I'm going to like soldiering," he said. "I think I would make a good professional soldier."

"A professional soldier?"

"Guys who hire themselves out for special military operations," he said. "Jobs like rescuing some rich man's daughter from kidnappers or hiring out to fight rebels for a banana republic."

"Those people are called mercenaries."

"Mercenaries. Yeah, that's the word."

***

Two mornings later, Jesse and I and the other members of Company B, Platoon C, were standing at parade rest on the tarmac at San Francisco International Airport waiting to board the C-130 that would take us to Vietnam. As we waited in the blazing sun, a young long-haired war protestor walked among us trying to pass out anti-war literature.

"You guys are idiots!" he shouted. "You're going over there to kill innocent women and children! Aren't you ashamed?"

After he was unable to find takers and shouted another round of insults, one of the soldiers suddenly swung the butt of his rifle upward and slammed it into his face. Immediately, the young long-hair, dazed by the blow, slumped to the tarmac.

"Who did that?" barked the sergeant.

Then, as a group, the entire company shouted: "I did, sir!"

Five minutes later, as the members of Company B filed past the prostrate protestor to board the C-130, Jesse turned to me.

"I'm glad we left all that behind us," he said.

"So am I."

***

The following day, 22 hours later, the C-130 landed in Saigon, Vietnam. After refueling and taking on a host of new recruits, the huge military transport lifted off the runway again en route to the coastal city of Da Nang, some 400 miles north of Saigon. It was then that Jesse and I met the other members of our Platoon C, the men who would be with us in the field. There was Carlos Rodriguez, a wiry, tough native Peruvian who grew up in East Los Angeles; Tyrone Washington, a tall, thin, African-American from Chicago's south side; and Tony Castellano, a short, stocky Italian man from Queens. Only moments after we met the others, Washington, Rodriguez and Castellano were involved in a card game on a wooden platform in the belly of the airplane.

"I call!" Washington said.

"Two kings and two fours!" Rodriguez said.

"I got three eights," Washington said.

"Beats me," Rodriguez said, throwing in his cards.

Washington raked in his winnings and started shuffling the cards again.

"When we get to Da Nang," Castellano said, "the first thing I'm going to do is get me one of those little oriental women."

"Not me!" said Rodriguez. "I'm going to the chicken fights. I can pick fighting chickens better than I can play cards."

Washington had finished shuffling.

"Cards coming," he said, dealing himself and the other two players two cards face down and one showing.

Castellano had a seven showing; Rodriguez had a king and Washington dealt himself a three.

"Bets?" Washington asked.

"Hold!" Rodriguez said.

"I'll hold too," Washington said.

"Same here!" Castellano said.

Washington dealt another round of cards.

Castellano now had two sevens showing; Rodriguez had a king and a four showing and Washington had a queen and a three.

"I bet ten dollars!" Castellano said.

Washington and Rodriguez looked at his cards.

"Mother of God!" Rodriguez said. "Ten dollars? You must really believe in that pair of sevens."

"I do," the Italian said, throwing a ten-dollar bill on to the wooden platform.

"I ain't betting against you," Washington said, throwing his cards on the table.

"I'm in!" Rodriguez said, throwing a ten-dollar bill in the pile.

"Last card coming! Down and dirty!" Washington said, dealing Rodriguez a four and the Italian one new card each face down.

Rodriguez looked at his cards, then turned to Castellano.

"What are you doing?"

"I'll bet twenty dollars!" Castellano said.

"Dios mio!" Rodriguez said. "You holding two pairs?"

"It will cost you twenty dollars to find out."

Washington, who considered himself an expert, turned to Rodriguez.

"Let me see your hand," he said.

Washington looked at Rodriguez's hand. He had a pair of kings.

"What do you think?" Rodriguez said.

"No!" Washington said. "If he's betting like that, he's got at least three of a kind. He's got another seven in the hole."

"You got three sevens?" Rodriguez said.

"It'll cost you twenty dollars to find out," Castellano replied.

Rodriguez looked back at Washington. Washington shook his head.

"It's all yours," Rodriguez said, throwing in his cards. "What you got?"

With that, Castellano turned over his cards. The pair of sevens was all he had. Rodriguez could have beaten him with the two kings.

"Well, kiss my ass!" Washington said. "He bluffed us out."

"Like my old granddaddy used to say," Castellano said as he raked in the winnings. "No weapon is more powerful than fear."

***

Before America's involvement in the war, Da Nang was little more than a sleepy fishing village on the coast of the South China Sea halfway between Saigon and Hanoi. After American involvement began to escalate in the early spring of 1964, however, Da Nang rapidly became a boom town. With the construction of a major military operations base just north of the city, complete with an ordnance depot, three landing strips, barracks and mess facilities for 20,000 American soldiers, Da Nang suddenly became a focal point for the thriving commercial enterprise known as war.

That night, after Jesse and I were settled in the barracks at the operations base, we went out to explore the city. Everywhere, it was alive with activity. The streets were crowded with pedicabs, bicycles, motor scooters, cars and pedestrians. At the open-air markets, local farmers, eager to take advantage of the new economy, squatted in groups and offered all manner of fresh meat and produce. Garlic, tomatoes, watermelon, squash, custard apples, guavas and fruit jacks were all readily available. Local hunters displayed freshly-killed monkey, cobra and wild parrot meat. All along the streets, little family soup stands offered their own version of Pho, the traditional Vietnamese noodle soup made from freshly boiled rice noodles, greens and chicken, beef or pork. Small neighborhood bars offered Vietnamese sake, cheeseburgers, American music, and women for sale.

***

Finally, after walking around the city for almost two hours, Jesse and I stopped in front of a huge pink building that stretched for half a block. The sign above the entrance read: "The Pink Pagoda." During the French occupation of Vietnam, the building had been a bright yellow color and served as a club for military officers. After the French were defeated in 1953, the new government converted the structure into a resort hotel for tourists. Now, after the new US-installed government had assumed control, the hotel had been painted pink and turned into a bar, restaurant and brothel.

For a moment, Jesse and I peered at the customers seated in the outside dining area.

Suddenly, someone called out.

"Chance! Trubble!"

We turned to the direction of the voice and saw Rodriguez sitting alone at a table in the outside dining area. He was waving.

"Come on!" I said. "Let's go sit with Rodriguez."

As we made our way to the table, we could see an assortment of women at the bar inside waiting to be negotiated with and taken to the rooms upstairs.

"Why don't we sit at the bar?" Jesse said.

"I'm not interested in women like that," I said. "Let's sit with Rodriguez."

Moments later, Jesse and I were seated with the Latino. We ordered beers and started to chat.

"I want to go to the chicken fights," Rodriguez said, "but nobody will tell me where they are."

"Why not?" I asked.

"They say it's a big secret."

"I want to go to the chicken fights too," I said. "Let's see if we can find out where they are."

Jesse couldn't keep his eyes off the women at the bar.

"Check out the small one at the end of the bar," he said.

"The one with the pouty lips and low-cut top."

Rodriguez laughed.

"God only knows how many men she's been with," he said. "If she had as many sticking out of her as she has had stuck in her, she'd look like a porcupine."

I laughed.

Moments later, we turned to see a small, middle-aged Vietnamese man, dressed in an impeccable white suit and hat, approaching our table.

"Good evening!" he said. "May I introduce myself?"

"Have a seat!" Rodriguez said.

"My name is Sammy Thieu," he said after taking a seat. "You three are new to Vietnam?"

"How did you know?" I said.

"I have been in Vietnam long enough to recognize new soldiers when I see them."

The little Vietnamese man lit a cigarette, which he held daintily in a plastic holder.

"I have been to your America," he said, dragging slowly on the cigarette. "I have a brother in Orange County, California. He owns a liquor store."

"What can we do for you, Mr. Thieu?" Jesse asked.

"The question is: what can I do for you?" the little man replied. "In Da Nang, if you have the... 'moola,' as they say in America, 'I can get you whatever you want'."

"Like what?" Johnny asked.

"Anything," the little man said. "Women, drugs, guns, military hardware, airplanes.... What did you have in mind?"

"There is one thing I need," Rodriguez said.

"What might that be?" the little man asked.

"Do you know where the cock fights are held?"

He smiled.

"Yes," he replied. "But it is very dangerous. In Vietnam, gambling is illegal outside of Saigon. The Buddhists feel that gambling is an unforgiveable sin."

"I know!" Rodriguez said.

The little man leaned over the table.

"The cock fights are at Do Lin," he said, almost in a whisper.

Then, the little man turned to the cluster of pedicabs and drivers waiting at the curb.

"Hong!" the little man called. Instantly, a young Vietnamese man, who had been leaning on an idle pedicab, rushed over. The little man spoke briefly in Vietnamese. The driver listened, then bowed in a gesture of submission.

"Go with Hong!" the little man said. "He will take you. Pay him fifty cents American."

"Great!" Rodriguez said, gulping down the last of his beer. "Come on!"

With that, Rodriguez and I got up to leave.

I turned to Jesse.

"You want to go?"

"No, I'm going to stay here. I'll see you back at the barracks later tonight."

I turned back to the little Vietnamese man.

"Thanks!"

"If you need anything else, just let me know." he said. "I'm usually somewhere close to the Pink Pagoda."

***

Moments later, Rodriguez and I were riding across the eastern section of Da Nang in a pedicab. As we rode, he was reading a Spanish language newspaper titled *La Verdad*. As he read, he seemed to becoming increasingly agitated. Finally, he stopped reading and threw the newspaper to the floor of the pedicab.

"Los bastardos!" he said.

"What's wrong?"

"Government troops have killed more of my people," he said. "Innocent people who were only standing up for their rights. Someday the bastards will pay."

Then he stopped his rant and took a deep breath.

"I'm sorry," he said. "I get very upset that I can't right the wrongs being done to my people."

We rode quietly for a moment

"Is all of your family still in Peru?"

"Only my younger brother and my mother. My sister is

living in a commune in Oregon."

"Do you ever hear from them?"

"I get letters now and then."

He seemed calmer now. I liked Rodriguez. Honest, forthright and fearless in a firefight, he and Washington were the two funniest soldiers of Platoon C. I was glad to be his friend.

***

The arena where the cock fights were held was an old, abandoned tire warehouse in the Chinese sector of Da Nang. A hot, dry, dusty place, it was little more than a roofed concrete floor with sawdust shavings scattered about. The smell of chicken manure hung heavily in the air. When Rodriguez and I arrived, the fights were already underway and some 200-250 men, mostly of Vietnamese and Chinese descent, were flailing the air, frenziedly placing bets and urging on their favorite fowl. Finally, when a new fight was set to begin, Rodriguez turned to me.

"Pick the red one," he said expertly. "It's a bantam and hatch mix. They'll fight to the death."

I placed a twenty-dollar bet on the red chicken, then Rodriguez placed his bet. Bets in place, the fight was ready to begin. The two small roosters, steel gaffes affixed to their legs with tiny leather thongs, circled one another in the fighting pit. Neck feathers flared, gaffes glinting in the light, the two combatants continued to circle, then suddenly the red one attacked. In a flurry of frenzied fighting and flying gaffes, the fight was over in an instant. In the furious attack, the red rooster delivered three quick stabs to the breast and neck of the black and now the black one lay on its side mortally wounded, its blood spurting out into the sawdust shavings. As the red chicken stood over his dying rival, the crowd erupted in a triumphant yell. Rodriguez and I collected our winnings.

Moments later, two new roosters were presented. The owner of a sleek little gray rooster held up his entrant for the bettors to see. Beside him, a second owner held up a black rooster, which had most of the feathers missing along the right side of its neck.

"That black has seen lots of action," Rodriguez said. "I'm going with the black."

Moments later, Rodriguez and I placed our money on the black. With that, the two roosters were placed in the pit and, with neck feathers fluffed angrily, they started circling one another. Suddenly, the black rooster charged in and, in a furious exchange, both roosters slashed and hacked at each other unmercifully. Then, as they started to circle one another again, the crowd could see that one of black rooster's gaffes were dragging behind it.

"No! No!" shouted the owner of the black. Quickly, he jumped into the pit to grab his bird to stop the fight. As he did, the owner of the gray rooster jumped in and pushed him away. For a moment, the two men glared at one another, then began cursing one another in Vietnamese. Suddenly, the owner of the black chicken turned and punched the other man in the face, then the two men went down into the wood shavings. The crowd scattered, some watching the fight between the roosters and others watching the fight between the two owners. Seconds later, the owner of the gray rooster escaped the grasp of the other man and stood up. Instantly, he pulled a pistol out of his hip pocket and fired a single shot. The owner of the black chicken fell to the concrete floor. For a moment, everything stopped. Then there was a sudden mad scramble for the exits.

"I'm out of here!" Rodriguez said. "I don't want to get arrested."

Quickly, the Latino darted to the nearest exit. For a moment, I looked around, unsure of what I should do. Then, like all the others, I rushed for the door. For several moments, I was caught up in a crush of humanity trying to get out the door. Finally, after some shoving and pushing, I was through the door.

Outside, the gamblers were running in all directions. Then I heard the sound of police sirens. Quickly, I turned and ran down the street in the opposite direction. After running for almost two blocks, I turned and ducked into an alleyway. Then, after running a short distance in the darkness, I could see that the alley had been sealed off by a wall. To the left, I saw a gate that led to an enclosed courtyard. I pushed the gate, but it was locked from the inside. Quickly, I pushed two fingers through the opening and flipped the latch. Then I went inside and closed the gate. For a moment, I stood perfectly still and listened. At the warehouse up the street, I could still hear a melee of shouting voices and police whistles.

Suddenly, somewhere in the darkness of the courtyard, I heard a woman's voice say something in Vietnamese. I turned.

In the shadows, I could make out the form of a young woman standing in the darkness. Again, she spoke in Vietnamese.

"I'm sorry," I said. "I'm leaving now."

I turned back to the gate.

"You speak English," the woman said. "Who are you?"

Surprised that the woman spoke English, I turned to face her.

"Who are you?" she asked again.

I moved closer.

"You're an American soldier?" she said. "You were at the cock fights?"

Still trying to get a read on the situation, I hesitated before answering.

"That's right," I said finally. "But I'll leave now."

"No!" the woman said. "Please don't. I haven't had a chance to speak English in over four years."

In the darkness, I could see her moving closer. Now, in the light of a street lamp, I could see a small, pretty Vietnamese woman in a white silk kimono coming toward me.

"My name is Phoung," she said, stepping forward and offering her hand. "I know your country well. I lived there for three years."

I smiled nervously, then shook her hand.

"Don't be afraid," she said. "Have a seat here in the courtyard. I'll bring some tea."

With that, I took a seat at a stone table in the courtyard. I was calmer now. Moments later, she reappeared, carrying a candle and two cups in one hand and a ceramic pot of steaming Chinese tea in the other.

"I don't have electricity," she said as she poured the tea. "I hope you don't mind the candle."

"That's fine," I said.

"Two weeks ago," she said, "there was a raid at the cock fights and a young German couple came here. They were from Munich."

"So I'm not the first to invade your privacy?"

"Oh, no!" she said, with a soft smile. "I'm happy to see you."

In the candlelight, I could see she was no more than five feet tall, with braided jet-black hair, a pretty face and dark eyes that shined in the candlelight.

She poured tea for each of us.

"Tell me about yourself," I said.

"I was born in Laos," she said, "in Bac Boa, a tiny village near the Kong River. My family and I came to Vietnam during the French Occupation when I was very small. During the Diem regime, my father was a high-ranking military officer, but after Diem was assassinated, the new government saw him as the enemy and he fled back to Laos."

"Where did you learn to speak English?"

"I studied English when I attended a girl's school in Hue," she said, "but I didn't get a chance to speak it until I went to California to live with my aunt in West Covina."

She poured more tea.

"I love America and Americans," she continued. "The three years I spent with my aunt were the happiest days of my life."

"Do you live alone?"

"Not exactly," she said. "I'll explain when I know you better."

I could see I had hit a sensitive spot. I got up from the stone table.

"I think I should go," I said.

"Please don't!" she said. "I can make some more tea. And I have fish cakes and Vietnamese sake."

"No." I said. "I really should be getting back to the base."

"Will you come again?"

"Yes! I would like that."

"When would you like to return?"

"Tomorrow night?"

"Perfect." she said. "The next time, go to the front of the building, then take the left passageway to the elephant tree and you will see this gate," she said, pointing to a second gate in the courtyard where I had entered originally. "Knock four times. I'll know it's you."

With that, I said good-bye. This time, I went out through the second gate, passed along a narrow passageway under a huge elephant tree, then walked to the street. At the street, I stopped and peered at the front of the building. It was an International Red Cross Relief Center.

***

The following night, I was back in the Chinese sector with Phuong. As instructed, I took the passageway along the side of the building to the gate under the elephant tree. I knocked four times. Moments later, she appeared.

"It's you!" she said, opening the door. "Please come in."

This time, she ushered me into her living quarters, a tiny two-room affair with a combination kitchen-sitting room and a small bedroom. After serving me a large helping of pho with strips of monkey and duck meat and a large glass of Vietnamese sake, we sat on a small straw mat and ate by candlelight. It was then she opened up about the details of her personal life.

"Why didn't you return to Laos with your parents when the Diem government fell?" I asked.

"I was in Hue attending college," she said. "The military coup was so fast, I didn't have time to escape."

"So…you're hiding here?"

The little woman, quiet fear in her eyes, peered at me.

"For almost a year," she said. "The director of the Red Cross mission is friends with my father and he lets me stay. I'd give anything in this world to get back to my family. I don't want to be captured by South Vietnamese intelligence."

"So how can I help?" I asked.

She looked at me, her dark eyes shining in the candlelight.

"I want you to help me get back to my family in Laos."

"Where is your family?"

"At Bac Boa," she said. "About twenty miles west of the Kong River. It's three days travel."

I didn't answer at first.

"I have it planned," she said. "It's one day by train to Hue, then twelve miles through the mountains to Muong Nong. There we will cross the Laotian border and go another seven miles to the Kong River. From there, it another twenty miles to Bac Boa."

"Why don't you cross the border into Laos at Bien Hein?" I said. "It's much closer."

"Oh, no!" she said. "At that point, the border is heavily guarded. It's too dangerous."

I studied her for a long moment.

"I have money," she said, "to pay for the journey."

I finished the pho and handed her the empty bowl.

"Let me see what I can do," I said.

Phuong took my bowl, placed it in a tiny dishpan, then she turned and went through the bamboo blind into the bedroom. Moments later, she returned wearing a black silk kimono with a scarlet hem. Without saying a word, she extended her hand. With that, I got up from the straw mat and she led me through the bamboo blind to the bedroom. Inside, I saw a bed, neatly laid out with fresh cotton linens on a straw mat. Above the bed was a statue of Buddha and a well-stocked bookshelf built of bricks and wood boards stacked atop one another. She sat on the bed and extended her arms. From the moment I took the tiny Vietnamese woman to my breast, I knew I would like her. She was a strong lover with intelligent, caring hands. As I thrust my body into hers again and again, I kept thinking about the line from Samuel Taylor Coleridge's poem "Xanadu": "A savage place, as holy and as enchanted as ever beneath a waning moon did woman wail for her demon lover." On orgasm, she whined softly like a hurt animal. It was a low, primal, haunting sound. Afterward, she lay in my arms.

"Will you help me?" she said.

"I don't want to see you dead."

"If South Vietnamese intelligence captures me, they will torture me to make me tell where my father is. I would rather die than be tortured."

"Let me see what I can do."

When I left that night, she asked when I would return.

"Not sure," I replied. "But I will try to make it soon."

"Please do," she said, standing on tiptoes to kiss me good-bye. "I'll be waiting."

***

During our first eight months as soldiers, Jesse and I spent most of our time on patrols, guarding prisoners, and performing search and destroy missions. Our platoon would go into a village, gather the people, then try to weed out the Viet Cong spies. Sometimes, once villagers were gathered, the spies, upon seeing they were about to be discovered, would turn and try to run off into the jungle. They were shot on the spot. A few spies were always discovered in each village and, once the operation was over, they had to be escorted back to the detention center in Da Nang. Patrols were basically scouting missions. When headquarters would report enemy activity in an area, Platoon C would be dispatched to investigate. Most of these forays ended up being nothing. Occasionally, we would kill a few, then escort the others back to Da Nang for incarceration. Meanwhile, our nights were spent at the Pink Pagoda, drinking Vietnamese beers at one of the city's many beer gardens or playing cards in the barracks. Then, in early September of 1965, Platoon C was dispatched on a special mission.

***

When Jesse and I went into the briefing room on that warm June morning, we saw Lieutenant James Greene, our platoon commander, standing in front of a topographical map. He was a medium height, stocky man in his early forties with a serious face and close-cropped dark hair.

"Good afternoon!" he said.

He turned to the map.

"The Viet Cong and North Vietnamese regulars are

mounting a new offensive in the northern part of the central highlands. To fuel this offensive, the enemy is receiving supplies—food, personnel and ordnance—from the north along the Ho Chi Minh trail. In Quang Tri province at Do Lung," he said, indicating on the map, "there is a bridge which spans a narrow gorge along the trail. As long as this bridge exists, the enemy can easily move supplies over the gorge into Do Lung. Without this bridge, five extra days are required to move supplies over an alternate route. Two weeks ago, our forces destroyed this bridge. Now, almost like magic, our intelligence says the bridge has been rebuilt. Your mission will be to destroy the bridge at Do Lung again. I'll be in charge. Any questions?"

No hands raised.

"That's it!" Lt. Greene said. "Get some sleep tonight. At 0600 tomorrow, you'll be seeing combat."

***

The following morning at daybreak, me, Jesse and the other members of Platoon C were in a convoy of Huey helicopters cruising high over the central highlands. Through the helicopter window, we could see the vibrant green, grassy expanses of the Vietnamese countryside unfolding beneath us. Here and there, we spotted farmers in black attire and conical straw hats tending the fields. Some were plowing with water buffalo, others with crude digging tools. As the Hueys passed overhead, the children of some of the farmers waved at us.

Washington, who was keeping time to Ray Charles' "Hit the Road Jack" on a portable tape player, looked out the window.

"Looks pretty safe down there," he said. "Nothing but farmers."

"There are lots of VC small artillery here," Lt. Greene said. "They love to take free shots at passing choppers."

For several more minutes, we rode quietly. Then suddenly, above the flock-flock-flock of the helicopter's blade, me and the others could hear the sounds of artillery fire. Quickly, the pilot yelled to the gunner manning the 60-caliber machine gun on the right side of the aircraft.

"Charley artillery!" he yelled.

Instantly, the port side gunner wheeled the weapon around and opened fire with a deafening, ear-pounding rhythm. For several minutes, the firing continued. Suddenly, a bullet ripped a hole through the bottom of the helicopter and a mass of wires and plastic pipes were exposed in the floor.

"Holy Christ!" Rodriguez said. "They're trying to shoot our balls off."

Washington grabbed his backpack from the floor.

"They aren't going get mine," he said, placing his backpack under him and sitting on it.

Then, just as suddenly as it had started, the firing stopped and the helicopter started to go down.

"Set her down along the edge of that rice paddy," Lt. Greene said to the pilot. "We're going into those mountains over there."

Then he turned to his charges.

"As soon as we're down, I'll be out first. I want you guys and your equipment right on my heels."

Moments later, the helicopter bumped down on a dry grassy knoll along the edge of a rice paddy.

"Let's go!" Lt. Greene said.

Then, holding one hand on top of his helmet and an M-16 in the other, he jumped out of the helicopter on the run. Instantly, the other members of Platoon C were behind him.

Once we were on the ground, I could hear the rhythmic rat-tat-tat of a machine gun coming from a grove of gypsum trees on the opposite side of the rice paddy.

"Take cover!" Lt. Greene shouted, pointing to a nearby stand of mangrove trees. Right away, Jesse and I and the others scrambled into the thick undergrowth surrounding the trees. Moments later, the lieutenant was training a set of field binoculars on the mangroves.

"There is a light machine gun in there," he said. "I can see three, maybe four North Vietnamese regulars."

He pondered for a moment.

"Chance! Rodriguez!" he said. "Take grenade launchers and go around the edge of the rice paddy to that hill on the left.

Once you're there, you should be able to see the machine gun nest. Put a couple of grenades in there."

Rodriguez and I nodded.

"Once you have destroyed it," Lt. Greene said, "blow this whistle!"

He handed a black toy whistle to Rodriguez.

"A toy whistle?" Rodriguez said.

"Just follow your orders," the lieutenant said. "When we hear the whistle, we'll know you've done your job."

Instantly, Rodriguez and I grabbed grenade launchers and grenades and got ready to make a run to the hill.

"Go!" the lieutenant said. "We'll cover you."

With that, the other members of Platoon C opened fire on the machine-gun nest and Rodriguez and I, ducking down low, darted out of the thick undergrowth, then we made our way around the rice paddy to the hill. Finally, we stopped and peered down into the mangrove trees.

Some forty yards ahead, we could see the helmets of two North Vietnamese Regular Army soldiers glinting in the sunlight. In front of them, on the ground, were two other NVRAs manning the machine gun.

"Well, look at that!" Rodriguez said. "Let me do the honors."

"Be my guest," I said.

Expertly, Rodriguez attached a grenade to the launcher, then taking careful aim, he fired. On explosion, the force of the grenade blast blew open the tops of the mangrove trees and the machine gunner, his feed man and one of the soldiers standing with them were killed instantly. The fourth enemy soldier looked around frantically to determine what had killed his comrades. Then, for a split second, he instinctively peered toward the hill where Rodriguez and I were standing. Quickly, he raised his rifle to fire, but I was faster. With a single shot from an M-16 spinner bullet, the fourth soldier fell, mortally wounded.

"Blow the whistle!" Rodriguez said.

Thirty minutes later, members of Platoon C were safely on the hill.

"Good job!" the captain said as he looked down at the dead

North Vietnamese soldiers. "Let's go. We've got some marching to do."

He turned to his charges.

"Chance! Rodriguez!" he barked. "I want you at point. Trubble! Washington! Bring up the rear!"

***

With that, Platoon C, laden with explosives, set out on a five-mile march through the Vietnamese countryside. For almost two hours, we trekked across a sandy, grassy plain. Then, after crossing a river with water up to our waists, we were in heavy, mountainous jungle. As we moved silently along the jungle trail, a rich canopy of greenery surrounded us. High overhead, black monkeys, ring-tailed lemurs, and wild parrots peered down curiously.

I turned to the lieutenant.

"Think we'll see a tiger?"

"We might," he said. "They're in here."

Ten minutes later, we came upon an abandoned hut along the side of the trail. Lt. Greene called a halt so he could inspect it.

"Enemy soldiers have slept here," he said, reading the labels of empty c-rations cans he found beside the doorway. "They were here less than a week ago."

Twenty minutes later, another mile up the jungle trail, the lieutenant called another halt and pointed to a huge mahogany tree ahead. The bodies of four badly-decomposed Viet Cong soldiers were hanging by their necks from the tree.

"Holy Christ!" Washington said as he peered at the bodies. "What happened to them?"

"They were hung by their own officers," Lt. Greene said. "Probably for desertion."

"Come on!" Washington said, holding his nose against the putrid smell. "Let's get the hell out of here!"

***

An hour later, Platoon C was out of the jungle and

marching along a verdant green valley floor with mountains on either side. Suddenly, Lt. Greene called another halt.

"We're getting close," he said. "The bridge at Do Lung is just around the side of this mountain."

Now the trail along the valley floor, overgrown by giant masses of veil moss, a leathery, southeast Asian lichen almost as hard as wood, narrowed to a point no more than three feet across. With that, me and the other members of Platoon C, holding our weapons and knapsacks in front of us, carefully squeezed through the narrow passageway into a clearing.

"Chance! Trubble!" Lt. Greene said. "Come with me! The rest of you stay here."

Moments later, Jesse and I were following the lieutenant up a heavily-vegetated trail along the side of the mountain. After walking some 30 feet off the trail, the lieutenant parted the branches of a small rubber tree and trained field glasses on the gorge below.

"Well, look at that!" Lt. Greene said, peering through the binoculars. "I don't know how the little bastards do it. Two weeks ago, we left that bridge a scrambled mess of logs and broken timbers. Now it looks like it was never destroyed!"

"Where are the people that rebuilt it?" I asked.

"Oh, we won't see them in the daylight," the lieutenant said. "They only work at night. That's why we've got to work fast."

Once we had shinnied back down the side of the mountain, the captain barked a new set of orders.

"Rodriguez! Castellano!" he said. "You and the other men take up a post here! Anybody comes down this trail from either direction, blow them away!"

Rodriguez and Castellano nodded.

"Me and Chance and Trubble are going down into the valley floor to the target," the lieutenant said, pointing to a small indentation between two gorges. "If we're not back in two hours, come looking for us."

Thirty minutes later, darkness had fallen and Jesse, I and Lt. Greene had scrambled down the side of the mountain into the narrow mouth of the gorge. Ahead of us, some 100 yards away, we could see the bridge.

"You two get up there on those rocks with your infra-red gear," the lieutenant said, pointing to some huge boulders some forty feet above us. "If there is resistance, they'll be on the opposite side of the bridge. Look closely along the support beams. That's where the guards will be. I'll wait here."

Ten minutes later, Jesse and I were on top of the boulders, then, using the infrared gear, we scanned the area around the bridge. Only seconds later, I spotted two VC guards. One was young and looked to be in his twenties. The other was older, maybe in his late thirties.

"I see two guards!" I said. "They're on the north end."

"I see them too," Jesse said. "You take the young one and I'll get the older one."

Then, training our M-16s with night vision scopes on the targets, we prepared to fire.

"Hold your fire!" Jesse said suddenly. "The young one has left his post."

"Where did he go?"

"He's going for a quickie," Jesse said.

"A quickie?"

"See the bridge support on the far side," Jesse said. "Look just to the left beyond the base of the last support, maybe 10-15 yards."

I adjusted the focus on my scope.

"Oh, yeah," I said. "He's got a girl. She can't be more than 14 or 15."

"I've got the older one in my sights. Ready?"

"No, wait!" I said. "Let's see how he makes out with this young chick."

"Let's blast them while we got the chance."

"No, wait!" I said. "Let's watch."

"You're a perverted bastard," he said.

For a moment, we waited. Then we watched as the young Viet Cong soldier undressed the young girl. Once they were naked, he escorted her to a straw mat on the ground nearby.

"Okay," I said, adjusting the focus on my infrared scope. "You got the older one?"

"Yeah," Jesse said. "I'm ready."

As the Viet Cong soldier mounted the young female and began penetrating her with unmerciful fury, I sighted him carefully through the infrared scope and took careful aim.

"Now!" I said, then Jesse and I fired simultaneously.

Through the infrared scope, I could see the impact of the M-16 spinner bullet literally knock the young Viet Cong soldier off the girl into a stand of nearby bamboo trees.

Then, I could hear the man's muffled scream echo against the mountainside as the young girl, her tiny breasts shining in the August moonlight, looked around in horror trying to determine what had happened. Quickly, she gathered her clothes and, still stark naked, ran off into the bamboo forest.

"I got mine," Jesse said.

"So did I. One thing I'll say, he went out happy."

Twenty minutes later, Jesse and I and Lieutenant Greene were at the support columns underneath the bridge. Immediately, Lt. Greene started unpacking nitroglycerine charges and securing them to the support beams.

"Christ, look at this!" the lieutenant said, pointing to the cross beams. "They've even placed steel bolts in the cross beams. It takes time to do that."

Over the next twenty minutes, we placed the charges among the support beams, running a leader wire from one to the other until we were on the opposite side of the gorge. Finally, we were finished.

"All the charges are in place," Jesse said.

With that, Jesse and I and Lt. Greene started back down the mountainside. Behind us, I was stringing a lead wire. Once we were at a safe distance, Jesse cut the lead wire, I attached a detonator and turned to the lieutenant.

"Ready?" I asked.

"Do it!" the lieutenant said.

With that, I pushed the plunger. Instantly, a chain reaction of loud explosions in tandem with a series of brilliant flashes of light shattered the serenity of the August night. Then, once the bridge's underpinnings were blasted away, its wood beam superstructure gave a groaning, creaking sound and, after twisting sideways, it crumpled downward and finally collapsed into the valley floor with a mighty thunderous crash. In the bright moonlight, Lt. Greene looked at the dust settling over the giant pile of splintered logs and support beams.

"Let's see how long it takes them to rebuild it this time."

With that, he picked up the field telephone.

"Lame Duck," he said into the receiver. "This is Popeye. We'll meet the chopper back at the pick-up point at 0800 hours."

***

Back at the base barracks two nights later, I told Jesse about Phuong's plan and asked him if he would accompany us.

"Let me get this straight," he said. "This woman wants you to take her across the Vietnamese border into Laos, then travel another 20 miles through enemy territory to deliver her to a little village in Laos?"

I nodded.

"You're nuts!" he said.

"We could do it."

"Yeah." Jesse added, "And in the process, we're end up being dog meat. Why won't she go on her own?"

"She would never make it."

"So she wants you to risk your life?"

I studied him for a moment

"You don't have to go," I said.

Jesse shook his head.

"Boy, she must have good foo-foo to talk you into something like this."

"I like her," I said. "She's a gentle soul that's got caught up in this crazy war. And yes, if you must know, I love to roll around with her."

"What if I say no," he said.

"She and I will go alone," I said.

"You're crazy. Wacko. Nuts."

***

The following morning, Lt. Greene rousted the members

156

of Platoon C out of their bunks at 0700.

"Listen up!" he barked. "Everybody report to the briefing room in one hour. Looks like we're going to Thanh Hoa Mountain."

Jesse sat up sleepily and threw his legs over the side of the army cot.

"What is Thanh Hoa Mountain?" he asked.

"I don't know. I guess we'll soon find out."

Deep in the rugged highlands of Quang Binh province, there was a high promontory known as Thanh Hoa Mountain, which, throughout the war, proved to be one of its most strategic points. At its very top, the mountain was a flat, grassy knoll shrouded with coconut palms, banyan trees and giant stands of red bamboo. From that point, an observer with field glasses could hide among the vegetation and monitor movements along the Ho Chi Minh trail five miles to the south and almost seven miles to the North. As a result, control of the mountaintop was of the greatest importance. If Charley controlled it, he could safely direct the southward movement of North Vietnamese supplies and ordnance along the trail. If US forces controlled it, they could seek out and destroy those same supplies and ordnance.

"For almost two months," Lt. Greene began, "we have had control of Thanh Hoa Mountain and effectively stopped the movement of enemy supplies southward. Now, two days ago, after heavy losses, the enemy has recaptured the mountain and supplies are flowing freely to the south again. Our mission is to retake Thanh Hoa Mountain."

***

Two hours later, Jesse and I and the other members of Platoon C were in a convoy of Huey Helicopters travelling northward across the central highlands toward Quang Binh province.

"What kind of fricking war is this?" Washington asked, peering down on the rugged mountains below. "We've captured this mountain once before. We take it, then Charley takes it back. Nobody ever wins in this war."

An hour later, the convoy of Huey helicopters sat down on a narrow ridge on the valley floor along the base of Thanh Hoa Mountain. Once the members of Platoon C disembarked, Lt. Greene ordered us up the mountainside through the thick, green undergrowth. For two hours, we scrambled over the rocks, ducking through groves of nipa palm and skirting endless stands of bamboo. Finally, the lieutenant called a halt. In the western skies, the sun was slowly beginning to sink behind the mountains.

"Chance! Trubble!" the captain called. "Get your infrared gear, crawl up on that ledge and see what they have on the top of the mountain it. Charley will start to move freely after dark."

As instructed, Jesse and I made our way up the mountainside, then mounted the ledge. For some thirty minutes, we trained our infra-red equipment on the top of the mountain. An hour later, we returned.

"What we got?" the lieutenant asked.

"Charley has got a command post and four of those little pop-pop anti-aircraft guns right on the very top," I said.

"What?" the lieutenant said.

"Pop-pops," I said. "Those little swivel chair anti-aircraft weapons like they have on ships."

"Those are Chinese-made LL-104s. How many men?"

"Looks like forty, maybe fifty North Vietnamese regulars," I said. "About half of them are part of a patrol along the front edge of the mountain."

Lt. Greene pondered for a moment, then reached for the field telephone.

"Popeye to Lame Duck," he said. "Do you read me?"

Lt. Greene listened.

"Lame Duck! This is Popeye at target #1033," he said. "We've got a company of fifty NVRAs and four Chinese-made LL-104s on the very top of the target. Please advise."

He listened.

"We're going to need air support."

Lt. Greene listened again.

"That's right," he said. "That's right."

Finally, he hung up the phone.

"Tomorrow, at 0600," he said, "F-14 fighters will bomb the top of the hill. While they are attacking, we'll move up the mountain and take positions. When the air force is finished, we'll go to the top and mop up. Let's get a good night's sleep and be ready tomorrow."

***

The next morning at 0500 hours, after an uncomfortable night of sleep on the rocky mountainside and a breakfast of C-rations, Jesse, I and the other members of Platoon C were ready. From our position halfway up the mountain, we waited for the air strike.

"The F-14s should be coming any minute," the lieutenant said, looking at his watch.

Suddenly, high overhead, we watched as four F-14 fighter jets screamed in low over the top of Thanh Hoa Mountain. The moment they came into view, the LL-104s started firing. Then, seconds later, there were the loud swooshes of laser-guided cluster bombs as they crashed into the anti-aircraft gun emplacements and exploded with ear-deafening loudness.

"Move out!" Lt. Greene said.

With that, members of Platoon C started up the side of the mountain. As we scrambled upward through thick groves of nipa palm and red bamboo, we could hear the battle raging at the top. One after another, the F-14 fighter jets swooped in low again and again and dropped their deadly cargo on the enemy weapons. The walls of the valley echoed with the explosions of the cluster bombs and the rhythmic *Pop! Pop! Pop!* of the LL-104s.

Finally, at a clearing halfway up the mountain, Lt. Greene called a halt. On the other side of a clearing, we could see a huge stand of red bamboo trees flanked on either side by tall elephant grass.

"Take cover in the bamboo trees," Lt. Greene shouted. "We'll take a position there until the action is finished on top."

Seconds later, Jesse and I and other members of the platoon raced across the narrow clearing then dove headfirst into the bamboo trees. Now, lying flat on our stomachs, our M-16s at the ready, Jesse and I lay side-by-side under the bamboo trees and listened as the battle raged above us.

Suddenly, Jesse rolled over on his side and looked up at the tops of the bamboo trees.

"What's wrong?" I asked.

"I'm getting a funny feeling about these bamboo trees."

"What do you mean?"

"Something tells me we're going to remember this grove of bamboo trees for the rest of our lives."

I laughed.

"There are millions of groves of bamboo trees like this in South Vietnam," I said. "What's so special about this one?"

"We've got some big-time karma tied up with these bamboo trees."

I laughed again.

"You've been hanging out with that Laotian woman too long," he said. "That foo-foo has got your brains scrambled."

At the top of the mountain, the sounds of battle between the F-14s and the LL-104s ceased.

"Move out!" the lieutenant barked.

Ten minutes later, Platoon C was out of the bamboo grove and scrambling up the side of the mountain.

Suddenly, some twenty yards ahead, we heard Lt. Greene.

"Take cover and commence firing!" he yelled.

Jesse looked toward the top of the hill.

"Oh hell!" he said. "It's an enemy charge."

Suddenly, from the top of the mountain, we could see a mass of NVRA soldiers, led by a middle-aged North Vietnamese officer waving a pistol, charging down the side of the mountain toward us, firing and shouting anti-American slogans.

"F*ck John Wayne!" one called.

"Mickey Mouse eats shit!" another shouted.

"LBJ, kiss my ass!" still another called.

Quickly, the soldiers of Platoon C took cover behind the grass-covered boulders and undergrowth and commenced firing. At first, as the enemy soldiers rushed forward in a human wave attack, me and the other members of Platoon C easily picked them off. After more than half of them had been killed or wounded, they retreated back up the mountainside and took positions among the boulders near the top. Behind one huge boulder, some fifteen NVRA soldiers had taken a position.

"Chance!" Lt. Greene called.

I looked over.

"Castellano is coming up with the grenade launcher," he said. "You two go around to the left and see if you can drop some grenades behind the big rock."

Moments later, Castellano, some ten grenades dangling from his waist and the grenade launcher in hand, plopped down beside me.

"Let's go!" he said.

Instantly, Castellano and I were on our feet and racing straight up the side of the mountain using a giant field of elephant grass for cover. After running some forty yards through the tall white grass, we stopped. Some fifty yards below, we could see the NVRA soldiers crouched behind a huge boulder, firing at the American position below.

Quickly, Castellano took a grenade from his belt and fitted it to the launcher. Then, taking careful aim, he fired.

"Good shot!" I said. "Now give them another one!"

With that, Castellano fitted another grenade on the launcher and took careful aim. Then, suddenly, before he could fire, he was blown back into the elephant grass.

"Tony! Tony!" I called.

Quickly, I rushed to him.

"Oh, no!" I said as I looked down. An enemy bullet had hit him in the lower neck and blood was pouring out of the wound. I looked at the stream of warm blood spurting out of the wound.

"Chance!" he said. "Don't let me die like this! Please don't let me die!"

"Hang on!" I said. "Hang on!"

Suddenly, I looked up and saw two North Vietnamese soldiers rushing through the elephant grass toward me. Instantly, I dropped to the ground. Then, putting my M-16 on automatic, I started firing. The first enemy soldier fell dead at my feet. The other was still coming. I jumped up and dashed off into the elephant grass. Moments later, the second NVRA soldier rushed into the area where I had been. Frantically, he looked around for me. Then, as he turned, I sent two M-16 spinner bullets into his chest and he fell mortally wounded.

Now, as I peered back down the hillside toward the rocks, I could see the remnants of the enemy force retreating along the opposite side of the mountain. As I watched, I could hear Platoon C rifles and machine guns firing after them. Finally, the firing stopped. The battle was over.

Suddenly, I remembered Castellano.

Instantly, I dashed back into the tall elephant grass. There, in a huge pool of blood exactly where he had fallen, he lay dead.

***

Some twenty minutes later, I was back down the side of the mountain and reported the death of Castellano.

"Where is he?" Lt. Greene asked.

I pointed toward the elephant grass.

"He was a good soldier," the lieutenant said. "I'll see that he is buried with full military honors."

I turned back to Jesse and Washington.

"Come on!" Washington said. "Let's go check out the dead gooks."

Twenty minutes later, Jesse, Washington, Rodriguez and I were moving among the enemy corpses scattered along the side of the mountain.

Rodriguez kicked over one of the bodies.

"Mother of God!" he said, staring down at the body. "It's a woman. She's got breasts and everything."

The three of us peered at the body. It was a young girl, not more than eighteen years old. She had a pretty face and closely-cropped hair. Her chest had been blown away by grenade shrapnel and we could see that her breasts had been tied down with a cloth band.

"God damn!" Rodriguez said. "You mean I killed a woman?"

With that, he looked up to the heavens and made the sign of the cross.

Washington stared at the woman's corpse.

"What a waste!" he said indignantly. "Gone forever. And for what?"

With that, Washington kneeled down beside one of the corpses. As Jesse and I watched, he opened the dead soldier's backpack and started throwing things out. There was a water canteen, a transistor radio, and an old Vietnamese newspaper with photos folded up inside. Then he pulled out a curious-looking, round black object.

"Hey!" Washington said with a big smile. "Look at this!"

Johnny and Jesse looked at the object.

"What is it?" I asked.

"Hash!" Washington said. "Black Thai hash!"

That night, Washington, Jesse and I snuck away from the other members of Platoon C into a grove of mahogany trees and smoked some of the black hash. As we passed the pipe, a cool breeze from the South China Sea wafted through the tops of the mahogany trees.

"It's really a shame about that young foo-foo," Washington said. "Such a waste. God! She was gorgeous..."

***

The following night, back in Da Nang, Jesse and I were back at the Pink Pagoda. Jesse wanted a woman. I wanted to talk to Sammy Thieu and, only moments after we arrived, I found him.

"How can I help you?" the little man asked.

"I need a Jeep and two automatic weapons."

"Where are you going?"

"Do you have to know that?"

"It would help me serve you better."

I peered at him for a moment.

"I want to take a Jeep into Laos."

"That's a tough one," he said. "Nobody is going to let you have a Jeep to go into Laos on your own."

"Why not?"

"Because you and the Jeep probably won't make it back. The people who own the Jeep don't give a damn about you, but they want their Jeep back."

"So, what can you do?"

"Where do you want to pick up the Jeep?" Sammy said.

"You're asking me to tell you all my plans. How do I know I can trust you?"

The little man peered at me.

"In my business, if I was not trustworthy, I would have been dead long ago."

"Hue!" I said finally. "I want to pick up the Jeep at Hue."

"Then you're going to need a guide. I know just the person to help you. He can get you into Laos to the Kong River, but you're on your own after that."

"How much for the Jeep, the guide and two automatic pistols?" I asked.

"Three hundred dollars American for the Jeep and another one hundred dollars for the guide."

"What about the pistols?" I asked.

"I can only get German-made .45 caliber at the moment," he said.

"How much?"

"Another two hundred dollars," the little man said.

"Who do I pay?"

"Pay me one hundred dollars to arrange the deal," he said. "Pay for the weapons, the Jeep and the guide when you arrive in Hue."

***

Later that night, as Jesse and I rode in a pedicab back to the barracks, I mentioned Phoung's plan again.

"Hell no!" he said. "No way. If this woman is hiding from South Vietnamese intelligence, then she is an enemy of the state. If you get caught trying to get her out of the country, you'll be seen as an accomplice."

"You always manage to find a way to not do things."

"I'm not looking to get court-martialed and end up spending the rest of my life in Leavenworth."

"We won't get caught," I said. "You're making this whole thing a much bigger deal than it actually is. Next week, I will have everything ready to go and I want you to go with me."

"How are we going to get away from the US Army long enough to pull this off? We can't go AWOL."

"We don't have to go AWOL," I said. "It won't take more than two or three days. A three-day pass is all we would need. If you don't go, Phuong and I are going alone."

He slowly shook his head.

"Remember you said you wanted some adventure and excitement in your life?"

Slowly, the scowl on his face slowly turned into a smile.

He laughed.

"So, when do you want to do this?"

"I want to leave for Hue on Saturday morning."

He pondered for a moment.

"That's September 25 and 26."

"That's right."

"Okay," he said, "Let's go talk to the lieutenant. If he'll give us a three-day leave, I'll go with you."

***

Thirty minutes later, we were in Lt. Greene's office.

"Why do you two want a three-day leave?"

"We want to visit Saigon, sir," I said. "We want to see the sights. The sounds. The rhythm of the city."

"Bullshit!" the lieutenant said. "You want to roll around some oriental women and smoke some hash. I know what you two and Washington were doing under the mahogany trees after the battle at Thanh Hoa Mountain."

I looked at Jesse. We wondered how he knew about that.

We waited.

"Okay!" he said. "You guys have done a good job and Charley is laying back right now."

He picked up a calendar on his desk.

"Three days?" he said, looking at the calendar. "That means you two want to take leave on September 25, 26 and 27?"

165

"That's right, sir!" I said.

"Granted!" the captain said. "Now at 1100 hours on the morning of September 27, I want your butts back on this base."

"Thank you, sir!" we said in unison.

***

Six days later, Jesse, I and Phuong, wearing sunglasses and dressed as my American wife, boarded a public train at Da Nang bound north to Hue. On the train, Jesse and I were happy to see other American soldiers travelling with Vietnamese women. This would help provide some cover. Once we were seated, I could see the other passengers represented every level of Vietnamese society. There were Vietnamese military officers, talking, laughing, smoking American-made cigarettes and sitting in groups; middle-aged Vietnamese war veterans with missing limbs; young mothers, many not more than twelve or thirteen years old, with crying babies; and old Vietnamese couples with toothless grins and nibbling on fish cakes. One farmer, travelling with his family, held a coop of chickens in his lap while his wife had three cobras in a cage. Their teenage son had a small pig, its legs tied with a stick, which sat on the floor and smelled up the passenger car. Throughout the journey, Phuong, Jesse and I rode silently.

After a two-hour journey, we arrived at Hue.

Once we got off the train, I hailed a pedicab.

"We want to go to the Diamond Star bar," I told the driver.

Moments later, we loaded our suitcases into the pedicab and were headed across town. Finally, the pedicab arrived in front of a small Vietnamese night club. I paid the driver and, as we got out, I turned to Phuong.

"The man we're looking for is Do Thi Ha," I said. "He owns the bar."

Inside, Phuong spoke briskly in Vietnamese to the bartender. For a moment, he looked at the three of us, then he turned and went to the back of the bar. Moments later, a middle-aged Vietnamese man appeared and came straight to me.

"You are Sammy Thieu's friend?" he said.

I nodded.

"I'm Do Thi Ha," he said. "Come with me!"

Outside, at the back of the bar, he led us out of the building into a small garage where we saw a young Vietnamese woman leaning against an old French-made Peugeot Jeep.

"This is Nhi Trac," he said. "She will be your driver and your guide."

I looked at Jesse. His eyebrows raised with interest.

Then the man reached up to a shelf in the garage and took down a navy-blue felt cloth.

"Here are the automatic weapons," he said. "And ammunition."

I took the felt cloth and opened it. There were the two German Lugers and 200 rounds of ammunition, exactly as Sammy had promised.

"I believe that's a total of five hundred dollars American?" I said.

"That's right."

Phuong opened a tiny purse and pulled out a wad of American dollars. She counted out five hundred dollars and placed it in the man's hand.

"Thank you," he said. "Also, you will find two days of supplies, food, water and blankets in the Jeep."

Then Phuong spoke briefly in Vietnamese to the woman guide and the four of us got into the Jeep. Moments later, we were on the main road headed west out of Hue.

***

Most of that afternoon was spent bouncing along the rugged mountain roads and valleys of the northern highlands. Nhi and Phuong sat in the front seat while Jesse and I sat in the back. As we rode, Phuong and Nhi chatted and nibbled on rice cakes. Finally, before sundown, we arrived in La Drang Valley.

"Nhi says we should wait until dark to cross the border," Phuong said. "Every three miles along the border, Laotian soldiers have checkpoints."

"How are we going to get past the checkpoints?" I asked.

167

"Nhi knows a backroad," she said. "We just have to wait until dark."

Phuong looked at Jesse.

"Nhi likes you," she said. "She wants you to ride in front with her."

"That's fine," Jesse said.

Three hours later, after darkness had fallen, the four of us were bouncing up and down along a bumpy mountain road. Finally, in heavy woods, we stopped and peered down the mountainside. Far below us, we could see the bright searchlights of a military checkpoint. Moments later, Nhi was negotiating the Jeep down a steep mountain grade. Suddenly, the Jeep stopped. In the moonlight, we could see what appeared to be the remains of an old border checkpoint. It was dark and deserted. Nhi pulled the Jeep off the road and waited.

"Why are we stopping?" I asked.

"Nhi says, although the checkpoint is no longer in use, sometimes guards will be dispatched to guard it at night."

Finally, after we were certain there were no hidden guards, Nhi took the Jeep through the checkpoint. Moments later, we were in Laos headed west to the Kong River.

"We're lucky to have Nhi," Phuong said. "Very lucky. She has made this trip many times."

***

By midnight, we had traversed the 18 miles through the mountains to a small, palm-covered ridge overlooking the Kong River.

"Nhi says we should spend the night here and cross the river tomorrow," Phuong said. "She says it's too late for her to return to Vietnam tonight. She wants to spend the night with us."

With that, Phuong and I spread blankets under the palm trees to sleep on. Without saying a word, Nhi took two blankets and spread them in the grass nearby, then she turned to Phuong and spoke to her in Vietnamese.

"Jesse," Phuong said. "Nhi wants you to lay with her

tonight."

"I think I'd like that," he said.

After we had eaten our fill of rice cakes covered with fish paste and drank Vietnamese Saki, Nhi pulled out a pipe and began stuffing the bowl with oily Thai hash. Once we had smoked two bowlfuls, each couple retired to their respective sleeping pallets.

***

The next morning, the four of us were up at dawn. Far below, we could see the vegetation along the banks of the Kong River.

Phuong spoke briefly to Nhi.

"Nhi says there is a monkey bridge about two miles up the river. That's where we will cross."

"A monkey bridge?" I asked. "What's a monkey bridge?"

"The locals build them," Phuong said. "It's a community bridge. I'll show you."

With that, Phuong and I said good-bye to Nhi. When it was her turn to say good-bye to Jesse, she kissed him and spoke to him in Vietnamese.

He turned to Phuong for translation.

"She said 'Thank you for a wonderful night.'"

Jesse smiled.

"Tell her I said 'You're welcome'!"

Phuong spoke briefly to Nhi.

Nhi smiled, then she waved good-bye and turned back to the Jeep. Moments later, we watched as the old French-made Jeep bounced along the bumpy road and disappeared into the mountains.

An hour later, Jesse, Phuong and I, carrying our supplies, were making our way down the mountainside to the Kong River.

Suddenly, Phoung stopped and pointed up the river.

"There's the bridge!"

Ahead of us, we could see a flimsy bridge constructed of bamboo and wooden poles spanning a narrow point in the river. It seemed to sway slightly with the movement of the current.

"That thing?" Jesse said. "You call that a bridge?"

"What choice do we have?" Phuong asked. "All the local people use it. If they weren't using it, it wouldn't be here."

Jesse peered warily at her.

"I'll go first," Phuong said.

Then, with her personal belongings tied to her back, she mounted the small platform, grabbed both hand rails and started walking across the row of narrow poles that served as the walkway. After going about thirty feet, she stopped.

"It's very sturdy," she said.

"It's swaying with the current," Jesse said.

"All monkey bridges do that," Phuong said. "Come on!"

With that, she started across the rows of narrow poles. I was right behind her. Once we were on the other side, we turned to face Jesse.

"See how easy it is!" she said. "Come on!"

Jesse unsteadily mounted the platform and took a few tentative steps.

"Hold the side rails," Phuong said. "And watch your footing."

Jesse gripped the side rails.

For a moment, he wavered, then he smiled.

"I can do this."

Twenty minutes later, as Phuong, Jesse and I stepped down from the bridge platform on the opposite bank of the river, a group of Vietnamese, two older women, an old man and a young Vietnamese woman were staring at us. For a moment, Phoung studied the group, then continued walking.

Suddenly, a young Vietnamese woman called out.

"Phuong Ho Fat?!"

Instantly, Phuong turned.

The young Vietnamese woman, still unsure of herself, stepped forward and peered closely at Phuong.

"Phuong?"

Instantly, Phuong recognized her.

"Lia!" she said. "Lia Won Bat!"

Then the two women rushed into each other's arms and kissed one another on the cheeks.

With that, Phuong took the young woman's hand and led her over to Jesse and me.

"Johnny! Jesse!" she said. "This is my cousin Lia! I haven't seen her in seven years. She's going to Bac Boa."

Introductions over, Phuong turned back to us.

"Let's go!" she said. "We've got another fifteen miles to go."

After we had walked another two miles along the mountain trail, we saw a farmer approaching in a two-wheeled, hay-filled cart drawn by a water buffalo.

"Let's get some transportation," Phoung said.

"That thing?" Jesse said. "You expect me to ride in that thing?"

"It's transportation," she said. "We do have quite a way to go."

Moments later, Phuong went up to the old man and started speaking to him in Vietnamese. As Jesse and I watched, she finally opened her little purse again and handed the old man a handful of American dollars. Then he handed her the reins.

"We now have transportation," she said.

Phuong and I climbed into the front seat and Jesse and Lia seated themselves in the pile of hay.

By late afternoon, we had travelled more than nine miles along the narrow dirt road into the mountains. Finally, we stopped

"The water buffalo is tired and hungry," Phuong said. "Let's stop and spend the night here. Bac Boa is another eight miles."

Following Phuong's instructions, I untied the water buffalo, then went down to a stream to fetch water for the animal. While I was gone, Phuong fed the animal fresh hay from the cart. Once the animal was cared for, Phuong and I settled on our blankets under the palm trees along the roadside. Lia opened a bundle she had been carrying. From it, she produced Vietnamese sake, fish cakes and several sticks of Thai hash. After we had eaten and smoked the Thai sticks, Jesse announced he and Lia were going to sleep in the hay in the cart.

***

Early the next morning, Jesse and I were up at sunrise. After we had fed and watered the water buffalo, we gathered our supplies and personal belongings and were on the trail again. By noon, we had traversed the last few miles of our journey. Phoung was excited at the thought of seeing her parents again.

"We're close!" she said. "We're very close."

Some thirty minutes later, as we rounded a curve in the road, Phuong pointed frantically.

"There! There!" she said, pointing to a thatched hut on a hillside. "There is my parents' home!"

Unable to contain herself any longer, Phuong jumped out of the cart and ran toward the thatched hut. In the yard, she was met by her mother, who hugged and kissed her. Then, her father and her sisters came out and embraced her.

***

That night, Phuong's mother prepared a traditional Vietnamese meal of roast duckling, ginger-flavored squash and French-style baguette bread with Vietnamese sake and sweet cakes.

"To America and Americans," Phuong's father said, holding up a glass of sake and proposing a toast.

"To America and Americans," Jesse and I answered.

That night, Phuong and I slept in one bed and Jesse and Lia in another in the family's guest quarters.

The next morning, for our trip back to Da Nang, Phuong's mother had prepared a huge stack of fish cakes along with fresh containers of water for our return journey.

"Thank you!"

Phuong's mother smiled and bowed.

I kissed Phuong good-bye. Jesse kissed Lia good-bye, and together, we waved to Phuong's family and started back down the mountain road.

"How in hell are we going to get back to Da Nang before

1100 hours tomorrow?" Jesse said.

"We've got more than a day to get back. You don't know what might happen between now and then."

"We're going to be AWOL and they're going to court-martial our asses!"

"Just keep walking," I said. "And stop worrying so much."

***

All that day, we walked along the mountain road back to the Kong River without seeing a soul. At first dusk, we stopped at a small stream within a shady mountain glade. I dropped my supply bundle and kneeled to drink from the stream.

"We've come about 12 miles," he said, wiping his mouth on the back of his hand. "It's another two to three miles to the river."

"Let's eat," I said. "I'm starving."

I opened the supply bundle and withdrew the fish cakes. For some fifteen minutes, we ate silently and watched the sun sink below the western horizon. Above us in the trees, we could hear the night sounds. The chatter of squirrel monkeys. The intermittent squawking of wild parrots.

Suddenly, I sprang upright.

"What is it?" Jesse said.

"I can hear Bob Dylan singing."

Jesse burst out in laughter.

"Bob Dylan?!"

"Yeah. He's singing 'Mr. Tambourine Man'."

"Bullsh*t!" he said. "You ARE losing it!"

"Shhhhhh!" I said, trying to fine tune my ears.

Instantly, both of us sat perfectly still and listened.

"Christ, you're right!" he said. "I hear it too."

"Come on!"

Quickly, both of us jumped up and listened for the direction of the sounds.

"This way!" Jesse said, darting off into the afternoon twilight.

***

For some ten minutes, we dodged through the jungle undergrowth following the sounds of Dylan's singing. Finally, at the edge of a jungle clearing, we stopped. In the darkness, we could see a Huey helicopter and a group of American soldiers gathered around a fire. Now the sounds of Bob Dylan's voice were perfectly clear.

"Hey, Mr. Tambourine Man, play a song for me, in the jingle-jangle morning, I'll come following you..."

Jesse and I walked out into the clearing.

"Hey!" I called.

Instantly, two of the soldiers turned and drew their weapons.

"Who goes there?" one called.

"American soldiers!"

Both cocked their weapons and leveled them at us.

"Show yourself!" one shouted.

We stepped out of the undergrowth into the light of the fire.

"Move forward!"

Now they could see that we were American infantrymen.

"What the hell are you two doing in Laos?" one soldier, a sergeant, asked.

"We were captured by VC and brought here for interrogation," I said.

"Twenty miles inside Laos?" he asked disbelievingly. "Let me see your dog tags!"

Still suspicious, the sergeant walked up to me and inspected our dog tags.

"Company B, Platoon C?" he said.

"That's right," I said. "We're trying to get back to our platoon."

"Where are you stationed?"

"Da Nang!" I said.

"We're going back tomorrow," he said, "as soon as we get this Huey back in the air."

"Can we go back with you?" Jesse said.

"I don't see why not," the sergeant said, "You guys look like you could use a shower and some hot food."

"What are YOU guys doing here?" I said.

"We were doing reconnaissance flights over the Ho Chi Minh trail and our chopper lost power," he said. "If we hadn't broken down, you guys could have been out here forever."

"Those are the sweetest words I've ever heard," I said.

***

The next morning at 1700 hours, Jesse and I walked back into Lt. Greene's office at command headquarters in Da Nang.

"I could have started court-martial proceedings against you two at 1100 hours yesterday," he said.

"We couldn't help it, Lieutenant," I said. "We were captured by VC and taken into Laos."

"Don't try to bullsh*t me, Chance!" he said. "You guys can get the pilot of that crippled helicopter to believe that crap, but not me. You and Trubble were off getting laid and doing drugs."

I shrugged.

"Have it your way."

"So, we're off the hook?" I said.

"Not exactly," the lieutenant said. "I've got to write a backdated memo saying I gave you two a four-day leave rather than a three-day leave. After that, everything will be okay."

"Thank you, sir!" we said in unison.

***

Two years passed. During that time, Jesse and I got an up-close look at the war. In our hearts, we knew it was unwinnable, but we continued to fight. Like the French and the Germans at no man's land in World War I, it became abundantly clear that the conflict had become little more than a war of attrition. Human lives were being lost, but no substantial military gains were being made by either side. We would take a strategic point, like Tran Hoa Mountain, then Charley would take it back. So far as a purpose to the war, the North Vietnamese people knew what they wanted, a sovereign state that would unite all of their people. Meanwhile, the US had no clarity of purpose. If they won the war, then what?

Meanwhile, the Chinese and the Russians were happy to provide weapons and supplies to Charley. While American jets were dropping bombs on Hanoi, it only alienated the local population and inspired the Viet Cong to fight harder.

Meanwhile, Jesse and I tried to make the most of our lives as soldiers. Days were spent working patrols, escorting prisoners in and out of the enemy detention center and performing special missions. Nights were spent at the Pink Pagoda, drinking beer in one of Da Nang's many beer gardens or playing cards in the platoon barracks. Then, in the early fall of 1967, we were dispatched to destroy the bridge at Do Lung for the third time.

***

When Platoon C crowded into the briefing room that cold September morning, a new face was standing on the podium with Lt. Greene.

"With us today," the lieutenant said, "is Colonel Frank Carnage, a tactical specialist on assignment from the Pentagon. Col. Carnage will not only brief you on this mission, but all of us will be under his command."

We looked up to see a young spit-and-shine officer, short in stature with a boyish face, blonde hair and a bird colonel designation on his arm. He could not have been more than twenty-five years of age.

"Good morning, men," he began. "As you all know, the war in Vietnam is new to America. The type of guerilla tactics the enemy is using calls for some special needs. That's why the Pentagon has sent me here to assess those needs."

Members of Platoon C looked at one another, not quite sure of what was happening.

"This afternoon," Col. Carnage continued, "we're going back to Do Lung to destroy the bridge again."

"Kiss my ass!" Washington, who was sitting beside me, whispered. "Not again!"

"In the past, we have used traditional explosives to destroy the bridge," he said. "This time, we will use air power."

Then he proceeded to explain that intelligence had reported

the bridge had been rebuilt a third time and was now heavily guarded with up to twenty enemy soldiers.

"Once Platoon C arrives at the target," he said, "we will wait for Air Force jets to destroy the bridge, then we will go in to kill or capture the surviving enemy."

***

Early that afternoon, members of Platoon C, under the command of Col. Carnage, were in a convoy of three Huey Helicopters headed once again to the rugged mountains near Do Lung. This time, rather than landing on the mountain opposite the bridge and marching to the target, Col. Carnage ordered the Hueys into the narrow valley floor directly below the target. Once the choppers were on the ground, our new commander took charge.

"Follow me, men!" he shouted, jumping out of the chopper and waving his charges forward.

Moments later, Jesse and I and the other members of Platoon C were on the ground. Only moments after we were out of the helicopter, we heard the sounds of a machine gun from somewhere along the base of the mountain.

"Take cover, men!" the colonel yelled.

Instantly, members of Platoon C ducked behind nearby trees, boulders and undergrowth. Around us, we could hear machine gun bullets whizzing through the air. Col. Carnage, with Lt. Greene at his side, was crouched behind a huge, grass-covered boulder for cover.

"Lieutenant!" the colonel yelled. "Hand me the heat-sensitive binoculars."

Lt. Greene located a brown leather case among the equipment and handed it to the colonel.

"These little bastards won't hide from these," he said as he opened the case and withdrew the special field glasses. "These babies will locate each and every one of them by their body heat."

For a moment, he adjusted the binoculars, then trained them on the mountain ledges high above the gorge.

"There's the new bridge," he said. "I can see at least eight or nine guards on the north end. The south end is unprotected."

Carefully, he adjusted the binoculars.

"Also, there is a machine gun nest in some coconut palms just below the north end."

Quickly, he lowered the binoculars and picked up the field telephone.

"Captain Marvel to Lame Duck!" he said. "Captain Marvel to Lame Duck!"

He listened.

"This is Captain Marvel at target #786," he said. "We need three helicopter gunships."

He listened.

"Ten minutes?" he said. "We'll be waiting."

Col. Carnage hung up the field telephone.

Meanwhile, above us, machine guns continued to spray the trees and boulders around us.

"Listen to that machine gun!" Lt. Greene said. "That's not a standard VC or NVRA weapon. That's a US-made .30 caliber machine gun. I can tell by the sound. Where did they get that?"

"They're using captured weapons," Col. Carnage said. "But we're going to blow them and the machine gun to kingdom come."

Some ten minutes later, me and the other members of Platoon C looked up and saw three helicopter gunships coming around the side of the mountain. Instantly, the colonel was back on the field telephone.

"Captain Marvel to Little Lulu!" he said. "Captain Marvel to Little Lulu! Do you read?"

He listened.

"The target is at two o'clock from your present position," he said. "The machine gun emplacement is about twenty yards below the target among the coconut palms."

He listened.

"What do you mean you can't see the machine gun nest?" he said, a note of irritation in his voice. "You have defoliant, don't you?"

He listened.

"Then drop it on the coconut palms," he shouted. "Once you can see them, use cluster bombs to blow the little bastards away!"

Then members of Platoon C watched as the gunships swept in low over the coconut palms, dropping canisters of defoliants. As the canisters reached the treetops, they exploded in brilliant flashes of orange and enveloped the palm trees in a huge cloud of orange. As the fronds of the coconut palms above the machine gun nest dissolved away, we could see there had been only three NVRA soldiers manning the machine gun. For a moment, the enemy soldiers looked up helplessly as the helicopter gunships took aim. They were sitting ducks.

Suddenly, there was a series of giant swooshes as laser-guided cluster bombs, trailing powder blue streamers, exploded with an ear-pounding blast into the machine gun nest. Instantly, body parts, palm trees, vegetation, huge clods of dirt and rocks were blasted high into the air. For some fifteen seconds after the blasts, objects were still falling to earth. Once the falling objects stopped, what had once been a grove of wild coconut palms was now nothing more than a gaping hole—some ten feet deep—in the earth.

Col. Carnage reached for the field phone.

"Captain Marvel to Little Lulu!" he said. "Now give me some cluster bombs on that bridge."

Instantly, the three helicopter gunships moved in again. After hovering momentarily, there was another series of loud swooshes and more ear-deafening explosions. Moments later, the huge logs and wooden support beams that comprised the new bridge were splintered into a million smaller pieces.

"Holy fricking Christ!" Washington said as he watched the mass of splintered wood crash to earth. Moments later, the gunships disappeared back around the side of the mountain.

Col. Carnage smiled.

"That'll teach those little bastards," he said. "These people can't beat us. No way in hell. Let's go up and see what damage we did."

Some ten minutes later, Col. Carnage and members of Platoon C were walking among the enemy dead. Washington, his eyes as big as saucers, was the first on the scene.

"Holy Christ!" he said, peering down into the giant hole.

The crater was littered with body parts, smoking clothing,

twisted metal that had once been weapons, the personal effects of enemy soldiers such as glasses, eating utensils, letters and stationery. Everything that had been part of the machine gun nest fifteen minutes earlier had now been blown to tiny bits.

"Look at this!" Col. Carnage said. "Isn't this beautiful? God, I love war!"

Then he turned to the members of Platoon C.

"We did a great job, men!"

"We did a fabulous job," Washington said. "We used three billion dollars' worth of military equipment to kill ten little gooks armed with an American-made machine gun."

"That's war, soldier!" Col. Carnage said. "We killed the enemy and we killed them well."

"You got that right, sir!" Washington said. "Here's part of one here," he said, pointing to an arm. "And another there," he added, indicating the upper half of a torso. "And if you look up there in that palm tree, you'll see one of 'em's balls hanging from a limb. Yes, sir! War is wonderful! No doubt about it! Flat fricking wonderful!"

***

Another six months passed. By the spring of 1968, many Americans, taking sides with the growing anti-war movement, were calling for an end to US involvement in the war. After watching the blood and violence on their televisions every night, the average American could see the conflict was unwinnable and felt it was wrong from a moral standpoint. Some claimed it was a war against Vietnamese independence and an intervention in a foreign war. President Johnson resolved to continue fighting until the US could have "peace with honor." Meanwhile, Jesse and I fought on. Then, in mid-summer of 1968, we were assigned to retake Thanh Hoa Mountain for the fourth time.

***

On the morning of July 14, three Huey Helicopters delivered the members of Platoon C, now under the command of Lt. Greene again, back to the base of Thanh Hoa Mountain. After disembarking, we spent almost an hour trekking up the mountainside. Finally, when we stopped, Lt. Greene trained field glasses on the top of the mountain. Jesse and I were at his side.

"Charley didn't learn much from last time," the lieutenant said. "He's got several anti-aircraft guns along the top and fifty, maybe sixty, men. Their emplacements are wide open from above."

He picked up the field telephone.

"Captain Marvel to Lame Duck," he said. "We're at target #304. Charley has got four new LL-104 anti-aircraft weapons at the top. We need for you to put some cluster bombs in there."

He listened.

"Fifteen minutes?" he said. "We'll be waiting."

Lt. Greene hung up the field telephone.

Suddenly, the air around us was filled with the booming sounds of enemy artillery.

"Incoming!" the captain shouted. "Incoming!"

Instantly, Jesse and I and the others ducked for cover. Around us, the earth exploded with artillery shells and behind us, we could hear the screams of other soldiers as the shrapnel ripped into their bodies.

"God damn!" Lt. Greene said. "Charley has got artillery hidden in the bamboo trees. We're pinned down."

Again and again, from the hill above us, we could hear the boom-boom sounds of the artillery pieces. Behind us, soldiers screamed in pain as the shells exploded around them.

Instantly, Lt. Greene was on the field phone again

"Lame Duck! Lame Duck!" he shouted. "Tell MEDEVAC to get to target #304 on the double. We're taking casualties. Enemy artillery has got us pinned down."

Lt. Greene turned to me.

"Chance!" he said. "You, Washington and Rodriguez go around the perimeter and take a position in the elephant grass on the edge of the bamboo trees. Once you are in, fire off some grenades at those artillery pieces."

"We can't see 'em in all that bamboo!" I said.

"Just fire at the smoke!" Lt. Greene said. "We've got to get some relief."

Instantly, Rodriguez, Washington and I, carrying grenade launchers, were racing through the dense undergrowth to the elephant grass. Seconds later, at a clearing some thirty yards from the elephant grass, we stopped.

"Charley is going to open up with small weapons when we start across this clearing," I said. "We're going to have to move fast. Real fast!"

"We will!" Washington said, poised to run. "I'll count. We'll go on three."

We waited.

On the count of three, Washington, Rodriguez and I were running as fast as our legs could carry us, in a mad dash across the clearing for the elephant grass. The minute we were in the clearing, the sound of enemy rifles erupted from the hillside above.

At my feet and in the trees beyond, I could hear bullets whizzing by. Seconds later, Washington and Rodriguez dove into the elephant grass. Then, at the very moment I dove in behind them, I felt a burning sensation in my lower right leg. I looked down. I had been shot. Blood was coming out of the wound and running down my leg.

"God damn!" I said, lying on my stomach within the elephant grass. "I've been hit."

"Stay here!" Washington said. "Me and Rodriguez will take care of this!"

Then Washington and Rodriguez, each carrying grenade launchers, raced off into the bamboo trees. I waited.

From the hill above me, I could hear the *Plock! Plock! Plock!* sounds of enemy grenade launchers. Instantly, I ducked down, then I heard three massive grenade explosions not more than fifty feet ahead of me in the bamboo grove.

"Washington! Rodriguez!" I called.

No reply.

"Washington! Rodriguez!" I called again.

Then I heard anguished moans and the sound of Rodriguez's voice.

"Oh hell!" I said to himself. "Rodriguez is hit!"

Then, with my M-16 held under my chin, I crawled on

elbows and knees to the edge of the elephant grass. Some twenty feet ahead, among the bamboo trees, I could see Rodriguez sprawled on the ground. Instantly, I rushed forward. When I reached him, I could see that shrapnel had ripped a gaping hole in his chest and his left side was a mess of bleeding, ragged flesh. Suddenly, I felt a terrible emptiness in my gut. I sat down beside him and took him into my arms. He looked up at me.

"I'm dying," he said.

"Hang on! We'll get the medics."

"Medics can't help me," he said. "Will you do me a favor?"

"Anything!"

"Look in my shirt pocket," he said. "There is a package."

I opened the shirt pocket and took out a small plastic bag.

"What can I do?"

"When you get back to the States, take that to my sister. She's living in a commune in Oregon. Her name is Consuelo."

"What's the name of the commune?"

"Nature's Blessings," he said. "The address is written on the letters."

"I'll take care of it."

"Promise!"

"Promise."

He stopped and, for a long moment, looked into my eyes.

"Do you think there's a heaven?"

"I don't know…"

Then he fell limp in my arms.

Quickly, I took the dog tag from around his neck, then stuffed it and the plastic bag in my shirt pocket. Still on my elbows and knees, I left Rodriguez's body and crawled deeper into the bamboo trees. After I had crawled some twenty feet, I could see another body. Immediately, I recognized Washington.

"Washington!" I called out. "Washington!"

No response.

I crawled on my hands and knees to the body. A heavy, fearful sensation seized the pit of my stomach as I turned the body over. Fragments from an enemy grenade had blown away the right side of his face; there was a gaping hole in the side of his head. As I looked into his eyes, still wide open and staring straight ahead, I threw up. The vomit just blew out of me.

I looked down. Blood was continuing to pour out of my leg wound. Quickly, I used a knife to slice open my pants leg. Then, removing my belt, I fashioned a crude tourniquet then tied it just above the wound. As I tightened the belt as tight as I could stand it, the blood flow became a tiny trickle. Tired and weary from the loss of blood, I lay back on the ground among the bamboo trees. *This is where I die*, I thought to myself. *This is where Jesse and the other members of Platoon C will find me.*

Suddenly, high above the canopy of trees, I could hear a helicopter gunship, then moments later, the dull *Plop! Plop! Plop!* sound of exploding canisters. With each explosion, a huge cloud of nauseating orange vapor formed above me, then began to slowly settle over the bamboo trees.

Suddenly, somewhere in the orange mist, I could hear Jesse's voice.

"Johnny! Johnny!"

"Over here! Over here!" I yelled

"Johnny! Johnny!"

His voice seemed to be further away now.

I waited.

Again, I heard his voice calling again. Now he seemed even further away.

I waited.

"Yoooodle, doodle, doodle, doodle, doodle, doodle!" I called in a shrill voice.

"Johnny! Johnny!"

Now his voice was nearer.

"Yoodle, doodle, doodle, doodle, doodle, doodle!" I called again.

Suddenly, through the thickening orange mist, I saw Jesse appear within the bamboo trees. Instantly, he was at my side.

"Come on!" he said. "We've got to get out of here."

In a single movement, he scooped me up in his arms and started running through the bamboo tress. By now, the grove of trees had been turned into one giant cloud of orange vapor. All around and above us, we could hear millions upon millions of crackling sounds as the defoliant dissolved away the leaves off the trees. For a moment, the vapors were so thick that Jesse couldn't see. He stopped, then peered through the orange mist trying to determine the best way out. For a single instant, the vapors cleared slightly and Jesse saw an opening through the bamboo trees to the elephant grass beyond. Instantly, he made a mad dash out of the trees and into the elephant grass. After he had run some fifty feet, he stopped at the front edge of the elephant grass. He waited several seconds, then raced out of the elephant grass and back across the clearing to the American position. Moments later, he dumped me on the ground, then collapsed in huge spasms of coughing. For several minutes, his body was racked with one unmerciful cough after another.

Suddenly, Lt. Greene came running up.

"Chance!" he said. "What happened?"

"Washington and Rodriguez are dead," I said. "I've got a leg wound."

The lieutenant looked over at Jesse, who was still rolling on the ground doubled over in spasms of coughing.

"Jesus!" the lieutenant said. "I'll get the medics!"

Moments later, two young medical officers appeared. One bent down to examine me.

"We've got to get you into surgery as soon as possible," he said.

Meanwhile, the second medical officer was examining Jesse.

"Get the oxygen!" he said.

Quickly, a subordinate was back with an oxygen tank. Moments later, he placed a mask over Jesse's face. Immediately, Jesse stopped coughing and breathed easier. The medic checked Jesse's pupils. Quickly, he turned back to his subordinates.

"Get this man to the hospital!" the medical officer barked. "His lungs are full of defoliant."

***

A week later, Jesse and I found ourselves in the US Army hospital in Saigon. At our request, our hospital beds were

185

placed side by side. The attending physician, Dr. Ahmad Hooshman, a dark, late-thirtyish Armenian man, stopped in to check on us.

"What's the prognosis?" Jesse asked.

The doctor looked from one to the other.

"You," Dr. Ahmad said, indicating me, "will be out of here and back in the States as soon as the leg wound heals."

He turned to Jesse.

"You're a different case," he said. "X-rays show that you have quite a bit of lung scarring as a result of inhaling such a massive amount of the defoliant. We're going to have to keep you for a while to see just how severe the damage is."

Jesse looked at him.

"What was the stuff I inhaled?"

"The chemical name is 2,2,4 diethyl prothambedamine carotate," the doctor said. "The commercial name is Agent Orange."

"Is it dangerous?" Jesse asked.

"The jury is still out," the doctor said. "Some tests have shown the active ingredient to be a cancer-causing agent. Others claim it is harmless."

Jesse looked at the doctor.

"So how long will I be in here?"

"At least two months."

***

A month later, on August 21, 1968, I walked out of the US Military Command Headquarters in Saigon with my honorable discharge papers. I was two months shy of finishing my enlistment. Once outside, I hailed a pedicab and started across town to the US Army Hospital to say good-bye to Jesse.

"I'll be back in the States day after tomorrow," I said.

"What are you going to do?"

"First thing I'm going to a commune in Oregon and give Rodriguez's sister his personal effects."

"A commune?"

"A place called Nature's Blessings. It's east of Portland somewhere in the Cascade Mountains. What are you going to do?"

"Once I get out of here, I want to stay in Vietnam for a while. I love Vietnam, the countryside, the people, the food, the women. I'll end up back in the States, but I want to spend some time in Vietnam first."

"Let me ask you a question."

"Shoot!"

"Remember when we were in the bamboo grove during the first battle at Thanh Hoa Mountain?"

"I remember."

"How did you know then that the bamboo grove would have such a drastic effect on our lives?"

"I don't know how I knew. I just knew."

I pondered his words for a moment, then shook his hand.

I'm out of here," I said.

"Stay in touch."

"I will."

5 – Hippie Commune

1974

Nature's Blessings, the sharing community where Rodriguez's sister was living, was a three-hundred-acre, fenced-off compound high in the Cascade Mountains some thirteen miles east of The Dalles, Oregon. When I got off the bus with my duffel bag, I saw a small, colorfully painted sign nailed to an oak tree that read "Nature's Blessings" with an arrow pointing along a dirt road leading into thick woods. After I had walked some one hundred yards from the highway, I saw a guard shack with a sign that read "All pedestrians and vehicles must check in before entering." When I approached, I found an early twenties, bearded man wearing long hair, a tie-dyed t-shirt and a string of beads inside. Although he was colorfully dressed, his demeanor was very serious.

"You got business at Nature's Blessing?" he said, looking me up and down.

"I'm here to see Consuelo Rodriguez."

"You got ID?"

I took out my Army ID and handed it to him.

He looked at the piece of plastic, studied me suspiciously, then scribbled a note on a piece of paper.

"This is a four-hour pass. To stay longer, you have to get approval from Lester."

"Lester?"

"Yes. Lester Huffman. He's commune counselor," the guard said. "The compound is just ahead. Go to the administration building and tell them you're looking for

Consuelo."

I thanked him, then, when the heavy metal bar blocking the road was raised, I passed through. Moments later, I was standing in front of a thriving hippie commune in the middle of thick woods. Before me, to the right, stood what appeared to be an administration building with a peace sign over the entrance. To the left, I could see several rows of large two-story buildings with designated numbers and names that apparently served as living quarters. Beyond that, I could see fields, a huge barn, a pasture with cattle and goats, and a sprawling vegetable garden.

At the administration building, I saw three people, an older man and two young women, loitering on the front porch. As I approached, one of the women turned to me.

"Welcome to Nature's Blessings," she said. "Can I help you?"

"I'm looking for Consuelo Rodriguez."

"She works in the candle shed. Go between the two buildings on the right," she said, pointing. "You'll see the candle shed on the left."

I thanked her and started walking in the direction she had indicated.

Moments later, I was standing in front of a long, rectangular wooden structure with a sign over the entrance which read: Candle Making.

Once I stepped inside, my senses were suddenly filled with a medley of exotic smells like being inside a perfumery. At a long table, I saw a statuesque, Latin-looking woman, early twenties and wearing a flowery dress, pouring hot wax into molds for making candles. Beyond her, I could see another woman, a late twenties brunette with flowers in her hair, carving huge chunks of wax off a block and tossing them into a fired vat.

Upon seeing me, the Latin woman stopped and peered at me.

"Are you Consuelo Rodriguez?"

"Yes!" she said with a bright smile.

I introduced myself and explained I had been with her brother in Viet Nam. As the thought registered, her face took on a sad expression.

"You were with Carlos when he died?"

"Yes. Before he died, he asked that I give you his personal effects."

I withdrew a small plastic bag and handed it to her.

She opened it. There was a tiny Bible, a turquoise brooch with a crucifix, several worn letters, old photos and a hank of hair in a plastic tube. She examined the strand of hair.

"This was our father's," she said. "It was taken at his death."

She thumbed through the Bible, briefly glanced through the photos and letters, then, looked up at me. For a moment, she stared blankly, then suddenly burst into tears.

"I'm sorry," I said.

After several moments, she wiped her eyes.

"Was he in pain when he died?"

"No!" I lied. "He died peacefully in my arms."

She stood up.

"Thank you!" she said. "Can I give you a hug?"

I stepped forward and she gave me a long, warm hug.

"Thanks so much for bringing this to me. My mother in Peru will want these."

She placed the items inside a small handbag on the workbench, then turned back to me.

"Where will you be going now?"

"I'm not sure."

"You ever thought about living in a commune?"

The suddenness of the thought caught me completely off guard.

I laughed.

"No, I haven't. What it's like?"

"Oh, we have a great life here. No bills. No bosses. You're completely free of the madness of the world. If you make your contribution, everything you need is provided."

"In California, I heard about communal living, but I never thought about doing it myself."

"You work forty hours a week and the rest of the time is your own. You have a roof over your head, three healthy meals a day, plenty of fresh air and sunshine. I've been here almost two years."

The more she spoke, the more intrigued I became. In my heart, I could feel a sense of wild adventure lurking behind her every word. This was the sort of sudden delicious impulse I lived for.

"Why don't you give it a try?" she said. "If you are interested, I'll introduce you to Emily. She's got political pull."

"How do you mean 'political pull'?"

"Her brother is the commune founder. Come on! I'll introduce you."

Quickly, she got up, then she led me past the tables where row upon row of scented candles were waiting to be boxed and shipped.

Emily was a tall, thin, late twenties brunette with green eyes, a plain face and a serious countenance. The minute Consuelo introduced me, she smiled broadly as she looked me up and down.

"Johnny wants to know more about joining the commune," Consuelo said. "Can you introduce him to Lester?"

"Sure!" she replied. "Give me a moment to finish this batch."

***

Ten minutes later, Emily and I were walking back across the commune grounds to the administration building.

"You were in Viet Nam?" she asked as we walked.

"Yes."

"Horrible tragedy, this war. It's doing far more evil than good. Killing babies. Destroying homes and families. Absolutely terrible!"

Moments later, we arrived at the administration building and went inside. In the foyer, she led me to a table where several forms had been neatly stacked. She picked up several.

"Fill these out," she said.

I sat down at the table and began filling out the forms. Thirty minutes later, I was finished. Emily examined the forms, then, satisfied they were complete, she turned to me.

"Let's go talk to Lester."

Lester Huffman was a stocky, slightly chubby man in his late forties with a red face, shoulder-length graying hair and faded overalls. He was seated behind an old wooden desk and wore a blue bandana with a peace symbol.

Emily introduced me and explained that I was interested in joining the commune.

"Good afternoon," he said, offering his hand. "Welcome to Nature's Blessings."

I stepped forward and shook his hand. He looked me up and down. Instantly, his eyes fell on the army duffel bag.

"You were in Vietnam?"

I nodded.

Are you physically fit to do a good day's work?"

"I think so."

"Do you know how to drive a tractor?"

I nodded again.

"When and where did you ever drive a tractor?"

"I was in an orphanage for five years when I was a teenager. I drove a tractor all five growing seasons."

"Excellent," he said. "Normally, there is a waiting list to join our community, but we've got spring plowing starting tomorrow, so we have an emergency of sorts."

He picked through several papers on the desk, then took one and handed it to me.

"These are the commune rules," he said. "Read them later and understand them."

I took the sheet of paper.

"We have our own lifestyle here at Nature's Blessings," he said. "Our primary goal is personal freedom and a stress-free way of life. Any kind of drugs are allowed. You can wear whatever you please and no one will judge you. We believe in polygamous relationships. That means any two people can have sex as long as its consensual. If a woman claims you forced yourself on her, you're out. Is that understood?"

"Yes, sir."

"We serve gourmet food, provide comfortable lodging and give qualified residents a one-hundred-fifty-a-month stipend. If you follow the rules, get along with other residents and pull your weight, you'll be fine. There is a three-week trial. We have to weed out the drunks and the slackers."

He paused.

"Understood?"

"Understood!" I replied.

Then he turned to a small key closet to the right of his desk. He opened it, took out a key and handed it to me.

"This is your room key. Report to 'Cowboy' Ferguson tomorrow morning at seven at the big hay barn. Emily will show you to your room."

***

Ten minutes later, Emily and I were strolling back across the commune grounds to the dormitories.

"I think you'll like it here," she said. "Are you married?"

"No."

"Significant other?"

"No."

"After you get settled tonight, you want to come up to my room and hang for a while? I've got the new Pink Floyd album and some dynamite Panama red."

"Can I take a rain check? I'm tired after the long bus ride. I want to get a good night's sleep."

"I understand."

"Who is Cowboy?"

"Cowboy Ferguson is in charge of the commune's farming operation," she said. "His real name is Ralph, but everybody calls him 'Cowboy' because he always dresses like one."

***

Each of the nine residential buildings at the commune were named after trees. My room, on the second story of the Aspen building, was a windowless, 8X10 cubicle with a cot, a small writing desk and a wash basin. Sanitation and showers were a community affair. The previous occupant had left a large photo of Bob Dylan over the head of the bed. The moment I saw it, I loved it.

193

Once I was unpacked, I went to the dining hall—a massive, two-story log structure located in the center of the compound—and I must say the food lived up to its billing. I had a large helping of chicken alfredo, squash casserole, green beans, au gratin potatoes and fresh baked rolls. Now, in the main dining hall, I could see how big the community truly was. There were easily 175-200 people present. After the meal, many of the residents retired to the recreation room adjacent to the dining hall to read, watch TV, and play ping-pong and board games. In front of the recreation room, there was a large swimming pool, but it was only open from May until August.

Back in my room, when I drifted off to sleep that night, I kept thinking communal living might not be so bad. I had done crazier things. One thing was for sure, a new adventure awaited me.

***

The following morning, when I arrived at the "big hay barn," I saw a tall, thin, late fortyish man with a sun-burned face gassing up a tractor. He was wearing faded jeans, western boots and a sweat-stained cowboy hat with a ponytail of salt and pepper hair dangling down his back. When I approached, he turned.

"You must be John Chance," he said, offering his hand.

"Pleased to meet you," I said, shaking his hand.

"Lester says you know how to drive a tractor."

"Yes."

"That one's yours," he said, indicating a smaller tractor sitting in front of the one being fueled. "It's gassed up and ready to go. Did you bring a lunch?"

"No."

"Do you like chicken salad sandwiches?"

"Love them!"

"Go into the barn and look in the refrigerator beside the desk. There are two chicken salad sandwiches and some root beers. Help yourself."

Moments later, inside the structure, I could now see the fullness of the "big hay barn." It was actually one enormous wooden building that had been split into two separate parts. On

one side, there was a large hayloft and below was storage space for tractors, farm implements, seed and fertilizer. On the opposite side were feeding and milking stalls for cows and goats, which supplied the full-scale dairy operation that produced milk, butter and cheese for the commune kitchen and local retail outlets.

That first morning, I plowed a total of four acres of new ground and Cowboy turned five more in the adjacent field to the south. Now that the two fields had been "cut," they would lie fallow for a few weeks, then be fertilized and sown with wheat. Out of the total eighty acres in cultivation at the commune, fifty was in wheat and the remainder planted in potatoes and alfalfa hay.

As I maneuvered the tractor around the barren dusty field, I had forgotten the beauty of plowing. Tilling the earth is about as close to nature as you can get. It brought me a sense of peace and comfort and provided a continuity between myself and the natural world. I guess the feeling arose from my having grown up in the country.

At noon, I saw Cowboy's tractor lumbering across the plowed field toward me, a giant cloud of clay-colored dust boiling in its wake.

"Let's go down to the creek and have lunch," he said, pointing to thick woods at the edge of the fields.

Five minutes later, after parking the tractors, we took our lunches then followed a narrow foot path through the woods to a quiet mountain stream. There we took seats on an old log, unwrapped our sandwiches and began to eat. The only sound was the gurgling stream and the wind in the trees.

Finally, I broke the silence.

"How'd you end up at Nature's Blessings?"

Cowboy didn't answer at first. He took a big bite of his sandwich then a long swig of root beer. After wiping his mouth on the back of his hand, he began to speak.

"All I ever wanted in this world was my freedom," he said. "When I was growing up in Sacramento, I watched my father go to his insurance office every day for eighteen years. At the time, I didn't say anything, but I knew I was never going to spend my life like that. Doing the same thing over and over day after day. Then, the summer after I graduated high school, I was in a bookstore in Oakland and bought a copy of Jack Kerouac's *On the Road*. Once I read it, I was never the same."

"How did it change you?"

"It gave me the courage to take control of my life. That book showed me I wasn't the only person in this world that didn't want to be tied down all their life to a job and a mortgage."

"What did you do?"

"I told my father I had no interest in being an insurance agent. I told him the world was too big and too interesting to stay in the same place all of my life. He said I was stupid and would never amount to anything. My mother cried. So I packed my bags and hit the road. My first stop was San Francisco. During the early sixties, there was no place on earth like that town. Talk about personal freedom. You could feel the revolution in the air. God! I miss those days."

He stopped and took another bite.

"Over the next three years, I rambled all over. Worked as a cowboy on ranches in Montana and Utah, spent time in the oil fields of southern Louisiana, traveled with a carnival all over the Midwest, picked beans and grapefruits in Florida… even once had a job painting eyes on Mickey Mouse dolls in North Carolina."

He took another bite of his sandwich, then a swig of root beer.

"Even before I came to Nature's Blessings, I had heard about the Messiah…"

I interrupted.

"Who is the messiah?"

"The Messiah is Harold Massey, the founder of the commune."

"Why do they call him the Messiah?"

"Some people in the commune believe he's a seer. That he can predict events before they happen."

"Do you believe that?"

He laughed.

"Gurus nowadays are a dime a dozen, but I wouldn't want

Harold to know I thought that. I love my life here at the commune. I wouldn't do anything to oppose the powers that be."

He took another bite of his sandwich.

"You'll meet Harold at some point," Cowboy continued. "He makes an appearance in front of the community every month or two. When you see him, you can judge for yourself."

A pause.

"The commune was the best thing that ever happened to me. It brought organization into my life. Good food. Outdoor living. Easy sex. Lots of drugs. You ever do drugs?'

"I've had my share," I said. "What about you?"

"Some people treat their body like a temple," he said. "I've treated mine like an amusement park."

I laughed.

"What year did you come to the commune?"

"Either '64 or '65. My memory is not as good as it once was. I did too much acid in '66. You ever done LSD?"

"Oh, yeah!"

"You'll have to come to the 'shroom party next Saturday night. They'll have all kinds of drugs. Acid, weed, pills and plenty of mushroom tea. There is no drug like mushroom tea."

***

Back at the barn that afternoon, I pulled my tractor back into its designated space. Once I shut down the engine, I could see there were a total of four tractors in the barn. The two main ones were the Ford and the Farmall that Cowboy and I had been driving, but two others, another Ford and an old Massey-Ferguson, were sitting idle.

"Do you ever use those other tractors?" I asked. "That Ford looks like it's newer than the one you're driving."

"It is, but it needs a new clutch and transmission," he said as he locked the barn door. "Costs seventeen hundred dollars to get it fixed, but the commune doesn't have the money. Your tractor needs two new tires, but they can't afford that either."

***

In the dining hall that night, Emily made a bee line for my table and, when she invited me to her room a second time, I accepted. Her quarters in the Ponderosa building were larger than mine and she had a separate bedroom with a picture window that looked out on thick woods. The moment I entered, my senses were hit with a strong scent of patchouli. The room's centerpiece was a portrait of a beautiful young woman in a supplicant pose by Czechoslovakian illustrator Alphonse Mucha. A giant red lava lamp stood in one corner and, since there was only one chair in the room, we seated ourselves on pillows scattered about the floor.

Moments later, she pulled out a bong, offered me a glass of wine and put on the Rolling Stones' album *Beggar's Banquet*. Then, while we smoked and listened to Mick Jagger belt out the words to "Jumping Jack Flash," she proceeded to show me her collection of Mucha illustrations.

"This is from his middle period," she said, pointing to one. "His work takes on a mystical quality here. See how the dark blues and the light purples give the work an ethereal effect."

Over the next fifteen minutes, she went on and on about the intricacies of Mucha's work. Once finished, she turned to her bookshelf, a stacked arrangement of wood slats and red bricks. She took down a copy of Ken Kesey's *Sometimes a Great Notion*.

"His most famous work is *One Flew Over the Cuckoo's Nest*, but this one is my favorite," she said. "Ken Kesey is the link between the beatniks and the hippies. The beatniks believed that even acknowledging the government and its corruption rooted its power further. The hippies, on the other hand, were active participants in the Civil Rights Movement as well as the anti-war protests."

Once she had finished the lecture on Ken Kesey, she turned to her personal life.

"I've been living at the commune since 1965," she said. "After I went through a bad divorce back in Ohio, Harold invited me to come live at the commune."

An hour later, when I announced I was ready to leave, she said she wanted to show me her king-size waterbed. The bedroom was equipped with the signatory features of the day. Over the bed was a giant black light poster of Jimi Hendrix and below sat a small shelf with an array of scented body oils.

"Consuelo's room is on the other side of this wall," she said. "These walls are paper-thin. I can hear her snoring at night."

Then she turned, threw herself on the bed and struck a seductive pose.

"Want to try it?" she said.

"Maybe later."

"Don't you like me?"

"I like you," I replied. "I just don't like to rush into things."

"Are you going to the 'shroom party Saturday night."

"Yes."

"Let's go together."

"I would like that."

She smiled and turned her face to mine.

I kissed her lightly on the lips.

"Meet me at the dining hall at seven."

"You're on."

***

The following morning, when I arrived at the big hay barn, I saw two women, a young one and an older one, struggling with a cart loaded with eight ten-gallon containers of fresh milk. They were transporting the milk from the barn to the dairy-processing shed when one of the wheels came off the cart. The younger one, a big blonde with glasses, pigtails and a leather vest, was trying to lift the cart high enough for the older woman to replace the wheel.

"Just a little higher!" the older woman said.

"Uhhhhh!" grunted the younger woman as she strained to lift the heavy weight.

"Here!" I said, rushing forward. "Let me help you."

Quickly, I grabbed the end of the cart and lifted it high off the ground.

"Hold it right there!" the older woman said.

Then she slipped the wheel back on the axle.

"You need a nut and a cotter key to hold it on the axle," I said.

The younger woman laughed.

"We lost that a long time ago," she said.

"If you like, I'll look through the toolbox in the barn and try to find one," I said.

"That would be great," said the younger woman. "Thanks for your help! What's your name?"

"I'm Johnny Chance. What's your name?"

"Honah Lee!" she said.

"Honah Lee? I've never heard that name before."

"Yes, you have! Remember the line in the song, 'Puff the Magic Dragon'? 'And frolicked in the autumn mist in a land called Honah Lee."

I smiled at the recollection.

"Cool!" I said.

"I'm Stella," said the older woman. "Thanks for the help."

"You're welcome," I replied, then watched as the two women, closely eyeing the errant wheel, turned and continued pushing the cart to the dairy shed.

***

That afternoon, when Cowboy and I arrived back at the barn, I rummaged through an old toolbox and found a washer and a cotter key. Moments later, I was in the dairy shed. At the back of the building, I could see Honah Lee working at a bench pouring melted cheese into a round mold. She looked up and saw me.

"Where's the broken-down milk cart?" I said.

"Over here!" she replied.

She set aside the container of molten cheese and led me to the cart. Seconds later, I had the new washer and cotter key installed.

"Good as new!" I said.

"Thanks a million!"

Now, as I started back out, I could see the fullness of the dairy operation. It was a beehive of activity with at least fifteen to twenty people working diligently to produce a variety of dairy products. Some were using cream separators, others were running pasteurization machines and still others were laboring with giant churns for making butter, yogurt and cheese. In the back, the final products were being packaged, labeled and prepared for shipment. It was quite an impressive operation.

***

That night, when I arrived at the dining hall, I had planned on eating alone. Once I had gone through the serving line, however, I glanced around the tables looking for a place to sit. Then I saw Honah Lee. She waved me over.

"Sit down and join me," she said.

Moments later, I was seated and we began to eat. I told her about my early years in Georgia and Texas and my service in Vietnam. When I asked about her past, she had the open innocence of a little child.

"I was born to be a hippie," she said. "My parents were two of the original beatniks and, during my early years, we were always on the road living out of a camper van. I was born in the parking lot of a McDonalds restaurant in Bismarck, North Dakota. At my fifth birthday party in Yosemite National Park, my parents and I abandoned the cake when a grizzly bear chased us back into our van. There we watched as the bear ate the entire cake. I cried, but my parents thought it was hilarious."

I laughed.

"My parents and I came to the commune in '64 when I was fourteen," she continued. We spent three years here, then my parents said they wanted to go traveling again. I told them I wanted to stay at the commune. I loved my parents, but I wanted to settle for a while. They said to do as I please. Since I was not of age, Harold legally adopted me. I've been here ever since."

Suddenly, she looked up and waved to someone across the dining hall.

"Here comes Stella and her girls," she said.

Moments later, Stella, the older woman I had seen earlier with the broken-down milk cart, and two young girls appeared at the table. The older girl made a bee line for Honah Lee, then hugged her and took a seat beside her.

"Will you braid my hair tonight?" she said.

"Of course."

"Will you help me with my homework?" said the younger one.

"You know I will," Honah Lee said.

Then she turned to me.

"Johnny, I want you to meet Carla," she said, indicating the older girl. "She's thirteen and a whiz at math."

"Hello!"

"Hi!" the teenager said with a shy smile. "He's handsome. Is he your boyfriend?"

"Just a good friend."

Honah Lee turned to the other girl.

"And this is Elaine. She's ten and she's learning to bake biscuits."

"And cakes," the younger child said.

Stella Gramling was a smallish, busty woman in her late thirties with streaks of gray in her dark hair and a face much older than her years. Now that I could see her up close, the lines around her eyes and lips testified to a life of hardship and worry.

"The commune has been a Godsend for me," she said. "After my husband abandoned me and my girls three years ago, I didn't have anywhere to go. Here I have a job and a home for me and my girls. If I lost Nature's Blessings, I'd be out on the street."

Finally, when the meal was finished, it was almost seven p.m., time for the monthly commune meeting.

Stella turned to her daughters.

"You girls go back to the dorm now," she said. "Me and Honah Lee are going to the Commons for the monthly meeting."

As the girls stood up to go, Carla turned to Honah Lee.

"When can you braid my hair?"

"As soon as the meeting is over."

***

"The Commons" was a sprawling open field directly behind the commune's administration building. It served as both a meeting area and a recreational space. In the meeting portion, logs had been arranged in rows to serve as seating. Adjacent was a scattering of wooden tables in a large, open field where residents could eat, hang out, picnic and participate in field games.

When Honah Lee, Stella and I arrived, a huge crowd of residents were already present. I saw Cowboy sitting in one of the back rows and, once I led the way, the three of us took seats beside him. Several minutes later, Lester appeared at the podium.

"Quiet, please!" he said. "Before I deliver the March report on commune finances, I have some announcements. First, I wanted to say that Barbara Hensley left the commune last week. Anyone who had contact with her should report to the free clinic in town."

This brought a ripple of laughter.

"There will be no more music playing in the recreation room. People watching TV and playing board games have complained again and again. At the moment, we need more volunteers to work in the wind chimes shed. We have a standing order for one thousand units and we are only making about ten per day. Anyone who puts in extra hours in the chimes shed will receive extra pay in their stipend."

Several hands went up.

"Come to the administration building after the meeting and we'll sign you up. Finally, we try to keep our place clean. Anyone caught littering will be assessed a five-dollar fine. We love our commune and we want to keep it clean. So, no littering…please!"

He stopped and looked at his notes.

"Now I want to give you a rundown of commune finances. During March, we had a total income of $7,890. Most of this came from the candle and the wind chimes shed. The dairy and the hammocks sheds continue to perform well and contribute to the commune's financial well-being. Thanks to Harold's excellent planning, we're heavily in the black so far this year."

***

The next day at lunch, I asked Cowboy about what Lester had said.

"Pure bullshit," he said. "Lester tries to make the balance sheets look all hunky-dory, but actually, the commune lives month to month. The most profitable ventures they have right now are the candles and the hammocks. The candles have always been the big moneymaker. Several years ago, they had a contract with a sporting goods store to manufacture ten thousand hammocks and everybody threw in, but when the contract ended, they had to go back to the candles."

Cowboy stopped and took another bite of his sandwich.

"Why do you think they haven't had the other tractor fixed? If they had more than seven thousand dollars on hand, why doesn't he have the other tractor fixed and buy tires for the one you're driving?"

***

Late that afternoon, I met Emily at the dining hall. After we finished our meal, we started across the grounds to the Commons for the 'shroom party. When we arrived, some thirty to forty other residents were already gathered for the festivities. Once we were seated, I saw a dark-haired man in his early twenties with long dark hair and a flowing beard standing over a large pot of boiling water fired by several small logs. He was slicing up wild mushrooms from a dishpan and tossing them into the boiling water.

"Who is that?" I asked.

"That's Stoner Wilson," Emily said. "His name is Edward, but everybody calls him 'Stoner' because he's always high. He's slicing up the psilocybin mushrooms he gathered from the cow patties in the pasture. He's in charge of making the 'shroom tea and the LSD."

"Where did he learn that?"

"He's has a degree in chemistry from Georgetown University in DC."

Moments later, Stoner had finished slicing the mushrooms.

"All right, folks," he said. "The tea will be ready in about thirty minutes. I'm going to pass out the acid."

Then he started moving through the crowd passing out hits of blotter acid. Moments later, he had reached us.

"Hi, Stoner," Emily said. "This is my friend Johnny."

"Hey, man!" Stoner said, looking down at me with a big smile. "If you're a friend of Emily's, you're a friend of mine. What flavor LSD you want?"

"What you got?" Emily said.

Stoner displayed three sheets of yellow paper divided into small squares with perforated lines.

"Mr. Natural, Orange Sunshine and Purple Haze. The Mellow Tuesday is all gone."

"Mr. Natural!" Emily said.

Stoner tore off a small square of yellow paper and handed it to her.

"I'll have the Purple Haze," I said.

I took the small square of yellow paper, then Stoner continued moving through the crowd.

"It takes about thirty minutes for the LSD to hit you," Emily said. "Let's smoke a joint and ease into it. Once the acid starts to take effect, we'll start drinking the tea."

Emily lit a joint and we started passing it back and forth. Soon, I began to feel the edges of a raging storm forming inside my mind. I tried to measure the sensation, but I couldn't remember anything to compare it to. At some point, over the next few minutes, Emily handed me a cup of mushroom tea and I drank it down.

***

Over the next five to six hours, my senses plunged through a carousel of different perceptions like I had never experienced. I knew the sensation of an LSD high, but the effect of the mushrooms I was not prepared for. It was like an Alice in Wonderland world. One moment, I found myself lying on my back in the middle of a bullring somewhere in Barcelona or Madrid and the crowds were shouting "Ole!" again and again. I was flat of my back on the ground, helpless to move, but I finally managed to raise myself on one elbow and utter a weak "Ole!" Then I found myself lost in a white mist. Intermittently, I could see a beautiful young woman reaching her hand out to me, but each time I tried to take it, she would slowly withdraw it. Then, as I lay back and peered up at the starry night, multi-colored rings began to form around the stars, then slowly descend rhythmically to earth. The rings, as if they were on springs, descended slowly… down, down, down until they almost touched my face, then, seconds before touching my face, they slowly sprang back upward to the heavens. Then, somewhere, far, far away, I could hear a familiar voice calling. Again, I raised myself on one elbow and tried to focus my eyes. Then I realized the voice was Emily's and I could see her face. She had leering, sex-hungry eyes like a lioness in heat and she was unbuttoning my shirt and kissing my chest. Suddenly, I could see the two of us tumbling naked through some sort of infinite purplish space; her dark hair and her breasts waving softly in an unseen wind and I could feel her breath coming fast and heavy. Suddenly, in my mind, I could see our two bodies being blended together like a painter mixes two different colors of paint on an easel.

The next morning when I awoke, Emily and I were rolled up in an old quilt among a pile of leaves under an oak tree. Her pants and panties were off, but she still had on her top.

"Oh, Johnny," she said. "I enjoy you so much."

***

I needed all day Saturday to recuperate from the 'shroom party. Never in my life had I bombarded my senses with such an avalanche of drugs. The LSD was the most damaging. I promised myself that, thereafter, I would stick with the weed and the wine. All of the others were too damaging to both mind and body.

After that night, Emily and I became a couple. Over the days that followed, when I was finished work in the fields, I would meet her in the dining hall. Once the meal was finished, we would go her room, smoke weed, listen to Bob Dylan, talk about the events of our day, then roll around on her waterbed.

It became a drill. It was too easy.

***

In early October, I saw Harold Massey, the so-called "Messiah," up close for the first time at the monthly meeting. After Lester delivered the latest financial report, Harold stepped forward. A full six-foot two inches, he was in his mid-forties with long, ill-kempt dark hair and a flowing salt and pepper beard. There was a bedraggled look to him and he wore a long-sleeve white robe, which came down to his sandaled feet. The residents grew quiet when he took the podium.

"On this day, we live within the blessing of this earth," he said. "The giver of all and the taker of all, this earth represents everything that is or shall ever be. It was here before us now and it shall remain as such after each and every one of us are returned to it. It is alpha and omega, the beginning and the end, and we are helpless to change it. We are its children. Its custodians and its benefactors. Let us not forget that. May this great earth continue to bless each and every one of us."

Then he stepped off the podium to mild applause. He struck me as weird, but harmless.

The following afternoon, when Cowboy and I left the fields, I had to stop by the administration building to get a new key for the small tractor. As I approached the administration building, I glanced up to the balcony of the great one's quarters and I saw Harold and Stella's two girls. Elaine was sitting on his knee and he was reading to her. Carla, the older one, was sitting nearby, eating an ice cream. It looked strange seeing two young girls with a middle-aged man who was not their father.

***

The following Saturday afternoon, while I was waiting for Emily to finish work, I found Honah Lee sitting at a picnic table at the commons. She was reading and watching Stella's daughters while their mother was working in town. The two girls played hopscotch and jump rope while Honah Lee and I chatted. As always, she had no filters on her personal life.

207

"I didn't have a happy girlhood," she said. "In school, I felt isolated from the other girls because I was taller and bigger and stood out from the other girls. I always wanted to be petite. Men don't like big women."

She seemed so terribly lonely when she said it.

"All I ever wanted was to find a nice guy to settle down with, have a home and a couple kids. But it never happened. It's because I'm a big girl that wears glasses. I'm not interested in the fly-by-night sex they have here. I'm afraid I'll catch something."

Long pause. I changed the subject.

"Last week, I saw Stella's two girls with Harold on the balcony of his quarters. Elaine was sitting on his knee and he was reading to her. Carla was nearby eating an ice cream. Doesn't that look strange?"

"How do you mean?"

"A thirteen and a ten-year-old being alone with a forty-year-old man in his quarters?"

"It's all very innocent," she said. "Harold gives them money; they help clean his room. Harold is a father figure to them. And it's fine with Stella. She wants to stay on Harold's good side."

Moments later, Emily arrived. I said goodbye to Honah Lee and we started back to Emily's quarters.

She was quiet as we walked. I sensed she was angry about something.

"All right, what is it?" I said.

"You were looking very cozy back there with Honah Lee."

"She's just a friend."

"Didn't look that way to me."

I stopped and studied her for a moment.

"Why are you so jealous?"

"I have to protect my property."

"You don't own me," I said. "Do you understand? Don't put chains on me because I will run."

"If you cheat on me, I'll chase you down."

"You're driving me away from you."

"You heard what I said."

I had heard enough.

"I'm going to my room," I said.

Then instantly, I broke from her side and started across the grounds to my own room.

***

On weekends, there was always plenty of activity and a cast of colorful characters at the Commons. On Sunday mornings, "Preacher Joe" Hinkle, the acid-dropping man of God, and his group of Jesus freaks would hold worship services. Preacher Joe would deliver a short sermon, then members would testify to their faith, pray for world peace and sing "I'll Fly Away" or "Rock of Ages" from hymn books. Another colorful character was Wanda Sue Carter, a failed country singer from Nashville who always had her guitar and wanted to play "I Want My Baby Back" a song she had written and recorded. Then there was Jimmy "Killer" Kilgannon, the former NFL quarterback who wanted to show everyone how far he could throw a football.

Occasionally, I would drop by the candle shed and visit with Consuelo. Down deep, she was a secret political revolutionary. On her workbench, she played the songs of Victor Jara, the Chilean revolutionary who spoke out against political oppression in South America. Also, there were copies of Marx and Engels' *The Communist Manifesto* and Lenin's *The State and Revolution* on her workbench.

"The present government in Peru is robbing the people blind," she would say off-handedly as she clipped wicks for a new batch of candles. "High taxes, low wages and oppression on every hand. They are taking the nation's wealth for themselves and leaving nothing for the people. Those who speak out against them suddenly disappear. It's horrible! Absolutely horrible! Someday, I'm going back to Peru to help my people."

***

Eight months passed. During the summer of 1969, some of my fondest memories were going to rock concerts in Portland.

For the Iron Butterfly concert in July, more than eighty residents piled into eight vans and three trucks for the trip. We packed sandwiches and drinks from the commune kitchen in ice chests. We brought plenty of weed and speed, then spent the weekend rocking out. When the band played "In-a-Gadda-da-Vida," the crowd of some seventy thousand fans went into hysterics. We didn't return to the commune until the following Sunday afternoon because we were too drugged out.

During that first year, I fell easily into the rhythm of communal living. At every hand, I found pleasure and fulfillment. I loved working outside and farming the land. I adored the wild and crazy people, the food, the easy drugs and sex, and the sense of personal freedom. Further, I made lots of good friends. Cowboy became my soulmate. He knew all of my secrets and I knew all of his. Then there was Honah Lee, Stella and her girls, Stoner, Consuelo and "Preacher Joe" Hinkle.

***

Five years passed. During that time, Emily, she of the green eyes and long nipples, had wormed her way into my heart, but it was not all sweetness and light. For me, the sex had become too easy, even routine. I enjoyed her, both body and mind, but I knew I could never be with her forever. Further, her jealousy was too burdensome. She was madly in love with me, but I knew it was a waiting game. That didn't mean I couldn't be with her and enjoy her for the time being.

***

In the spring of 1974, I wrote a letter to Jesse. I hadn't heard from him in almost three years.

April 12, 1974

Dear Jesse:
Hope all is well with you.

What are you doing with your life these days?

I was thinking about you today and thought I would write.

I've been living at the Nature Blessings commune for almost four years. This is the same place Rodriguez's sister lives and is located high in the mountains just east of The Dalles, Oregon. I must tell you I believe I have found paradise.

It has everything I could ask for. Healthy outdoor living. Gourmet food, easy sex and drugs, lots of personal freedom.

I would love for you to come join me. We could have a great life together here.

Looking forward to hearing from you.

Johnny

I addressed it to the US Army Hospital in Saigon. Jesse said that was the address to write him. If he had been released from the hospital, he said, they would forward it to the Red Cross headquarters nearby, who would then send it to his last known address.

***

It would be three months before I got a reply.

July 3, 1974
Dear Johnny:
I received your letter today. It sat for two months at the US Army hospital in Saigon then, three days ago, was forwarded to the Red Cross headquarters. I received it today.

I was released from the hospital in Saigon in the spring of 1969. While there, I met a nurse, a Vietnamese woman named Houng Pham, and, when I was released from the hospital, we started living together. After two years with her, my Vietnamese became quite good and, last year, we moved to Pleiku where I started a job with a language school teaching English.

As you know, I love this country and its people and, even now, I still feel guilty about how we destroyed it.

At the moment, I'm getting bored. Bored with the work, bored with Huong, bored with everything. I long to see the USA again.

My contract with the agency will be up in August. Once that occurs, I will make a decision. I would love to see you and the States again.

I'll be in touch.
Yours,
Jesse

When I looked up from the letter, my heart soared with happiness at the thought of seeing my old friend again. My life always seemed to be fuller when he was in it.

The following morning, when I arrived at the big hay barn, Stella burst through the door of the dairy shed.

"Johnny! Johnny!" she said. "Have you heard the news?"

"What news?"

"Honah Lee is dead."

I was stunned.

"What happened?"

"She and Lester were going into town yesterday afternoon and the pickup truck swerved to miss an elk and ran off the road into a reservoir. Honah Lee was drowned. Lester made it out alive."

"Oh, no! Where is the body?"

"In the morgue in town. They're doing an autopsy."

Later in the barn, I asked Cowboy about the incident.

"Nobody seems to know," he said. "Lester and Honah Lee were going into town when the pickup ran off the road and flipped over into the reservoir. Lester was lucky to get out alive."

That afternoon, I went to the county morgue. The coroner was a stocky, fiftyish man with thick glasses and a paunch.

"I would like to see the body of Honah Lee Freeman?"

"Are you a family member?"

"Just a friend."

He studied me for a moment.

"I guess it won't hurt anything," he said.

When he pulled back the sheet, I could see the bruises on her face and a huge wound across the front of her head.

"She received the head wound when the pickup truck

crashed into the rim of the reservoir," the coroner said. "The blow knocked her unconscious and she was helpless to escape the sinking vehicle."

My eyes filled with tears as I peered at the body.

***

Over the next week, commune and local authorities were unable to reach Honah Lee's next of kin. Stella, fearing she would be buried in the local potter's field, took up a collection from other commune members to pay for a simple church burial. Some fifty to sixty members of the commune attended her funeral at a small church in The Dalles. As I watched her casket being lowered into the grave, I wept like a little child. She was the kindest, gentlest soul I had ever known.

***

In September, I received another letter from Jesse.

September 9, 1974
Dear Johnny:
My contract with the language school has ended and the time has come for me to close out my life in Vietnam. Whatever good I could have done here, whatever karma I had to pay back for what we did to this nation and its people should have been paid in full by now.

I left Huong and Pleiku last week and I am currently staying at a hotel in Saigon. Next Tuesday, I'm going to board a plane from Saigon to San Francisco. Then I'm catching a bus to this Nature's Blessings commune.

Does the commune have room for another member? If so, I'd like to try it for a while.

I will arrive in San Francisco on September 22 and should arrive at The Dalles on the afternoon of the 23rd. Can you pick me up at the bus station?

I'm looking forward to seeing you again.
All the best,
Jesse

***

One afternoon two weeks later, I was cruising westward along I-84 from the commune to The Dalles in a commune pickup to pick up Jesse. When I arrived at the bus station and saw him walk out of the train station with a suitcase in one hand and a duffel bag over his shoulder, my heart smiled. He looked a little older, but he still had a confident step and a fearless face. The very sight of him aroused in me that same sense of excitement. I was going to touch the magic again.

"Jesse!" I called.

He turned at the sound of my voice. When he saw me, he rushed forward, shook my hand and hugged me.

Ten minutes later, we were in the pickup headed to the commune. As we rode, I described my life at the commune and explained the reasons I loved it.

"Sounds like another back-to-the-earth trip," he said.

"You're going to love it," I said.

He laughed.

"I'll try anything once. At least it will be different."

***

Back at the commune, Jesse filled out the forms and I took him straight to Lester and explained he wanted to become a new member.

"We do need someone to drive a truck to pick up supplies and make deliveries in town," Lester said. "When you're not driving, you can work in the wind chimes shed."

"Fine with me," Jesse said.

"You understand you may be doing something else next week. We like to move our people around as needed."

"I understand."

"Has Johnny explained all of the rules?"

Jesse nodded.

"Do you understand them?"

"Yes."

For a moment, he studied Jesse, then turned to the key

closet.

"I'm going to put you on the third floor of the Aspen building. That's the same one Johnny is in."

"Thanks," Jesse said.

***

The night, Stella and her girls joined Jesse and me in the dining hall. Over the past four years, I had watched Carla and Elaine grow up at the commune. When I first arrived, they were flat-chested, skinny-legged schoolgirls. Now, at eighteen, Carla was in the full flower of maidenhood. Elaine, at fifteen, was not far behind.

I introduced them to Jesse.

"How long have you and Johnny been friends?" Carla asked.

"More than twenty-five years," I replied.

Her face took on a look of sheer wonder.

"You two have been friends longer than I've been alive."

I laughed.

"Yeah," I replied. "I guess we have."

***

Over the next month, Jesse fell into the rhythm of communal living. Mornings, he spent cutting joints of dried bamboo, then knotting and stringing them together to make wind chimes. In the afternoon, he made pickups and deliveries in town. During the second week, he attended the 'shroom party. He took an instant liking to Cowboy and he would spend hours talking to Stoner and questioning him about making LSD. Upon seeing the great one at the October meeting, Jesse had a big laugh and deemed him a "weird wacko." Also, he made friends with Preacher Joe and Wanda Sue. At one point, she sang "I Want My Baby Back" for him and, at the time, he told her he liked it. Later, when we were alone, he broke up in uproarious laughter at the thought. Jesse liked living in the commune.

On Monday afternoon of the fourth week, the head of the commune kitchen dispatched Jesse into town to pick up a month's supply of flour, corn meal and cooking oil at the wholesale grocers. A kitchen employee was dispatched to go with him to sign for the goods. Her name was Francesca Pope and word around the commune was that she was New York Italian and had been an actress. I had seen her several times in the dining hall and, when you saw her, you didn't forget her. She was a striking beauty in her early twenties with dark, sultry good looks and a shape that made Italian women famous for being Italian.

I'm not sure what happened during the trip into town, but that night, when Francesca and Jesse sat down with me and Emily to have dinner, I could see he was absolutely enthralled with Francesca. He couldn't keep his eyes off her. He was attentive to her every move and facial expression. I had never seen him like that. Once we started to eat, we were joined by Stella and her two girls. During the meal, Francesca was in the spotlight.

"I grew up in a luxury high-rise overlooking Central Park," she said. "My father owned a mutual fund company on Wall Street and had more money than God. My mother was a socialite and knew all the right people. I went to the best schools, wore the most expensive clothing and spent summers in the Hamptons. You've heard of being raised with a silver spoon. Well, that's me."

"We've never had anybody like you before," Stella said. "Why did you leave all the wealth and privilege?"

"Because it was fake. False. A total lie. I realized that my parents and their lives were as fake as the performances I delivered as an actress on Broadway."

"Were you a star?" Stella asked.

"No! I had several small parts on Broadway, but I never landed a big role."

"Think you'll ever go back?" Stella asked.

"Not sure. I've been thinking about going to Alaska. It's clean up there. The air, the water, the skies are all clear and pure. Not all this filth we have to breathe here in the lower states."

Throughout the meal, Jesse and Francesca were laughing, putting food into one another's mouth and playing footsie under the table. When the meal was finished, they got up to say good-bye. Then, as they started from the table, Jesse turned to me and winked. I knew he had her in the bag.

***

The true beauty of living at the commune was that, once your work was done, you had plenty of time to do exactly what you pleased. And Jesse and I wasted no time exploiting that freedom. That November, we decided to do some reading and, every Saturday morning, we would go into town to the local library and check out a stack of books. We started with the Greek philosophers, Aristotle, Plato and Diogenes. In January and February came a slew of classic novels, including Hemingway, Steinbeck, Tolstoy and Dickens. Jesse loved Dickens, especially *Oliver Twist* and *Great Expectations*. He thought Hemingway was over-rated.

"All of Hemingway's works are nothing more than daydreams for teenage boys," he said. "Everything he wrote was an expression of his manliness, his machismo."

I laughed. I could see the truth of what he was saying.

"Dickens, on the other hand, is pure genius. You can put him up there with Tolstoy, Balzac and Hugo. The greatest American author was Steinbeck. *East of Eden* is probably the greatest American novel ever written. Faulkner was good, but personally, I lean more toward Steinbeck."

***

Then one morning three days later, while I was gassing up the tractor, I saw Stella and a new member pushing the milk cart from the barn to the dairy shed. She was a tall, thin blonde with blue eyes, a confident gait and a shy, retiring demeanor. The moment my eyes fell on her, I was drawn to her.

"Good morning, Stella!" I said.

"Hi, Johnny! This is my friend Susan."

"Hello, Susan!"

Susan glanced at me with a shy smile.

"Hi, Johnny!" she said. "Nice to meet you."

Then she dropped her head and returned her attention to pushing the cart to the dairy shed.

***

A week later, Jesse and I returned to the library in town, returned a stack of books and checked out a pile of new ones. While rummaging through the stacks, Jesse found a new book sitting on one of the display tables. He picked it up and examined it.

"I've been looking for this," he said.

"Who is the author?"

"Carlos Castaneda. He's the one Bob Dylan wrote the song to."

"Which song?"

"Remember the song 'Senor,' subtitled 'Tales of Yankee Power'? That's Mr. Dylan's take-off on Castaneda's book *Tales of Power*. If you listen to the words, you know immediately the song was addressed to Carlos."

"I remember that song," I said. "But I had no idea it was dedicated to anyone. Let me see it."

I took the book and examined it.

The title was *The Teachings of Don Juan: A Yaqui way of knowledge*.

"The author was an anthropology student at UCLA doing research about psychedelic drugs in Mexico. During his work, he travelled throughout Northern Mexico and, one day, while waiting at a bus station, an old Indian man kept staring at him. It was very disturbing to him."

"Later, after Carlos was on the next bus, he was unable to forget the old Indian. When he reached the next stop, he took the bus back to where he saw the old Indian and chased him down. He spent the next twenty-six years as a student of the old Indian and writing books based on his teachings."

"Twenty-six years? Who was the old Indian?"

"A sorcerer and shaman. His name was Don Juan."

"A sorcerer? Sounds like a bunch of mumbo jumbo. What

were his teachings?"

"I'll tell you once I read the book."

***

Two nights later, I was at the Commons with Cowboy. We were smoking a joint and talking about Nixon and Watergate when we saw a lone figure with a flashlight coming through the darkness toward us. The figure stopped in front of us. It was Susan. She was carrying an oblong box.

"Where is the pathway that leads through the woods to the creek?"

"It's about thirty yards down," I said, pointing into the darkness. "See the big oak tree? The path is just to the right."

"Thanks!"

She turned to go.

"Where are you going?" I asked.

"To the deep woods to set up my telescope. The Pleiades should be beautiful tonight."

"Can I go? I might learn something."

"Sure."

Quickly, I said goodbye to Cowboy and went to her side.

"Since you know the way, you take the flashlight."

Ten minutes later, with me leading the way, we were walking along the foot path through thick woods to Kitchens Creek.

"Tell me about yourself," I said.

"There's not a lot to tell," she said. "I grew up in Chicago. My father was an attorney and spent his life in a high-rise office on Michigan Avenue. We lived in an upper middle-class neighborhood north of the Loop. Graduated Adlai Stevenson High, attended Northwestern for a while then dropped out. I was an only child. I lost my mother when I was twelve…"

"Your mother was killed?"

"No. she was committed to an institution."

"Sorry."

"It's all right. I got over it long ago."

"How long have you been into astronomy?"

"At the age of nine, I was in the Girl Scouts and earned a

merit badge in astronomy. I was at summer camp up in Waukegan when I saw Orion for the first time. I was hooked. My father bought me a reflecting telescope for my tenth birthday."

It was a clear, moonless night and high overhead, I could see a million stars. After we had walked for more than thirty yards along the wooded trail, the only sound was the crushing of leaves under our feet. Finally, we were at the creek.

"How's this?" I asked.

She looked up.

"Too many trees. We need an open space to the western sky."

"I know just the place."

We walked another fifty yards along the creek bank to a point where the trees had been clear-cut and exposed a wide expanse of open sky.

"Perfect!" Susan said.

I held the flashlight while she unpacked the telescope. I watched as she set up the mount, attached the telescope and began scanning the sky. Expertly, she made one adjustment, then another and still another. Finally, she stopped.

"Oh my! Look at the stars in Orion."

I peered into the eyepiece.

"Orion was a hunter in Greek Mythology," she said. "The bright star on the left is Betelgeuse and represents his right shoulder. The star to the right is Belarus and represents his left shoulder. The three side-by-side stars underneath are his belt."

"Magnificent!" I said.

"Betelgeuse is 642 light years from earth," she said. "Do you know how far that is?"

"The distance light travels in 642 years?"

"Very good! Many people cannot even comprehend a number like that."

She started to make another adjustment.

"Let's see what Taurus is doing tonight."

"Can I make the adjustment?" I asked.

"Sure. Here's the knob to make the westward adjustment."

She took my hand and placed it on the knob. Her hand was trembling. I glanced briefly into her eyes, then turned back to the telescope.

"Give it a slight turn clockwise," she said.

I did as she instructed.

She peered through the eyepiece.

"Too far. Go back just a hair."

I made the adjustment.

"It's still slightly out of focus," she said

Again, her hand guided mine. The trembling was still there. In the darkness, she turned her face to mine. Our eyes met. At that point, I knew there was no turning back. Instinctively, my lips moved to hers. She held the kiss for a long moment, then my hand went under her top. She wasn't wearing a bra.

"No! Not here," she said, breaking the kiss. "Let's pack up the telescope and go to my room. That way, I can get ready for you."

Back in her room, no words needed to be spoken. There was a bit of foreplay, then we were naked in bed thrusting our bodies together. She was a wonderful lover. She had good hands and a soft, gentle approach. Later that night, when I left Susan's room, I knew it was time to say goodbye to Emily.

***

The following afternoon after I left the fields, I met Emily at the dining hall. I wasn't sure how I was going to break it to her. I wanted to be delicate, but I knew she had a temper. When we left the dining hall and started back to her room, she was drinking a soda. I was quiet as we walked. She sensed something was amiss.

"What's wrong?" she said finally. "Are you mad at me?"

"I need to talk to you."

"What about?"

"About us?"

"What about us? You aren't happy with the relationship?"

"I want to find someone else."

Suddenly, she stopped and glared at me. I could see the fire in her eyes.

"What do you mean? Haven't I been faithful to you? Haven't I devoted myself to you?"

"You've done all of those things."

"Is there someone else?"

"No!" I lied. "I just want my freedom."

For a long moment, she peered at me, then burst into tears and ran to me. She hugged me.

"Oh Johnny! Please don't leave me! I love you so much."

"I need my freedom," I said.

For a long moment, she clasped me tightly. Then, just as suddenly as the mournful tears began, they became tears of rage.

"All right! You son of a bitch! Go on!" she said, blinking through tears. "Do as you like. I can live without you. Get away from me!"

She turned and started walking to her quarters alone.

Suddenly, she turned.

"I won't let you get away with this," she said. "You understand. You won't get away with it."

Then, in livid anger, she threw the half-empty can of soda at me. I ducked and it missed. Then I watched as she disappeared up the stairs to her room.

Moments later, I was walking up the steps to my quarters. I was glad it was over.

***

Over the next few weeks, Susan and I became a couple. Almost every weeknight, we would be in the woods with the telescope. On Monday, it would be the trapezium nebulae, on Tuesday, the Cassini rings in Saturn, and Wednesday, the stars in Cancer. After the star gazing, we would return to her quarters, smoke weed and roll around on her waterbed. One of the traits I truly appreciated about her was her love of poetry. Many Saturdays, we would walk in the woods or loiter at the Commons reading poetry to one another. She would read Emily Dickinson to me and I would read Matthew Arnold to her. She especially loved his poem *Dover Beach*.

***

One night in early April of 1975, as we were returning to her quarters, Susan said she had been granted a request to move from the dairy operation to the candle shed.

"As a teenager, I made candles as a hobby and I loved it. I think I could create some new designs for the commune."

"What about Consuelo? She's been in the candle shed for some time."

"Oh, she's moving to the dairy shed," Susan said. "She says she wants to do something different."

***

On Saturdays, Jesse and I would walk in the woods, smoke weed and discuss our reading.

"You've got to read Carlos Castaneda," he said. "He is the only author I've ever read who understands the essence of both worlds."

"I have no interest in medicine man crap. Books about mysterious sorcerers are a dime a dozen."

"Carlos is different," he said. "If you read him, you'll understand why."

I shook my head disapprovingly.

"I'm not going to buy in to a bunch of fake crap."

"Your scientific learning has led you to stick your head straight up your butt," he said. "In your little 2+2=4 world, everything has to make sense. It must be logical and reasonable. In the spirit world, reason and logic is meaningless."

I laughed out loud.

"What kind of mumbo jumbo is that? What basis do we have for understanding our world if it isn't based on reason? Why did God or evolution or whatever created us give us reason if it was not to be used?"

"Read the book!" he said, holding up a copy of Castaneda's *Tales of Power*. "It doesn't say not to use your reason, only to keep it in its place. The exact quote is: 'Reason makes a great tool, but a very poor master.' You have allowed your sense of reason to become your master."

I laughed.

"Oh, ye of little faith," he continued. "One of these days, I'll take you to the other world. I'll show you the great beyond."

"The great beyond?"

"Yes. Where the spirits reside."

I shook my head and laughed in disbelief.

"Sure you will! You're going to take me to the land of milk and honey. Where all the angels dance around God's golden throne and sing songs all day?"

"Your mind will not allow you to think thoughts that run afoul of your precious logic."

"Do you see this?" I said, rapping on the side of a nearby tree. "This is real," I said. "This is something I can touch and feel and smell. Not some fairy tale crap dancing around in thin air."

He peered at me.

"I'm trying to make you understand one of the most valuable pieces of knowledge you will ever have. I'm trying to get you to see both worlds."

"I'm not buying into some medicine man crap."

"You're hopeless. Absolutely hopeless. Your head will be stuck up your butt for the rest of your life. Once you have pushed your reason aside, only then you can see the fullness, the totality of the other world. Until then, you will remain at the mercy of your reason. You only look at the world. You don't see it."

"Screw you!" I said. "When did you get so high and mighty that you can tell me what to believe?"

"You're always telling me about your pursuit of truth," he said. "I'm trying to make you understand the greatest of all truths."

"Your truths. Not mine."

Jesse inhaled and stepped back.

"You're hopeless! Like I said, someday I'll show you the great beyond."

"Sure! Sure!" I replied.

"Come on!" he said. "Let's go to the dining hall and eat."

***

On the following Monday afternoon, Cowboy and I worked until almost sunset planting potatoes. When we arrived back at the barn, Cowboy sent me to the administration building to see if the new tires for my tractor had been delivered. I went to Lester's office, but the door was locked. A sign read "Will return in one hour."

I turned and started back to the barn when, suddenly, I heard loud screams and shouts coming from the Messiah's compound behind the administration building. I turned and saw Carla, distraught and sobbing, running out of the back door. The Messiah, looking angry and agitated, was right behind her.

"Come back here!" he shouted.

Suddenly, Stella appeared.

Instantly, Carla ran frantically into her arms.

"Oh, Mama, he's got a gun," Carla said. "He threatened to kill me."

Stella turned angrily to the great one.

"What were you doing to her?"

The great one paused, then shook his head.

"Get her out of here!" he said. "Now!"

"Oh, Mama!" Carla said, clinging to her mother. "I'm afraid. I'm so afraid."

"Shhhh!" Stella said, putting her fingers to her lips. "Come on. Let's go back to the dorm."

Carla, quieter now and with Stella's arm protectively around her shoulder, started back across the grounds.

Instantly, the great one ducked back into his quarters.

Then Stella looked up and saw me standing in the middle of the walkway.

"Stella! What's wrong?" I said.

"This doesn't concern you."

"Tell me what's wrong!"

"Go away! Mind your own business!"

Then, still holding tightly to Carla, Stella brushed past me and continued escorting her daughter along the sidewalk to their quarters.

***

At lunch the next day, I mentioned to Cowboy what I had witnessed.

"I'm not sure what goes on between Harold and Stella's girls," he said. "I do know it's been going on for a while. Whatever it is, it's their business. The best policy here is to see no evil, hear no evil, say no evil."

"That's not good enough for me," I said. "Carla and Elaine are just kids."

"You're being stupid!" Cowboy said. "Harold has total control over Stella. If Harold sent her away from the commune, she wouldn't have a home for herself and her girls."

"So, Stella allows the girls to visit with him because, if she didn't, she wouldn't have a home."

"That pretty well sums it up."

I shook my head in disgust.

"It's not right."

Cowboy laughed.

"Let's get back to the field," he said. "Take my advice and let sleeping dogs lie."

***

Cowboy and I spent all that day planting potatoes. That afternoon, when we arrived back at the barn, I saw the old Ford tractor, which had been broken down for over three years, was missing.

"Where's the old Ford?"

"The repair shop came and picked it up today. They're going to install a new clutch and transmission."

I peered at him.

"When did the commune get the money all of a sudden?"

"From the insurance money."

"What insurance money?"

"For Honah Lee. The commune had an insurance policy on her."

I stopped and stood aghast.

"When Honah Lee's parents left her at the commune,

Harold adopted her and took out an insurance policy."

"This smells to high heaven," I said.

At that moment, my worst suspicions were aroused. There were some dark secrets lurking at the commune. All was not as it seemed. There was something rotten—terribly rotten—at Nature's Blessings.

***

The following morning, Consuelo joined me for breakfast in the dining hall and I mentioned the incident between Stella's daughter and the Messiah.

"I've heard whispers," she said. "But I never witnessed anything first-hand. When I first came here nine years ago, I knew a girl who claimed she and her sister she had been raped multiple times by the Messiah."

"Did she provide details?"

"She said he threatened them with a gun and promised to kill their parents if they ever told anyone."

I studied her for a moment.

"Another time, she told me that she had witnessed a murder at the swimming pool."

"A murder?"

"She said she had watched Lester and another resident drown a woman in the swimming pool. She said she was told, if anyone asked, she should say the victim slipped, hit her head on the concrete and drowned before anyone could help."

"That's some scary stuff. What happened to her?"

"I'm not sure. Shortly afterward, she and her sister disappeared."

"Do you know where she is now?"

"No."

"What was her name?"

"Laura. Laura Elders."

***

Two nights later, Cowboy and I were at the Commons when we were joined by "Preacher Joe." Joseph Hinkle was a smallish man in his late forties with a lean face, a sad smile and a constant stubble of beard. Originally from North Carolina, he was one of the commune's longest-standing members. I decided to ask him about my concerns.

"Did you know Stella Gramling's girls were visiting the Messiah's compound at night?"

"Harold is a father figure for those girls. It's all very innocent."

I told him about the scene I had witnessed several nights earlier.

"They must have got into an argument."

"They're just kids."

Preacher Joe shook his head.

A pause.

"And what about all the money the commune received from Honah Lee's insurance?" I said.

"Harold adopted Honah Lee and later took out an insurance policy on her. It's all legal and above board."

"I wouldn't want them to have a policy on me," I said. "I'm afraid I might end up dead."

Preacher Joe's facial expression changed. That was when I knew I had struck a nerve. He turned from me, looked ominously at Cowboy, then quickly stood up to leave.

"I'm going to call it a night," he said. "Got to get up early tomorrow and make some hammocks."

We said our good-byes, then I watched as Preacher Joe disappeared into the darkness.

Moments later, Cowboy and I were walking back to our quarters.

"You just tipped off Lester about your suspicions," he said. "That's not good."

"How do you mean?"

"Lester and Preacher Joe are tight," he said. "Lester depends on Preacher Joe to control the Jesus Freaks. They all look up to Preacher Joe and he will tell them anything Lester wants. Now, he's going straight to Lester and tell him your suspicions."

"We'll see what happens."

***

The following afternoon, when Cowboy and I arrived back at the barn, Lester was waiting. He waited while Cowboy locked up the barn and left, then he took me aside.

"I've heard some talk that you're asking questions about the commune," he said.

"Yes."

"If you've got questions, you can ask me. I know what's going on. What questions do you have?"

"What are Stella Grambling's girls doing in Harold's quarters late at night? Doesn't that appear strange?"

"Harold is a father to those girls."

"They're just kids."

"You're reading it all wrong," Lester said. "Harold Massey is a man that wants to help his fellow human beings. There is nothing wrong or evil about the man."

I was flabbergasted. He was doing everything in his power to allay my suspicions.

A long pause.

"Any more questions?"

"How many residents do you have insurance policies on?"

"That's private information. In the case of Honah Lee, the commune took out a policy after Harold adopted her. Everybody knows that."

Another pause.

"You're letting your imagination run wild," Lester continued in a fatherly tone. "You've been a good resident. We like you and want to keep you. Didn't I move your friend right into the commune?"

"Yes."

"So why can't you learn to just live and let live? Peace and harmony are what we strive for here. Don't be a troublemaker."

I studied him for a moment.

"Let's be friends and have peace," he said, offering his hand.

I shook it.

"Thanks!"

As I watched him turn and start walking back across the

grounds to the administration building, I knew I was being led down the primrose path. I knew he was trying to throw me off the trail, but I had only begun to fight.

***

That night, when I met Jesse in the dining hall, he announced he was leaving the commune.

"Leaving? Why?"

"You've fallen in with a bunch of drag-asses," he said. "Now you've become one yourself. These people are afraid to go out and face to world on their own. They need the commune and the great Messiah to protect them."

"I love my life here," I said. "It takes away all the worries I'd have to deal with if I were living outside."

"I'm bored out of my skull." he said. "The only good thing I found here was Francesca."

I peered at him.

"Look! I've been here almost a year," he continued. "I said I would give it a try, but now I'm finished. You've been lured into the trap we've tried to escape all these years. Doing the same thing over and over day after day."

"It has its rewards."

"One hundred fifty a month? What kind of reward is that? I'm telling you there is something crooked about this place. The so-called Messiah is a drugged-out wacko. And this thing about Stella's girls going to his quarters at night stinks to high heaven."

"I agree," I said.

"So why do you stay here?"

"I like it here."

He paused and studied me for a moment. I could see his mind was made up.

"So, what are you going to do when you move out?" I said.

"I've fallen in love with Francesca. She wants to move into town, get an apartment and start a coffee shop and bakery business."

"Where's the money going to come from?"

"She's got money. So do I."

230

"You're going to start serving hot coffee and bran muffins to yuppies?"

"It will be more interesting than making fricking wind chimes and driving a pickup truck."

***

That afternoon, Jesse and Francesca moved out of the commune and took an apartment in town. Once they bought a car, they rented a small business space in a strip mall on the south side of town and proceeded to prepare it for a coffee and sweets shop. Luckily, the previous business had been a bakery, and ovens, dough-making machines, flour sifters and such were already installed, but coffee-brewing equipment, tables and chairs were needed before they could open for business. Over the next two weekends, I helped them paint, repair, clean and move equipment. Francesca was a savvy businesswoman and, while Jesse gave his input, she made the final decisions. Finally, on the first day of May, 1975, she proudly hung out the sign, The Dark Bean Coffee Shop, and they opened for business.

That afternoon, I dropped in to visit. The place was bustling with people when I entered. Couples, singles and families were anxiously waiting in line to be served. Others were crowding around the display cases to see the bran muffins, chocolate croissants and fruit Danishes. Francesca was working the cash register and dispensing coffee while two waitresses were busy serving tables.

Francesca saw me and smiled.

"Are you a millionaire yet?" I asked.

She smiled.

"No, but I'm working on it."

I brushed past her and went into the kitchen.

I laughed out loud when I saw Jesse wearing a large white chef's apron and mixing dough with his hands in a big stainless steel bowl.

"Well, looks like our boy has been domesticated," I said.

He looked up. His hands were covered with white dough and he had a streak of white on the side of his face.

"I've got to please the missus."

***

The following morning when I arrived at the big hay barn, Cowboy was gassing up his tractor. He seemed agitated.

"I'm not sure what happened, but you've unleashed the dogs of war," he said.

"What do you mean?"

"Lester called me into his office last night and gave me the third degree. He wanted to know what I had been telling you about the commune. He was hot!"

"What did you tell him?"

"I lied and told him I didn't tell you anything."

"What did he say?"

"Nothing, but I can promise you this won't be the end of it. They're going to nail you."

"Who is they?"

"Lester and Harold. I'm not sure what they're going to do, but they're going to get back at you."

"I haven't done anything illegal."

He laughed.

"Illegal has got nothing to do with it. Like I said, if I were you, I'd be getting the hell out."

"I can't just drop everything. This is my life."

He studied me for a moment.

"Tonight, meet me at the creek where we have lunch. And don't tell anyone."

"Why so secretive?"

"Just do as I ask. Meet me there at seven."

***

That night, when I arrived at the creek, Cowboy was waiting. He had a suitcase.

"I'm leaving," he said.

"I thought you liked living here."

"I've been here thirteen years," he said. "That's long enough to be in any one place."

"Where will you go?"

"I don't know. I got a little money saved. I want to see the streets of San Francisco again. Might even go wandering again. I'm forty-four now. Wandering at this age is not as easy as it was when I was twenty-five."

I offered my hand.

"Again, I would advise you to get out," he said as he shook my hand. "If you don't listen, then so be it."

"I wish you the best," I said.

"So long!" he said, picking up the suitcase. Then he waved and disappeared into the darkness.

Later that night when I crawled into bed, I was fearful of Cowboy's warning. Two of my closest allies, Cowboy and Jesse, were no longer at the commune. I sensed there were evil forces gathering around me, but I couldn't just drop everything and flee into the night. I decided to wait a few days. Maybe things would settle down, then I would make my escape. I didn't sleep well that night.

***

A month passed. The Procol Harum concert was set for the night of June 4, 1975 in Portland. Around 4:30 that afternoon, some seventy to eighty members of the commune loaded into three trucks and eight vans—well-stocked with food and drugs—and left for the concert. Personally, I didn't care to go. Procol Harum was not one of my favorite bands. They had only one song, "A Whiter Shade of Pale," that I truly liked. My favorite groups were Led Zeppelin, Pink Floyd and the Grateful Dead. Further, Susan didn't want to go and I had to put new tires on my tractor.

After dinner with Susan that night in an almost-deserted dining hall, I went to the barn and started the tire project. Replacing the tires was a two-man job, but since I didn't have Cowboy, it took me almost four hours. The hardest part was slipping the new tires on the huge wheel rims. It had to be started on one side, then slowly worked all the way around the rim until the tire was in place. Finally, just before midnight, the job was finished. When I closed and locked the barn door, I glanced at the clock. It was 12:10 and I decided to drop by the candle shed to see Susan.

When I arrived, I saw Emily.

"Hi, Emily!" I said.

She glanced up at me, then proceeded to ignore me.

I turned to Susan.

"I'm working late tonight," she said. "I've got another three batches to finish for delivery tomorrow morning."

"How late will you be?"

"Probably two or three. If I get tired, I'll take a nap on the cot in the office."

"Don't work too late!"

"I won't."

I turned to go.

"Bye, Emily!"

She didn't look up.

When I arrived at my room, it was 12:45. I was dog-tired after putting the tires on the tractor and I fell straight into bed. Only moments after I pulled the covers over me, I was sound asleep.

***

Around 2 a.m., I was awakened by a loud explosion, which rattled the walls of the Aspen building. Seconds later, I heard frantic shouts. Instantly, I jumped out of bed, threw on my clothes and raced down the stairs. Outside, residents were running back and forth.

"What's wrong?" I yelled to a man who rushed past me carrying a bucket of water in each hand.

"The candle shed has exploded!"

"Susan!"

Frantically, I turned and raced across the grounds to the candle shed. When I turned the corner, I could see the office end of the shed was a raging inferno.

"Susan! Susan!" I shouted.

I made my way through the smoke to the office door. There was a lock on it. I tried to force open the door, but I turned back quickly because the heat was too intense.

Meanwhile, other residents were spraying the flames with garden hoses and throwing buckets of water on the blaze, but I could see it was useless. Susan was my concern now.

Quickly, I turned and rushed up the stairs to Susan's room in the Ponderosa building. The door was locked. I beat my fist on the door.

"Susan! Susan!" I yelled again and again. No answer. It was then that my worst fears were confirmed. Susan was in the burning building.

As I raced back down the steps, I heard the sirens of fire trucks. Back at the candle shed, firemen were spraying the flames with giant fire hoses and bringing the fire under control. A crowd of residents, including Lester, most in sleeping clothes, were milling around the scene.

"Was anybody in there?" one fireman asked.

"If they were, they're gone now," said another fireman.

Lester turned to address the other residents.

"It's all over," he said. "Nobody can do anything now. The fire department can handle it from here."

I was heartsick as I returned to my room.

***

The next morning, when I was awake, I went straight to the candle shed. All that remained intact was the production end of the building. The office end was a rubble of charred timbers, ashes and the smoking remnants of office equipment. Several other residents were gathered to view the scene.

"The coroner's office found a body in the ashes," said one.

"Who was it?" said another.

"Susan Rawlings."

My heart leapt into my mouth at the sound of her name. In my heart, I knew it, but my mind didn't want to accept it. All that day, while I was working, I was crying inside. I kept thinking about Susan and all the good times we had together. Again and again, I searched my mind for the chain of forces that might have caused her death, but I was coming up with nothing.

***

That afternoon, I was not prepared for the nightmare that was about to unfold. When I arrived back at the barn after work, I saw a Wasco County sheriff's car and two deputies waiting. Once I pulled the tractor into the barnyard, they approached me.

"John David Chance?" one deputy asked.

"That's me."

"You're under arrest."

"For what?

"For the murder of Susan Anne Rawlings," the deputy said. "You have to go with us."

I was in shock at his words. Suddenly, I remembered Cowboy's warning.

Once the first deputy put handcuffs on me, the second escorted me to the squad car.

***

The Wasco County Courthouse in The Dalles was a two-story, gray marble structure on Main Street that had the fortified look of an English medieval castle. The jail annex was located at the rear and, between the two structures, a sheltered walkway had been built to transport prisoners in and out of jail. Late that afternoon, the two deputies were escorting me along that walkway. In the booking room, a sleepy-eyed, middle-aged man made a mug shot and fingerprinted me, then gave me a striped jail uniform and a pair of sandals. Finally, with chained hands and feet, I was led up the stairs to the cellblock on the fourth floor. The jail was a dingy affair. The smell of urine hung in the air, the lighting was poor, and, as the cellblock door clanged shut behind me, I saw a rat skitter across the floor.

"No. 3," the deputy said.

I stopped in front of the designated cell. The deputy unlocked the door.

"Go on in!" he said.

I shuffled inside and the deputy removed the chains.

"Breakfast at seven," he said. "If you're not up to get your food, you don't get none."

Then he turned and, seconds later, I heard the steel door clang shut behind me. I looked around. The cell was an eight-by-ten rectangle with steel walls on either side, a sink and a toilet, and a barred window at the rear with heavy mesh wire on the outside. The bunkbed was made of steel springs and a thin mattress. It was cold. I grabbed a blanket off the top bunk, removed my clothes to my shorts, then crawled under the blanket. Before I drifted off to sleep, I wondered what was happening to me. Whatever it was, it was out of my control.

***

The next morning, I was awakened by a jailer rapping on the bars to notify me that breakfast was being served. After a meal of fried baloney sandwiches, powdered eggs and dry grits, the jailer was back.

"You've got a visitor, he said.

Moments later, downstairs, I saw Consuelo in the visiting room.

"Johnny! What happened?"

"I have no idea."

"You didn't really murder Susan?"

"Of course not."

"I knew you didn't," she said.

"I want you to go into town and get Jesse."

"Where is he?"

"He moved into town and opened a coffee shop with Francesca."

"What's the name of the shop?"

"The Dark Bean. Tell him I need his help."

***

That afternoon, Jesse appeared in the visitor's room.

"What in hell have you gotten yourself into now?" he said.

"Somebody is trying to pin a murder rap on me."

"The big man and his henchmen have come down on you

for asking too many questions about their playhouse. I told you that place was not on the up and up."

"No lectures. Okay? You've got to help me get out of there."

"That may be easier said than done. Have you got a lawyer?"

"I've got a public defender."

"Public defender! You've got to have a real lawyer."

"Can you help me get one?"

"Let me see what I can do."

Late that afternoon, Jesse was back.

"I found a good lawyer," he said. "He wants five thousand dollars to take the case."

"I don't have that much," I said. "I got maybe twenty-five hundred saved. Can you lend me the other twenty-five hundred?"

"Will you pay me back?"

"You know I will."

***

The following morning, before the arraignment, I met attorney Paul Scofield in the jail detention room. He was a stocky man in his early fifties with sad eyes and a gaunt, frail appearance. Despite this, he had a sincere smile and a perceptive twinkle in his eye.

"The arraignment will be short and simple," he said. "Enter your plea, then once we see what evidence the state has, we'll know how to build our case. Let's go to court."

Moments later, two county deputies were escorting me down the courthouse corridor. Inside the courtroom, a hubbub of voices filled the air as I walked down the center aisle to the defense counsel table. Once I was seated, I glanced through the gallery. On one side, I saw Jesse and Consuelo. On the opposite side, there was Lester and Harold. On the bench, the judge shuffled through some papers, then peered down at me.

"John David Chance," he said, his voice booming across the courtroom. "You have been charged with one count of capital murder in the death of Susan Anne Rawlings at the Nature's Blessings commune on the night of June 4, 1975. How do you plead?"

"Not guilty!"

"Let the defendant's plea be noted in the record," the judge said. "Bond has been set at one hundred thousand dollars and trial will be held July 6, 1975. Anything further?"

"No, your honor," Scofield said.

"Court dismissed," the judge said.

The entire affair had lasted five minutes.

***

Thirty minutes later, back in the detention room, Jesse, Consuelo and the attorney sat down with me. Over the next two hours, the attorney grilled me about my whereabouts on the night of the murder. Consuelo provided details about the commune and Jesse provided what background information he could. Finally, the attorney said he enough information to start building the case.

"It's going to be a month before the trial begins," he said. "Until then, I'd try to make the best of the jail time. The food is not worth a damn, but you got a warm, dry place to sleep every night."

When they got up to leave, Consuelo turned to me.

"I want to help you with this," she said. "I know you're innocent."

"Thanks!" I said. "Did you see Lester and Harold giving you the evil eye at the arraignment?"

"I could see they weren't happy."

"They know now whose side you're on in the trial. You're now their enemy and they're not going to let you remain at the commune."

"What should I do?"

I turned to Jesse.

"Can you go to the commune with Consuelo, get her belongings and help her find a new place?"

"I can even put her to work," he said. "Business at the Dark Bean has been brisk lately and we need another waitress. She can sleep on our couch until we can find something."

***

During the month of June, I saw first-hand what the life of a convicted criminal was like. There was nothing pretty about it. These men represented wasted lives with no clue as to how to turn themselves around. I became accustomed to seeing men who only knew lives of incarceration, men whose lives testified to a life of crime. The days dragged on and on. In the cell next to me was Tom Faulkner, a middle-aged, life-long criminal who openly bragged about his armed robberies.

"If I hadn't stopped to grab a piece of cherry pie, I could have got away clean in that robbery in Eugene," he said.

Jim Clinton, a smallish, late twenties career criminal with chain-gang tattoos covering his neck, was waiting to be transferred from the county jail to the state prison in Portland. He was serving fifteen years for armed robbery. His mind always had some sort of sexual bent.

"You boys should have seen this woman public defender I had during my last trial. Man, oh man, was she gorgeous! She had legs all the way up to her butt."

My favorite fellow prisoner was Moses Williams, an older black man from Washington state who was serving time for manslaughter. He had gotten into an argument with another man at a bar and, during the ensuing fight, the other man ended up dead. His cell was directly beside mine and we played a lot of chess.

"My biggest regret about prison was my mother," he said. "After I was sent to prison, her health started declining real fast. It got worse and worse until they put her in the hospital. She died last year. I know my incarceration led to her death."

The hot days of late June dragged on and on. Finally, when the day of my trial arrived, I was happy beyond words.

***

My murder trial was scheduled for July 6, 1975 and, as my attorney predicted, it was a circus. For years, the locals had heard stories about mysterious happenings at the commune. These included sex orgies, rampant drug use, animal sacrifices, bizarre cult rituals and mysterious deaths. Now that the trial was at hand, they expected their suspicions to be confirmed.

Just after 8:30 a.m. that morning, two deputies led me down the courthouse corridor and up the stairs to the second-floor courtroom. The hallways were crammed with court spectators, curiosity seekers, newspaper reporters, photographers and other interested parties. Inside the courtroom, the wooden pews were packed with spectators—many of them commune residents—who strained to get a glimpse of me as I was led down the center aisle to the defense counsel table. Among the spectators, seated several pews back, I saw Jesse and Consuelo. When my eyes met Consuelo's, she smiled and winked. Jesse flashed a V with his fingers. Across the aisle, District Attorney Glenn O'Donnell, a medium-height man with the look of a bulldog, was waiting in front of a stack of court documents. In the pews behind the DA, I saw Lester, Harold and Emily.

To the left of the judge's bench, a jury of eight men and four women were seated. There was a hardware store owner, two cherry farmers, an insurance agent, a furniture store proprietor and a bakery shop owner. Two of the four women were housewives. All of the jurors were white.

A hush fell on the crowd as the court bailiff stepped forward.

"Hear ye, hear ye!!" he said. "The seventh judicial circuit court of Wasco County, Oregon is now in session. All rise!!"

Behind the bench, the chamber door opened and Judge Tom Murphy, who had presided at the arraignment, stepped forth and took a seat on the bench. With a lean, serious face and decked out in his judicial robe, he had the solemn air of a churchman.

"Gentlemen," he said, rapping the gavel. "Court is now in session. Mr. Prosecutor, please proceed."

States Attorney O'Donnell stood to address the court.

"Your honor, the state will show that the defendant, John David Chance, with malice and forethought, murdered Susan Anne Rawlings on the night of June 4, 1975 at the Nature's Blessings commune. After a lover's quarrel, he went to the commune's candle shed where he knew she would be sleeping. There he cut a small slice in the hose which runs from the propane tank to the shed's fired vat. Moments later, this action caused a huge fire and an explosion, which resulted in her death."

He stopped and returned to his seat.

Seconds later, Scofield stood up.

"Your honor, the defense will prove that John David Chance is innocent of all charges, charges that were brought as the result of a heinous plot to convict an innocent man. The murderer has not been apprehended and may well be in this courtroom."

Scofield returned to his seat.

"Mr. Prosecutor," said the judge. "Call your first witness."

"The state calls Willard Bobo."

Moments later, an early fifties, heavy-set, red-faced man took the stand and was sworn in.

"Name and occupation," said the DA.

"Willard Bobo, Wasco County Fire Marshal."

"You investigated the fire at Nature's Blessings commune on the night of June 4?"

"I did."

"What were your conclusions?"

"A small cut had been made in the line between the vat used to melt wax and the propane tank which feeds it. Once the leaking gas reached the fire under the vat, the building exploded and a raging fire ensued. The sleeping victim died of smoke inhalation. She had no chance of escape."

"Why do you say that?"

"Even if she had awakened before the explosion, she would have had little time to escape."

"Please explain."

"Someone had placed a lock on the front door of the shed."

"Was it customary to have a lock on the door?"

"I don't know."

"Has the lock been presented into evidence?"

"It's on the evidence table."

O'Donnell turned to Scofield.

"Your witness."

"No questions."

The fire marshal stepped down.

O'Donnell turned to the judge.

"Your honor, the state calls Emily Massey."

Moments later, Emily appeared before the court and, after being sworn in, took the stand.

"State your name and occupation."

"Emily Sandra Massey," she said. "I am employed at the Nature's Blessing commune."

"Miss Massey, can you tell the court your whereabouts on the night of June 4, 1975?"

"I was busy at work in the candle shed until 11:30 p.m. After I finished a final batch, I left the shed and was in bed asleep at 11:45."

"Can you tell the court what happened on the night of the murder between the defendant and the victim?"

"As I was finishing the final batch for the night, the defendant came into the candle shed and began arguing with the victim."

"What were they arguing about?"

"I'm not sure."

"Would you call it a loud argument?"

"He didn't raise his voice, but I could see both of them were very angry with the other when he left the shed."

At the counsel table, I whispered into my attorney's ear.

"Lies! All lies! She wants revenge for me dumping her."

He studied me for a moment, then made a note.

"What did you do then?" O'Donnell continued.

"I left the shed, went to my room and went to sleep."

"You didn't see the defendant again that night?"

"Correct."

The DA turned to my attorney.

"Your witness," he said.

Scofield studied her for a moment, then stood up.

"Now, Miss Massey," he began. "At the Nature's Blessings commune, did you know the defendant?"

"I did."

"How did you know him?"

"We had a relationship for five years."

"You and he were lovers?"

"Yes."

"What happened with the relationship?"

"He broke it off."

"You mean he jilted you?"

"Yes."

"Would the fact he jilted you have anything to do with your testimony before this court?"

"No."

"Are you sure?"

"I am sure."

My attorney studied Emily for a moment, then turned back to the judge.

"No more questions."

Emily stepped down.

"Ladies and gentlemen," the judge said. "We have reached the noon hour. We will take a lunch break and reconvene again promptly at 1 p.m."

***

After lunch, when the afternoon court session began, Scofield called Consuelo. Moments later, Consuelo took the stand and was sworn in.

"Where were you on the night of June 4, 1975?"

"In my quarters."

"Your room is directly adjacent to the Emily Massey's room?"

"That is correct."

"To your knowledge, was she in her room on the night in question?"

"She was in her room until around midnight. Then, from midnight until around 12:30, she was gone."

"How do you know she was not in her room at those times?"

"I didn't hear her. The walls are so thin that, when she is present, I know every minute she's in the room."

"Do you know where she went?"

"No."

"No more questions," Scofield said, returning to his seat at the counsel table.

Before closing the day's court session, Judge Murphy warned jurors they were not to speak to anyone about the trial except one another. Also, they were to be together at all times and he cautioned them to not read any newspaper articles or watch television shows dealing with the case. The jury foreman assured the judge those requirements would be met.

***

After the court session was finished that day, Scofield, Jesse, Consuelo and I were in the detention room discussing the case.

"The key to solving this case is to find the person who placed the lock on the candle shed door," the attorney said. "That person is the killer."

"The person who placed it there probably bought the lock locally," Consuelo said. "The Dalles is not that big, so it should be easy to find where the lock was bought."

"That's a great idea," Jesse said. "If we could find out where the lock was bought and who bought it, we could blow this thing wide open."

"You're right," I said.

"Consuelo," Jesse said. "Let's go into town tomorrow morning and try to find out where the lock was bought."

He turned to Scofield.

"Have you examined the lock on the evidence table?"

"It's a Secure Pro model padlock," Scofield said. "The stock number is 10314."

"Great! That's what we'll need," Jesse said.

***

When court opened again the following morning, the district attorney called the first witness.

"The state calls Lester Huffman."

Lester took the stand and was sworn in.

"Where were you on the night of the murder?"

"I couldn't sleep, so I went out on the balcony of my quarters to drink a glass of iced tea."

"Where are your quarters relative to the candle shed?"

"It's fifty yards away on the second floor."

"Tell the court what you saw on the night of the murder."

"It was a quiet evening. Most of the commune residents were at the rock concert. As I sat sipping the iced tea, I glanced toward the candle shed and saw John Chance come out of the Aspen Building and go into the candle shed."

"What time was that?"

"About 12:15."

"What was he doing at the candle shed?"

"I don't know. I couldn't see him."

"How long was he out of his room?"

"About fifteen minutes."

"So at 12:15, you saw him go into the candle shed, then fifteen minutes later, go back up the stairs at the Aspen Building?"

"That is correct."

"So that would have given the defendant plenty of time to cut the gas line and put the lock on the door?"

Scofield quickly interrupted.

"I object, your honor," he said. "The district attorney in putting words into the witness' mouth."

"Sustained," the judge said.

The district attorney took a deep breath, then turned to Scofield.

"Your witness."

Scofield stood up from the counsel table. Then he turned, stepped behind me and placed his hands on my shoulders.

"You are telling this court that you are absolutely certain that the person you saw that night was this man?"

"Yes, sir!!"

"You could not have been mistaken?"

"No, sir!!"

"Do you understand there at severe penalties for lying in court?"

"Yes, sir!!"

For a long moment, Scofield peered at the witness, then he

spoke.

"There was a lock on the door to the candle shed on the night of the murder," he said. "Is there normally a lock on that door?"

"Not usually."

"Don't you think it is strange the candle shed would be locked up for the first time on the night of the murder of Susan Rawlings?"

"I guess so."

"No more questions," Scofield said, taking his seat at the counsel table again.

"Ladies and gentlemen," the judge said, "the noon hour is upon us. We will break for lunch and return promptly at 1 p.m."

***

An hour later, when Judge Murphy rapped his gavel for the afternoon session to begin, Jesse and Consuelo suddenly appeared in the courtroom and went straight to the defense table.

"Did you find anything?" I asked.

Consuelo smiled.

"We sure did!"

After a whispered conversation with my attorney, Jesse and Consuelo took seats in the defense gallery. Across the aisle, behind the prosecutor's table were Harold, Lester and Emily.

"Mr. Scofield!" the judge said. "Call your first witness."

"Your honor, the defense calls Glenn Hudson."

Glenn Hudson was a tall, gangly youth in his early twenties with a thin face and a shock of unruly blonde hair. Once he had been sworn in, he took the stand.

"Name and occupation," Scofield said.

"Glenn Hudson, employee of Hudson's Hardware Store in The Dalles."

"Your father is the owner of the hardware store?"

"Yes, sir."

Scofield turned from the witness, strode to the evidence table and picked up the lock. Then he returned to the witness and showed him the lock.

"Have you ever seen this lock before?"

"Yes, sir."

"When?"

"On June 1, 1975."

"Under what circumstances did you see it?"

"I sold it to a customer."

"Would you recognize the person you sold the lock to if you saw them again?"

"Yes."

"Do you see that person in this courtroom?"

"Yes."

"Can you please point them out?"

Hudson turned from Scofield and pointed straight at Emily.

"That's her!"

Suddenly, there was a ripple of ooohs and aaahs from the packed courtroom as all eyes turned to Emily.

"Order! Order!" Judge Murphy said, rapping this gavel. "Mr. Scofield, please continue."

Scofield turned back to the witness.

"You're sure it's the same person?"

"I'm sure!"

"You're sure it's the same lock?"

"The stock number is on both the receipt and the lock."

Scofield turned back to the judge.

"Your honor, let the record show that the witness identified Emily Massey as the purchaser of the lock that was on the shed door on the night of the murder. I submit to you that Emily Sandra Massey is the murderer of Susan Rawlings. Further, if you will issue a bench warrant and have Emily Massey's quarters searched, you will find the key to this lock."

Suddenly, the courtroom was filled with a loud scream.

"No! No!" shouted Emily.

Then she jumped up from her seat in the gallery and burst through the courtroom doors.

"Arrest that woman!" Judge Murphy shouted.

Instantly, two deputies shot through the courtroom doors and returned moments later holding Emily by the arms.

"No! It's not true!" she shouted. "I'm not the murderer."

Suddenly, Lester jumped out of his seat.

"You stupid bitch! I told you it wouldn't work."

"Shut up!" said the Messiah. "Shut up now!"

A hubbub of voices suddenly erupted in the courtroom.

"Order! Order!" shouted the judge, rapping his gavel.

Lester sat back down and the courtroom grew quiet again.

"In light of the new evidence, I am calling a mistrial. I hereby order that that the charges against John David Chance are dismissed and new murder charges be brought against Emily Sandra Massey. Court is adjourned."

My heart soared with happiness at the judge's words. Moments later, I watched as deputies put handcuffs on Emily and led her away. She was sobbing like a little child. Across the aisle, the great one, all dressed up in his white robe and sandals, looked at me as if he could run through me.

Moments later, Consuelo and Jesse were at my side.

"Congratulations," she said.

She smiled and hugged me. I had never seen her look more beautiful than at that moment.

Jesse turned to me.

"What are you going to do now?"

"I'm not sure."

"Come stay with me and Francesca for a while. Your personal belongings are already there."

***

That afternoon, I hung out at the Dark Bean. Consuelo was serving tables, Jesse was busy baking muffins and Francesca attended the cash register. I tried to help any way I could. I washed dishes, moved heavy bags of flour from the storage room to the kitchen, took out the trash and, after the shop closed that night, I put the chairs on the tables and swept the floor. Promptly at eight that night, Jesse turned off the lights, locked the door and we started walking the two blocks to the apartment.

"You and Francesca have got a good business," I said.

"Actually, it's more than we can handle. We need at least one more waitress. I put an ad in the paper today. Maybe I can hire another one tomorrow."

When we arrived back at the apartment, Consuelo and Francesca were already there. That night, the four of us made a dinner of pizza and beer. Afterward, Consuelo and I went for a walk in the public park behind the apartments. I had been waiting for this moment for some time.

"I wanted to say thanks for helping me through my ordeal."

"I was happy to do it," she said. "I have a strong sense of right and wrong."

"There's something I wanted to tell you," I said.

"What might that be?"

"I have developed a certain fondness for you over these past few weeks."

She smiled.

"Are you saying you're physically attracted to me?"

"Yes."

She laughed.

"I feel the same way about you," she said. "I thought you were never going to mention it."

"Sometimes, I'm a little slow on the uptake."

For a moment, she held my eyes, then I stepped forward and kissed her lightly on the lips. When she broke the kiss and peered into my eyes, I felt like I had known her all my life.

Back at the apartment that night, we made love for the first time. She was a strong lover with good hands and a soft, gentle approach. Afterward, we lay in one another's arms on the apartment floor.

"I think I've fallen in love with you," I said.

"I've been in love with you since the first time I saw you in the candle shed."

"Why didn't you say something?"

"The time wasn't right."

***

The following day, I was at the Dark Bean all day. As before, I helped however I could. Washing dishes, sweeping the floor, moving supplies from the storage room to the kitchen and watching Consuelo dart about the dining area serving tables. Around 7:45 that night, I started putting chairs on tables to prepare for closing. Once the floors were swept, Jesse flipped off the lights, locked the doors and we started walking the two blocks from the shop to the apartment.

As we walked along the street, we passed in front of several closed businesses. There was an insurance company, a tire store and a cab company. As we approached an alleyway past the cab company, two dark figures suddenly jumped out.

"Look out!" Jesse shouted.

In the street light, I could see their faces were covered. One had a baseball bat and the other had what appeared to be a knife. The one with the baseball bat came straight at me and swung the bat. I quickly side-stepped and, as he lunged past, I caught him with a hard right in the jaw. He went down. For a moment, he was stunned. As he lay on the ground, I grabbed the baseball bat and tried to take it away. For several moments, we struggled for possession of the bat. Then, with one mighty twist, I wrested the weapon from his hands. For a moment, he peered up at me, then as I drew back the bat to strike him, he jumped up and ran off into the darkness.

Meanwhile, Jesse and the other assailant, armed with a knife, were circling one another. Several times, the other man lunged at Jesse and made a thrusting motion. Each time, Jesse dodged. Finally, on the fifth attempt, Jesse managed to grab his knife hand, spin him around and catch him in a headlock. Seconds later, with one hand firmly grasping the knife hand, Jesse used his free hand to pull the covering off the man's face.

"No! No!" the man said.

Then, with a terrified look on his face, he looked from Jesse to me, then turned and disappeared into the darkness.

"Did you get a look at his face?" Jesse said.

"His name is Jacob," I replied. "He's a member of the commune. He was sent here by Harold. Are you okay?" I asked.

"I'm fine."

***

The following morning, I was back at the Dark Bean. Again, I tried to help any way I could. I cleaned off tables,

251

washed dishes and moved supplies from the stockroom to the kitchen. Consuelo waited tables and handled the cash register while Francesca interviewed candidates for the new waitress job. After talking to several candidates, she hired a smallish, dark-haired woman in her early twenties named Jody Caldwell. Once the deal was struck, Francesca brought her around to meet Jesse and Consuelo. After introductions and small talk, Jody mentioned she had been a member of Nature Blessings.

"What years were you there?" Consuelo asked.

"Early 1966 until 1971."

Consuelo studied her for a moment.

"Oh, yes," she said. "I faintly remember you. Did you know a girl named Laura Elders?"

"She was one of my best friends. I still get letters from her."

"Do you know where she is?"

"She's in Montana. Kalispell, Montana."

"Do you have an address?"

"I can get it."

"Can you have it when you report for work tomorrow?"

"Sure."

***

That night, Jesse and I closed the coffee shop promptly at 8, then returned to the apartment. After a dinner of burgers, fries and cokes, we watched television for a couple hours then went to bed. Around 3 a.m. we were awakened by loud knocking on the door. It was a neighbor from downstairs.

"Your coffee shop is on fire," he said. "You better get down there."

Quickly, Jesse and I had our clothes on and were out the door.

When we arrived at the Dark Bean, the front of the building was engulfed in flames. Two fire trucks and six firemen were on the scene. Already the fire had destroyed most of the walls and the tables and chairs in the front dining area. The back of the store had been largely untouched and the work benches, baking equipment, mixing bowls, flour and such had been untouched. After some forty minutes, the fireman had the blaze extinguished.

By now, Francesca and Consuelo were at the scene. When Francesca saw the smoking, smoldering ruins of the coffee shop, she broke down in tears. Instantly, Jesse went to comfort her. For several minutes, the four of us peered at the smoldering ruins.

"Lester and Harold's shills failed in their attack," Consuelo said. "So now they've tried to destroy your business."

Instantly, at the thought, rage formed in Jesse's face. He turned to me.

"Let's go down there and kill Harold."

"You'd end up in prison," Consuelo said. "Let's go to Montana and find Laura Elders. If she will testify to some of things she told me years ago, we can send Harold off for a long time."

"You're right," Jesse said. "We'll go to Montana tomorrow."

***

The following morning, we went to Jody's home on the south side of town. She was surprised to see us. Jesse explained that the coffee shop had burned down during the previous night and there was no job.

"Can we get the address for Laura Elders?" Consuelo said.

Quickly, Jody stepped back into her apartment and returned moments later with an empty envelope. She handed it to Jesse. At the top left corner was scrawled an address. 11407 Highway 93, Kalispell, Montana.

"In her last letter, she said she was working at Kelso's Plant Nursery at Kalispell. I think that address is for the nursery."

***

Two hours later, the four of us were cruising eastward along I-80 through the rugged mountains of Idaho in Jesse's 1967 Chevrolet. When we crossed the state line at Lookout Pass, Montana, I was absolutely enthralled by the scenery. This was the first time I had been to Montana and, as we cruised along the highway, I knew I was having an epiphany. Never had I seen country like this except in my dreams. The towering mountains, the wide, spacious skies, the clear blue lakes, herds of elk and antelope grazing in the open fields, the overall western feel of the place enthralled me.

"Look at all this!" I said. "Now I know why they call this place 'Big Sky.' It's the most beautiful country I've ever seen."

Just after 1 p.m., we arrived in Kalispell and, after some searching, we found Kelso's Nursery.

"All four of us shouldn't go in," Consuelo said. "We don't want to scare her off. Just me and Johnny will go in."

"That's fine," Jesse said. "Me and Francesca will stay in the car."

Inside the nursery office, we were greeted by a bulky, middle-aged woman with a drawn face and a pile of gray hair piled high on her head.

"I'm looking for Laura Elders," Consuelo said.

The woman looked Consuelo up and down.

"Are you a relative?"

"I'm an old friend. We were in a commune together in Oregon."

"I heard her talk about those days."

"Is she here?"

"Her last name is not Elders anymore. She got married last spring. Her name is Laura Payne now."

"Can we talk to her?"

"She's working in the perennial shed," the woman said, pointing to a set of double doors. "Go through the doors and you'll see her."

Moments later, inside the greenhouse, we saw a smallish, frumpy-looking woman with glasses down on her knees planting lilacs.

"Laura?" Consuelo said.

The woman looked up.

"I'm Consuelo Rodriguez. Do you remember me from Nature's Blessings?"

She pushed her glasses up on her nose, then peered at Consuelo.

"Oh, yes! Consuelo! How are you?"

Quickly, she stood up, went to Consuelo and hugged her.

"I never dreamed I would ever see you again," she said. "What brings you here?"

Consuelo reminded her of the stories of sexual abuse she had suffered at the hands of the Messiah while she was at the commune.

"Now we have an opportunity to right the wrongs that were done to you and your sister. Will you come back to Oregon with us and testify against Harold in court?"

"I'd love to see him behind bars, but we have a problem."

"What's that?"

"I don't have the money for the transportation to Oregon."

"We'll buy you a bus ticket," Consuelo said. "Also, we'll provide lodging while you're there."

"When do you want me to go?"

"As soon as possible."

"I do have a vacation coming up next week. I could go then."

Laura studied Consuelo for a moment.

"If you like, I could have my sister come with me. She suffered as much at the hands of Harold as I did."

"Perfect!" Consuelo said.

Suddenly, Laura started crying.

"Why are you weeping?" Consuelo said.

"My sister and I thought we would never get justice. Now maybe the time has come."

***

An hour later, as we were cruising westward along I-80 back to The Dalles, I realized what a success the trip to Montana had been. Not only did we find Laura and win her cooperation, I had discovered Montana. This was the place I had been dreaming of for many years. It epitomized all the western locales I had seen in cowboy movies, on TV and in comic books. I was in love. I knew that someday I would come back here to live out my final days.

***

Ten days later, Consuelo and I picked up Laura and her sister Clara at the bus station in The Dalles and took them straight to the office of District Attorney O'Donnell. When Consuelo told him about Laura and her sister's potential testimony, he was elated. That afternoon, he took depositions from both women. They provided testimony about the times and places they had been sexually assaulted by Harold as well the murder of another commune resident who had been killed for the insurance proceeds. Once depositions were finished, O'Donnell said he would get a court date set in a month and asked her to return to provide live testimony. When Laura asked about transportation and lodging expenses, he said the state would foot the bill for both of them.

"Now the truth about Nature's Blessings is finally going to come out," he said.

***

Two days later, Harold Massey was arrested at the commune and charged with two counts of insurance fraud, two counts of murder and 118 counts of sex crimes against children. Lester Huffman, upon learning about Laura's testimony, turned state's evidence and blew the case wide open. He confessed that he and Harold had drowned commune member Patricia Hughes in the swimming one night while she was drunk to collect the insurance. Also, he admitted, while he and Honah Lee were going into town, they had stopped at a restaurant, where he drugged her drink before he intentionally ran the pickup off the road into the reservoir. In a plea deal, he was sentenced to fifteen years in state prison.

***

Once authorities began investigating the Messiah, they discovered his real name was Juan Gabriel Ortiz of Oklahoma City, Oklahoma, a fugitive from justice for crimes against children in Kansas. At his trial, both Laura and Clara testified

Harold had raped and sodomized them multiple times over a period of eight months, vowing to kill their mother, a commune member, if they ever told. Once the trial was over, a jury convicted him of two counts of insurance fraud, two counts of murder and multiple sex crimes against children. He was sentenced to a total of 83 years in prison. In Emily's case, she pleaded guilty to second-degree murder in the death of Susan Rawlings and received a sentence of 25 years. On the first day of August, two weeks after Harold's trial, Nature's Blessings was closed and the State of Oregon seized the commune property under the state's criminal enterprise laws.

***

A week later, Consuelo and I moved out of Jesse and Francesca's apartment in The Dalles and took new quarters in another apartment building less than a block away. I bought a car and took a job at a lumber mill on the outskirts of town while Consuelo continued working at the Dark Bean, which had since been rebuilt from insurance money. Tips were good and she liked to meet the public.

Over the next two months, I feel madly in love with Consuelo. I quickly discovered her deep, abiding intellect. She was as widely read as I and had an interest in a broad range of subjects, including history, biology, literature, psychology and philosophy. She was a good cook and made a strawberry dessert called crema de frases, which I simply adored. Many nights, after making love, we would lie in bed discussing Plato, Marx, Locke, Hume and Whitehead. As a lover, she was everything I could have asked for.

In late April of 1976, after we had been living together for six months, she announced she wanted to return to Peru.

"What's in Peru?"

"My mother. And my younger brother."

"That's Javier?"

"How did you know?"

"I heard Carlos speak of him."

"Also, I want to help my people right some of the political wrongs in my country. I want you to go with me."

"Where would we live?"

"We could live with my mother until we found our own place."

"Will you help me learn Spanish?"

"I'd love to."

"Will you prepare that little strawberry dessert for me?"

"Crema de frases? Of course."

"Will you make love with me each and every night and take me to the final frontiers of sexual satisfaction?"

She laughed.

"I wouldn't miss it."

"When do you want to leave?"

"In two weeks, I'll have enough money saved."

"Let's get married," I said.

She was startled.

"Marriage? Why would you want to get married?"

"I love you."

She laughed.

"Everything changes in a relationship when a couple gets married. Without marriage vows, the bond is free and unfettered. After you take the vows, the relationship becomes a chore."

I didn't answer at first.

"Maybe you're right," I said finally.

***

A month later, in early May of 1976, Jesse and I were sitting on the balcony of his apartment in The Dalles. We were sipping beers and passing a joint when I announced I was going to Peru.

He studied me for a moment.

"How old are you now?"

"I turned thirty-six last month."

"You planning on leaving any sperm on this earth?"

"I'd like to have at least one child before I die."

He studied me for a moment.

"I don't think I would have the patience to raise a child," he said. "What are you going to do in Peru?"

"I'm not sure," I said. "I just want to be near Consuelo. Living in the Amazon would have to be an awesome adventure."

"I'd love to come down and visit."

"You know you'll be welcome."

A pause.

"I always told myself I would be rich by the time I was forty," he said.

"How do you plan on doing it?"

"Not sure. I'd like to make a big hit for a quick score."

"Such as?"

"A big adventure that pays a lot of money. You know, rescuing some bank president's daughter from kidnappers. Fighting with rebels in a banana republic as a mercenary. I'm telling you… I could be a professional soldier."

I laughed.

"Well, if you find something, let me know. I'll join up with you."

When I said good-bye that night, I hugged him and wished him well.

"I'll be in touch," I said.

"Take care."

As I walked away, he called after me.

"Johnny!"

I turned.

"You're got my address at the Dark Bean."

"You'll be hearing from me."

6 – Peru

1983

The Amazon River Basin is a world unto itself. Stretching more than 1400 miles across the South American Continent, the mighty river hosts an infinitely-variegated ecosystem of plants, animals, birds and fish like no other in the world. It is home to the pink dolphin, the red-bellied piranha and the black caiman; there are howler monkeys, three-toed sloths, saddleback tamarins and shaggy-tail Saki monkeys; birds include the scarlet macaws, nine species of toucans and the hoatzin, the mysterious reptile bird that has claws on its wings; among insects, there are giant leeches and red centipedes that grow to more than a foot long. In its journey eastward, the river wanders snakelike through the dense rainforests and endless floodplains of northern South America and touches the nations of Peru, Colombia and Brazil before finally dumping into the Atlantic Ocean on the opposite side of the continent. Despite its majestic beauty, it is a world fraught with danger, darkness and mystery.

***

On the morning of May 12, 1976, the plane carrying Consuelo and I touched down in Lima, Peru, the nation's capital and a major port city on its Pacific Coast. From there, we took a two-hour flight due east to Iquitos, the largest city in the world without access to roads and the gateway to the river towns and tribal villages of the upper Amazon River. Upon arrival at the airport, a motocab, a motor scooter outfitted to

carry two passengers, delivered us to Consuelo's mother's home in the heart of downtown Iquitos. It was a white, stucco structure with a metal roof and tiled floors and, by local standards, could be considered solid middle class. When we arrived, we saw her mother Maria, a smallish woman in her late sixties with a drawn face and salt and pepper hair, bent over in a small garden at the side of the house. When the old woman looked up and saw Consuelo, a big smile flashed across her face and she came hurrying across the yard to greet us. Once Consuelo introduced me, Maria hugged me, then we went inside and she began preparing a meal.

Once we had eaten, Consuelo gave her mother the package from Carlos. The old woman went through the package piece by piece, closely fingering each and every one. The letters, the hank of hair, the photos, the crucifix and the dog tags. As she did, huge tears rolled down her cheeks. Finally, she put away the mementoes and asked us to go to the market.

* * *

That afternoon, Consuelo and I explored Iquitos. A town of just over half a million, Iquitos was settled by Spanish Jesuits in 1757 on the banks of the Nanay River. In the late 19th century, it became the major export center for rubber products from the Amazon basin and, in the early 20th century, its population exploded as European businessmen and North African traders arrived to exploit its vast wealth and natural resources. Famous for its massive open-air street market and rustic stilt houses lining the Itaya River, Iquitos's historic center, La Plaza de Armas, was surrounded by European-influenced buildings dating back to the region's turn-of-the-20th-century boom in rubber production.

As Consuelo and I browsed the markets, I saw a wide assortment of meats, fruits and vegetables I had never seen before. The bulky little women, with their colorful hats perched high atop their heads and decked out in costumes in hues of blue, yellow, red and green, hawked their crafts and products to passersby. There were hand-painted dining plates featuring family scenes and small children; wire sculptures of sloths, anacondas and howler monkeys; painted ceramic teapot sets; intricately carved onyx figurines of toucans, parrots and macaws. When we left the market, we had bought a basket of guava fruit, two dressed chickens, a large basket of strawberries, a sack of flour and five pounds of potatoes. Back at the house that night, we dined on chicken tacos, rice and beans, and a large helping of crema de frases, the dessert Consuelo made from strawberries. After dinner, Consuelo and her mother talked about her life in the commune.

***

That night in our bedroom, after making love, Consuelo lay in my arms.

"Javier will be here tomorrow," she said. "He's my youngest brother. He runs a ferry boat up and down the river."

"I'd heard Carlos speak of him."

"You want to work on the ferry boat?"

"Sounds like fun."

"We'll both go. He always needs some extra help."

"How long will we be gone?"

"Six days. Three days to Tefe, Brazil and three days back. You'll have to pack some clothes."

That first night, once she was asleep in my arms, I was so happy. I was with the woman I loved and I had a new adventure awaiting me. Through the open bedroom window, a gentle breeze was blowing and, in the distance, I could see a giant yellow moon hovering over the stark silhouette of the rainforest. As I drifted off to sleep, I could hear the pitter-patter of raindrops on the metal roof, and somewhere far, far away, I could hear the mournful cry of a scarlet macaw. My heart was soaring.

***

Early the next morning at the breakfast table, I met Javier. Medium height and in his late thirties, he had a thin face with dark eyes, a well-trimmed mustache and a stout, capable look about him. After introductions, Consuelo explained that I was with Carlos in Vietnam when he died. He crossed himself. Then, after offering some words of solace for his mother, Javier began telling me about his ferry service.

"When I first started the business, I was making runs with *La Senora* between Iquitos and Manaus, Brazil. After a few months, however, I realized it was too dangerous."

"Dangerous?" I said.

"There is no law on the Amazon River," he said. "Pirates are on every hand waiting to rush in and rob you."

"What do they want?"

"Mostly drugs and fuel, but they will take anything they can get."

I studied him for a moment.

"Where did you learn your English?" I said.

"When I was a teenager, I worked four years on a rubber plantation in Tefe. It was owned by an Englishman from Liverpool. Most of the workers were from Ireland and Scotland."

"Consuelo has promised to help me learn Spanish," I said.

"You've got a good teacher," he said.

***

An hour later, when we arrived at the docks and *La Senora*, passengers were already waiting to buy tickets. There were tourists from France and Germany; workers going to the rubber plantations and oil fields at Tefe, Brazil; a family of thirteen was going to Leticia, Colombia; a teenaged boy and his mother with a home-made cage filled with twelve piglets; an old couple going to visit grandchildren in Fonte Boa. The cargo included a shipment of truck tires going to Santa Rosa, a machine for processing rubber, and two bales of cotton bound for a small textile company in Tefe. When we untied from the docks at Iquitos and started upriver, the cargo portion of the boat's lower deck was full and we were carrying about fifty passengers.

La Senora was a sleek, well-maintained wooden vessel, powered with two 250-horsepower diesel engines. Just over fifty feet long, she had an upper deck, which contained a pilothouse and six cabins, which served as living quarters for the crew. The front portion of the lower deck served as an enclosed seating area for passengers while the stern was reserved for cargo. Also, on the lower deck, there was a small kitchen for preparing snacks and short orders for passengers. Passengers could rent hammocks to sleep in during the trip and usually they brought their own food.

Ignacio, a late twenties, long-haired Brazilian, was a crew member who performed whatever chores were necessary. He would collect fares, serve snacks to passengers, clean the restrooms and tie up and release the vessel when it was docking. His main chore was to guard the vessel at night while other crew members slept. Piloting chores were left to Alejandro, an older man with gray hair and missing teeth, who had operated the boat up and down the river before he sold it to Javier. Although Javier knew how to operate the boat, usually, Alejandro was at the helm.

"Alejandro is a good man," Javier said. "He knows this river like the back of his hand. Every little eddy, every tributary, every snag, every sand bar. I'm very lucky to have him."

***

Once *La Senora* was underway that first day, I could see the majestic beauty of the river unfolding around me. The rainforests were a towering ocean of deep greens broken up only by the blues, the reds and the yellows of the birds and mammals that lived among its dense foliage. Since it was the wet season, floodplains extended far beyond the usual width of the river on either side. As we skimmed along, I saw floating meadows of white hyacinth—some twenty to thirty feet across—bobbing up and down in the water. Giant stands of water lilies with flowers more than four feet across dotted the water's surface along the shore. After we were about an hour upriver, I saw a herd of capybara for the first time. These furry creatures are evolutionary cousins of the gopher rat and can grow as large as a small cow. As we passed close to the shore, I saw a giant green anaconda, more than twenty feet long, trying to swallow a howler monkey it had squeezed to death.

Further upriver, the small villages of indigenous peoples began to pop up along the shoreline. These homes were mostly simple square or round wood structures with roofs made of thatch. Some were little more than walls that had been fashioned by tying small logs together, then chinking the cracks with river mud and using palm branches for framing and thatch panels for a roof. Small children, most of them naked, played along the river's edge. Many waved at us as we passed. Here was a mysterious, unexplored world of native tribes, cannibals, blow guns and shrunken heads.

***

Late that afternoon, we arrived at Santa Rosa, Peru. For years, Santa Rosa had been little more than a quiet fishing village, but, in the late seventies, after international travel companies began to offer sight-seeing tours, hotels, restaurants and the other trappings of modern society began to spring up. Located on an island, Santa Rosa was the Peruvian contribution to Tres Fronteras, the triple border on the river which separates Peru, Brazil and Colombia. Each nation has its own city represented at the crossing. Santa Rosa for Peru, Leticia for Colombia and Tabatinga for Brazil.

Once *La Senora* was docked at Santa Rosa, Javier said we needed to refuel. When he asked the supplier at the docks to buy fuel, the man said his tanks were empty and we would have to go into town to buy directly from the Petrobras distributor. Since each barrel of diesel fuel weighed above 200 pounds, we took two hand trolleys with us to transport them back to the boat.

Thirty minutes later, as we were rolling the hand trolleys along the sidewalk back to the city's the main street, we saw a group of some fifty to seventy-five protestors, mostly men, parading down the middle of the street toward us. They were carrying crudely drawn signs that protested against taxes and called Belaundre, the nation's current president, a fascist.

"Fools!" Javier said, when he saw them. "Don't they know they could be killed for protesting against Belaundre?"

***

Thirty minutes later, at the local Petrobras distributor, we purchased two 55-gallon drums of diesel fuel, then loaded them on the hand trolleys and started back down the city's main street. As we rounded a corner to the street that led back to the docks, we suddenly heard loud voices and shouting.

Ahead of us, a group of some twenty government troops, known to locals as Federales, were holding guns on the protestors. The protest leader and the commandant of the troops were arguing violently with one another. Suddenly, without warning, the commandant pulled a sidearm and shot the protest leader point-blank in the chest. The leader fell to the ground, mortally wounded. Instantly, pandemonium ensued and the remaining protestors, shouting frantically, started running in the opposite direction. As they did, the troops opened fire. Many fell where they stood. Some who had been wounded limped off into alleyways or took refuge into shops along the street. Even after the crowd dispersed, the Federales continued firing.

I was horrified. I turned to Javier.

"That's cold-blooded murder," I said.

"I know," he replied. "There's nothing to be done."

"Shouldn't we try to help those poor people?"

"No! Then the Federales will turn on you."

"Holy Christ! What kind of country is this?"

"That's the Belaundre way. If you oppose him, you will be killed."

Back at the boat, Javier told Consuelo what we had witnessed.

"Los bastardos," she said. "Someday our people will have their revenge on those dogs."

***

Two hours later, we were cruising through a quiet, uninhabited stretch of the river some twenty kilometers east of Santa Rosa. Now, on either bank, all we could see was raw,

dense jungle and the towering canopy of the rainforest with puffs of mist hovering overhead. I was in the pilothouse with Javier. He was at the helm while Alejandro took a break.

"We'll be approaching San Juan Bautista in the next few minutes," he said. "Take one of the rifles and ammunition out of the case," he said, pointing to a gun closet next to the helm, "and go stand at the stern of the boat and keep watch."

"Why?"

"Water rats! Pirates!" he said. "There is a huge bend in the river at San Juan Bautista and the current whips boats around the bend with great force. When the current catches a vessel, particularly a small one, it can quickly flip it around the bend and ground it on the sandbar on the other side. Once the boat is stuck on the sand bar, the pirates will come rushing in to attack."

"How will I recognize them?"

"They'll usually be in speedboats. Something that is small and fast and easily maneuvered in and out the tributaries."

"What if I see them and they try to board *La Senora*?"

He laughed.

"You kill them," he said. "You kill them or they will board and rob us and our passengers. Last year, pirates attacked a sight-seeing boat at Fonte Boa and not only were the passengers robbed of their jewelry and personal possessions, but thirteen were killed. They like to sneak up on you when you're sleeping. I'm more afraid of the pirates than I am the Federales."

I turned from him, opened the gun case and took out an aging World War II German Mauser rifle and six rounds of ammunition.

"Chances are you won't see anything," Javier said. "I just like to keep my passengers safe. If water rats were to board and rob the passengers, I would be out of business."

Moments later, I was at the stern keeping watch when *La Senora* entered the bend in the river. Suddenly, I could feel the tremendous force of the water pulling on the vessel. Instantly, in the pilothouse, Javier revved the engines to counter the force of the current and, for several minutes, it was the power of the current against the power of the diesel engines. Finally, we were past the bend and into quiet water again. Now I could see the huge sand bar Javier was referring to and how easy it would be for smaller boats to become helplessly stuck on it once it cleared the bend.

***

Later that afternoon, as we cruised eastward toward Tefe, Consuelo was busy cooking meals for passengers while I loitered in the pilothouse with Alejandro. He was in a philosophical mood.

"At night, this river is like an old woman," he said. "Serious, demanding and treacherous. During the daylight hours, she is like a young girl: happy, gay and prancing about without a care in the world. She can be a loving mother one moment, then become a raving monster. After you've made as many runs as I have, you learn all of her different moods."

"How long did you operate *La Senora* before you sold it to Javier?"

"Thirteen years. When I turned sixty, I sold it to Javier because I was getting too old. After he paid me for my business, he asked me to stay on as his pilot."

"So, it's Javier's boat now?"

"Not exactly, he paid me, but we haven't had the title transferred into his name."

"Don't you think you ought to get that done?"

"We'll get it done some time," Alejandro said, dismissing the matter with a wave of the hand.

***

On the afternoon of the third day, *La Senora* tied up to the docks at Tefe, Brazil, a sprawling town built around a lake, appropriately named Lake Tefe. As early as 1620, Portuguese Carmelites were converting the Muras, the indigenous tribe that had lived on the lake's shores for centuries, into Christianity. By 1783, the missionaries had established a total of eight monasteries around the lake and, in 1760, the principal one, Parauarí, was converted into a municipality which was officially named Tefe. By the 1860s, as word filtered back to

Europe about cheap land and labor, traders, businessmen and adventurers began flocking to the region to establish rubber and sugar plantations. In the early 1930s, oil drillers from both the states and Europe arrived to exploit its vast petroleum reserves. By early 1976, now with a population of 60,000, Jefe was a bustling river town whose economy depended principally on sugar, rubber and oil production.

Once we were docked, *La Senora* was empty of both cargo and passengers within an hour. Over the next two hours, Consuelo, Ignacio and I set about cleaning up the boat and preparing it for a new run back down the river the following day. After darkness fell, Consuelo and I had a meal of chicken tacos, beans, rice and crema de frases, then we retired for the night.

* * *

The following morning, before we started loading passengers, Javier disappeared into town while Consuelo and I and the other crew members waited on *La Senora*. Three hours later, he reappeared. On his return, he had a copy of a Spanish-language newspaper titled "*La Verdad.*" It was filled with articles and editorials about the suffering of native Peruvians at the hands of Belaundre's government. The headline blared out the news that government troops had killed twenty-two protestors in Santa Rosa. The moment he boarded *La Senora,* Javier showed it to Consuelo.

"This is what Johnny and I witnessed," he said.

Consuelo took the newspaper and shook her head in anger.

"Someday the people will rise up and make them pay," she said.

Moments later, we started boarding passengers and loading cargo. There were oil field and rubber plantation workers going to visit their families in Iquitos, a young couple going to Santa Rosa to be married; a family of six with a small child that would not stop crying. One older couple wanted to board a cow, but Javier refused to allow it. Among the cargo was a punch press for a machine shop, eight truck tires and two huge crates of women's hats going to a milliner in Santa Rosa.

Once passengers and cargo were loaded, Ignacio pulled up the gangplank, Alejandro fired up the engines and *La Senora* was back on the river headed to Iquitos. Over the first hour, Consuelo was busy preparing food for passengers, selling hammocks for sleeping and helping passengers find seating. Finally, when the initial rush was over, Consuelo came and sat with me in the pilothouse.

"Where did Javier disappear to for three hours?" I asked.

For a long moment, she peered at me without answering.

"Can you keep a secret?" she said finally.

"Yes."

"He is a member of the organization."

"What organization?"

"Tupac Amaru."

At the sound of the words, I turned quickly back to her.

"The guerilla group that is trying to overthrow the Peruvian government?"

"That's right."

"Isn't that dangerous?"

"Very dangerous. If the Federales get wind of it, Javier would be shot."

I pondered her words.

"You must never breathe a word to anyone," she said.

"Don't worry. I wouldn't want anything to happen to Javier. I like and respect him too much."

***

Seven years passed. During that time, Javier, Consuelo and I made many, many trips up and down the river loading and unloading passengers and cargo day after day. My nights were spent at the breast of my beloved Consuelo. We were two great spirits constantly winding in and out of one another at several different levels. She would drill me on Spanish verbs and sentence structure, then we would discuss the animal imagery in Shakespeare, Freud's theories on sexuality and famous military campaigns. She had an intimate knowledge of

Hannibal's crossing the Alps, Napoleon's campaign in Russia and Patton in Northern France after D-Day.

Over that period, my Spanish became quite good and my fascination for the sheer beauty and wonder of the Amazon River increased a hundredfold. Every time we were in Tefe, Javier would disappear into town and not return for several hours. Once, in the summer of 1979, we were attacked by pirates near San Juan Bautista, but we managed to fight them off. During the skirmish, Ignacio suffered a leg wound, but after receiving medical attention at Tefe, he was fine.

Being with Consuelo day after day, learning the language and witnessing the history and culture of the Amazon firsthand engendered a deep appreciation of Latino heritage within me. At night, as I lay on top of her thrusting my body into hers, I would look down into her face and all of the Latin beauty and history and culture lurking within her spirit would come shining forth through her dark eyes. In her face, I could see the glory of the Inca Empire, the artistry and genius of Machu Picchu and the majesty of the ancient civilization at Cuzco. Until that moment, I never dreamed there was a woman on this earth that could reach that part of me.

***

In early June of 1983, I wrote a letter to Jesse. I addressed it to the Dark Bean.

June 7, 1983
Dear Jesse:
I'm loving my life here in South America.
Everywhere I turn, I find something new and different that interests me.
The people, the history, the wildlife, the river, the rainforests, my beautiful Consuelo. There is adventure and excitement on every hand.
Didn't you tell me you wanted to see the Amazon before you die?
How are you and Francesca doing? Is she still the great love of your life?

*Can you get away from her long enough to pay me a visit?
I'd love to see you.
Johnny*

P.S. Try to arrive on a Sunday. Six days a week, I'm on the river. Sunday is the only day I can come to the airport to get you.

***

Two months later, I got a response.

*August 4, 1983
Dear Johnny:
Francesca and I are still devoted to one another and still running the Dark Bean.*

Business is good and Francesca loves it, but I'm getting bored.

I'll bet I've baked at least ten million muffins since we opened and, from all appearances, the pace is not slowing down.

Running a business is very confining and I only get one day a week off.

I'll talk to Francesca tonight about paying you a visit.

When you get this letter, call me and we'll discuss my coming down for a visit.

The number at the Dark Bean is 203-428-1192.

*I'll be waiting to hear from you.
Jesse*

***

Three weeks later, on Sunday, August 25, 1983, I was waiting at the Iquitos Airfield to meet Jesse. As I watched him stride across the airport tarmac, suitcase in hand, I could see he hadn't changed much. At 44, he was a little grayer and the wrinkles around his eyes were a little deeper, but the same confident gait and carriage was still there. When he saw me, his face broke out in a big smile and he hugged me. I was going to touch the magic once again.

Moments later, we were walking from the tarmac to the airport cabstand.

"Was Francesca all right with you coming down?"

"She had to hire another cook while I'm gone, but she'll be fine. If truth be told, I think we need a break from one another."

Moments later, we were in a motocab trundling across downtown Iquitos to Maria's home. As we rode, Jesse pulled out a newspaper he had taken from the plane.

"What are you reading?"

"This article says that the postwar baby boomers, now that they're in their forties, are abandoning their freedom-loving ways and trying to get rich. You think that will happen to us?"

I laughed.

"I'd still like to make a quick score that pays a lot of money," he continued.

"Like rescuing the banker's daughter from the kidnappers?" I said.

"Yeah. An adventurous job that pays a lot of money."

We were quiet for a moment.

"Are you still in love with Francesca?"

"Oh, yes!" he said. "I get bored with her at times and we argue, but I don't stop loving her."

***

When we arrived at Maria's house, Consuelo was waiting on the front stoop to greet Jesse. She hugged him, then introduced him to Javier and her mother.

"Where are you going to stay?" Consuelo said.

"I'm not sure."

"We have a small anteroom with a cot," she said. "You could stay here with us."

"I don't want to impose."

"We'd love to have you," she said. "Javier might even put you to work on *La Senora*."

"I would love that," Jesse said.

Later, while Maria prepared dinner, Jesse, I, Consuelo and Javier went into town and bought four bottles of wine. Back at the house, we wolfed down a sumptuous meal of roast chicken, boiled potatoes, green vegetables and crema de frases, then proceeded to demolish the wine. We didn't go to bed until 1 a.m. that night. The more stories about Vietnam Jesse told, the more Javier wanted to hear. We reminisced about our days at Nature's Blessings. He asked about Carlos and the circumstances of his death. At least three times, Jesse told about the third battle for Tran Hoa Mountain where Jesse rescued me from the bamboo grove. Javier was fascinated with Jesse.

"You come to work on *La Senora* tomorrow," he said. "There is no better way to appreciate the beauty of the river."

***

The following morning, Jesse joined the crew of *La Senora*. Javier showed him his cabin, introduced him to Alejandro and Ignacio and put him to work helping Ignacio rearrange passenger's baggage. Once some forty passengers and cargo were loaded, Ignacio untied the boat and we were cruising up the river. That first day, as *La Senora* skimmed along the water's surface, I pointed out the wonders of the river to Jesse. He was fascinated by a herd of capybara and marveled at the sight of a blue macaw. Late that afternoon, we arrived at Santa Rosa and passed into Brazil. Two hours later, as darkness fell, Javier, Jesse and I were in the pilothouse when Javier gave the order to dock for the night.

"What about the pirates?" Alejandro said.

"The river rats won't attack on the west side of the bend," Javier said. "At least, they never have. Ignacio will be on guard. We'll be safe."

He turned to Jesse.

"I want to show you where the guns are located," he said.

Then, he turned and opened the gun case.

Jesse peeked inside and saw the array of weapons.

"There is a constant threat of pirates on the river," Javier said. "They usually attack at night, but they have been known to rob and pillage during the daylight hours."

***

Later that night, Consuelo and I retired to our cabin and were asleep within an hour. Around 2 a.m., I was awakened when I felt someone poking me in the chest. I opened my eyes and, in the galley's dim light, I could see a dark figure standing over me. He had been poking me with the barrel of a rifle. Instantly, I knew it was pirates. Consuelo was sound asleep beside me.

"Levantarse!" the man said, ordering me to get out of bed.

Slowly, I raised myself out of bed.

"Traiga su esposa!" he said, pointing to Consuelo.

I bent over her and shook her shoulder.

"Consuelo! Consuelo!"

She sat up and rubbed her eyes.

"Who is that?" she said when she saw the dark figure holding the rifle.

"Pirates!"

Moments later, we were out of our cabin and the dark figure was pushing us toward the stairs leading to the lower deck. Once we were on the lower deck, I could see that the passengers had all been awakened and were standing, hands raised high, beside their hammocks in their bed clothes. Four of the pirates were holding guns on the passengers while a fifth, a short man with a bushy black beard and a three-corner hat, was holding a flashlight and going from one passenger to the other taking their possessions. When an older woman pleaded with him to not take a gold pendant from around her neck, he jerked it off, breaking the chain. Seeing what he had done, she slapped him across the face. Anger filled his eyes, then he drew his sidearm and hit the woman full in the face. Instantly, she went down, crying and moaning.

Next, the man in the three-cornered hat moved to Javier and began rifling through his pockets. There was a worn billfold, some change and a small pocket knife.

"Por favor!" Javier said in protest.

"Silencio!" replied the short man.

Suddenly, from the upper deck, a shot rang out and the short man in the three-corner hat, a surprised expression on his face, fell dead to the lower deck floor. Then I heard Jesse's voice from the upper desk.

"Here!"

I glanced up.

He threw a pistol to me.

I caught it.

"Get the two on your left!" he said.

Quickly, I turned and started firing. Instantly, one of the men fell. Then the other raised his rifle, but, before he could fire, Jesse dropped him. As he did, I fired point blank and killed the third one. Now, upon seeing three of their comrades dead, the other two turned and headed for the stern of the boat. Seconds later, Jesse and I were chasing them across the lower deck to their craft, which was tied to the stern of *La Senora*. As one tried to start the engine, the other raised his rifle. Quickly, Jesse fired, and he fell overboard.

"Let go check on the others," Jesse said.

As we started back down the galley way toward the others, we saw the body of Ignacio lying atop a pile of docking rope. His throat had been cut.

Moments later, we were back in the passenger area, which was now illuminated with flood lights. Javier went through the pockets of the pirate leader and returned valuables to passengers. After possessions were returned, I asked Javier what he wanted to do with the pirates' boat. He said to cut it loose and sink it. Two hours later, calm was restored and passengers were asleep again. Javier and Jesse said they would stand guard for the rest of the night.

***

Two days later, we were back in Tefe. As usual, Javier left the boat and disappeared into town for several hours. Once he was back on board, he went straight to Jesse.

"I want to talk to you and Johnny," he said.

He turned to Consuelo.

"Come on! You might as well hear this too."

Moments later, we were in the pilothouse seated at a table.

"I liked the way you handled yourself during the pirate

attack yesterday," Javier said. "I could see that you two, like Consuelo said, are born soldiers. I have a proposal for you."

"What kind of proposal?" Jesse said.

Javier looked to Consuelo, then at me. Finally, he took a deep breath.

"I'm a member of Tupac Amaru, the underground group that has been fighting the Belaundre government."

"What's that got to do with us?" Jesse said.

"I'm about to tell you," Javier said. "Our group wants to move a cache of arms from Tefe to a safehouse on the Purus River to arm our comrades to the South. We need two men to plan and execute the mission. Two men with strong military experience."

"Those two men are me and Johnny?" Jesse said.

"That's right!" Javier said. "I'm going to propose to the organization leader that you two plan and carry out the mission."

Sheer disbelief crossed Jesse's face.

"What?" he said. "You want me and Johnny to lead a special mission to run illegal arms down the river?"

"That's right."

Jesse began laughing in disbelief.

He looked around.

None of the others were laughing.

Moments later, serious again, he turned to me.

"Is this on the level?"

"Javier is dead serious."

He looked to Consuelo for an answer.

She nodded.

There was a long silence.

"Think you would be interested?" Javier said finally.

"I would be interested," Jesse said.

He turned to me.

"What about you?"

"Oh yes!"

"You realize Johnny and I have no political interest in an operation like that," Jesse said. "We would only do it for the money."

"I know that," Javier replied.

"How much does it pay?"

"Not sure. You'll have to talk to El Jefe."

"When can we do that?"

"Tonight."

***

That afternoon, *La Senora* remained docked at Tefe harbor, empty of passengers and cargo. Just before sundown, a strange-looking man appeared at the docks, boarded *La Senora* and went straight to Javier. Tall and in his late twenties, he was dressed in military fatigues, wore glasses and had a flowing black beard that came down to his waist. When Javier saw the man, he embraced him as if he were an old friend. Then the mysterious man ushered Javier, Jesse, Consuelo and me down the docks to a small speedboat. Once we were all safely inside, the man fired up the engine, maneuvered the boat out of the harbor and headed west up the Amazon River.

As the small boat glided across the water's surface, Javier was at the helm with the bearded man while Consuelo, Jesse and I were riding at the stern. I turned to Consuelo.

"Who is El Jefe?"

"His real name is Joaquin Pablo Guzman," she said. "He grew up on Figueroa Avenue in East LA with me and my brothers. I've known him since I was a little girl. In the late seventies, he left East LA and returned to Peru. For a while, he was a member of the Shining Path, but became disillusioned and formed his own movement. Once he found wealthy sympathizers among the copper miners, his movement began to grow. He now has almost five thousand guerilla fighters in the Peruvian jungles. His movement has since moved into Colombia, where he has more than two thousand fighters."

"Who is the man that met us?" Jesse asked.

"That's Romero. That's his lieutenant."

We were quiet for a moment.

"This is like being back in Vietnam," Jesse said.

***

Thirty minutes later, as the speedboat cruised northward up the tributary, the darkness ahead of us was suddenly interrupted by three quick flashes of bright light on the east bank. At the helm, Romero quickly returned three quick flashes of light from a flood lamp on the boat's bow, then guided the boat toward land. When the bow bumped into the shoreline, two more dark figures, dressed in military fatigues, rushed forward and pulled the small vessel ashore.

"Vamanos!" said Romero.

Moments later, our group was out of the speedboat and trekking along a jungle trail through heavy undergrowth. After we had walked some one hundred yards, we came to a clearing that had been hacked out of the jungle. In the bright moonlight, I could see a large wooden building in one corner, two small planes and a landing strip. Beyond the building, at the edge of the jungle, I could see several small thatched huts. Over the next few minutes, we walked across the clearing to the huts.

"Espera aqui!" Romero said.

Then he turned and went inside. As we waited, we could hear several voices inside speaking Portuguese, then Romero stepped outside again.

"Passe!" he said.

Inside, we saw a crudely-constructed meeting room. On an elevated platform at the front, there were three tables lined up end to end and four chairs on a dirt floor. Directly behind the tables was a large placard of a freedom fighter with a rifle in his hand and a war cry in his face, the symbol of Tupac Amaru. Seated at the middle table was El Jefe, a late thirties man with a beard and a sun-burned face. To his right sat a large white man, early fifties, and dressed in a white suit and a Panama hat. He was every inch of six feet five inches and weighed at least three hundred pounds. In the chair to El Jefe's left sat Romero.

Once our group was seated before them, El Jefe turned to Javier.

"You may begin," he said.

Javier cleared his throat, then began speaking.

"For some time now, the organization has been seeking men to lead a military operation down the Purus River to arm our comrades in the south.

"I am here tonight to recommend two men I feel would be well qualified for the task. Both are veterans of Vietnam and one was awarded a purple heart for his bravery."

He stopped.

"What are their names?" El Jefe said.

"Johnny Chance," Javier said, pointing to me, "and Jesse Trubble," he added, indicating Jesse.

"Chance and Trubble?" El Jefe said with a laugh. "Is that their real names?"

"That's their real names."

"Which one won the purple heart?" El Jefe said.

"That would be Jesse," Javier said.

El Jefe turned to Jesse.

"How many men did you kill in Vietnam?"

Jesse paused before answering.

"I never counted," he said. "Probably ten to twelve. Maybe more."

"How were they killed?"

"When a patrol would go into a village looking for VC spies, the platoon commander would order that everyone stay in their places. If anyone ran, they were shot on the spot. In combat situations, using grenade launchers, I killed seven or eight more."

He studied Jesse for a moment, then turned to me.

"How many men have you killed?"

"Probably seven, eight… ten," I said. "Like Jesse, I killed suspected spies on patrols and used grenade launchers to destroy enemy machine gun nests. I don't know how many I killed that way."

El Jefe was quiet for a moment.

"Why don't you lead the mission?" Jesse said.

"There are wanted posters with my face all over the nation of Peru. There is nothing the Federales would love more than to get their hands on me. If I was captured or killed, the whole movement would collapse."

"You don't have underlings that could handle the job?"

"The men under my command are uneducated day laborers… fishermen and rubber and sugar plantation workers. They know nothing about fighting tactics."

The fat man spoke up.

"They don't know the river," he said. "They don't know the jungle. Why would they be qualified to lead?"

"Both are born soldiers," Consuelo interjected. "They understand weapons, field tactics and the psychology of war."

"The psychology of war?" El Jefe said with a big laugh. "Now there is a mouthful."

Quickly, he grew serious again, then turned back to Jesse.

"How do I know I can trust you?"

"You don't. We were brought here at Javier's request."

"I know them," Consuelo said. "They are both men of their word. They were with Carlos in Vietnam."

"I heard about that," El Jefe said. "I am sorry."

El Jefe paused for a moment then turned back to Consuelo.

"When did you return from America?"

"Seven years ago. Since then, Johnny and I have been helping Javier run his ferry boat business."

"Remember the days on Figueroa Avenue playing stickball?"

"I'll never forget it," she said.

El Jefe smiled, paused for a moment, then turned to the fat man.

"Any questions?"

"Why would you want to undertake such a job as this?" the fat man said.

"We need the money," Jesse said.

El Jefe laughed.

"Everybody needs money," he said. "How much are you looking for?"

"Fifty thousand dollars!" Jesse said quickly.

"That's a lot of money," El Jefe replied.

"It's a dangerous job," Jesse said. "We could lose our lives."

"That's true," he said.

He turned back to the fat man in the white suit.

"Thoughts?"

"We would expect all of the weapons to be in the hands of our comrades once the job is finished."

"That's the agreement," Jesse said.

El Jefe turned back to the fat man.

"Are you in agreement with the fee?"

"Yes."

"How will we be paid?" Jesse said.

"Three days after the job is complete, you will go to El Banco de Brasileo in Tefe where an account has already been set up in your names. Once you identify yourselves, you will have access to the agreed-upon amount."

A pause.

"How soon do you want the mission accomplished?" Jesse said.

"As soon as possible," El Jefe said.

"So, do we have an agreement?" the fat man said.

"Agreed!" Jesse said.

"Agreed!" I replied.

***

Thirty minutes later, El Jefe, Romero and our group were striding across the clearing to the building near the airfield. Once Romero unlocked the door, we went inside. The front of the building was filled with equipment to harvest and process rubber, but, after El Jefe escorted us to the rear, we saw the back wall lined with crates of weapons. There were Chinese-made assault rifles, boxes of pistols, grenade launchers, ammunition, mortars and mortar rounds stacked to the ceiling.

"Twelve crates of rifles, fifty boxes of ammunition, eight grenade launchers, and four mortars and loads will be moved to our comrades in the south," El Jefe said.

Jesse stepped forward and, using his hand, began to measure the size of the containers.

"What are you doing?" El Jefe asked.

"We're going to need to know the exact size of our cargo," he said as he moved expertly from one container to the next. Finally, he was finished.

"That's a total of 120 square feet of cargo space."

Then he peered at the other weapons stacked neatly along the back wall.

"What about the others?"

"We haven't decided on those yet," El Jefe said.

Thirty minutes later, on the return trip to the docks at Tefe, Javier announced that ferry operations would be suspended until the mission was complete.

"I want to be part of this mission," Consuelo said.

"No!" Javier said. "It's too dangerous. I want you to return to Iquitos and wait until this is over."

"I can handle a gun just like a man," she said.

"If anything happens to me, you need to be here to take care of Mother."

She studied him for a moment.

"Maybe you're right. I'll take another ferry back to Iquitos in the morning."

***

The following morning, Jesse, Javier and I were in the pilothouse of *La Senora* planning the mission. Jesse was standing in front of a topographical map of the river.

"*La Senora* will be the perfect cover for the operation," he said. "It has been seen going up and down the river carrying passengers for years."

"It's never been down the Purus," Javier said.

"Why not?"

"There are not enough passengers to turn a profit," Javier said. "I would go broke in the first week."

"That could be a problem," Jesse said. "Since it's the first time, they're going to be checking your paperwork."

"We'll have to deal with that when the time comes."

Jesse studied Javier for a moment, then turned back to the map.

"The entire operation should take about eight hours," he said. "The goods will be picked up here," he said, indicating the jungle hideout on the map.

I interrupted.

"We can't take *La Senora* up the tributary to the hideout," I said. "The channels are too shallow."

Javier turned to me.

"You're right," he said. "I hadn't thought of that. I'll arrange for Romero to get a small boat to move the goods back downriver to *La Senora*. Alejandro can stay with *La Senora* while we're retrieving the goods."

"Once we're back to the river, we can stack the crates four feet high and thirty feet long and put them in the regular cargo space of *La Senora*."

"We couldn't leave it exposed," I said.

"We could throw a covering over it," Javier added. "That's what we do with regular cargo."

"What about the men under your command?"

"There will be six of them," Javier said. "We will dress them in civilian clothes and pose them as passengers on deck. All will be armed."

"They should have pistols that can be easily concealed," Jesse said.

"I'll see that they have pistols."

Jesse turned back to the map.

"So, once we have the goods, we'll go sixty kilometers downriver to the Purus."

He turned to Javier.

"Once we enter the Purus, how far is it to the drop-off point?"

"Around four, maybe five kilometers," Javier said. "Once we enter the mouth of the river, there is a Federales checkpoint less than two kilometers to the south."

"Getting past that checkpoint will be the key to our success," Jesse said. "We should start the operation in the late afternoon "That way, we will have plenty of daylight to load the goods and move them back to *La Senora*. Once we have the goods on board, darkness will be our best friend."

"The sun sets around 5:30," Javier said. "I'll have Romero meet us at *La Senora* at 3:30."

"That should give us plenty of time," Jesse said. "So, when do you want to do it?"

"Day after tomorrow," Javier replied. "I'll need time to talk to El Jefe and Romero about the small boat."

*****

Two days later, in the late afternoon, Jesse, Javier and I were waiting on *La Senora* at Tefe Harbor when Romero appeared. Once Javier saw Romero, he instructed Alejandro to take *La Senora* upriver to the mouth of the Sao Feliz tributary and wait. Then, we strode down the docks with Romero and boarded the same small boat that had taken us to the jungle hideout three days earlier. We rode quietly as Romero guided the speedboat eastward on the Amazon River, then turned northward up the Sao Feliz tributary to the jungle hideout. When we arrived, we were met by six men who accompanied us across the clearing to the storage building. Over the next hour, Jesse, Javier, myself and the six men who would accompany us began lugging the heavy boxes across the clearing to the boat. Finally, once we were loaded, Javier turned to Romero and explained in Spanish that the six men under his command were to be dressed in civilian clothing. Instantly, Romero produced two other large boxes and explained they contained the requested items.

Over the next twenty minutes, we cruised back down the tributary to the main river channel. There, as planned, Alejandro and *La Senora* were waiting. Over the next hour, we unloaded all of the weapons, placed them in neat stacks on the lower deck, then covered them with a canvas tarpaulin.

Then, the men under Javier's command went below deck, then appeared several minutes later in civilian clothes.

"We're ready," Jesse said.

***

Darkness had fallen when *La Senora* pulled away from its moorings at the mouth of the tributary. As Alejandro guided *La Senora* eastward toward the Purus River, the vessel's engines hummed quietly and the only light in the pitch-black darkness was the two flood lamps on its bow. The river was calm and, along its banks, the towering rainforests stood like giant ghosts against the night sky. Intermittently, from the shore, I could hear the mournful cry of a howler monkey or the screech of scarlet macaw.

Four hours later, when *La Senora* arrived at the mouth of the Purus River, we could see the dim lights of the Federales checkpoint in the distance. Javier, Jesse and I were in the pilothouse.

"How should we do this?" Javier said.

"If they see two Americans on board, I think they'll be suspicious," Jesse said. "You and Alejandro talk to them and Johnny and I will hide in the storage room below and listen. If there's a problem, rap twice on the deck with your foot and we'll come out."

"That's a good idea," Javier said. "Anything else?"

"Tell your men we are approaching the checkpoint," Jesse said. "Tell them to stay calm and do nothing unless ordered."

Javier turned and barked the orders to his men.

Ten minutes later, *La Senora* was approaching the security checkpoint. Now, in the bright moonlight, we could see the guardhouse and boarding pier fast approaching. Constructed of concrete and steel, we could see two uniformed guards on the platform awaiting us. From the guardhouse, a giant steel arm extended across the river channel for some 40 yards to prevent any unauthorized vessels from passing. Atop the guardhouse, we could see two giant flood lights.

As Alejandro slowed the engines to a crawl, Jesse and I left the pilothouse and went into the storage area on the lower deck. Once we were safely inside, we heard the engines being reversed then, seconds later, *La Senora* came to a stop. Above us, we could hear Javier and Alejandro speaking Portuguese to the guards.

Jesse turned to me.

"What are they saying?" he said.

"They are checking Alejandro's and Javier's identities and the boat's registration," I said.

We waited several minutes as the conversation above us continued. Now we could hear Javier arguing with the guards. We could hear tempers flaring and raised voices.

"What are they doing?" Jesse said.

"The guards are claiming that the boat's registration papers are not legal. They're claiming the name on title doesn't match the IDs."

Suddenly, I remembered what Alejandro told me about the registration.

"Holy Christ! I had forgotten," I said. "Javier bought this boat from Alejandro, but the names were never transferred."

Above us, we could hear one of the guards shouting.

"No pueden pasar!" he said. "Regresa! Regresa!"

"They are refusing passage," I said.

"You mean we can't pass because the boat's registration is not in order?"

"That's right."

Then we heard the *La Senora*'s engines start again and the transmission shift into reverse. For several seconds, we waited as the vessel backed up for some 30 yards, then turned and headed back north. Once we were at a safe distance, Jesse and I came out of our hiding place.

"What happened?" Jesse said.

Javier had a dumbfounded look about him.

"The fault is mine," he said. "Our papers are not in order."

Then he proceeded to explain that, although he had paid Alejandro for the boat when he bought it, the title had not been transferred out of Alejandro's name.

Jesse should his head in frustration.

"So, what we do now, smart guy?" Javier said, shaking his head in frustration. "We can't take the weapons back."

"Give me a minute," Jesse said. "I'm thinking."

He turned to Alejandro.

"Is there a tributary on the east side of the Amazon which runs south and reconnects with the Purus?"

"There is," he said. "But you could never make it through there with *La Senora*. The water is too shallow and the channels are too narrow. She would run aground very quickly."

I studied him for a moment.

"Now, on the west side," he continued, "there is a tributary that runs south and reconnects with the Purus."

"How far is it to the tributary?"

"Three, maybe four kilometers."

"And how far before it joins the Purus?"

"Probably ten kilometers."

"Do you think *La Senora* could negotiate it?"

"Possibly," he said. "It's the wet season, so the channels should be full. On the map, it's called the Juan Gabriel tributary."

"Let go back upriver and try it."

Ten minutes later, we were back on the Amazon cruising westward to the Juan Gabriel tributary. When we arrived, the bow lights revealed a wide mouth from the Amazon into the tributary's main channel.

"I've been here before," Alejandro said. "Many years ago, I was here to deliver a woman and two children to a man that worked on a rubber plantation. As I recall, it's clear sailing to a point about six kilometers downriver, but there the channel starts to narrow."

"How narrow does it get?"

Alejandro laughed.

"Very narrow. Ten to twelve feet across."

***

Over the next thirty minutes, we had clear sailing with a wide berth on either side of the river, then, in *La Senora*'s bow lights, we could see the river channel starting to narrow. Moments later, Alejandro was slowing the engines to a crawl.

"This is the narrow point," he said.

In the lights, we could see that the channel narrowed down to a point no more than ten feet wide. At that point, the opening was clogged with an accumulation of river debris, which included downed trees, small limbs, plastic bottles, an old rusty bicycle and the rotting carcass of a dead cow.

"We'll never get through there," Javier said.

As the engine idled, Jesse, Javier and I stood on the ship's bow to decide our next move.

"Do you see that one large dead tree is holding most of the rubbish on the right side?" he said. "We could take a dinghy to shore, tie a rope to that one tree and, with nine of us pulling, we should be able to dislodge it. If we could move it, even slightly, the force of the water would send the collection of rubbish downstream and clear the way."

Then he turned.

"Alejandro," he said. "You stay with the boat and keep the lights steadied on the channel."

Moments later, Jesse, I, Javier and his six charges were paddling to shore in a dinghy. Once we were on land, we exited the dinghy and walked along the riverbank to a tiny spit of land that narrowed to a point where the river debris had accumulated.

For a long moment, Jesse studied the accumulation of debris, then he turned to Javier.

"Do you see how the large tree is situated?" he said. "If we could get the rope around the lower branches and pull it to the left, the entire mess should come apart."

"I think you're right," Javier said.

Jesse took his shirt off, then took one end of the rope and waded into the water. Then we watched as Jesse, waist deep in water, tied the end of the rope around several of the small tree's lower branches. Once he was back on dry land, all of us grasped the end of the rope and awaited Jesse's command.

"Pull toward yourselves at an angle," he said.

Javier barked the command to the others in Spanish.

Then, with the strength of all nine men, we all pulled in unison on the rope and, as we did, it barely moved.

"Hold it!" Jesse shouted.

He waded back into the water, retied the rope to the very end of the tree trunk, then returned to shore.

"That will give us more leverage," he said.

Then together, we all pulled again in unison. As we did, the small tree moved slightly. As it did, the force of the water rushed in and quickly swept away the accumulation of debris, leaving an opening in the channel some thirty feet wide.

Javier clapped his hands in sheer delight.

Thirty minutes later, we were back on *La Senora* and cruising down the main channel of the Purus to our drop-off point, a slight bend in the river that had a cross sitting high atop the riverbank. When Javier spotted the cross, he sent out three short flashes of light, which were answered in kind. When *La*

Senora pulled into shore, we were met with several men in military garb. Quickly, the weapons were unloaded and taken ashore. Once the goods were removed, we headed back up the Juan Gabriel tributary to the Amazon, then headed west. Around 1 a.m., *La Senora* docked again at the harbor at Tefe. Javier was ecstatic.

***

The following morning, Jesse and I left *La Senora* and took a motocab across town to El Banco de Brasiliero. There, upon presenting our identification, we collected $25,000 each. The money had been deposited by Cobre Consolidated Inc. in Rio de Janeiro. When we walked out of the bank, I turned to Jesse.

"What are you going to do now?"

"I'm not ready to go back to the States," he said. "I want to do some more exploring."

***

Two days later, *La Senora* was back in Iquitos and I was back at the breasts of my beloved Consuelo.

"I'm so happy to have you back safe and sound," she said.

"We've got money now," I said. "Let's get married."

She studied me for a moment.

"I could see myself as the matron of a rubber plantation," she said wistfully. "With a spacious, elegant house, lots of servants, lavish social outings and afternoon teas with friends. What do you think?"

I studied her for a moment.

"Are you giving up your militant ways?"

She laughed.

"It's time for me to settle down," she said. "I'll soon be 38. If I'm ever going to have a child, it's going to have to be soon."

We were quiet for a moment.

"I've seen ads in El Brasilero for small plantations near Tefe," she continued. "I saw one for R$112,000 reals, which claims to produce three thousand pounds of rubber a year. With the money we have, we could make a down payment and have funds left to operate on.”

“How close to town is it?”

“About six miles.”

“Let’s find something closer to Iquitos. I don’t want to get too far from Mother.”

“I must tell you I know nothing about rubber production.”

“Javier can teach you,” she said. “He worked four years on a rubber plantation.”

“So do you want to get married?” I said again.

“Why?”

“I want to have a child before I die.”

“We can have a child without getting married.”

“I want it to be legal and proper. For the child’s sake.”

She hesitated before answering.

“When you take the marriage vows, the spirit of a relationship changes. Without the vows, there is freedom. With the vows, the relationship becomes a chore. It becomes something you have to do rather than something you want to do. Let me think about it.”

***

The following morning, Javier made an announcement at the breakfast table.

“I am happy to report that *La Senora* is now officially in my name. All legal and official.”

“That’s a good thing,” Consuelo said. “I heard about what happened during the first mission.”

“That’s history now,” Javier said, dismissing the matter. “I have one more bit of news. El Jefe has another job.”

Both Jesse and I turned quickly to Javier.

“What is it this time?”

“He wants us to go into Colombia.”

***

Our second meeting with El Jefe and the fat man was three days later in an old hotel in Tabatinga. After *La Senora* was docked, we met Romero and he guided Jesse, Javier and me through the city's back streets to a dilapidated five-story hotel on the outskirts of town. High above, a neon sign read: Excelsior Hotel. After we walked up three flights of stairs, Romero guided us to a room. Once we went inside, we found El Jefe, the fat man and three guards. Instantly, El Jefe dismissed the guards and we sat down to talk. It was a short meeting.

"We want to move arms from a safehouse at Tabatinga to a point just north of Tres Fronteras in Columbia," El Jefe said. "There will be sixty rifles and ammunition, fifteen grenade launchers, and six mortars and loads. These will be delivered to a safehouse in Nuestra Madre, Colombia. **Once the weapons are in the new safehouse, there will be a small plane waiting that will return you to Tabatinga.**"

"Sounds more dangerous than the previous job," Javier said.

"It probably is," El Jefe said. "Security is tighter and it will take more planning."

"The fee will remain the same?" Jesse said.

El Jefe looked at the fat man.

"That is correct," he said. "The fifty thousand will be paid again."

***

An hour later, back in the pilothouse on *La Senora*, Javier was standing in front of a map of the Amazon.

"The goods will be picked up here," he said, indicating a point on the river just east of Tabatinga. "It is a small river village, so it should be secure. The pickup will be at a fish market."

"How are we going to get the goods from the fish market to the boat?" I asked.

"The goods will be in crates marked as machinery," Javier said. "We can pick them up, take them to *La Senora* and load them."

"How will we get them to *La Senora*?"

"The organization will provide a truck and driver," Javier said. "Once loaded, we will travel to the checkpoint at Leticia,

Colombia. Once we cross the border, we'll deliver the goods eight kilometers up the Arauca River to an abandoned oil field at Nuestra Madre."

The three of us fell silent.

"Once again, getting through the checkpoint will be the crucial part of the operation," Jesse said.

"How do you want to proceed?" Javier said.

"Before we plan anything," Jesse said, "let's make a dry run up the river to see what we're facing. This will give us clues as to how we can prepare ourselves."

"That's a good idea," Javier said.

***

The following morning, *La Senora*, with Alejandro at the helm, was back at Tres Fronteras, fast approaching the security checkpoint into Colombia at Leticia. As we neared, we could see the water gateway was up the Arauca River, a winding body of muddy water that snaked its way to the Putamayo River some sixty kilometers to the north. In many ways, the checkpoint was similar to the checkpoint we had seen on the Purus. A concrete and steel guardhouse with a boarding pier was jutting out into the water so passing vessels, once docked, could be boarded by guards. Beyond the boarding pier was a steel guard rail, some forty feet long, which opened and closed to allow or prevent vessels to pass. High atop the guard house, we could see two searchlights and a flag pole bearing the Colombian national flag.

Slowly, Alejandro eased *La Senora* up to the boarding pier, then shut down the engines. Moments later, a security officer, a short, chubby man in his late thirties with glasses, boarded *La Senora*.

"Registration! Identification!" he barked in Spanish.

Once Javier presented the registration papers and identification, the officer asked about what cargo we had and Javier explained the boat was empty since we were going upriver to pick up some machinery at Ponte Vedra. The officer then asked if we were carrying any drugs. When Javier said no, the officer then announced he wanted to check. He turned to the boarding pier and whistled. Instantly, a man with a drug-sniffing dog on a leash stepped out on the boarding pier and boarded *La Senora*. We waited while the officer and the dog went through the cargo hold and the empty passenger area. He asked about Jesse and me, and Javier explained we were crew members. Finally, satisfied that all was in order, he exited *La Senora*. Once he was back on the boarding pier, he motioned to another officer inside the guardhouse to open the security gate.

"Passe," he said.

Then he and the man with the dog exited La Senora.

Alejandro started the engines, then as *La Senora* eased away from the boarding pier, Jesse turned to me and Javier.

"How many total guards do you see?"

"Five," Javier said. "The one who came on board, the one with the dog and three others in the guardhouse."

"What about the one in the tower?" I asked.

"Where?" Javier said.

I pointed to the tower above the guardhouse.

Javier peered to the tower.

"Oh yeah. I see him now."

"So, there's a total of six guards. Let's make a note of that," Jesse said.

Once we had passed through the checkpoint gates, Jesse pointed ahead to two speedboats, one hidden on either side of the river channel.

"See those," he said. "Those are primary intercepts. Any unauthorized vessels that pass through the gate will have to deal with those."

Over the next ten minutes, *La Senora* glided quietly up the narrow river channel past small villages of indigenous people and intermittent groups of local fishermen plying their trade.

Moments later, after we rounded a sharp bend in the river, we could see another small guardhouse and two more speedboats. As before, high above the guardhouse, we saw floodlights.

"These are the secondary intercepts," Jesse said. "Any unauthorized boat that makes it past the primary will be pursued by these."

He turned to Javier.

"How much further to the drop-off point?"

"About eight kilometers to Nuestra Madre," Javier said. "There is a fork in the river ahead and Nuestra Madre is to the right. I haven't been here in several years."

Thirty minutes later, *La Senora* arrived at Nuestra Madre. On shore, the first thing we saw was a small group of thatched huts which were part of a fishing village and, beyond them, rusting oil derricks jutting into the morning sky.

"This is the drop-off point," Javier said. "El Jefe's men will meet us here. There is a landing strip on the backside of the oil field."

Ten minutes later, we were cruising back down the Arauca River toward Tres Fronteras. Inside the pilothouse, Jesse turned to Javier.

"We can't use *La Senora* for this job," Jesse said.

"Why not?"

"It's too slow and unwieldy. We need a speedboat that is fast and agile. We know the guards at the checkpoint are going to board every vessel to look for drugs. If they board and discover the weapons, we're going to have to fight our way out."

Javier peered at Jesse with a stupefied expression.

"We need a speedboat disguised as a fishing vessel," Jesse continued. "The sides should have reinforced steel, a steel-reinforced bow and a machine gun mounted on the rear."

"Machine gun?" Javier said.

"We can pretend to be fisherman and try to pass through quietly," Jesse said. "If they discover our goods, we'll have to make a run for it. When we do, they'll send the primary and secondary speedboats after us. With a detachable machine gun on the rear of our vessel, we can blow them away."

"Why detachable?" Javier asked.

"We can't pull up to the checkpoint in a boat with a machine gun mounted on the back!"

Javier laughed.

"I see your point."

"Here!" Jesse said. "Let me show you what we need."

Then he sat down at a table and began drawing a picture of the vessel he had in mind.

"The vessel should look like a fishing boat with nets dangling over both sides. We should have a detachable machine gun at the rear with the cargo hold and the bow protected by reinforced steel."

"Why do you need the steel plating around the cargo hold?"

"We're going to be carrying live ammunition and mortar rounds. If one of the speedboats pulls up beside us and starts firing, a single bullet into the mortar rounds will blow us all to kingdom come."

"And the steel reinforcements on the bow?"

"If we're discovered and have to make a run for it, we'll have to crash through the metal gate guarding the river's entrance. The steel reinforcements on the bow will protect the boat."

Javier peered at Jesse for a long moment.

"Where are we going to get a boat like that?"

"You'll have to talk to El Jefe," Jesse said. "Our success depends only on how well we plan."

***

On Thursday of the following week, Javier announced that the boat was ready for inspection. That afternoon, we made the trip back downriver to Tabatinga. At the harbor, we met Romero, who took us to a small boatyard on the outskirts of town. Upon arrival, he led us into a cluttered work shed where we saw the retooled fishing boat for the first time. *La Rosa* was a thirty-foot black and green fiberglass fishing boat with a pilothouse and lifts along the sides for hauling fishing nets in and out of the water. Once Javier had led us onboard, he opened the lower compartment and showed us the two 250-horse diesel engines with protected fuel tanks. Then, in the cargo hold, we looked at the steel plating for the sides and the bow.

"Looks good!" Jesse said. "It's one-inch steel and that's what we need."

"Now, what about the machine gun?" Javier said. "The

workmen are not quite clear about how you want the machine gun."

"I'll show you," Jesse said.

Then we returned to the stern.

"A base for the machine gun will be installed here," Jesse said, indicating the center of the stern. Once the base is installed, a .30 machine gun can be quickly mounted on it."

"Where will be machine gun be stored?" Javier asked.

Jesse looked around. He opened several storage compartments along the deck until he found one large enough to store a machine gun.

"In here," he said, showing the large compartment. "Also, be sure we have several thousand rounds of ammunition."

Javier turned and opened another storage compartment.

"It's in here," Javier said.

Jesse peered inside where he saw six boxes of .30 caliber ammunition.

"Good!" Jesse said.

"We'll take four men," Javier said.

"That's too many, Jesse said. "We only need two. Two men with rifles on the bow to destroy the flood lights at the secondary checkpoint. Also, be sure they're dressed as deck hands on a fishing boat."

"It will be done."

"What about registration?" Jesse said.

"It will be registered to The Brazilian Maritime commission in my name," Javier said. "All of the papers will be in order."

"I think that's everything," Jesse said. "What about *La Senora*?"

"She'll remain at Tabatinga until the mission is over."

"When do you want to do it?" Javier asked.

"Isn't there a full moon in the next few days?"

"Day after tomorrow night."

"We'll do it then," Jesse said.

"We'll be ready."

***

That night, back in Iquitos, I lay in Consuelo's arms.

"I want to get married after this mission," I said. "We'll have money and we can have whatever life your little heart desires."

"Are you sure that's what you want?" she said.

"I'm sure."

"You know I love you with all of my heart," she said.

"I know that. So, will you marry me?"

She smiled.

"Yes, I will."

A rush of pure joy filled my soul.

"I love you," I said.

"I love you too."

***

Two days later at twilight, *La Rosa*, the fishing boat that had been retooled for the second mission pulled out of the harbor at Tabatinga and headed upriver toward the security checkpoint at Leticia, Colombia. The dark green and black craft, with Javier at the helm, glided quietly across the brown water past the closed stores and shuttered markets of downtown Tabatinga. In the hold, covered with fishing nets, were twelve crates holding sixty rifles and ammunition, thirty grenade launchers and six mortars with loads. On board were Javier, Jesse, me and two soldiers from the organization, all dressed as fishermen. As we approached the security checkpoint, Jesse turned to Javier.

"Tell your men to keep their weapons out of sight and make no move unless ordered."

Quickly, Javier issued the orders.

Moments later, as we approached the boarding pier, we could see two uniformed guards waiting to meet us. Once the engines stopped, the first officer, a medium-height, late thirties man with a well-trimmed mustache, boarded *La Rosa*. From the first, he was all business.

"Registration and identification!" he said in Spanish.

Javier presented the requested papers.

After checking the documents, he asked Javier why he had

two Americans working on a fishing boat and Javier explained we were good fishermen. Then he went into the cargo hold. Upon seeing the fishing nets, he asked what was under them. Javier said more fishing nets. Then he asked if we were carrying any drugs. Javier said no.

For a moment, he studied Javier, then pulled a toy whistle out of his pocket and blew it. Moments later, another officer appeared on the boarding pier with a drug-sniffing dog. For several minutes, the dog sniffed around the boat, the nets in the hold and the pilothouse. Finally, the officer came back out to announce he had found nothing.

Then, the first officer, seeming satisfied that all was in order, started to exit the boat. As he did, he saw a copy of *La Verdad* sitting on the dashboard at the helm. Instantly, he froze.

"*La Verdad*? La papel de los Communistas?" he blurted out.

Instantly, he drew his side arm and pointed it at Javier.

"No! No!" Javier said. "We're only poor fishermen."

Then, the officer with the dog drew his sidearm and the first officer ordered Javier, Jesse and me off the boat and into the guardhouse.

Moments later, in the guardhouse, the first officer was going from one to the other of us asking again and again in Spanish who we were. Javier replied that we were simple fishermen who only wanted to fish the Arauca River. When the officer asked about *La Verdad,* Javier explained that we were not communists and the publication was a street hand-out he had received in Tabatinga. Finally, the first officer ordered the second one to stand guard over us, then went to a desk and started shuffling through papers.

Suddenly, Jesse fell to the floor, holding his chest. I knew he was putting on his heart attack routine as a diversion.

Startled, the first officer arose from the desk, turned to Javier and asked what was the matter with Jesse.

"He has a heart condition," I said in Spanish.

For a moment, the first officer knelt and leaned over Jesse. Then, seeing his guard was down, Jesse quickly reached up, grabbed his shirt in both hands and, in a single motion, stood up, spun him around up and threw him to the floor. As he did, his weapon fell out of its holster and Jesse grabbed it. As he did, I grabbed the gun hand of the second officer, wrested the gun from his grasp and pointed it at him. He raised his hands.

"Let's go!" Jesse said.

Moments later, we were racing back across the boarding pier to the boat. Once we were on board, the second officer rushed out of the guardhouse pointing a rifle at Jesse. Using the pistol I had taken from the second guard, I fired a single round and dropped him where he stood. Seconds later, the three of us had reboarded *La Rosa* and the twin engines roared to life. Then, at full power, the vessel lurched forward and crashed through the steel bars guarding the entranceway. Instantly, we heard a siren. Now the two diesel engines were at full power and *La Rosa* was racing up the Arauca River.

"It will take them at least five minutes to get their boats started and catch up with us," Jesse said. "Let's put as much distance between them and us as we can."

With that, Javier revved the engines and *La Rosa* was skimming across the moonlit water at break-neck speed. For several minutes, there was only the sound of *La Rosa*'s engines. Then, in the distance, we could hear the roar of the government speedboats behind us.

"Here they come," Jesse said. "Let's mount the machine gun."

Moments later, the machine gun was in place and ready for action.

Jesse turned to Javier.

"There is a bend up ahead," he said. "When we round the bend, slow down and let them catch up."

Then he turned to me.

"The moment you see their lights come around the bend, open up," he said.

Five minutes later, just as *La Rosa* rounded the bend, the two pursuit vessels were right behind us.

"Now!" Jesse said. "Aim for the lights!"

At the order, I opened up with the machine gun. Instantly, the lead boat exploded. In the resulting flash of light, we could see pieces of the boat, body parts and weapons flying into the water.

"Good aim!" Jesse said. "We've got another."

Now the second boat was closing fast behind us.

"Give her all she's got," Jesse yelled to Javier in the pilothouse. Suddenly, the engines revved and the vessel lurched forward at higher speed. The government boat was gaining.

"Now!" Jesse said.

Again, I opened up with the machine gun. Instantly, I heard the rounds glancing off the speedboat, then suddenly, it stopped and everything went dark.

"What happened?" Jesse said.

"I think I hit the engine and stopped it cold."

Over the next few minutes, all was quiet save for the roaring sound on *La Rosa*'s engines. Then, in the darkness ahead, we could see the black silhouette of the secondary checkpoint.

Jesse turned to Javier.

"Tell your men to take placements on the bow and destroy the searchlights. They can't hit us if they can't see us."

Quickly, the two men were in place.

Seconds later, the waterway ahead of us was suddenly flooded with light from the second guardhouse tower. Instantly, the fire from the two soldiers on the bow plunged the river into total darkness again. Behind us, closing fast, we could see the lights of the secondary speedboats.

"They're gaining!" I said.

"Let him have it!" Jesse said.

With that, I pulled the triggers on the machine gun again. No response.

"Holy Christ!" I said. "The machine gun has jammed."

Quickly, Jesse ducked inside the hold, pulled back the nets and took one of the grenade launchers from its case. Then, after I loaded it, Jesse put it to his shoulder and took careful aim. At the sound of the shot, the boat behind us exploded, sending shrapnel, boat pieces and men flying into the water.

Then silence returned to the river.

"I think that's all of them," Jesse said.

Then silence, save for the screech of a howler monkey or the squawk of a blue macaw, returned to the river.

"Looks like we did it again," Javier said.

Thirty minutes later, we reached the fork in the river, then took the channel northward. After another twenty minutes, we arrived at Nuestra Madre. In the moonlit night, the oil derricks in the abandoned oil field stood like giant ghosts against the night sky. Once we were docked, we were met with El Jefe and several other men in military fatigues. Quickly, *La Rosa* was unloaded and the weapons transported to a storage building on the backside of the oil field.

"Let's go!" El Jefe said.

"What about the boat?" Jesse asked.

"It will be destroyed," El Jefe said. "We can't leave any evidence."

Thirty minutes later, we were in a small plane soaring over the rainforests back to Tabatinga. Once the plane landed, we returned to the old hotel where the fat man was waiting.

"Good work!" he said. "The additional funds to your Banco de Brasiliero account will be deposited tomorrow morning."

After leaving the hotel, we returned to *La Senora* and went to sleep for the night.

***

The following morning, as *La Senora* headed upriver back to Iquitos, Jesse announced he was returning to the States.

"I'm missing Francesca," he said. "It's been three weeks since I've talked to her."

"When do you plan to leave?"

"Day after tomorrow."

"Can you delay it until after Sunday?"

"Why?

"I'm going to be married. I want you to be my best man."

He laughed, shook my hand and hugged me.

"Congratulations!"

***

Three days later, Consuelo and I were married at **Santa Monica Monastery,** a small Catholic Church in downtown

Iquitos that had been on the same site for 176 years. Maria and two of her friends made a wedding dress. Guests included Maria's friends, relatives and well-wishers. In the ceremony, Javier gave away the bride and Maria served as ring bearer. Jesse, in an ill-fitting black suit, served as the best man. The old women, mostly friends of Maria's, dabbed their eyes when Monsignor Gorge Valdez asked the groom to kiss the bride. Later, celebrants feasted on roast duck, green vegetables and boiled potatoes and red wine. Both Jesse and Javier danced with the bride and wished her many years of happy marriage.

That night, back at Maria's house, I asked Consuelo if there was anything else I could do to make her happy.

"I want a dog," she said.

"What kind of dog?"

"A small one with a happy face and fluffy ears. I can't be the matron of a rubber plantation without a dog."

"We'll buy one tomorrow."

She smiled.

"What can I do to make you happy?" she said.

"I want you to give me a child. A son."

"It shall be as you wish."

That night, as I drifted off to sleep, my heart was full. I had money in my pocket, the woman I loved as my wife and firm plans to make a new life with her.

***

Two days later, I saw Jesse off at the Iquitos airport.

"I talked to Francesca last night," he said, as we waited on the airport tarmac. "She can't wait for me to get back. She says she has decided to sell the Dark Bean and go back to New York. This fifty thousand dollars will probably be our ticket."

"How do you mean?"

"Uncle Marvin is in New York now and he has a small investment firm on Wall Street. With that money, he says he can arrange to make me a junior partner in the firm."

"So, you're giving up your freedom-loving ways and going for the gold?"

"I'm forty-four," he said. "Not getting any younger."

I laughed.

"What are you going to tell her when she asks about the extra fifty thousand dollars you have in your pocket?"

"I'm going to tell her you and I ran guns up and down the Amazon for a rebel guerilla organization."

I laughed.

"Do you think she'll believe it?"

"I'll have to wait and see."

I shook his hand, hugged him, then watched as he walked across the tarmac and boarded the plane that would take him to Lima, then back to the States. Once the plane taxied down the runway and lifted off into the air, I waved good-bye one last time. It would be twelve years before I would see him again.

***

Over the next few days, I settled in with Consuelo. I bought her a small dog at a local pet shop, a black and white terrier mix which she named "Coco." The following week, when *La Senora* started back upriver again for its regular run, the dog was with us in our cabin. Consuelo had bought all of the accessories needed to maintain him. A cage, a leash, toys and treats. He had quickly become a member of the family.

For several days now, Consuelo had been canvassing real estate offices near Iquitos for a small rubber plantation. We looked at one near Santa Rosa, but, at forty acres and 115,000 Brazilian reals, it was out of our price range. Now, as we cruised back downriver, we planned to inspect another at Sao Feliz.

When *La Senora* pulled into the small lagoon which served was Sao Feliz's harbor that afternoon, Alejandro dropped anchor and tied up the vessel. Once Consuelo and I were off the boat to go inspect the new plantation, she peered at the white sandy beach which ran along the edge of the water in front of the dock.

"When we return," she said. "I want to get some sun and let Coco play in the water."

Ten minutes later, we were in a motocab travelling across

town to the plantation we had seen advertised in the Iquitos newspaper. Upon arrival, we went to the main house and inquired about the owner. A servant said he had gone upriver, but would return around two that afternoon. We explained we would be back at the designated time.

Once we returned to *La Senora*, Consuelo took a beach towel and Coco, and started off the boat to the beach area in front of the dock.

"Be careful!" I said. "There are black caimans on the far side of the lagoon."

"I'll be watching," she said. "We'll be fine."

From the deck of *La Senora*, I watched as Consuelo, holding the dog, a beach towel and sun tan lotion, went down the gangplank to the sandy beach area along the shore. After spreading out the beach towel, she took Coco to the edge of the water. For several minutes, I watched as Consuelo threw a small rubber ball into the water, then giggled with delight each time the dog leapt in the water, retrieved it and returned it to her. Finally, believing she was safe, I left my vantage point on the deck and went into the pilothouse with Javier.

I had been in the pilothouse only a few minutes when, suddenly, I heard Coco barking frantically. Quickly, I ran back outside to the railing. Coco had swum out into some eight to ten feet of water and apparently could not make it back to shore. Consuelo, who had been dozing on the beach towel, suddenly awoke to the dog's barking and realized its dilemma. Quickly, she waded into the water to rescue it. As she did, I saw four black caimans, who already had their eyes on the dog, launched themselves off the shore and into the water.

"No! No!" I shouted, pointing to the caimans who were headed straight for the dog. "Caimans!"

She looked first to the dog, then to the caimans, the black ridges of their backs skimming through the water toward her. Despite the danger, she was determined to rescue the dog. Moments later, she had the dog and was rushing back to shore. Then, in sheer horror, my heart flew into my mouth as I watched the first caiman grasp her waist in its massive jaws, then go into a death roll to drown its victim. Again and again, I could see the creature's white belly flash on the water's surface as it completed its murderous task.

***

Over the next few days, I was lost in my misery. The ultimate depths of my sorrow had been reached. At the very moment I had achieved my greatest happiness, fate had suddenly snatched it away. I was like a small child lost in a great forest filled with savage monsters too fearsome to behold. For three days, I suffered living in a world without Consuelo. Then, I realized the only way to rid myself of this sorrow was to leave Peru. She was the reason I arrived and, now that she was gone, there was no point to remain. Two days later, I said my goodbyes to Maria and Javier. The old woman made the sign of the cross and blessed me. Javier hugged me and wished me good luck.

On the morning of September 29, 1983, I bought an airline ticket from Iquitos to Lima, Peru, then to Denver, Colorado. I knew Montana would be my final destination.

7 – Montana

1995

When I first decided to go to Montana to pursue my cowboy dream, I really didn't know where to begin. At the Denver airport, the airline agent said she had only one flight to Montana and that was to Missoula, so that was where I started. Once I got off the plane, I went straight to the airport rental car office to get a vehicle with plans to visit three towns: Big Fork, Colombia Falls and Kalispell. At the rental car counter, I saw a long line, so I decided to take a seat in the waiting area. As I seated myself, I noticed someone had left behind a newspaper, a small community publication that featured color photos of high-country properties surrounded by snow-capped mountains, crystal streams and giant stands of ponderosa pine. As I unfolded the paper, I glanced up at the masthead. It read: "*Hungry Horse News*, Hungry Horse, Montana."

As I waited, I thumbed through the pages, admiring the photos and glancing through the articles. Finally, I turned to the classified ads and, instantly, at the top of the page under "Ranch Properties," my eyes fell on an ad that was captioned: "Old-time rancher wants out." I read the details: "Working cattle ranch, 30 fenced acres, three-bedroom house, small cherry orchard, large barn, horse corrals, twenty-two head of polled Hereford cattle. $65,000."

Forty minutes later, when I finally rented a car, my earlier plans to visit the three towns on my list was forgotten. My thoughts were fixed on the property I had seen in the *Hungry Horse News*. So, when I pulled out of the Missoula airport, I headed straight north on Highway 93 toward Hungry Horse.

Over that afternoon, I drove the 70 miles from Missoula to Kalispell where I got a room for the night.

***

The next morning, I called the real estate agent in Hungry Horse and made arrangements to view the ranch. That afternoon, after almost an hour of following a constantly-winding road along the banks of the middle fork of the Flathead River, the agent negotiated his car up a steep mountain road to the ranch entrance. As we waited for the caretaker to open the gate, I could see that, at the ranch entrance, two log rails had been erected on either side of a swinging gate and a third had been bolted across the tops of the first two. High atop the third rail, in hand-carved letters, were the words "The Rocking J." The J had a little rocker on it like a rocking chair. I smiled at the sight. Finally, a weathered old cowboy, who later introduced himself as Joe Batters, emerged from the ranch house. As I watched him saunter across the yard, I liked what I saw. This was a real cowboy.

That afternoon, the real estate agent, Joe and I toured the ranch in a four-wheel drive vehicle. Just before sundown, we finished the tour and returned to the ranch house.

"This place can handle ten times more cattle than it has now," Joe said. "Mr. Russell has let it go down to almost nothing."

"Why are there so few cattle?" I asked.

"The owner's wife has been sick in a hospital up in Minnesota," the old cowboy said. "He hasn't been here in over a year."

"When is he coming back?" I asked.

"Not until he sells it," Joe said. "You can get it cheaper than the sixty-five thousand he's advertising. He accepted two previous offers, but the financing fell through both times."

"Do you know what the other offers were?"

"One was fifty-five thousand and the other was sixty-three thousand," Joe said.

"Thanks for the tip," I said.

Thirty minutes later, as the real estate agent pulled his car

back through the swinging gate, I asked him to stop. Then I got out and walked back to the entrance. There, standing in the ranch entrance with the "The Rocking J" logo overhead, I framed the spread—the ranch house, the barns, the corral, the pastures, the cattle and the snow-capped mountains beyond—in my mind. I loved what I saw. I knew this would be my new home. Ten days later, I closed the deal. I paid fifty-nine thousand dollars.

After the purchase, I kept Joe on as ranch foreman and explained that my long-term plan was to have eighty head of cattle on the ranch in two years. I made it clear that his job was to oversee the day-to-day ranch operations while I managed the business end. Before settling in, I hired Socorro Molina, a local, early thirties Mexican woman, as a housekeeper. Her duties were to manage the household and ensure that plenty of Sonoran-style Mexican food, my favorite, was kept on the table.

***

I guess it was only fitting that I, like any good cowboy, should marry the school marm. In February of 1984, I was attending a ranchers' convention in Great Falls when I met Sally Jean Ferguson. Sally, who was sixteen years my junior, was a history teacher at the local high and the daughter of a Missoula cattleman. From the first moment I saw her, a petite blonde with blue eyes, dressed in a navy-blue suit and escorting conventioneers down the aisles to their seats, I knew I was interested. Very interested. Later, at a convention luncheon, I negotiated myself to a seat at her table and, once the food was served, I lost no time making conversation. When the convention ended, I returned to Hungry Horse and she returned to Missoula, but I continued to pursue her. Finally, three weeks after the convention ended, she agreed to a date and I drove down to Missoula.

"That's a long way to drive for a date," she said that night as we ate Italian food in a Missoula restaurant.

"I told you I was interested," I said. "I'm just living up to my word."

Over the next two months, the 75-mile drive from Hungry Horse to Missoula became a standard part of my weekend routine. Finally, after dating for six months, we were married in the October of 1984 and, in early August of 1985, she bore me a son whom we named Joshua. After that, we settled in at the Rocking J to raise our son and build the ranch.

***

Ten years passed. Now, in mid-May of 1995, almost twelve years after leaving Peru, I had settled into an entirely new life. Our son Josh was now nine years old and a third-grader at the local elementary school. Sally Jean, who had taken a new teaching position in Hungry Horse after we were married, had recently been promoted to assistant principal. Both Joe and Socorro were still at the ranch and the Rocking J now had three hired hands, ninety-one head of cattle, fourteen calves and nine horses. Over the past ten years, horses and horsemanship had become a driving passion with me. I had become an expert horseman and I owned a magnificent Appaloosa stallion I had named Rebel.

***

On Sunday afternoons, Sally Jean and I made it a habit to clear the hired help out of the ranch house so we could have some private time. On one such Sunday afternoon, we were lounging in the sunroom and sipping iced tea. Our son Josh was gone with friends to a soccer game in Coram.

"The coyotes have been in the garbage again," I said, peering out the sunroom window at the strewn garbage and overturned cans at the corral.

"You've got to put secure lids on them," she said. "And fix them upright so the coyotes can't turn them over."

"I'll have Joe take care of it."

On the nearby coffee table, the telephone rang. I picked it up.

"Hello!"

"Johnny?"

Instantly, I recognized Jesse's voice.

"Jesse! What's happening?"

"It's hot as hell in New York," he said. "The market is down and the bears are growling."

"That's nothing new," I said. "All the bears know how to do is growl. What are you doing?"

"I'm bored," he said. "Bored. Bored. Bored. I need a change."

"So what are you going to do?"

"I been thinking about coming out there."

"To visit?"

"To live."

"Bullsh*t!" I said. "You can't drag your capitalist butt out of New York long enough."

"I'm serious."

"I'll believe it when I see it."

"I'm weary of New York," he said. "The rat race, the crazy people, the constant struggle. I don't need the money anymore."

"You haven't needed the money in years."

"Yeah, I know," he said. "But I've had it up to here this time."

A long pause.

"Montana is the most beautiful place on earth," I said.

"You say that about every place you go."

"Yeah, but I mean it this time. This is the last place on earth that's real. A man can put his feet on the ground."

"So, what's your situation these days?"

"I have a ranch to run," I said. "Every day, my life is occupied with cattle, employees, fences and livestock shows. I'm a busy man."

"My! My! You have settled in. So what do you think about me coming out for a visit?"

"Quit talking and do it."

"When would be a good time?"

"Anytime," I said. "I'd love to see you."

"Same here."

A long pause.

"I've got a limited partnership deal to close up in Montreal next week, then I'll start making plans to come out there."

"You really going to do it?"

"I sure am."

"I'll believe it when I see it."

"You're going see it."

"You're just talking."

"Give me a couple of weeks. This is the 15th of May," he said. "I'll call you right around June 5th and tell you when I'll be there."

"I'll be waiting."

"You'll be seeing me," he said. "Bye."

"Bye."

As I hung up the phone, Sally Jean peered curiously at me. "Who was that?"

"That was Jesse," I said. "He says he's coming to visit."

"Jesse? The one you spent all those years with?"

I nodded.

"What's he like?"

"Jesse?" I said, with a laugh. "He's crazy, funny, intelligent, complex, ambivalent.... I can't describe him. There are too many sides."

"Don't you think you should have spoken to me before you approved his visit?"

"You'll like Jesse," I said, trying to sound reassuring. "Jesse's a good guy."

"I probably will," she said finally. "If he's a friend of yours, I'm sure I'll like him."

***

On the evening of June 4th, it was long after dark when I returned to the ranch house. All that day, me, Joe and the other two hired hands had been at a swollen creek near Lost Horse Mountain where we had thirteen head of cattle trapped in mud. Heavy spring rains had flooded the stream along the base of the mountain, and when the waters receded with warming temperatures, huge swaths of deep mud were left along the banks. When the cattle tried to get to the stream to drink, they waded into the mud and become hopelessly ensnared. The more the animals struggled to free themselves, the deeper into the muck they sank. Of the thirteen animals that had become trapped, we managed to save only seven head.

When I came into the kitchen that night, Sally Jean and Socorro had dinner ready.

"There was a call from your friend Jesse," Sally Jean said, placing a platter of hot tortillas on the table. "He wants you to call him."

"I've got to get this mud off me first," I said.

***

Later that night, after a long, hot shower and a dinner of Socorro's extra-hot beef enchiladas, I called Jesse.

"The plane gets into Kalispell about 4 in the afternoon. We should be there around 5 p.m. on the afternoon of the 6th."

"Who is we?"

"Me and Francesca."

"She's coming too?"

"I can't spend nights without her."

"You think a New York City girl like her will be okay out here?"

"I don't see why not. If she doesn't like it, she can always leave."

I didn't want to belabor the point.

"I'll be waiting."

***

On the afternoon of June 6th, Sally Jean and I were waiting in the sun room when we heard the sound of a car horn at the ranch entrance. When I looked out the sun room window, I saw a black Lincoln Town car waiting at the gate.

Moments later, I was striding across the yard. After I swung the gate open, the Lincoln pulled into the ranch house yard.

"Welcome to the Rocking J," I said as Jesse got out.

"What a trip!" Jesse said, peering around at the mountains, the sky and finally at me.

We shook hands, then hugged one another.

"Hi, Francesca!" I said, as she came around the side of the car. "Long time, no see."

"Johnny! How are you?"

I pecked her on the cheek.

"It's good to see you again," she said.

I turned back to Jesse.

"Welcome to paradise," I said. "Feel that breeze?"

"Yeah."

"See those mountains?" I said, pointing to the peaks of Tea Kettle Mountain to the east.

He nodded.

"See that sky?"

Jesse peered toward the horizon.

"It's called Big Sky," I said, emphasizing the word "big." "Well, you haven't seen anything yet. Wait 'til I get you on a horse. I'm going to show you paradise."

"We'll see," Jesse said.

He reached out and touched my shoulder-length hair.

"What is this?"

"Well! When in Rome..."

"You used to say that was the mark of a hippie."

"Those days are gone," I said with a big laugh. "You and Francesca come on in the house. I want you to meet my wife."

***

Long before Jesse arrived, I had been making plans. Several days earlier, I had instructed Socorro to spruce up the guest room with fresh linens, new curtains and flowers. Also, I asked her to start planning a welcome party. That night, as planned, the table in the main dining room was set for eight people and included three huge platters of Socorro's extra-hot chicken fajitas, double chocolate fudge cake and four bottles of chilled chardonnay wine. At 6 p.m. sharp, the welcoming party, which included me, Sally Jean, my ten-year-old son Josh, Joe and Ticker Martin, a young, long-haired cowboy and the ranch's assistant foreman, were seated for the big event.

"All right, everybody," I said, rapping a spoon on the table

to get everyone's attention. "We're all here tonight to welcome my long-time best friend to the Rocking J. Anybody that knows me has heard me talk about this man at one time or another. So, without further ado, let me introduce my old friend Jesse Trubble."

This brought a round of mild applause.

"I want to propose a toast," I continued, offering up my glass of wine. "Here's hoping that Jesse and Francesca have a long and happy stay at the Rocking J."

With that, wine glasses clinked all around and the party was underway.

Over the next three hours, we ate fajitas, drank wine and chatted. From the moment they met, Jesse took an instant liking to Ticker and spent most of the night regaling him with stories about my and his adventures.

"Sounds like you two were quite a team," Ticker said.

"We did everything we ever set out to do," Jesse said. "Not everybody can say that."

After the meal, Socorro cleared the table and served more chardonnay. Then I passed around old photos of Jesse and myself down through the years. Near the end of the evening, the group sang "For He's a Jolly Good Fellow" in honor of Jesse. Finally, just after 11 p.m., when the last bottle of wine was empty, Joe announced that he and Ticker had to get to bed. After the cowboys left, Sally Jean showed Francesca the guest room and Jesse and I, with fresh glasses of wine, went out on the sun porch.

"What are you looking for out here?" I said.

"I just wanted to hang out for a while. I've got a bad case of the blues."

I studied him for a moment.

"Things can't be too bad," I said. "You've got your health. You're not broke and you're not dead. What else do you need?"

"I'm not sure," he said. "From time to time, I have this need to do something totally insane."

"That's nothing new."

"Yeah. I guess I always had a crazy streak in me."

"Anyway, I'm glad you're here," I said. "Let's do some

cowboying and enjoy ourselves. You and Francesca are welcome to stay as long as you like."

***

Later that night, in the ranch house's master bedroom, Sally Jean and I were getting ready for bed.

"So, what do you think of Jesse?" I asked.

"I'm not sure I can tell you."

"Tell me anyway."

"Are you aware of what happens to you when he's around?" she said.

"What do you mean?"

"You become a different person. He brings out your wild and crazy side."

I studied her for a moment.

"You're probably right," I said. "Jesse and I have done some pretty crazy things."

"It's almost like he casts a spell on you."

I laughed.

"It's not THAT weird."

"Yes, it is!"

I laughed again.

"I think you had too much wine."

"No!" she said. "I know what I see."

***

The following morning, Jesse and I went to the local veterinarian's office in Kalispell to get some paregoric for the calves that had the scours. Once we left the vet's office, I took Jesse to the local western store. When we walked out an hour later, he was wearing new jeans, cowboy boots, a hat and a western shirt. Back at the ranch, Jesse, dressed in his new cowboy duds, and I went to the corral where Joe and Ticker were installing an automatic watering device in a trough.

"Hey, boss!" Ticker said, when he saw Jesse. "Who is that dude you got with you?"

"Some polecat I caught in a trap up in the mountains," I

said. "He says he wants to play cowboy."

Ticker laughed.

"Let me smell them clothes," he said.

Then he stepped over and playfully sniffed Jesse's new clothes.

"Woooo-wee," he said, looking Jesse up and down. "He's a real dude now."

"Get out of here!" Jesse said, laughing good-naturedly.

The fun over, I turned to Joe.

"You got a horse saddled for Jesse?" I asked.

Joe pointed to a strawberry roan at the hitching rail.

Jesse looked at the horse.

"Think you can ride him?" I asked.

Jesse smiled.

"I learned to ride horses before I learned to ride girls."

"Well, show me your stuff."

With that, Jesse stepped up to the horse, grabbed the saddle horn and instantly swung up into the saddle.

"So far, so good," I said.

Jesse took the reins and calmly turned the horse from the hitching rail. Suddenly, he dug his boot heels into the horse's side. The animal instantly lurched forward and loped across the corral.

"Open the gate and let me take him for a run in the pasture," Jesse said.

Joe opened the corral gate. Then, like a true expert, Jesse arose in the saddle and the animal launched forward into a full gallop across the open pasture. Finally, on the opposite side of the pasture, Jesse turned the animal, then galloped back into the corral.

"Wow!" he said, with a hearty. "I haven't done that in thirty years."

"Where did you learn to ride?" I asked.

"When I was seventeen, my Uncle Marvin sent me to a dude ranch at San Angelo, Texas for the summer."

"You never told me that."

"You never asked."

***

The Red Dog Saloon was a little roadside honky-tonk along Highway 93 between Kalispell and Hungry Horse where local cowboys would go to shoot pool, drink beer and swap tales. That night, Jesse, I, Ticker and Joe went in to avail ourselves of its services.

"I see that you really love being on a horse," I said. "I'm glad to see that."

"Oh yeah," Jesse said. "I think I'm going to buy my own. Can I keep him in your barn?"

"Of course," I said. "What do you have in mind?"

"Maybe an Appaloosa or an Arabian," he said. "A horse that's fast and looks good."

"Tomorrow, we'll go over to the Lazy W," I said. "They've got a herd of prize Arabians for sale."

***

The following morning, which was a Saturday, Jesse, Ticker and I drove to the Lazy W Ranch at Coram. Once we arrived, the ranch owner, a fiftyish, red-faced Irishman, led us out to a corral where he had eight Arabians, five mares and three stallions.

"Arabians are gorgeous animals," Jesse said, as he, Ticker and I leaned on the corral fence. "Look at the big stallion. I'll bet that horse can outrun the wind."

"I'll bet he's got a good price tag too," Ticker said.

Jesse turned to the ranch owner.

"Could you saddle up the big stallion?" he said. "I'd like to ride him."

"That's a lot of horse," the owner said.

"I'm a lot of rider," Jesse replied.

While a hired hand saddled the stallion, Jesse turned back to the ranch owner.

"How much are you asking for him?"

"Seventeen fifty."

Ticker looked at Jesse.

"Seventeen fifty?" he asked disbelievingly. "You're going to pay seventeen fifty for a horse?"

"Seventeen fifty is nothing to me," Jesse said.

Ticker peered at him.

"It must be nice to be rich."

***

Some twenty minutes later, the stallion was ready and Jesse swung up into the saddle and put the horse through its paces. First, a trot, a slow walk and then a lope. Finally, Jesse took the horse out into the open pasture and put the animal into a full gallop. For several minutes, Jesse rode the Arabian back and forth across the pasture at full gallop. Finally, he returned to the corral. Once he dismounted, he walked back over to Ticker and me.

"What do you think?" I said.

"That is one running horse," Jesse said. "You can feel all that strength and power under you. That horse can sprout wings and fly."

For a moment, the three of us studied the animal.

"Look at his lines," Jesse said. "The small hooves, the thin legs. The strong, muscular back. What a gorgeous animal!"

"I think you like him," I said.

"I'm going to buy him," Jesse said.

"What are you going to call him?"

"Sultan!"

***

Over the next five days, with his own horse, Jesse got a good taste of life as a cowboy. Every morning, he would get up at dawn, have breakfast with the hands, then go with them to do whatever work was necessary on the ranch that day. Two days were spent mending fences near the base of Lost Horse Mountain. Another was spent building a feeding parlor in the north pasture. Still another day was spent dehorning young steers. By the fifth day, Jesse had become one of the boys.

***

At the Red Dog the following night, Jesse, Ticker, Joe and I were seated at the bar having some beers and waiting for a vacant table to play eight ball.

"I'm really happy with Sultan," Jesse said. "I tell you, that horse is greased lightning."

"He's fast," Ticker said, "but only on short runs. In a race of a mile or more, he wouldn't last."

"Why do you say that?"

"I know horses." Ticker said. "Those Arabians look good, but they don't have the fire and the grit to run a long race."

Jesse peered at him.

"Sultan will outrun anything at the Rocking J."

"Naw!" Ticker said. "He can't outrun my Jonah."

Jesse laughed.

"You think that little brown horse of yours can outrun Sultan?"

"Yep!" Ticker said confidently. "In a race of a mile or more, I guarantee that Jonah can outrun him. A smaller horse like Jonah will outlast that Arabian every time."

"I got five hundred dollars that says your little brown horse can't outrun Sultan."

"Five hundred dollars?" Ticker said.

"Yeah," Jesse said again. "My five hundred dollars says your horse can't outrun Sultan."

"Look!" Ticker said. "I been around horses a lot longer than you and I know what I'm talking about."

"Then prove it!" Jesse said.

"Okay," Ticker said. "Let's have a race."

Ticker looked over at me.

"Do you think Jesse's Arabian can outrun Jonah?"

I laughed, not wanting to take sides.

"I've seen Jonah run and I can tell you he's tough, real tough in a long race."

"That's what I told him," Ticker said, "but he doesn't want to believe it."

Jesse was adamant.

"Again, I've got five hundred dollars cold cash that says Sultan can outrun your little horse."

Ticker, obviously irritated, looked at Jesse.

"You know," he said, "I get sick and tired of listening to you bragging about your money. Money is not everything."

Jesse smiled.

"It's not everything, but if you've got it, you might as well use it to prove your point."

The answer only served to rub salt in the wound.

"Okay," Ticker said. "We'll race."

"You got five hundred dollars?" Jesse said.

"I can get it."

"Who will hold the money?" Jesse said.

He looked at Joe.

"No, not me!" Joe said, "I don't want any part of this."

"Then let Johnny hold the money," Jesse said.

"I'm not sure I want any part of this either," I said.

"You're the one that should hold the money," Jesse said. "We want to settle this."

I looked from one to the other.

"You guys sure you want to do this?"

"I'm sure," Jesse said.

"Same here."

"Okay! I'll hold the money."

"When do we race?" Jesse said.

"Saturday," I answered. "The regular course."

***

That night, in the ranch house's master bedroom, Sally Jean called my hand about spending so much time with Jesse.

"Why have you been neglecting me?" she said.

"What are you talking about?"

"Over the past week, you've ignored me," she said. "Ever since Jesse arrived, you don't have time for anybody but him."

"That's not true," I replied.

"It is true!" she countered. "Outside of this bedroom, you haven't spent ten minutes alone with me since he arrived."

I studied her for a moment.

"I don't mean for it to appear that way. Me and Jesse go back a long way."

"I know," she said, "but I feel like an outsider when he's

around. That man puts some kind of spell on you."

"Please!" I said, reaching to turn out the light. "Don't start that again. Let's go to sleep."

***

The following morning, Jesse and I shored up the fence posts at a gap at Tea Kettle Mountain. Once we were finished, we gathered the tools, mounted our horses and started back to the ranch.

"Francesca is unhappy," he said. "She wants to go back to New York. She's bored. She says after she's done her nails and her hair, there's nothing to do but watch television."

"Why did you ask her to come here?"

"I wanted her with me. If I had left her in New York, I would have missed her. She and your wife are like day and night. Sally Jean is a cowgirl and grew up around horses and these mountains. Francesca didn't."

"I was afraid of that," I said. "When is she leaving?"

"When we get back to the ranch, I'm taking her to the airport at Kalispell."

***

On Thursday, two days before the race, I took Jesse around the race course. The "course," as the local cowboys called it, was a two-mile stretch from the Rocking J's front entrance along the dirt road to Tea Kettle Mountain, then across a pasture to the granite peak called Cathedral Rock. From there, it was a straight shot through an aspen grove to Piute Canyon, then along a dry creek bed for a quarter of a mile and finally back along the road to the Rocking J entrance.

"Riders are always on their own along the road," I said as we rode along the dirt road to Tea Kettle Mountain. "If a car is coming during the race, each rider has to handle his horse the best way he can. It's a test of nerves."

A mile later, at Cathedral Rock, I counselled him further.

"Now, here the trail through the aspens is a straight shot. For almost two hundred yards, you can just give your horse its head. Let him run as fast as he can because speed is what's important here."

Twenty minutes later, as we rode along the dry creek bed, I offered more advice.

"It's usually pretty soft in the middle of the trail here," I said. "Especially after a rain. When it's soft, the horse will mire up and this will slow it down. That's why it's best to stay on the edges where it's dry and the trail is firmer."

As I approached the point in the "course" where the creek bed leg ended and the dirt road began again, I stopped and pointed through the trees.

"See right there?" I said. "As you come up on the road again, you can look through there and see if any cars are coming."

"I noticed that," Jesse said. "There is a very definite advantage in that."

Finally, as we rode back along the dirt road to the ranch entrance, I had one more piece of advice.

"Look how the loose gravels have collected along the edge," I said, indicating the small rows of heaped gravels along the edge of the dirt road. "Be sure you keep your horse out of those. If he gets in those loose gravels, he'll go down and so will you."

Quietly, we rode back along the dirt road to the ranch entrance.

"Remember, don't wear your horse out too fast. Save most of him for the stretch along the road back to the ranch. That's where most races are won or lost."

"Thanks for the advice," he said.

"If I were you, I would make some practice runs," I said. "I'm telling you, Ticker's little roan is tough to beat. I've seen him race other cowboys and his Jonah is small, but gritty and mean in a race."

***

By 9 a.m. the following Saturday morning, a huge crowd of cowboys from the surrounding ranches had gathered at the Rocking J entrance for the big race. Over the past two days,

Jesse had taken the Arabian around the course seven or eight times, learning the trail, strategizing, trying to determine the advantages and disadvantages. Now the moment of truth was near.

At 9:30, I stood at the ranch entrance with a small starting pistol in my hand. Behind me, Ticker and Jesse were standing by their horses.

"Okay," I said. "The race will start here and be run around the regular course that both of you are familiar with. The finish line is right here," I said, indicating a line I had drawn in the gravels. "The first rider to cross this line will be declared the winner and get the thousand dollars."

I turned back at Jesse and Ticker.

"Mount up!"

With that, both Jesse and Ticker swung up in the saddle, then I backed up both horses and riders behind the starting line.

"Ready?"

Jesse nodded.

Ticker nodded.

I fired the starting gun and, instantly, the two horses lunged forward into a full gallop along the dirt road toward Tea Kettle Mountain. Off the starting line, the Arabian took the lead. By the time the horses had vanished out of sight around the curve of the mountain, the gathered cowboys could see the Arabian had a commanding lead.

Several minutes later, the two horses came into view again as they made the turn from the road to the pasture. At that point, the Arabian was ahead of the roan by some thirty to forty lengths. Then, as they streaked across the pasture, the little roan, its short legs churning ferociously, pulled to within five lengths of the Arabian.

As the riders turned at Cathedral Rock to make the run through the aspens, the Arabian seemed to take on new life. During the straightaway, Jesse gave the horse its head and, by the time the horses reached the dry creek bed, the Arabian still held a commanding lead. Now, as the two riders raced along the creek bed back to the dirt road, me and the cowboys lost sight of them again and waited for them to appear again on the road. Seconds later, the two horses darted out of the creek bed on to the dirt road.

Now, all of the cowboys stepped out into the middle of the road to watch as the two horses headed for the finish line. With some 200 yards left in the race, they were urging on Ticker and his horse.

"Run, Jonah! Run!" shouted one cowboy.

"Spur him!" shouted another.

Instantly, the little roan came alive. All the reserves Ticker had been saving were now being released. Although the Arabian was galloping at full speed, the roan pulled up beside it. The two horses were running neck and neck.

Suddenly, the smaller horse, its eyes fiery with competitiveness, bit out at the Arabian.

"Hey!" Jesse shouted. "Stop that!"

With that, the Arabian, fearful of the other animal's teeth, found new strength and pulled ahead again. Moments later, Ticker started whipping the roan and, suddenly, the smaller horse, snorting and running for all it was worth, was running side-by-side with the Arabian again. Then, as the two horses— each galloping neck in neck with every ounce of energy they possessed—headed for the finish line, the roan savagely bit out at the neck of the Arabian a second time.

"Stop that!" Jesse shouted again.

But it was too late.

The Arabian, fearing the roan's teeth, threw its neck to the side to escape the smaller horse's attack. As it did, the roan moved in closer to bite again and, in doing so, sharply bumped the Arabian's shoulder and sent it into the loose gravels along the edge of the road. Instantly, the Arabian lost its footing and, after slipping momentarily in the gravels, went down on all fours. As the animal went down, Jesse was thrown off its back into an embankment along the side of the road.

Immediately, Jesse got up and dusted himself off. He seemed okay. Then he turned to the horse. The Arabian, its eyes still wide with fear, struggled to its feet. Finally, after ascertaining that the animal had no broken bones, Jesse remounted, then dug his spurs into the horse's side and galloped back toward the ranch.

When he arrived back at the ranch entrance, he could see

all the cowboys gathered around Ticker, congratulating him.

"Tough luck!" Ticker said when Jesse came riding up.

"Tough luck, my ass!" he said. "You cheated!"

"What?!" Ticker asked.

"You know what happened!" Jesse said. "Your horse bumped Sultan while he was trying to bite him, we got into the gravels and went down."

"I didn't do anything," Ticker said. "The horse did it."

"You're a liar!" Jesse said angrily, dismounting. "You deliberately bumped your horse into mine."

"Nobody cheated you," Ticker said. "You can't stop a horse from trying to bite another horse in a race."

Jesse glared at Ticker.

"I know what happened!" he said. "You cheated, you son-of-a-bitch!"

Ticker's hair curled at the words.

"Don't you call me a son-of a bitch," he said, and started for Jesse.

Instantly, I stepped between the two.

"Cool it!" I said. "Just cool it! Both of you!"

I looked around at the other cowboys. They were waiting for me to announce the winner.

"Okay, boys," I said, holding up the thousand dollars. "The winner in this race is Ticker Martin. He crossed the line first and I'm declaring him the winner."

A triumphant yell went up from Ticker and the assembled cowboys.

With that, I turned to Ticker and counted out ten one-hundred-dollar bills. Ticker, money in hand, raised his arms in a victory gesture. The assemblage of cowboys, toasting with beer cans, gave a round of joyous yells.

For a moment, Jesse watched the victory celebration, then sullenly turned and led his horse back toward the stables.

***

For two days, the matter wasn't mentioned.

On the third night after the race, we were all drinking beer at the Red Dog when Joe told Jesse his horse had run well and, for somebody who had been riding regularly for only a month, he ran an extraordinarily good race.

"I won the race as far as I'm concerned," Jesse said.

"Forget it," Joe said. "It was all done in good fun."

"Losing five hundred dollars is not my idea of good fun," Jesse said. "Especially when I feel like I was cheated."

***

The following morning, Johnny and I were up at 8 a.m., had breakfast and were in the saddle headed for the mountains. At the corral, we saw Joe, Ticker and two other cowboys branding calves.

"Joe!" I called. "Are you going to need me today?"

"Naw! We only got about twenty head," Joe said. "We should be finished by lunch."

"Me and Jesse are going to ride over to Dead Man's Mountain," I said. "We should be back before lunch."

Joe nodded.

With that, Jesse and I trotted our horses out of the corral and into the open pasture.

"Come on," Jesse said. "I'll race you to Cathedral Rock."

Instantly, both horses lurched forward into a full gallop and raced some 200 yards across the pasture. By the time we reached the upturned granite spires of Cathedral Rock, the Arabian was ahead of my Rebel by some fifty feet. Finally, we pulled up and put the horses into a walk at the foot of Cathedral Rock. Both animals were breathing heavily.

"Boy!" I said. "That Arabian can run."

"Sultan is the fastest horse around," he said. "He didn't really get a chance to show his stuff in the race. If he had, he would have won."

"Come on!" I said. "Forget it! It was just a horse race."

"I got f*cked," he said. "And you know it."

"No, you didn't," I said. "Ticker won the race. It's nothing new for one horse to try to bite another horse during a race."

"Johnny!" he said. "He deliberately bumped his horse into mine. That's cheating as far as I'm concerned."

"Horses will do that," I said. "When two horses are racing

side by side, they will fight each other to get ahead and the riders have nothing to do with it."

"I don't see it that way," he said.

"Let it go," I said. "It's no big deal. These cowboys race horses all the time. When they lose, they accept it and go on."

"I don't want to let it go," he said. "I don't need these f*cking rednecks."

I could feel my anger rising at his comment.

"You're a cry-baby," I said. "You hear me! You lost and now you can't take it."

"F*ck you!" he said. "Just whose side are you on here?"

"I'm on the side of what's fair! You aren't man enough to admit that the horse might have done it. You're a cry-baby!"

"F*ck you!" he said, reaching out and shoving my shoulder.

For a moment, I glared at him.

"What are you doing?" I said, "You don't shove me."

Instantly, I reached out and roughly shoved his shoulder.

"Come on!" he said, red-hot anger in his face. "Get off that horse!"

Instantly, both of us dismounted. For a moment, we glared at one another, then we circled one another. Suddenly, Jesse threw out a right hand and hit me in the face.

I raked my hand across my face. I felt blood.

"You never slap me!" I said. "You understand?"

With that, I lunged at him and threw a hard right hand into his mid-section. For a moment, he doubled over in pain.

Then, his face livid with anger, he straightened up and, with a running go, tackled me. Then together, we fell on the ground tumbling, rolling, fighting, rolling, tumbling, fighting.

When the tumbling stopped, I was sitting on top of Jesse, hitting him again and again in the face. Suddenly, he threw his legs over my head from behind like a wrestler and flung me off. Now, on his feet again, he waited for me to get up. Once I was on my feet again, we circled one another and I unloaded a huge right hand to his jaw. For a moment, he was dazed, then, after regaining his senses, he suddenly lunged forward and tackled me again. This time, when the tumbling stopped, my head was in a rock pile and Jesse, using both hands, was banging my head against the rocks. Then, in a desperate effort to find something to defend himself with, my hand found a small rock within the pile. Grasping the rock firmly, I brought the rock around and slammed it into the side of his head. For a moment, his eyes took on a glazed look, then he fell backward. He was out cold.

For several minutes, I tried to regain my senses. Finally, I managed to raise myself on one knee. Then I felt the side of my head. A huge, hard knot was forming. I stood up and staggered to a nearby stream where I wet a handkerchief and held it to my bleeding face. Then, I saw Jesse, who had regained consciousness, sitting upright on the ground.

"Ohhhhhh..." he said, touching his head.

Still holding the wet handkerchief to my face, I walked over.

"Come on!" I said, calmly offering my hand. "Let me help you..."

"Get the f*ck away from me!" he shouted.

"Come on!" I said. "This whole thing was stupid. Just plain silly."

Again, I offered my hand.

He glared at me.

"I told you to get away from me."

"I'm sorry all this happened. Let me help you."

"F*ck you!" Jesse said, trying again to get up. "All these years I thought you were my friend. Now I know what an asshole you are."

"I'm not going to let you shove me around," I said. "Now come on. I'm sorry."

"Kiss my ass!" he said. "You're no friend of mine."

Slowly, as I watched, Jesse dragged himself to his feet, staggered uncertainly for a moment, then went to his horse and mounted. Then, turning the animal back toward the ranch, he galloped off.

***

Ten minutes later, when I arrived back at the ranch, I saw Joe, Ticker and the other cowboys were still branding calves at the corral. Then I saw Jesse's horse, standing untethered nearby. For a moment, I glanced at the cowboys, then quickly dismounted. Suddenly, at the ranch house, I heard a door slam and I saw Jesse, suitcase in hand, striding across the yard.

"Jesse!" I called.

"I'm out of here!" he shouted.

"Please don't do this!" I said. "There's too much karma!"

"F*ck the karma!" he said, unlocking the trunk of the Lincoln.

With that, he slung the suitcase into the trunk, then turned and got into the car. In an instant, the mighty engine roared to life.

"What about your horse?" I said.

"F*ck the horse!" he shouted as he pulled the Lincoln across the yard to the gate. "Open the God-damn gate!"

"Jesse, don't do this!"

"I can do what I damn well please," he shouted. "Open the gate!"

The nose of the Lincoln, eager to get out, was bumping the metal cross bars of the gate.

"Wait a minute!" I said.

With that, I walked briskly across the yard and opened the gate.

"Don't leave it like this!" I pleaded. "Please don't leave it like this!"

"F*ck you!" he shouted again through the open car window. "You're no friend of mine!"

With that, he gunned the engine, and the Lincoln, with spinning tires and a flurry of flying gravel, passed under the Rocking J entrance.

"F*ck YOU!" I said, in a full flush of red-hot anger.

Then, grabbing several rocks from the side of the road, I threw them at the retreating Lincoln as it stormed off down the mountain road. One of the stones glanced off the rear window. Helplessly, I watched as the car disappeared around the curve of Tea Kettle Mountain in a huge cloud of dust.

Angry beyond words, I kicked the gravels, slammed the gate shut and started back across the yard. The cowboys at the corral, who had been watching, quietly returned to their calf branding. As I strode back to the house, I saw Sally Jean standing under the carport. She had seen the entire episode.

"I've never seen you act like that," she said.

"Well, you have NOW," I said angrily, brushing past her. "That son-of-a-bitch. I'll never talk to that cry-baby again. Never."

Sally Jean, shaking her head incredulously, watched as I opened the door and started into the house.

"If you ask me, it's the best thing that could have happened," she continued. "Now maybe you'll start paying some attention to me and Josh."

I peered angrily at her. Then, without a word, I went inside and slammed the door behind me.

8 – Montana II

2005

The year was 2005. In April of that year, Sally Jean and I celebrated my sixty-fifth birthday with a big cake and a bash at the ranch. All of the cowboys, except Joe Batters, were present. In the spring of 2003, Joe and Ticker had been branding calves at Piute Pass. They were almost finished when Ticker noted that the branding fire needed to be replenished. As Joe turned to put more wood on the fire, he suddenly stopped, grabbed his chest, then fell to the ground. Quickly, Ticker threw him over his horse and started back to the ranch. Back at the ranch, we rushed him to the local hospital, where he was pronounced dead of a heart attack. The following day, I named Ticker the new ranch foreman.

Our son Josh was now twenty years old and a junior at the University of Montana in Missoula, where he was studying ranch management. On weekends, he would return to the Rocking J to pursue his interest in mountain bikes. Most Saturdays would find Josh and me under the ranch carport tinkering with one of his bikes. On one particular Saturday morning, Sally Jean was watching as Josh and I put a new front tire on one of the bikes. The tire had been mounted on the rim and now I was tightening the bolts to secure it on the fork.

"Come on, Daddy!" Josh said. "Tighter."

I tugged again on the socket wrench.

"Uhhhh!" I grunted.

"More!" he said. "I don't want the wheel to come off during a race."

"It's tight enough."

"No! It needs at least another half a turn."

Amused, I studied him for a moment, then shook my head.

"He's just like his father," Sally Jean said. "He's got a mind of his own."

I laughed.

"I'll tighten it some more."

"I'll tell you when it's tight enough," he said.

I placed the socket wrench over the axle bolt again and slowly started turning, all the while watching Josh for a signal.

"A little more...little more....little more....Whoa!" he said, holding up his hand like a traffic cop.

I removed the wrench.

"Perfect!" he said. "Absolutely perfect."

Seconds later, Josh had the bicycle upright and was about to mount.

"Whoa!" I said, reaching down to squeeze the bicycle's rear tire.

"You're going to need a new tire on the back too," I said, pinching the rubber to demonstrate the worn spot. "It's worse than the front."

"Yeah," he replied. "Can we go into town and buy a new one?"

"We'll do that next Saturday," I said.

Satisfied, he mounted the bicycle and started pedaling around the ranch house yard. As I watched him ride the mountain bike, I suddenly heard the phone ring in the kitchen.

"I'll get it," said Sally Jean.

Then, as I bent down and started gathering up the tools, I heard her call.

"Johnny!"

"Yeah."

"It's a telephone call for you."

"Who is it?"

"I don't know. It's long distance."

I tossed the wrenches into the toolbox and closed the lid. Then I walked up the steps, opened the kitchen door and took the telephone.

"Hello."

"Long distance calling for Mr. John Chance," the operator

said.

"This is he."

"Go ahead," said the operator.

For a moment, I listened and heard nothing.

"Johnny?" the voice said.

The first syllable of the first word was the only clue I needed to know it was Jesse. At first, I didn't respond.

"Johnny?" the voice said again.

"Hey, Jesse!" I said finally.

A long, chilly pause.

"How you doing?" he asked.

"I'm doing okay."

Another long, chilly pause.

"Why are you calling?" I asked.

Another long pause.

"I want to come see you."

When I first heard the words, I couldn't believe it.

"You want to come see me?"

"Yeah."

"Last time I talked to you, you said you'd had enough of me."

"That was a long time ago."

"What's different now?"

Another long pause.

"I didn't call you to fight with you," he said.

I could hear him coughing in the background.

"I can't change what I said or did ten years ago," he said. "I was pissed, you were pissed. Both of us said some things we shouldn't have."

"You didn't have to leave it like you did," I said. "You could have tried to patch things up before you stormed off."

"The past is the past," he said. "We've got too much karma tied up together to let one incident keep us apart."

Another long pause. More coughing.

"My life has changed a lot since the last time I saw you," I said finally. "I'm a busy man."

"Too busy to spend a few days with me?"

I was totally lost for an answer.

"You know, Jesse," I said. "Your calling like this is sort

of.... surprising."

"I guess it is," he said. "I didn't call you to beg. Somehow, I thought you might have forgotten what happened all those years ago. I see you haven't."

Another long pause.

"I can't see that anything positive could come of it," I said. "Like I told you, I'm really busy these days."

Another long pause.

"Any chance you'll change your mind?"

"I don't think so."

"Okay," he said. "Take care of yourself. Bye."

With that, I heard the other end of the phone go dead. Then, as I slowly hung up the telephone, I heard Sally Jean call from the sun room.

"Who was it?"

I didn't answer at first.

"Honey, I'm talking to you."

"I heard you," I said.

"Who was it?" she asked again.

"It was Jesse."

Instantly, she was back in the kitchen.

"What does HE want?" she said.

"He wants to come visit."

"To visit?" she said. "And....??!"

"I said 'no'!"

"You remember what happened last time. You and he tried to kill each other."

I didn't reply. I was lost in thought.

"You're not going let him come back again, are you?"

I didn't answer.

"Well, ARE you?"

"No!" I said. "It's over."

"That man is trouble," she said. "I can tell you that."

I peered at her.

"There is nothing you can tell me about him," I said. "I've known him all my life."

"You're a fool if you let him come back."

"I told you I said 'no.' Okay?"

With that, I started back to the carport.

"Where are you going?"

"I've got to fix the water trough in the corral," I said, not looking back.

***

That night, Sally Jean, Josh and I were seated at the dinner table in the main dining room preparing to dive into a feast of Socorro's chili rellenos with rice, beans and flour tortillas when the phone rang.

"I'll get it," Sally Jean said.

She got up from the table and went to the phone.

"Hello!"

A short pause.

"Who's calling?" Sally Jean asked, looking warily at me.

She put her hand over the mouthpiece and listened.

"It's Francesca," she said.

For a moment, I didn't get up. I knew that something was amiss. For a long moment, I peered at Sally Jean as she held the telephone with her hand over the receiver. Then, suddenly, deciding to face whatever was awaiting, I got up and took the telephone.

"Francesca!" I said. "This is Johnny. What's going on?"

"Jesse wants to come see you."

"Why?" I said. "You know what happened last time."

"Yeah, I know," she said. "He got pissed and you got pissed and..." She didn't finish.

"I don't want to see him," I said. "He destroyed all the karma we had when he threw his little fit."

"What a total idiot you are, Johnny Chance," she said. "Jesse is the best friend you ever had. Now, over one little incident, you're going to write him off."

"He didn't hesitate to write me off ten years ago," I said.

A long pause.

"He's dying, Johnny," she said, her voice breaking. "The chemical he inhaled while you and he were in Vietnam has eaten up his lungs."

The instant I heard those words, I felt a cold chill course up and down my spine.

"Doctors removed his right lung two weeks ago," she continued. "They sewed him up and said there was nothing else they could do. He's not going to live long."

I drew a quivering breath. For several seconds, I didn't answer.

"Johnny?" she said. "Are you still there?"

"I'm here," I said finally. "I didn't know he was ill."

"Well, he is," she said. "Very ill."

I didn't respond. My mind was racing in all directions.

"You're all he ever talks about," she said. "He just wants to come see you one last time."

I heard the words, but I didn't reply. There was a whirlwind in his mind.

"The least you could do is call him," she continued. "It would mean so much to him."

I didn't know what to say.

"Could you do that, Johnny?" she said. "Could you just please call him?"

Another pause.

"What's the number?"

As I reached for a pen, I could see my hand was trembling.

"Will you call him?"

"Just give me the number."

"In New York, 212-908-6604."

I jotted down the number.

"212-908-6604?" I said, reading back the number.

"That's right."

With that, I said good-bye and hung up the telephone.

"What is it now?" Sally Jean asked.

I inhaled, shook my head indecisively and retook my seat at the dinner table.

"Jesse's dying," I said finally. "He wants to come see me one last time."

She took a long, hard look at me.

"So, are you going to let him come?"

"I'm not sure."

"This morning, it was 'no.' Now it's 'not sure.' Which is it?"

"Let's eat. We can discuss it later."

***

That night, something truly strange happened to me. The tiny whirlwind that had been forming in my mind with the telephone call now became a mighty storm. When I went to bed, I knew I wouldn't be able to sleep. At 2 a.m., I got out of bed, restless and fitful. To calm my nerves, I tossed off a shot of straight whiskey. Finally, at 3:30, I managed to doze off.

The following morning, after breakfast, I met Ticker at the corral and we went to the barn to check the saddle sores on an Appaloosa stallion. As I ran my fingers along the horse's underbelly, feeling the lumpy knots where the cinch strap had worn callouses in the flesh, my mind was far, far away. When I withdrew my hand, Ticker waited for an appraisal. There was none. With that, he bent down to inspect the saddle sores himself.

"They should be healed in a few more days," he said, withdrawing his hand. "I'll put more medicine on and I think he'll be fine."

He peered at me. He knew I hadn't heard a word he said.

"The herd over at Tea Kettle Mountain needs to be moved to the north pasture," he said finally. "Me and Slats are going to do that today."

"That's fine," I said, "Go ahead."

I turned and started back to the ranch house.

"Boss?" Ticker called.

I stopped and turned.

"Is everything okay?" he said.

I took a deep breath. I was trying to calm himself.

"Yeah," I said. "Go ahead and move the cattle to the north pasture. I'll talk to you tonight."

Back at the ranch house, Sally Jean and Socorro were cleaning up the breakfast dishes. I walked into the kitchen, stopped at the sink and poured myself a glass of water.

"I thought you were going to move the herd to the north pasture today," Sally Jean said.

I didn't answer. I took a long drink of water and stared out the window.

"What's wrong?" she asked.

I shook my head.

"It's Jesse, isn't it?" she said. "That man has cast his spell on you again."

Suddenly, I turned and glared at her.

"Don't start that again!"

"My advice," she said, "is to leave that man out of your life."

"It's nothing you understand."

With that, I quickly tossed off the rest of the water, set down the empty glass and started to the door.

"Where are you going?" she said.

"I'll be back."

At the barn, I saddled up Rebel and rode off into the mountains.

For almost an hour, my heart beat to the rhythm of the horse's hooves. Galloping along the lush, green valley floor. Trotting rhythmically through the groves of aspen and ponderosa pines. Walking the horse through the shallow streams. It was here in the saddle, with the birds, the trees and the mighty Montana sky that I could reach inside and touch my innermost self. As I reviewed the sum of my life, there was no escaping the conclusion that I had more karma tied up with Jesse than with any other human being on earth. Our days together as boys, high school punks, soldiers, hippies and gun runners represented the highlights of my existence on this earth. While I dearly loved Sally Jean and Josh, at that moment in time, I realized it would be impossible to deny Jesse his single dying wish.

Back at the ranch, I put the horse in the barn and went straight into the house. Sally Jean, who was washing clothes, looked up when I walked in.

"I'm going to call Jesse," I said.

Somehow, she didn't seem surprised. In fact, it was if she had been expecting it.

"What are you going to tell him?"

"I'm going to tell him he can come visit."

"You're crazy," she said. "Stark raving mad."

I peered at her.

"He's dying, God-damn it! The man once saved my life. Now he's dying because of it. I can't say no. Don't you understand?"

"I'm sorry he's dying," she said. "We all have to die some time."

"I owe the man my life. If it hadn't been for Jesse, I wouldn't be standing here right now."

She rolled her eyes.

"Please," she said indignantly. "Spare me the details."

For a moment, I stared at her.

"It's nothing you would understand."

"I don't WANT to understand," she said. "That man has been a threat to my marriage and my home from the very first day I ever saw him. Now he is threatening my home and my marriage again."

"He is NOT threatening our home and our marriage," I said. "He just wants to come visit for a few days before he dies. Is that too much to ask?"

"I know the effect he has on you. The minute he comes in this house, the minute he darkens that doorway," she said, pointing to the front door, "I'm out of here."

"Please, let me do this!" I said. "Don't you understand this is something I have to do. I can't let him pass without seeing him again."

"I told you. The minute he walks through that door, I'm out of here."

I could see I was getting nowhere.

"Do as you like," I said. "This is something I have to do."

Then I turned and picked up the phone.

"Do you think I'm just bluffing?"

"I've got to do what I've got to do."

"You could tell him to go to hell."

"That's not going to happen," I said as I dialed the number.

I heard one ring. Then, on the second ring, I heard someone answer.

"Hello!"

"Jesse Trubble," I said.

"Just a moment," the voice replied.

As I waited, I watched as Sally Jean suddenly threw a salad bowl resting on the sink against the splashboard. It shattered into multiple pieces of broken glass. Then, wiping her hands on a small towel, she threw the cloth in the sink with the broken glass and stormed out of the kitchen.

"Hello!" Jesse said on the other end of the phone.

"Jesse?"

"Yeah, Johnny," he said. "What's up?"

"When did you want to come visit?"

"Will it be okay?"

"It will be fine," I said. "When do you want to come?"

"I could be there in four days," he said.

"On Sunday?"

"That's right. There is an afternoon flight that gets into Kalispell around 3 p.m. I'll rent a car at the airport and drive up to Hungry Horse."

"I'll be waiting," I said.

***

Five days later, on a Saturday morning, Josh and I were en route to Kalispell to the mountain biker shop. When we left the ranch house, he had grabbed the company's latest catalog and, as we rode, he was paging through it.

"Now, Dad," he said, eyeing the page that featured tires, "we've got to have the chain-link tread on the back because that's what I already have on the front."

"That's what we'll get."

For several minutes, we rode quietly.

"Look at this!" he said. "They have a sale on new steel carriers for the back of my bike. Can we get one of those?"

"We'll look at them," I said. "You don't want to buy some cheap thing that will break as soon as you put it on."

"Here's a picture," he said, holding up the catalog.

I glanced from the highway to the photo.

"We'll look at them when we get there."

***

Some thirty minutes later in Kalispell, we bought a new bicycle tire with the chain-link tread. After careful inspection by both of us, we also bought a steel carrier rack. Back in the pickup truck, Josh was proud of the new purchase.

"Thanks, Dad," he said. "This new carrier rack is so cool."

With that, he put the rack in the back seat and turned to me.

"Dad, why were you and Mom fighting?"

"Sometimes parents disagree," I said. "Adults don't always see everything the same way."

"It's about your friend, isn't it?"

I nodded.

"Why doesn't Mom like your friend?"

"She thinks he is not good for me."

"Why would she think that?"

"She just does."

For several moments, he was quiet and stared absently out the pickup truck window.

"There are some things your mother just doesn't understand," I said.

"Is it because she's a woman?"

"That's a pretty good explanation," I said. "I love your mother and she knows it."

We rode quietly.

"When my friend comes tomorrow, she's going to your grandmother's for a few days. Are you coming home next weekend?"

"I'm not sure."

"If you decide to leave the campus, can you go to stay with your mother?"

"That's fine," he said. "I know you want to be alone with your friend. This will be the last time you'll ever see him."

"That's right."

Then, satisfied with my answers, he returned his attention to the mountain bike catalog. As I drove, I suddenly realized the truth of my son's innocent statement. What an incredible mistake I would have made to not see Jesse one last time! How childish and shallow it was of me to hold a grudge for all those years! I remembered how I hated pettiness and vengefulness in other people, now I was having to face it in myself.

Moments later, he put aside the catalog and turned to me.

"Dad! Why are you crying?"

"I'm not crying," I said, wiping my eyes on the sleeve of my shirt.

"Yes, you are. It's your friend, isn't it? You're crying because your friend is going to die."

I didn't respond.

A long pause.

"Me and Mom will be just fine at Grandma's."

I looked at my son. I wondered how a father could ask more of a son. Then, tears welling in my eyes, I pulled the pickup off to the side of the road and stopped.

"I love you," I said.

"I love you too, Dad."

***

The following morning, Sally Jean and Josh, their suitcases packed and ready, were waiting under the ranch house carport.

"Daddy!" Josh called. "Me and Mom are leaving."

"Come give me a hug," I said.

He came over to me and I hugged him.

I turned to Sally Jean. She stared coldly at me.

"You know where I'll be," she said, handing me a scrap of paper. "Here's the number."

For a moment, I peered at her.

"I just wanted you to know..."

"I don't want to hear it," she said with a wave of her hand. "Just call when this madness is over. Come on, Josh!"

With that, she and Josh climbed into the family car. Sally Jean started the engine and backed the car out of the carport. Then, as I held the gate open, they waved goodbye and I watched as the car, in a cloud of dust, vanished around the curve of Tea Kettle Mountain.

As I strode back across the yard, I saw Ticker at the corral.

"My friend Jesse is coming to visit for a few days," I said. "We'll be wanting to ride and just hang out, so I'll be looking to you to run things."

"Is everything okay between you two now?" he asked.

I nodded.

***

At 3:30 p.m. that afternoon, I was sitting in the ranch house sunroom, sipping iced tea and intermittently peering up the road toward the base of Tea Kettle Mountain, trying to see a little tell-tale cloud of rising dust that would signal an approaching car. Jesse had said the plane would be in around 3 p.m. Mountain time. He would need some time to rent a car, then drive the 20 miles from Kalispell to Hungry Horse. Finally, after another glance, I left my vantage point and went back to the refrigerator to refill my glass with tea. When I returned, I peered back out the window again. As I did, I saw a dust cloud slowly rising from the base of Tea Kettle Mountain.

Moments later, I was in the yard. When I saw the black Cadillac round the curve, I went to the gate, flipped the latch and swung it open. Moments later, the car passed under the Rocking J entrance and into the yard.

When the car door opened and Jesse got out, I stood aghast. He looked like a dead man. His eyes were sunken and his face was pale and drawn. His hair was totally gray and his face, around the eyes and the chin, was seamed with long, heavy lines. As he emerged from the car, I could see his movements were painfully slow. All the pure, boundless energy I had taken for granted in earlier years was now gone. Physically, the person I had known over the past fifty-four years was little more than a shadow of his former self. Francesca was right. He didn't have long.

"Hey!" I said as he closed the car door.

"Hey, yourself!" he answered. We shook hands, then hugged one another. "Thanks for letting me come visit."

"I'm sorry I ever refused," I said.

"That's okay."

As before, Jesse took the guest room in the ranch house. Once I had helped him bring his bags inside, I watched him unpack. There were the same jeans, the western shirts, the hat and the pair of cowboy boots he had purchased during the previous visit.

"I'd say you came prepared," I said.

He smiled.

"Yeah. One last ride."

As I watched him hang clothes in the guest room closet, I was touched with a quiet nostalgia. Inside myself, I could feel the same sense of carefree excitement I always felt around Jesse beginning to emerge. Finally, he took a handful of medicine bottles out the suitcase.

"These are supposed to keep me alive," he said, placing them on the bedside table.

Then I watched as he closed the empty suitcase and placed it in the closet.

"What's the first thing you want to do?"

"I want to ride."

***

Fifteen minutes later, at the corral, Ticker had Rebel and a second horse, a black stallion, saddled and waiting.

"Ticker!" Jesse called when he saw the ranch foreman waiting with the horses. "Good to see you again."

The two men shook hands, then Ticker handed the stallion's reins to Jesse.

"His name is Omar," Ticker said. "He's the son of Sultan, your old horse."

Jesse looked at me.

"Whatever happened to Sultan?"

"He died last spring," I said. "He's buried out there beyond that stand of birch trees. He sired twelve colts before he died."

Jesse smiled.

"I'm glad to know he died happy."

I chuckled, then swung up in the saddle.

***

Some twenty minutes later, we were riding the switchbacks along the side of Lost Horse Mountain and Jesse was telling me about his career as a Wall Street investor.

"Then, in 1998, I started investing in computer software companies. Especially companies that were producing educational programs. I learned to pick the company, not based on quarterly earnings or PEs or any of the regular economic criteria, but on the number of hit programs it had produced. It was a market where a company would make $10 million a month for three months, then go belly-up. Christ, I was good. I never made so much money in all my life."

"How much did you make?" I said.

"Almost 18 million dollars in just over a year."

I shook my head with amazement.

"That's when I knew I would never have to work another day in my life. I had a net worth of almost $21 million. If I put that money into tax-free municipal bonds, I knew I could have $600,000 a year coming in. I thought I could live on that."

"So why didn't you stop investing?"

"I couldn't," he said. "I loved playing the market too much. For me, it's a challenge like nothing else. It's just..." He couldn't come up with the words. "What can I say? I just love it."

We rode quietly for several minutes.

"What do you think it's like to die?" he said.

"I don't know," I said. "How did Hemingway put it? 'Death is like jerking a handkerchief out of your pocket.'"

"What do you think he meant?"

I didn't answer at first.

"He meant that the act of life leaving the body is swift and clean and sure."

"I think you're right. Clean and swift and sure."

***

Later that night, after I went to bed, I could hear Jesse in the guest room listening to the soundtrack from the *Rocky Horror Picture Show* on a portable CD player. Intermittently, I would hear coughing above the sounds of the CD player. At times, the coughing spells came in short spurts; then at others, they seemed to last forever. At one point, during one particularly long spell, I wondered if Jesse was ever going to stop coughing. Finally, the coughing ended and he went to sleep. Around 2:30 a.m., he awoke again.

From the guest room, I could hear:

"There's a liiiiight over at the Frankenstein place, there's a li-hi-hi-hi-hi-hi-hi-hi-hi-hight...   burning   in   the fiiiiireplaaaace..."

***

Early the next morning, we were up at 7:30. In the kitchen, Socorro offered to fix breakfast, but I said I wasn't hungry. Even before I went to the guest room, I could hear Jesse coughing. I rapped on the door. Finally, he opened it. He was fully dressed in his cowboy outfit.

"Are you hungry?" I said.

"Not really. Let's go!"

"You don't think you should rest some?"

"Oh, no!" he said. "It's not going to be in a bed. It's going to be outside. I want to see mountains. I want to hear birds. And wind and water."

"Come on!" I said.

As we left the ranch house, Socorro handed me a package.

"This is for your lunch. It's some Kentucky Fried Chicken that has been in the refrigerator. It's still good."

"Thanks," I said, taking the package.

At the corral, Ticker had both Rebel and Omar ready to ride. After placing the food in a saddlebag, I swung up in the saddle, then we started out of the corral.

"Let's go to back to Dead Man's Mountain," he said. "I love the thick aspen groves and the ponderosa pines along the base of the mountain."

***

For almost an hour, we rode quietly up the switchbacks to the top of Dead Man's Mountain. Then, at the very top, I guided Rebel off the main trail to a shaded rock overhang which jutted out of the side of the mountain. Moments later, Jesse and his horse were beside me and Rebel.

We peered across the valley below.

"Look at that!" I said.

Some three thousand feet below, we could see the middle fork of the Flathead River slowly snaking its way along the lush, tree-laden valley floor. To the west, at the base on the Cascade Mountains, a herd of elk, maybe three hundred or more, grazed lazily in a spring meadow, lush with grass and wildflowers.

"Look," I said, pointing to the east. "There's a rain."

I peered up the valley. Standing tall and defiant in the eastern sky, I could see a long column of gray-leaden thunderheads dumping a fresh, spring rain on the valley below.

"It's beautiful," he said. "Absolutely beautiful."

"Let's go down to the valley floor."

***

A hour later, as we neared the bottom of the mountain, Jesse was struck with a tremendous fit of coughing. For several moments, his body was bent over in the saddle with the violent coughing. Finally, he stopped.

"Are you okay?" I asked.

"I'll be..." he said, but before he could finish the sentence, his body was racked with more coughing. Finally, he stopped again.

"Is there anything I can do?"

"I've got to stop and rest," he said.

His face was pale and his breathing was coming in short, labored gasps. I could see that he was helpless. The simple effort of breathing, coupled with the intense coughing, had left him so weak, he was holding on to the saddle horn to keep from falling off the horse.

Quickly, I dismounted and tied up the horses.

Then I helped him off his horse and carefully seated him on a patch of grass at the horses' feet.

"I've got to take my pills," he said.

I went back to my horse and got the canteen.

For a moment, I watched as he tried to raise himself on one elbow and remove the bottle of pills from his shirt pocket, but he was too weak.

"I'll get them," I said.

Quickly, I retrieved the bottle, popped the lid and handed him two of the white pills. Then, without looking, he tossed the pills into his mouth.

"Here!" I said, offering the canteen.

He took a swig of water and swallowed the pills.

"If you're hungry, I brought some Kentucky Fried Chicken," I said.

"Is it regular or extra crispy?"

"Regular."

"Damn!" he kidded. "I wanted extra crispy."

I laughed.

For several minutes, we sat quietly. Some thirty feet below us, winding its way through a stand of ponderosa pines, we could hear a small stream gurgling.

"Let's go down by the stream," he said.

"Can you make it?"

"You might have to help me."

Quickly, I stood up and offered my hands. He grasped them and I pulled him to his feet. Then, firmly holding his shoulder with my arm, I helped him down the rocky slope to the stream. There, on a grassy knoll beside the gurgling water, I helped him sit down.

High overhead in the ponderosa pines, a mockingbird sang.

"Hear that mockingbird?" he said. "He wants to tell the world about his sadness. What's the line in *Dover Beach*?"

I knew he wanted me to quote the last lines of the first stanza of Matthew Arnold's famous poem.

"You hear the grating roar of pebbles which the waves draw back, and fling, at their return, up the high strand," I quoted. "Begin and cease and then begin again, with tremulous cadence slow and bring the eternal note of sadness in."

"That's it," he said. "'With tremulous cadence slow and bring the eternal note of sadness in.' That's what that mockingbird is doing. He is trying to release his sadness."

For several minutes, we sat silently. High overhead, the wind softly nudged the tops of the ponderosa pines. Nearby, the horses whinnied.

Suddenly, Jesse was struck with another fit of coughing. For several moments, I watched as his body was racked with one unmerciful cough after another. Never had I seen anyone cough like that. Finally, he stopped.

"Just one little note," he said.

"What's that?"

"In October of 2021, I'll be back to get you."

I wanted to humor him.

"To show me the other world?" I said. "The great beyond?"

"That is correct."

"How will I know it's you?"

"You'll hear the distress call. At the place where you are, there will be a body of water in front of you. The water will be a surrounded by a white fence that has a tall door and a rounded top. Once you come through the door, I'll be waiting."

I knew to hold my tongue.

"Can I have a drink of water?" he said.

I reached for the canteen.

Jesse, resting on his elbows on the ground, tried to raise himself to drink from the canteen, but he didn't have the strength. I sat down beside him and held my hand under his head so he could drink.

"You okay now?" I said, withdrawing the canteen.

"That's better."

"There's something I should tell you," I said.

"What's that?"

"There's blood running out of your nose."

He raised himself on one elbow and touched his upper lip. A small stream of blood was running out of his nose, down his chin and dripping on to his western shirt.

"That's from the stitches," he said. "The doctor said they would bleed some."

"Want me to wipe it?"

"Yeah."

I used my handkerchief to wipe the blood off his face and shirt.

"I'm going to close my eyes for a minute," he said, lying back in the grass. "I want to rest."

For several minutes, we sat quietly.

Finally, he spoke.

"Of all the women you ever knew, which one was the sexiest?"

"The sexiest ever?"

"Yeah. Tell me about her."

I looked up and stared off into space.

"That would have to be Rita," I said finally. "You remember Rita Hallmark, the long-legged redhead that worked at the English pub in Santa Monica. Great God! I could just see that little tuft of carrot-colored hair sitting atop her pubis and I would go stark raving mad. Everything about her turned me on. Even the little things. The way she smiled. The way she would curl her lips after a sip of wine. I even liked the way she ironed my shirts. She always started ironing the cuffs first. Most women will start with the collar or the shoulders. I thought that was SO original," I said, still staring off into space.

I waited for Jesse to respond.

"Don't you think that was original?" I said again.

I looked down at him.

His eyes were closed.

"Jesse?"

No response.

"Jesse?" I said again.

Still no response.

I raised him into a sitting position and held him in my arms. His chin fell limply on my chest and, at that moment, I knew the breath of life had left him. I could see that his lips were turning a deep blue color. I placed my hand softly on his forehead and, holding it there for several seconds, I could feel his body heat slowly fading away. Then, I peered down at the cold, stiffening form in my arms. High overhead, the mockingbird had stopped singing. For a brief moment, all of nature, the trees, the mountains, the skies and the wind itself fell deathly silent. Even the little creek ceased to gurgle. The only sound was my sobbing as I rocked Jesse's lifeless body in my arms.

9 – Calvin and Lamar II

October, 2021

Back at the Golden Years Retirement Home, twilight—the crack between the two worlds—was fast approaching. On the veranda, eighty-one-year-old John David Chance, still leaning back and forth in his rocking chair, had finished his story.

"There you have it," he said. "That's the story of me and Jesse."

George didn't answer at first.

"Interesting," he said finally. "You and Jesse were quite a pair."

"Lots of wild and crazy times. You could never know how much I long to see him."

"Did you get back together with your wife?"

"Oh, yes! Sally Jean and I had a happy marriage for another ten years. We raised our son Josh and retired from our jobs. Sally Jean has been dead six years now. My son Josh is married and has his own family in California."

"Did you believe him when he said he'd come back to get you?"

"Oh no!" John said, with a laugh. "I didn't believe it any more than the man in the moon. Jesse was the kind of person who had a lot of fantasies. He told a lot of fibs just for pure fun. That's the kind of person he was."

They were quiet for a moment.

In the distance, beyond the lake, the two men could see the sun completing its daily arc across the western sky. The shadows of the tall Georgia pines that surrounded the retirement home fell long and lazy across its front lawn and parking lot.

Calvin and Lamar appeared on the veranda.

"It's going to be dark pretty soon," Calvin said. "Y'all ready to call it a day?"

"Just a few more minutes," said George. "I love this evening air."

Calvin and Lamar went back inside.

Suddenly, John heard a low shrill warbling sound.

"Yooooodle, doodle, doodle, doodle, doodle, doodle, doodle."

Instantly, he sat upright in the rocking chair.

"What's that sound?"

"I didn't hear anything," George said.

John looked around him, his eyes and ears wide with interest.

Then he heard the sound again.

"Yoooodle, doodle, doodle, doodle, doodle, doodle, doodle."

Instantly, a look of horrified shock flashed across his face.

"Oh, my God!" he said. "It's Jesse! It's him! I know its him! There IS another world."

Beside himself with excitement, he quickly arose from rocking chair and reached for his walking cane.

"He said there would be water surrounded with a white picket fence and a white door with a rounded top."

Seeing John was about to rush off, George grabbed his sleeve.

"Where are you going?"

"It's Jesse! It's Jesse! I know it's him!"

Instantly, John jerked his arm out of George's grasp, then, leaning on the cane, he strode across the floor to the veranda steps. Once he was on the ground, he was walking as fast as his eighty-one-year-old legs would carry him. Then, seeing the cane as a hindrance, he threw it aside and, with some superhuman effort, started running down the walkway toward the lake.

For a moment, George watched incredulously as John raced down the walkway.

"Calvin! Lamar!" he called.

Instantly, Calvin and Lamar appeared on the veranda.

"Something has happened to John!" George said, pointing to the figure running down the walkway.

Calvin squinted his eyes to peer into the twilight.

"Mr. Chance! Mr. Chance!"

John Chance didn't hear his words.

Calvin turned to George.

"Where's he going?"

"To meet his friend…"

"Friend? What friend?"

"His friend Jesse."

Calvin shook his head disapprovingly and turned to Lamar.

"You stay with George," Calvin said. "I'll go get Mr. Chance."

Then Calvin leapt off the porch.

"Mr. Chance! Mr. Chance!"

Moments later, he was racing down the walkway.

Quickly, George turned to Lamar.

"Lamar, take me down to the lake!"

"There's nothing you can do!"

"No! I demand you take me! I want to see what happens!"

Reluctantly, Lamar grasped the handles of George's wheelchair and they started down the ramp to the walkway.

Now, Calvin, racing down the walkway, could see John had reached the door.

"Mr. Chance! You can't get in! The door's locked!"

Then Calvin watched incredulously as John grasped the knob, opened the gate and went inside. The door slammed shut behind him.

Seconds later, Calvin arrived at the door. Quickly, he grasped the knob and twisted it, but the door refused to open. For a moment, he shook the door physically, but it wouldn't budge. Moments later, he peered through the pickets to the other side of the fence. He could see John David Chance lying on the ground. Now, Lamar and George had arrived. Then, all three men peered through the pickets into the twilight darkness on the other side of the fence. Suddenly, a great burst of thunder reverberated across the lake and a blinding white light illuminated the entire area on the other side of the fence.

"Oh, sweet mother of Jesus!" Calvin said.

Then, as they watched, a green mist arose from John's body, then evaporated into the twilight.

"Oh, God!" Calvin said. "Did y'all see that green smoke?"

"That was his spirit leaving his body," George said. "He went to be with his friend in the great beyond."

Then, just as suddenly as the rolling thunder and the blinding light had appeared, it disappeared.

All was quiet again.

Calvin turned from the fence. His face was white as a sheet.

"I have seen the face of God," he said. "I'm a changed man."

Then he turned and started walking back along the walkway to the facility.

"Where are you going?" Lamar said.

"I'm going to change my ways," Calvin said. "I've seen great God almighty."

"What about Mr. Chance?" Lamar said. "We can't leave him like this!"

Calvin continued walking, oblivious to Lamar's words.

Lamar turned back to the body.

"Oh, Lord! A dead patient? I'm going to lose my job for sure!"

Quickly, Lamar turned the wheelchair around and headed it back down the walkway.

"Calvin! Calvin!" he called into the darkness. "Wait! Wait! What are we going to tell the supervisor?"

In the darkness, they could hear Calvin's voice.

"The Lord is my shepherd. I shall not want. He maketh me to lay down in green pastures for his name's sake… He restoreth my soul…"

His voice trailed off in the darkness.

"Calvin!" Lamar called frantically. "Wait! Wait! Please don't leave me. What am I going to tell the supervisor?" he shouted into the darkness. "What am I going to tell the supervisor?"

The End

Other books by John Isaac Jones

A Quiet Madness: A biographical novel of Edgar Allan Poe

The Hand of God

Alabama Stories

The Duck Springs Affair

Thanks, PG!: Memoirs of a Tabloid Reporter

Thirteen Stories

The Angel Years